Victor Hugo

Dramas

Vol. 3

Victor Hugo

Dramas
Vol. 3

ISBN/EAN: 9783337306120

Printed in Europe, USA, Canada, Australia, Japan

Cover: Foto ©Andreas Hilbeck / pixelio.de

More available books at **www.hansebooks.com**

NATIONAL EDITION

VICTOR HUGO

DRAMAS

LUCREZIA BORGIA   MARY TUDOR
ANGELO, TYRANT OF PADUA

TRANSLATED BY

I. G. BURNHAM

PHILADELPHIA: GEORGE BARRIE & SON

TABLE OF CONTENTS

ACT FIRST

INSULT UPON INSULT

DONNA LUCREZIA (believing herself to be alone).

'T is he! at last it is vouchsafed to me to gaze on him an instant without peril! No, even in my dreams, he did not seem more beautiful!

LUCREZIA BORGIA

PREFACE

As he promised to do in the preface to his last drama, the author has reverted to the occupation of his whole life, art. He has resumed his favorite task, even before he has altogether adjusted matters with the petty political opponents who have been annoying him for two months past. And then, to bring forth a new drama six weeks after the proscription of the other was one way of speaking plainly to the present government. It was equivalent to showing it that its trouble was thrown away. It was equivalent to proving to it that art and liberty can spring up again in one night beneath the very foot which tramples on them. It is his purpose, therefore, to go forward henceforth with his political strife, so far as occasion requires, and his literary work, *pari passu*. One can do his duty and his task at the same time. The one does not interfere with the other. Man has two hands.

Le Roi s'Amuse and *Lucrèce Borgia* resemble each other not at all either in form or substance, and the fate of the two works has been so different, that the one will perhaps some day mark the principal political date, and the other the principal literary date in the author's life. He deems it his duty to say, however, that the two dramas, different as they are in form, substance and destiny, are very closely coupled in his thought. The idea which gave birth to *Le Roi s'Amuse*, and the idea which gave birth to *Lucrèce Borgia*, were born at the same moment in the same corner of the heart. What is, in fact, the fundamental thought, concealed under three or four concentric envelopes, in *Le Roi s'Amuse ?* It is this. Take the most hideous, the most repulsive, the most unrelieved *physical* deformity: place it where it stands out most prominently,—on the lowest, the farthest underground, the most despised

7

story of the social structure: let the glaring light of contrast shine in from all sides upon the wretched creature: and then cast into it a soul, and endow that soul with the purest sentiment which man can feel, the sentiment of paternity. What will take place? The sublime sentiment, warmed to life according to certain conditions, will transform the degraded creature under your eyes: the petty will become great: the deformed will become beautiful. That is the substance of *Le Roi s'Amuse*. And now, what is *Lucrèce Borgia?* Take the most hideous, the most repulsive, the most unrelieved moral deformity: place it where it stands out most prominently,—in a woman's heart, with all the surroundings of physical beauty and regal grandeur, which give notoriety to crime! and now mingle with all this moral deformity, a single pure sentiment, the purest and holiest that a woman can feel, the sentiment of maternity: inject a touch of the mother into your monster, and the monster will arouse your interest, and the monster will bring tears to your eyes: the creature which terrified you will move you to pity, and the deformed soul will become almost beautiful to look upon. Thus *Le Roi s'Amuse* represents paternity sanctifying physical deformity: *Lucrèce Borgia*, maternity purifying moral deformity. If *bilogie* were not a vulgar word, the author could well express his thought by saying that the two pieces were naught but a *bilogie sui generis*, the title of which might well be "The Father and Mother." Fate separated them, however, and what does it matter? One has been successful, the other was paralyzed by a *lettre de cachet!* the idea upon which the first is based will, it is probable, be hidden from many eyes for a long time to come, by innumerable prejudices! the idea which gave birth to the second, seems, if we are not deluded, to be accepted and understood every evening by an intelligent and sympathetic multitude. *Habent sua fata!* but whatever may be the fate of the two plays, which have no other merit than, the consideration which the public has been pleased to bestow upon them, they are twin sisters, the laurel-crowned and the proscribed were planted side by side, like Louis XIV. and the Iron Mask.

Corneille and Molière were accustomed to answer in detail the criticisms called forth by their works, and it is extremely interesting to-day to see how these giants of the stage struggled and squirmed in *prefaces* and *notices to the reader*, under the inextricable network of criticisms which contemporary critics were constantly weaving about them. The author of this drama deems himself unworthy to follow such great examples. He prefers to hold his peace in the face of criticism. That which becomes men of authority, like Molière and Corneille, does not become others. Moreover, there has probably never been any other than Corneille in the world, who could remain grand, yes, sublime, at the moment when he was on his knees to Scudéri or Chapelain, inditing a preface. The author is far from being a Corneille; the author is equally far from having a Scudéri or a Chapelain to deal with. The critics, with a few noticeable exceptions, have been loyal and kindly to him. Doubtless he might be able to meet more than one objection. To those, for example, who consider that Gennaro in the second act allows himself to be poisoned by the duke altogether too meekly, he might propound the question, whether Gennaro, a character originating in the poet's brain, is required to be drawn more in accordance with *probability*, than the historical Drusus, of Tacitus, *ignarus et juveniliter hauriens*. To those who reproach him for exaggerating the crimes of Lucrezia Borgia, he might say: "Read Tomasi, read Guicciardini, and above all read the

Diarium.'' To those who blame him for having given credence to certain popular, half-fabulous rumors touching the deaths of Lucrezia's various husbands, he might reply that the fables of the people are often the poet's verities; and thereon he might once more cite Tacitus, the historian being under greater obligations than the dramatic poet to be careful as to the accuracy of his facts. *Quamvis fabulosa et immania credebantur, atrociore semper fama erga dominantium exitus.* He might go much more into detail with his explanations, and examine with the critics all the parts of his structure one by one; but he takes greater pleasure in thanking than in contradicting them; and, after all, he prefers that the reader should find the replies he might make to their criticisms in the drama itself, if they are to be found there, rather than in the preface.

He trusts that he may be forgiven for saying nothing more on the purely æsthetic part of his work. There is an altogether different line of thought, no less lofty in his opinion, which he would be glad to have the leisure to suggest and examine into apropos of this play of *Lucrèce Borgia*. In his view many social questions are involved in literary questions, and every work in the field of letters is a fact to be considered. That is the subject upon which he would gladly dilate if time and space were not lacking. It cannot be repeated too frequently that the stage in our day is of immense importance, and its importance tends to keep pace with the advance of civilization itself. The stage is a platform. The stage is a pulpit. The stage speaks loud and strong. When Corneille says:

Pour être plus qu'un roi tu te crois quelque chose,[1]

Corneille is Mirabeau. When Shakespeare says: *To die, to sleep,* Shakespeare is Bossuet.

The author of this drama is well aware how great and how serious a thing the stage is. He knows that the drama, without going beyond the impartial bounds of true art, has a national, a social, a human mission. When, evening after evening, he sees the intellectual, cultivated people, who have made Paris the very centre of the world's progress, swarming before a curtain, which is to rise a moment later upon the creature of his, a paltry poet's, brain, he feels how small a thing he is, in the face of all that expectation and interest: he feels that if his talent amounts to nothing, his probity must be everything; he catechises himself sternly and collectedly as to the philosophical tendency of his work; for he realizes his responsibility, and he does not wish that that audience should call him to account some day for what he may have taught them. The poet also has the custody of souls. The multitude must not be allowed to go forth from the theatre, without having imbibed some austere and profound moral precepts. And so he hopes, that, with God's help, he may never exhibit upon the stage (at least while the present grave and serious times endure) any work that does not overflow with useful lessons and sound advice. He will always gladly introduce the coffin into the banquet-hall: the prayers for the dead will mingle with the refrain of drinking songs, and the monk's hood appear beside the mask. If he sometimes allows the carnival to figure in scant attire in the foreground, he will not cease to cry out to it from the rear of the stage: *Memento quia pulvis es.* He knows full well that art alone, pure art, art properly so-called does not demand all this of the poet: but he is of opinion that on the stage, of all places, it is not enough to satisfy the bare requirements of art. As for the wounds and suffering of mankind, whenever he exhibits them in his drama, he will endeavor to throw the veil of a solemn, comforting thought over what might otherwise be too painful in their nakedness. He will not bring Marion de Lorme upon the stage, without purifying the courtesan with a touch of real love: he will endow Triboulet the hunchback with a father's heart: he will give to Lucrezia, the monster, a mother's entrails. And by this means, he will at least ensure the tranquillity and repose of his conscience touching his work. The drama of which he has dreamed, and which he is trying to make an accomplished fact, will be able to touch on any and every subject, without being defiled. Let a compassionate, moral thought pervade whatever you do, and nothing will be deformed or repulsive. With the most hideous conception mingle the idea of true religion, and it will become pure and holy. Nail God to the gibbet, and you have the cross.

12TH FEBRUARY, 1833.

NOTE

[1] Because thou art more than a king, thou thinkest thyself of some importance.

DRAMATIS PERSONÆ

DONNA LUCREZIA BORGIA

DON ALPHONSO D'ESTE

GENNARO

GUBETTA

MAFFIO ORSINI

JEPPO LIVERETTO

DON APOSTOLO GAZELLA

ASCANIO PETRUCCI

OLOFERNO VITELLOZZO

RUSTIGHELLO

ASTOLFO

THE PRINCESS NEGRONI

AN USHER

MONKS

NOBLEMEN, PAGES, GUARDS

Venice—Ferrara

15 . . .

ACT FIRST

INSULT UPON INSULT

FIRST PART

A terrace of the Barbarigo Palace at Venice. An evening party is in progress. Masks are crossing and recrossing the stage. At both sides of the terrace the palace is seen, brilliantly illuminated, and a flourish of trumpets is heard at intervals. The terrace is in shadow, and covered with plants and greenery. In the background, at the foot of the terrace, the Zuecca Canal is supposed to flow, and gondolas are constantly seen passing back and forth in the dim light, laden with masks and musicians. From each gondola, as it glides across the back of the stage, arise strains of music, sometimes graceful and lively, at other times sad and plaintive; they gradually die away in the distance. In the background lies Venice in the moonlight.

SCENE I

Young noblemen, magnificently dressed, holding their masks in their hands, are talking together on the terrace.

GUBETTA, GENNARO, in a captain's uniform; DON APOSTOLO GAZELLA, MAFFIO ORSINI, ASCANIO PETRUCCI, OLOFERNO VITEL-LOZZO, JEPPO LIVERETTO.

OLOFERNO.

We live in days when ghastly deeds are done so commonly that men long since have ceased to speak of this; yet surely never aught befell more damnable and more mysterious.

ASCANIO.

A fiendish deed and done by fiendish men.

JEPPO.

I know the facts, my lords, I hold them from my cousin, the most eminent Cardinal

13

Carriale—Cardinal Carriale, you know, who
had the fierce dispute with Cardinal Riario,
touching the war against Charles Eighth of
France.

GENNARO (yawning).

Ah! Jeppo has one of his tedious tales
to tell! For my part I 'll not listen to it.
I 'm spent enough already without that.

MAFFIO.

Such matters have no interest for thee,
Gennaro, nor is the reason far to seek.
Thou art a gallant captain of adventure. The
name thou bearest is imaginary. Thou
knowest not thy father nor thy mother. None
can doubt that thou art gently born who ever
saw thee handle thy good sword; but all we
know of thy nobility is that thou fightest like
a very lion. Upon my soul, we are true
comrades in arms, and what I say, I say not
to offend thee. At Rimini thou didst save my
life, and at Vicenza I saved thine. We swore
a solemn oath always to bear each other aid
in danger as in love, each to avenge the other
when occasion called, and to know no other
foes, I than thine and thou than mine. A
soothsayer foretold that we should die the self-
same day, whereon we gave him ten gold
sequins for his prophecy. We are not friends,
but brothers. But thou hast the good fortune
to be called simple Gennaro, thou hast no ties
of kindred, and at thy heels do follow none of
those fatalities, often hereditary, which cling
to names that have a history. Happy thou art
in that! What matters it to thee what happens now, or what has happened, so that there
be always men for war, and women for love?
What hast thou to do with towns and families,
—thou, child of the flag, who hast no family
or town? But with us, Gennaro, 't is different,
as thou seest. It is our right to feel an interest
in the catastrophes of our time. In tragedies

like this our fathers and our mothers have
themselves had part, and almost all our families are bleeding still. Now, Jeppo, tell us
what thou knowest.

GENNARO. (Throws himself into an arm-chair, and
      composes himself to sleep.)

Wake me, I pray you, when Jeppo 's done.

JEPPO.

Well, 't was thus. In fourteen hundred
eighty . . .

GUBETTA (in a corner of the stage).

Ninety-seven.

JEPPO.

E'en so. In fourteen ninety-seven. Upon
a certain night betwixt a Wednesday and a
Thursday . . .

GUBETTA.

No, no! betwixt a Tuesday and a Wednesday.

JEPPO.

As you will. Upon that night a Tiber
boatman, sleeping aboard his craft, moored to
the bank, the better to keep watch upon his
freight, saw something terrible. 'T was just
below the church of Santo Hieronimo. The
time was some five hours after midnight. The
boatman saw two men afoot come from the
street which lies to the left of the church,
peering on this side and on that, as if in
dread; after them appeared two others, and
then three—seven in all. One only of the
seven was on horseback. The darkness was
intense. 'Mongst all the houses looking on
the Tiber, only a single window showed a
light. The seven men drew near the river
bank. He who was mounted turned his
horse's croup toward the Tiber, and then the
boatman could distinctly see a pair of legs
hanging upon one side, and on the other side
a head and arms—in short a lifeless body of a

man. While their companions stood on guard at the street corners, two of those on foot took down the body, swung it twice or thrice with vigor to and fro, then cast it far away into the river. Scarce had the body touched the water when the horseman asked some question of the others, to which they both made answer: "Yes, my lord." With that, the horseman turned toward the Tiber, and spied a something black floating upon the water. He asked them what it was. "My lord," they answered him, "'t is my lord's cloak who 's dead." And one among the number pelted the cloak with stones until it sank from sight. This done they all decamped in company, and took the street which leads to San Giacomo. This did the boatman see.

MAFFIO.

A grewsome sight, indeed. Was he a man of mark, whom these men thus did cast into the stream? That horse makes my flesh creep: the murderer in the saddle, and his victim riding on behind.

GUBETTA.

Upon that horse there were two brothers.

JEPPO.

You have said it, Signor di Belverana. The corpse was Giovanni Borgia; the horseman Cæsar Borgia.

MAFFIO.

A veritable family of demons are these Borgias! But tell us, Jeppo, why did the brother slay his brother thus?

JEPPO.

I will not tell you. The motive for the murder was so execrable that it should be a deadly sin merely to speak of it.

GUBETTA.

I will tell you why. Cæsar, Cardinal of Valentia, slew Giovanni, Duke of Gandia, because both brothers were enamored of the same woman.

MAFFIO.

And this woman was . . . ?

GUBETTA (still in the background).

Their sister.

JEPPO.

Enough, Signor di Belverana. Do not, I pray you, utter before us the name of that most monstrous woman. There 's not one of our families she has not wounded to the very quick.

MAFFIO.

And was there not a child involved in the affair?

JEPPO.

Yes, a child whose father only do I care to name: 't was Giovanni Borgia.

MAFFIO.

That child should be a man ere now.

OLOFERNO.

He disappeared.

JEPPO.

Did Cæsar succeed in abducting him from his mother? Did the mother succeed in removing him from Cæsar's ken? That none can say.

DON APOSTOLO.

If 't was the mother who concealed her son, she took the wisest course. Since Cæsar Borgia, Cardinal of Valentia, became Duke of Valentinois, he has put to death, as you all know, without counting his brother Giovanni, his two nephews, sons of Guifry Borgia, Prince of Squillace, and of his cousin, Cardinal Francesco Borgia. The man has a downright mania for killing all his kindred.

JEPPO.

Per Bacco! he intends to be the only Borgia, and so inherit all the pope's estate.

ASCANIO.

Did not this sister, Jeppo, whom you will not name, make at this time a pilgrimage in secret to the monastery of Saint Sixtus, and seek seclusion there, for reasons known to no one but herself?

JEPPO.

I think she did. Her purpose was to bring about a separation from her second husband, Giovanni Sforza.

MAFFIO.

What is the boatman's name who saw all this?

JEPPO.

I know it not.

GUBETTA.

His name is Giorgio Schiavone, and his trade to carry wood up Tiber to Ripetta.

MAFFIO (aside to Ascanio).

This Spaniard seems to know much more about our business than we Romans do.

ASCANIO (aside).

I have the same distrust that thou hast of this Signor di Belverana. But let us go no deeper into this. There may be danger lurking underneath.

JEPPO.

Ah! my friends, my friends! what times are these we live in! Tell me, do you know one single human being who is sure of living more than one to-morrow in this poor Italy of ours, so racked and rent by wars and plagues and Borgias?

DON APOSTOLO.

Methinks, my lords, that all of us here present are named as members of the embassy, forthwith to be dispatched by the Serene Republic to Ferrara, with her felicitations to the duke upon the conquest of Rimini from the Malatesta. When do we set out upon our mission?

OLOFERNO.

Two days hence, if all goes well. The two ambassadors, you know, have been selected— Senator Tiopolo and General Grimani.

DON APOSTOLO.

Will Captain Gennaro be one of us?

MAFFIO.

Doubt it not! Gennaro and I never part.

ASCANIO.

Gentlemen, there is a momentous fact to which I desire to call your attention: they are drinking all the good Spanish wine without us.

MAFFIO.

Let us go in.—Ho! Gennaro!

(To Jeppo.)

Why, verily he fell asleep during your story, Jeppo.

JEPPO.

Let him sleep.

(Exit all, except Gubetta.)

SCENE II

GUBETTA, then DONNA LUCREZIA. GENNARO, asleep.

GUBETTA (alone).

Indeed I do know more of their affairs than they: they told each other so in undertones. I know much more than they, but Donna Lucrezia knows much more than I, Signor di Valentinois knows much more than Donna Lucrezia, the devil knows much more than Signor di Valentinois, and Pope Alexander Sixth knows vastly more than the devil.

(Looking at Gennaro.)

How these young people sleep!

(Donna Lucrezia enters, masked. She perceives Gennaro asleep, and stands gazing at him in a sort of ecstasy, mingled with respect.)

DONNA LUCREZIA (aside).

He sleeps.—Doubtless this *fête* has wearied him.—How beautiful he is!

(She turns her head.)

Gubetta!

GUBETTA.

Speak lower, madame.—Here my name 's not Gubetta, but the Count of Belverana, a noble of Castile: while you, madame, are Marchioness of Pontequadrato, a Neapolitan dame. We must not seem to recognize each other. Such I understood to be your Highness's commands. You are not now upon your own domain: you are at Venice.

DONNA LUCREZIA.

Well said, Gubetta. But there is no one on this terrace save yonder sleeping youth. We may exchange a word or two.

GUBETTA.

As your Highness pleases. I venture to advance one word of counsel more: do not remove your mask. Even here you might be recognized.

DONNA LUCREZIA.

And what care I? If they know not who I am, I 've naught to fear. If they know who I am, 't is for them to fear.

GUBETTA.

We are in Venice, madame. Here you have many enemies, and enemies whose hands are free to strike. Doubtless the Most Serene Republic would not suffer aught to be done against your Highness's person, but you might be insulted.

DONNA LUCREZIA.

Ah, me! thou 'rt right. In truth, my very name arouses horror.

GUBETTA.

In Venice there are others than Venetians. There are Romans here, and Neapolitans, and Romagnese and Lombards, Italians from every part of Italy.

DONNA LUCREZIA.

And every part of Italy holds me in detestation. Yes, thou 'rt right. But I must look to it that it be so no longer. I was not born to cast a blight where'er I go; now, more than ever, I feel certain of it. 'T was the example of my kindred drew me on and made me what I am, Gubetta!

GUBETTA.

Madame.

DONNA LUCREZIA.

Dispatch at once the orders we now give thee to our duchy of Spoleto.

GUBETTA.

Say on, madame: four mules are always saddled and four couriers always ready to depart.

DONNA LUCREZIA.

What has been done with Galeas Accaioli?

GUBETTA.

He is still in prison awaiting your Highness's command that he be hanged.

DONNA LUCREZIA.

And Guifry Buondelmonte?

GUBETTA.

In the dungeons. You have not yet given the word to have him strangled.

DONNA LUCREZIA.

And Manfredi de Curzola?

GUBETTA.

He 's not yet strangled either.

DONNA LUCREZIA.

And Spadacappa?

GUBETTA.

As you have ordered the poison is to be administered to him in the host on Easter Day. That will be six weeks hence. 'T is Carnival time now.

DONNA LUCREZIA.

And Pietro Capra?

GUBETTA.

Still Bishop of Pesaro, and Regent of the Chancellor's office. But ere a month has passed he will be nothing but a bit of dust. For His Holiness the Pope has caused his apprehension upon your complaint, and holds him closely guarded in the dungeons of the Vatican.

DONNA LUCREZIA.

Gubetta, write on the instant to the Holy Father that I entreat Pietro Capra's pardon. Order Accaioli set at liberty, Gubetta! And Manfredi de Curzola, give him his freedom, too! And Buondelmonte! And Spadacappa!

GUBETTA.

Stay, madame! stay! and give me time to breathe! In God's name what commands are these to issue from your lips? Why, it rains pardons, and hails mercy! I am fairly submerged in clemency! I shall never make my escape from this frightful deluge of good deeds!

DONNA LUCREZIA.

Good or bad, what matters it to thee, so that I pay thee for them?

GUBETTA.

Ah! but a good deed is so much more difficult to do than a bad one! Alas! poor, poor Gubetta! Now that the whim has seized you to be merciful, what will become of me?

DONNA LUCREZIA.

Hark ye, Gubetta: thou art my oldest and most trusty confidant.

GUBETTA.

For fifteen years I have had the honor of working with and for you.

DONNA LUCREZIA.

So! Tell me then, Gubetta, my old friend, and my long-time accomplice, dost thou not begin to feel the need to change thy mode of life? dost thou not thirst to have men bless us, thee and me, as cordially as they have cursed us? hast thou not had thy fill of crime?

GUBETTA.

I see that you are on the way to be transformed into the most virtuous of all highnesses.

DONNA LUCREZIA.

Does not our shared renown, our infamous renown, renown as murderers and poisoners, begin to weigh thee down, Gubetta?

GUBETTA.

Not at all. When I pass through the streets of Spoleto, I often hear the blockheads buzzing about my ears: "See! here comes Gubetta, —Gubetta-poison, Gubetta-dagger, Gubetta-gallows!" for they've adorned my name with a long, flaring tail of sobriquets. They say all this, and when their voices say it not they say it with their eyes. But what is that to me? I am as wonted to my unsavory reputation as one of the pope's soldiers to assist the priest at mass.

DONNA LUCREZIA.

But dost thou not feel that all these hateful names with which they overwhelm thee, and myself as well, may perchance arouse the scorn and hatred of a heart by which thou wouldst be loved? Dost thou love no one in the world, Gubetta?

GUBETTA.

I would be well content to know whom you love, madame.

DONNA LUCREZIA.

What wouldst thou know? With thee I am all frankness, and yet I will say naught to thee of father, nor of brother, of husband, nor of lovers.

GUBETTA.

But I can scarcely see what other one can love.

DONNA LUCREZIA.

There is another, Gubetta.

GUBETTA.

Heaven save the mark! can it be that you have gone virtuous for love of God?

DONNA LUCREZIA.

Gubetta! Gubetta! if to-day there were in Italy, in fatal blood-stained Italy, one pure and noble heart, one heart instinct with lofty, manly virtues, one angel's heart beneath a soldier's cuirass; if there remained to me, poor, hated, scorned, abhorred woman, accursed of Heaven and cursed by all mankind, poor, pitiable creature that I am for all my unmeasured power; if there remained to me, in the distressful state wherein my heart now battles with its pain, one only thought, one hope, and that to merit and obtain before my death a little space, Gubetta, a trifle of affection and esteem within that proud, pure heart; if I had no thought save the ambition to feel it beat some day freely and joyously against my own; wouldst thou in that case understand, Gubetta, why I do long so to redeem my past, to purge my reputation, wash away the stains of every sort which my whole being bears, and change the thoughts of infamy and blood, to which my name gives rise throughout all Italy, to thoughts of glory, penitence and virtue?

GUBETTA.

Good lack! madame, what hermit have you trodden on to-day?

DONNA LUCREZIA.

Laugh not, Gubetta! long have I had such thoughts and dared not tell them thee. Once launched on crime's swift current, one does not stop at will. Within my breast my good and evil angels are waging deadly war, but I find faith to think the good will win the fight, and that ere long.

GUBETTA.

In that event, *te Deum laudamus, magnificat anima mea Dominum!* Do you know, madame, that I fail utterly to understand you, and that, some time since, you became a riddle unsolvable by me? A month agone your Highness did make known your purpose to depart for Spoleto, took leave of Don Alphonso d'Este, your noble spouse, who 's as fond of you as any turtle dove, and jealous as a tiger. Your Highness thereupon did truly leave Ferrara, but came to Venice here most secretly, almost without attendants, buried beneath a Neapolitan, and I beneath a Spanish pseudonym. Arrived at Venice, your Highness cut adrift from me, and ordered me to make no sign that we were aught but strangers. Then you began to frequent all the fêtes, concerts and *tertullias*, taking advantage of the carnival always to wear a mask, unknown to all, disguised, exchanging a brief word with me between two doors each night: and now behold this pretty masquerade ends with a sermon preached by you at me! A sermon preached by you at me, madame! is it not truly past all comprehension? You have metamorphosed your name, you have metamorphosed your dress, and now you metamorphose your nature! Upon my soul, this is carrying the carnival beyond all bounds. My brain is in a whirl. Tell me, in God's name, what may be the cause that leads your Highness to perform such freaks?

DONNA LUCREZIA (seizing his arm, and leading him to where Gennaro lies asleep).

Seest thou this youth?

GUBETTA.

This youth's face is not strange to me, and well I know that you 've been running after him, under your mask, since you have been in Venice.

DONNA LUCREZIA.

What hast thou to say of him?

GUBETTA.

I say that he is a young man, now sleeping on a bench, who would, 't is likely, have fallen asleep standing, had he been present during the edifying, moral interview with which I have been honored by your Highness.

DONNA LUCREZIA.

Dost thou not think him more than passing fair?

GUBETTA.

He would be fairer, were his eyes not closed. An eyeless face is like a palace without windows.

DONNA LUCREZIA.

If thou didst but know how I do love him!

GUBETTA.

That 's the concern of Don Alphonso, your royal husband. And yet I can but warn your Highness that your trouble 's lost. This youth, so I am told, is mad with love for a lovely girl named Fiammetta.

DONNA LUCREZIA.

And loves she him?

GUBETTA.

So 't is said.

DONNA LUCREZIA.

So much the better! how happy should I be to know that he is happy!

GUBETTA.

A strange thing that, and little like your Highness. I should have thought you more inclined to jealousy.

DONNA LUCREZIA (gazing at Gennaro).

What a noble face!

GUBETTA.

Methinks that he resembles some . . .

DONNA LUCREZIA (hastily).

No matter whom he seems to thee to resemble! Leave me.

(Gubetta goes off. Donna Lucrezia stands for some
moments at Gennaro's side, as if in a trance: she
does not notice two masked men who come in at the
rear of the stage and watch her closely.)

DONNA LUCREZIA (believing herself to be alone).

'T is he! at last it is vouchsafed to me to
gaze on him an instant without peril! No,
even in my dreams, he did not seem more
beautiful! O God! spare me the agony of
ever being hated and despised by him. Thou
knowest that he is the only being under
heaven who is dear to me! I tremble to
remove my mask, and yet I needs must wipe
away my tears.

(She takes off her mask to wipe her eyes. The two
masked men talk together in undertones, while she
continues to gaze in rapt admiration at Gennaro.)

FIRST MASKED MAN.

This is enough. I may return now to Ferrara. I came to Venice only to make sure of
her unfaithfulness: I have seen enough. My
absence from Ferrara may not be prolonged.
That youth 's her lover. What 's his name,
Rustighello?

SECOND MASKED MAN.

Gennaro. He 's a soldier of fortune, a
gallant fellow, fatherless and motherless, and
nobody knows whence he came. He is in
the service of the Republic of Venice.

FIRST MAN.

Arrange it so that he will come to Ferrara.

SECOND MAN.

That will arrange itself, my lord. He will
set forth for Ferrara two days hence with
several friends, who make part of the embassy
of Senators Tiopolo and Grimani.

FIRST MAN.

'T is well. The reports that came to me
were most exact. Again I tell thee I have
seen enough. We may return.

(They go off.)

DONNA LUCREZIA (clasping her hands, and almost
kneeling at Gennaro's side).

Oh! my God, grant that there may be as
much happiness in store for him, as I have
known of misery!

(She kisses Gennaro on the forehead, and he awakes
with a start.)

GENNARO (seizing Lucrezia, who is deeply embarrassed, by both arms).

A kiss! a woman! 'Pon honor, madame,
were you but a queen and I a poet, this would
be a veritable duplication of Messire Alain
Chartier's adventure, the French rhymer.
But who you are I know not, and I am but a
soldier.

DONNA LUCREZIA.

Release me, Signor Gennaro!

GENNARO.

Not so, madame.

DONNA LUCREZIA.

Some one comes.

(She runs off. Gennaro follows her.)

SCENE III

JEPPO, afterward MAFFIO.

JEPPO (entering on the opposite side of the stage).

What face is that? 'T is she in very truth !
That woman in Venice! Ho, there! Maffio !

MAFFIO (entering).
What 's the matter?

JEPPO.
Come, let me tell thee something past belief.
(He whispers in Maffio's ear.)

MAFFIO.
Art sure of it?

JEPPO.
Sure as that we are in the Palace Barbarigo,
and not the Palace Labbia.

MAFFIO.
And she was in soft converse with Gennaro?

JEPPO.
With Gennaro.

MAFFIO.
I must set free Gennaro, my dear brother,
from this spider's toils.

JEPPO.
Come—let us notify our friends.
(They go off. For some time the stage remains empty
except for the gondolas with music which pass to
and fro in the background. Donna Lucrezia and
Gennaro enter, wearing masks.)

SCENE IV

GENNARO, DONNA LUCREZIA.

DONNA LUCREZIA.

The light is dim here on the terrace, and there's no one by. Now I may unmask. I wish that you should see my face.

(She removes her mask.)

GENNARO.

You are very beautiful.

DONNA LUCREZIA.

Look well on me, Gennaro, and tell me that my aspect horrifies thee not.

GENNARO.

You horrify me, madame? Why should it be so? Contrariwise, I feel within my heart something that draws me to you.

DONNA LUCREZIA.

Dost thou then think, Gennaro, thou couldst love me?

GENNARO.

Wherefore not? But, madame, I've no purpose to deceive you; there's one whom I love even more than I'd love you.

DONNA LUCREZIA (smiling).

I know. 'T is little Fiammetta.

GENNARO.

No.

DONNA LUCREZIA.

Who then?

GENNARO.

My mother.

DONNA LUCREZIA.

Thy mother! thy mother! O Gennaro! Thou dost dearly love thy mother, dost thou not?

GENNARO.

And yet I ne'er have seen her. That must seem strange to you, I know full well. I cannot say whence comes my impulse to confide in you; and yet I feel disposed to trust to you a secret, which hitherto I have not lisped to any mortal ear, not even my sworn friend and brother's, not even Maffio Orsini's. Strange it is thus to lay bare one's heart to the first comer, but to me it seems as if to me you were not the first comer. I am a soldier who knows nothing of his family. I was reared by a Calabrian fisherman whose son I thought myself. The day that I attained my sixteenth year, I learned from the good fisherman that he was not my father. Then after but a little time a signor came, equipped me as a knight, and rode away without having raised the visor of his casque. Again a little time, and a man clad in black brought me a letter. In haste I opened it. 'T was written to me by my mother whom I did not know, —my mother whom in my dreams I saw, gentle and kind and sweet and fair as you— my mother, whom I adored with all the strength and vigor of my heart. The letter, though it told me not my name, gave me to know that I was nobly born and of a mighty

race, and that my mother was most wretched
and unhappy.   Poor mother !

DONNA LUCREZIA.

Dear Gennaro !

GENNARO.

That very day I chose war for my trade, for
much I wished to win distinction by my
sword to equal the distinction of my birth. I
have served since throughout the length and
breadth of Italy; but just so surely as month
follows month, on the first day the self-same
messenger appears, the bearer of a letter from
my mother. He gives it me, takes my reply
and goes ; and each of us says nothing to the
other, because he 's deaf and dumb.

DONNA LUCREZIA.

And so thou knowest nothing of thy
family ?

GENNARO.

I know that I 've a mother, that she 's most
unhappy, and that I would give my life in this
world just to see her weep, and my life in the
other just to see her smile. That 's all I know.

DONNA LUCREZIA.

What dost thou with her letters ?

GENNARO.

I have them here, all here against my heart.
We men of war must oft expose our breasts
to risk of sword-thrust.   A mother's letters
form an impenetrable cuirass.

DONNA LUCREZIA.

Noble nature !

GENNARO.

Look, do you wish to see her hand ? here 's
one of her letters.

(He takes from his breast a paper, which he kisses and
then hands it to Donna Lucrezia.)

Read that.

DONNA LUCREZIA (reading).

" Do not seek to know me, my Gennaro,
until such time as I determine. I am greatly
to be pitied. I am surrounded by heartless
kindred, who would kill thee even as they
killed thy father. I wish to be the only one
who knows the secret of thy birth, my child.
If thou didst know, it is at once so sad and so
illustrious, that thou couldst not keep silent.
Youth is trustful, and thou knowest not the
perils which surround thee as I know them.
Who can say ? thou mightest defy them with
the audacity of youth, thou mightest speak,
or let thy identity be divined, and then thou
wouldst not live two days. Oh, no I be content to know thou hast a mother who adores
thee, and keeps guard night and day upon
thy life. My Gennaro, my son, thou art all
that I love on earth. My heart bursts when I
think of thee . . ."

(She pauses to force back a tear.)

GENNARO.

How movingly you read it !   It is as if you
were saying it, not reading. Ah ! you weep !
You are most kind, madame, and my heart
goes out to you for weeping over what my
mother writes.

(He takes the letter, kisses it again, and replaces it in
his breast.)

Yes, as you see, my cradle was encompassed
with crime. Poor mother ! It must be that
you now can understand why I 've but little
taste for gallantry and wenching, when my
whole heart is filled with the one thought—
my mother. Oh I to deliver her ! to serve,
console, avenge her ! oh I what bliss I Then
might I think of love. All that I do, I do to
make me worthy of my mother. Many there
are, adventurers like me, who are not scrupu-
lous, and would fight cheerfully for Satan after
fighting for Saint Michael ; but I serve none but

righteous causes. I choose to have it in my power some day to lay at my dear mother's feet a sword as pure and loyal as an emperor's. Why, madame, it was once proposed to me to enter the employ of that vile creature Donna Lucrezia Borgia. I refused.

DONNA LUCREZIA.

Gennaro! Gennaro! have pity on the wicked. You cannot know the movement of their hearts.

GENNARO.

I have no pity for the pitiless. But, madame, a truce to that. Now that I 've told you who I am, do you the same, and tell me who you are.

DONNA LUCREZIA.

A woman who loves thee, Gennaro.

GENNARO.

But your name?

DONNA LUCREZIA.

Ask me no more.

(*Torches. Maffio and Jeppo enter with much noise. Donna Lucrezia hastily resumes her mask.*)

SCENE V

The Same : JEPPO LIVERETTO, MAFFIO ORSINI, ASCANIO PETRUCCI, OLOFERNO VITEL-LOZZO, DON APOSTOLO GAZELLA. Lords and Ladies. Pages, carrying torches.

MAFFIO (with a torch in his hand).

Gennaro, dost thou care to know her name to whom thou speak'st of love?

DONNA LUCREZIA (aside, under her mask).

Just Heaven !

GENNARO.

You are all my friends, and yet God hears my oath that he will venture much who first lays hand upon this lady's mask. A lady's mask is no less sacred than a man's face unmasked.

MAFFIO.

For that the lady must first be a lady, Gennaro. But we 've no purpose to insult this woman ; we simply wish that she should know our names.

(Taking a step toward Donna Lucrezia.)

I, madame, am Maffio Orsini, brother of the Duke of Gravina, whom your sbirri strangled while he lay asleep.

JEPPO.

And I am Jeppo Liveretto, nephew of Liveretto Vitelli, whom you had stabbed to death in the vaults of the Vatican.

ASCANIO.

I am Ascanio Petrucci, madame, the cousin of Pandolfo Petrucci, Lord of Sienna, murdered by your command that you might the more easily purloin his city.

OLOFERNO.

Madame, my name is Oloferno Vitellozzo, nephew of that Iago of Appiani, whom you did to death by poison at a party, after treacherously cozening him out of his seignorial citadel of Piombino.

DON APOSTOLO.

Madame, you put to death upon the scaffold Don Francesco Gazella, maternal uncle of Don Alphonso of Aragon, who died upon the staircase of Saint Peter's, beaten to death by halberds in your pay. I am Don Apostolo Gazella, of one the cousin, and the other's son.

DONNA LUCREZIA.

O God !

GENNARO.

Who is this woman ?

MAFFIO.

And now that we have told you our names, madame, is it your wish that we should tell you yours?

DONNA LUCREZIA.

No ! no ! my lords, have pity ! Not before him !

MAFFIO (removing her mask).

Off with your mask, madame, that we may see whether you still possess the power to blush.

DON APOSTOLO.

Gennaro, she to whom thou speakest of love is a base poisoner and adulteress.

JEPPO.

A vile, incestuous creature, too. Guilty of incest with her brothers, who sought each other's lives for love of her !

DONNA LUCREZIA.
Mercy !

ASCANIO.

And with her father, who is pope to-day !

DONNA LUCREZIA.

Have pity !

OLOFERNO.

Doubtless she would have had incestuous commerce with her sons, had sons been born to her, but Heaven denies sweet motherhood to monsters !

DONNA LUCREZIA.

Enough ! enough !

MAFFIO.

Wilt thou know her name, Gennaro ?

DONNA LUCREZIA.

Mercy ! mercy ! my lords !

MAFFIO.

Gennaro, wilt thou know her name ?

DONNA LUCREZIA (kneeling at Gennaro's feet).

Do not listen, my Gennaro !

MAFFIO (raising his arm).

She is Lucrezia Borgia !

GENNARO (pushing her away).

Oh ! . . .

ALL.

Lucrezia Borgia !

(She falls fainting at Gennaro's feet.)

SECOND PART

A public square in Ferrara. At the right a palace with a balcony furnished with Venetian blinds, and a low door. Under the balcony a large stone escutcheon bearing a coat of arms with the word: BORGIA, in great raised letters of copper, gilded at the base. At the left a small house with a door opening on the square. In the background, houses and steeples.

SCENE I

DONNA LUCREZIA, GUBETTA.

DONNA LUCREZIA.

Is everything made ready for to-night, Gubetta?

GUBETTA.
Yes, madame.

DONNA LUCREZIA.
Will all the five be there?

GUBETTA.
All five.

DONNA LUCREZIA.
They did most grievously insult me to my face, Gubetta.

GUBETTA.
I was not there to see.

DONNA LUCREZIA.
They showed no mercy.

GUBETTA.
Did they speak your name aloud?

DONNA LUCREZIA.
They spoke my name, Gubetta, and fairly spat it in my face.

GUBETTA.
In presence of the guests?

DONNA LUCREZIA.

In presence of Gennaro.

GUBETTA.

Shallow-brained idiots they must needs be to leave Venice for Ferrara. And yet they could not well do otherwise, being appointed by the Senate to the embassy that came but lately hither.

DONNA LUCREZIA.

Oh! now he hates me and despises me, and all the fault is theirs. I 'll be revenged on them, Gubetta!

GUBETTA.

Good! that 's the way to talk. Your merciful humor has left you, God be praised! I am far more at my ease with your Highness when you are like your natural self, as now. I know at least what ground I stand on. A lake, you see, madame, is the opposite of an island; a tower is the opposite of a well; an aqueduct is the opposite of a bridge; and I have the honor to be the opposite of a virtuous person.

DONNA LUCREZIA.

Gennaro is with them. Look well to it that naught befalls him.

GUBETTA.

If we should severally be transformed, you to a good woman, and I to a good man, 't would be a monstrous thing.

DONNA LUCREZIA.

Look well to it, I say, that naught befalls Gennaro!

GUBETTA.

Have no fear.

DONNA LUCREZIA.

I would gladly see him once again.

GUBETTA.

God's love! madame, your Highness sees him every day. You bought his valet so that he should persuade his master to fix his quarters in that hovel yonder opposite your balcony, and from your latticed window every day you have the unspeakable delight of seeing the said gentleman go in and out.

DONNA LUCREZIA.

I mean that I would gladly speak with him, Gubetta.

GUBETTA.

Nothing more simple. Send, by Astolfo, your cloak-bearer, to say to him that your Highness will await his coming at such or such an hour at the palace.

DONNA LUCREZIA.

That will I do, Gubetta. But think'st thou he will come?

GUBETTA.

Go you in, madame; I fancy that he soon will pass this way with the witlings in question.

DONNA LUCREZIA.

Do they still take thee for the Count of Belverana?

GUBETTA.

They believe me a true Spaniard from heel to eyebrow. I am among their dearest friends. I borrow money from them.

DONNA LUCREZIA.

Money! and wherefore?

GUBETTA.

Per Bacco! to have it. Furthermore there is nothing more Spanish than to have a beggarly air and to pull the devil by the tail.

DONNA LUCREZIA (aside).

Oh, my God! grant that my Gennaro may not come to harm!

GUBETTA.

And, apropos, madame, that suggests something to my mind.

DONNA LUCREZIA.

What is it?

GUBETTA.

That the devil's tail must be welded and screwed and fastened most securely to his spine to withstand the exhaustless multitude of people who are forever pulling at it!

DONNA LUCREZIA.

Thou hast a laugh for everything, Gubetta.

GUBETTA.

That way 's as good as another.

DONNA LUCREZIA.

Methinks they come. Slight none of my commands.

(She enters the palace by the small door under the balcony.)

SCENE II

GUBETTA (alone).

Who in God's name may this Gennaro be, and what the devil can she want with him? I am not cognizant of all my lady's secrets, far from it: but this one stirs my curiosity. 'Faith! she has chosen not to confide in me this time, and she must by no means fancy that she can depend on me. Let her conduct her intrigue with Gennaro as she can. But what strange way is this to love a man, when one is daughter of the Vanozza and Rodrigo Borgia: when one has in her veins the blood of a harlot, and the blood of a pope! Donna Lucrezia indulging in Platonic love! There's nothing could arouse my wonder now—not even were I to be well assured that Alexander Sixth believes in God.

(He looks down the nearest street.)

Ah! here come our young madmen from the carnival at Venice. A shrewd idea it was of theirs to leave a free and neutral state, and come to Ferrara, after they'd mortally insulted the Duchess of Ferrara! Had I been in their place, most certainly I would have held aloof from helping swell the suite of the Venetian ambassadors. But so young men are made. Of all things sublunary, they seem most eager to jump into the wolf's maw.

(The young noblemen enter, but at first do not see Gubetta, who has stationed himself to watch their movements behind one of the pillars which sustain the balcony. They talk together in undertones and with evident uneasiness.)

SCENE III

GUBETTA: GENNARO, MAFFIO, JEPPO, ASCANIO, DON APOSTOLO, OLOFERNO.

MAFFIO (in a whisper).

You may say what you will, gentlemen: it would have been as well to avoid Ferrara, when we had wounded Donna Lucrezia Borgia to the quick.

DON APOSTOLO.

But what choice had we? The Senate sends us hither. What means exist by which one may evade the behests of that most serene body? Once designated to perform the duty, one can do naught but go. Yet do I not gainsay thee, Maffio, that the fair Borgia's a most redoubtable foe. She is the mistress here.

JEPPO.

What dost thou fear that she may do to us, Apostolo? Are we not in the service of the Republic of Venice? Are we not attached to her embassy? To touch but one hair of our heads would be to levy war upon the Doge, and Ferrara's none too anxious to measure swords with Venice.

GENNARO (musing, in a corner of the stage, and taking no part in the conversation).

O mother! mother! Will not some one tell me how I may succor my poor mother?

MAFFIO.

They can lay thee at full length in thy tomb, Jeppo, without once touching a hair of thy head. There are poisons which arrange matters for the Borgias without a hue and cry

and much more comfortably than club and dagger. Why, dost thou not recall how Alexander Sixth sent to the other world young Sultan Zizim, brother of Bajazet?

OLOFERNO.

And many others.

DON APOSTOLO.

A strange tale that of Bajazet's young brother, and no less diabolical than strange. The pope persuaded him that Charles of France did poison him the day they dined together. Zizim believed it all, and from the fair hands of Lucrezia Borgia received a so-called antidote, which rid his brother Bajazet of him in two short hours.

JEPPO.

'T would seem the honest Turk was little versed in politics.

MAFFIO.

Yes, the Borgias have poisons that kill one in a day, or in a year, at their will. They are infernal poisons, too: they make wine taste the better, and give the greater zest to emptying the flagon. You think you 're drunk, but you are dead. Or it may be a man's oppressed with deathly languor, his skin grows wrinkled, his hair turns white, his eyes sink in his head, and his teeth break like glass against the bread he eats: he walks no more, but drags himself along: he breathes no more but has the death rattle always in his throat: he laughs no more, nor sleeps, and shivers in the sunshine at high noon: young though he be, he seems an old, old man: and thus some little time he lingers on in agony, then dies at last. He dies: and then his friends remember that some six months or a year since he drank a glass of Cyprus at a Borgia's table.

(He turns.)

Look, my lords, there 's Montefeltro yonder: perhaps you know him: he 's a Ferraran, and these very things are happening to him e'en now. See, he crosses the end of the square. Observe him.

(A man passes across the stage at the back; he has snow-white hair, is thin and limps weakly along, leaning on a cane, and wrapped in a cloak.)

ASCANIO.

Poor Montefeltro !

DON APOSTOLO.

How old is he ?

MAFFIO.

Of my own age. Some nine and twenty.

OLOFERNO.

I saw him not a year ago as fresh and plump as you.

MAFFIO.

'T is three months since he supped at Villa Belvedera with the Holy Father.

ASCANIO.

How horrible !

MAFFIO.

Ah ! strange tales are told of these supper-parties of the Borgias.

ASCANIO.

They are unbridled debauches, seasoned with poisonings.

MAFFIO.

Observe, my lords, how desert is the square about us. The people do not risk their lives so near the ducal palace as do we. They fear the poisons, which are brewing night and day therein, may filter through the walls.

ASCANIO.

Well, gentlemen, the ambassadors had their audience yesterday of the duke. Our mission 's nearly ended. The retinue consists of fifty knights. Our disappearance would hardly be observed among so many. To my mind we should do extremely well to leave Ferrara.

MAFFIO.

This very day !

JEPPO.

To-morrow it will still be time, my friends. This evening I am bidden to sup with Princess Negroni, to whom I have completely lost my heart, and I 'm most loath to seem to fly before the prettiest woman in Ferrara.

OLOFERNO.

You are bidden to sup with Princess Negroni this evening ?

JEPPO.

Yes.

OLOFERNO.

And so am I.

ASCANIO.

And I.

DON APOSTOLO.

And I.

MAFFIO.

And I.

GUBETTA (coming out from the shadow of the pillar).

And I, gentlemen.

JEPPO.

Ah ! Signor di Belverana. 'T is well ! we will all go together. 'T will be a charming evening. Good-day to you, Signor di Belverana.

GUBETTA.

May God lengthen your days, Signor Jeppo!

MAFFIO (aside to Jeppo).

You 'll think me very timid, Jeppo, but, if you give heed to me, we shall not go to this same supper-party. The Palace Negroni adjoins the ducal palace, and I have no great confidence in the amiable expressions of this Signor Belverana.

JEPPO (in an undertone).

You are mad, Maffio. The Negroni is a fascinating creature, I tell you I am madly in love with her, and Belverana is an honest fellow. I have made inquiries touching him and his family. My father was with his at the siege of Grenada, in fourteen eighty something.

MAFFIO.

But that 's no proof that this man is the son of the father who was with your father.

JEPPO.

You 're under no duress to join the party, Maffio.

MAFFIO.

If you go, Jeppo, I shall go.

JEPPO.

Then, long live Jupiter! say I. How is 't with thee, Gennaro? Art thou not one of us this evening?

ASCANIO.

Did not the princess invite thee?

GENNARO.

No. She doubtless deemed my birth too humble.

MAFFIO (smiling).

In that case, brother, thou hast some tryst to keep thyself; am I not right?

JEPPO.

By the by, tell us, pray, of what Donna Lucrezia talked with thee the evening that thou know'st of. It seems that she is mad with love of thee. She must have told thee so at weary length. The freedom of the ball gave her full opportunity. Women disguise their persons, but the more boldly to expose their hearts. Masked the face, the heart laid bare.

(For some moments Donna Lucrezia has been upon the balcony, and has drawn the blind partly aside. She listens.)

MAFFIO.

Ah! thou hast taken thy lodgings directly opposite her balcony. Gennaro! Gennaro!

DON APOSTOLO.

There is much danger in that step, my friend; for the worthy duke is said to be most jealous of his wife.

OLOFERNO.

Tell us, Gennaro, how thou hast prospered in thy *amourette* with the fair Borgia.

GENNARO.

My lords! if you say more to me of that vile woman, our swords will soon be flashing in the sun!

DONNA LUCREZIA (on the balcony).

Alas!

MAFFIO.

It is sheer foolery, Gennaro. But methinks we well may speak to thee of that same lady, since thou wearest her colors.

GENNARO.

What meanest thou?

MAFFIO (pointing to Gennaro's scarf).

That scarf?

JEPPO.

Those are indeed Lucrezia Borgia's colors.

GENNARO.

'T was Fiammetta sent it to me.

MAFFIO.

So thou believest; Lucrezia caused thee to be so informed. But she, with her own hands, fashioned the scarf for thee.

GENNARO.

Maffio, art thou assured of that? From whom dost know it?

MAFFIO.

From thy own valet whom she bought, and who gave thee the scarf.

GENNARO.

Damnation!

(He tears the scarf to ribbons, and tramples on it.)

DONNA LUCREZIA (aside).

Woe 's me!

(She closes the blind and withdraws.)

MAFFIO.

And yet the woman is most beautiful.

JEPPO.

True, but there 's a something sinister engrafted on her beauty.

MAFFIO.

She is a golden ducat, bearing Satan's effigy.

GENNARO.

Oh! curses on Lucrezia Borgia! You say she loves me! that that woman loves me! Ah, well! 't is better so! and let this be her punishment! she fills my soul with horror! Yes, with horror! Thou knowest, Maffio, it is always thus. We cannot be indifferent to a woman who 's in love with us. We must return her love either with love or hate. And how could one love her? 'T is likewise true that the more pertinaciously one is beset by

such a woman's love, the deeper goes one's hatred. This one haunts me, invests me, lays siege to me. What have I done to earn the love of a Lucrezia Borgia? Is it not shameful and deplorable? You cannot dream how odious the bare thought of that vile spawn of hell has come to be to me since the night when you made known her name in such dramatic fashion. Before, I saw her only from afar, a fearful phantom, trampling upon Italy, the terrifying spectre of the world. But now that spectre has become my own, it sits beside my pillow; yes, the spectre loves me, and would share my bed! By my mother's soul, it 's more than horrible! Ah! Maffio, she killed Signor di Gravina, yes, she killed thy brother. So! I will take thy brother's place with thee, and will avenge his death on her! Behold her execrable palace! palace of wantonness, palace of treason and of murder, palace of incest and adultery, palace of the whole calendar of crime, palace of Lucrezia Borgia! Oh! the brand of infamy I cannot stamp upon that woman's brow, by Heaven! I will stamp upon her palace!

(He steps upon the stone bench under the balcony, and with his dagger, strikes off the first letter of the name—Borgia—upon the escutcheon, so that the word ORGIA remains.)

MAFFIO.

What in God's name is he doing?

JEPPO.

Gennaro, that one letter the less in Donna Lucrezia's name means a head the less on thy shoulders.

GUBETTA.

Signor Gennaro, that pleasantry will cause half of the city to be put to the question.

GENNARO.

If she seeks the culprit, I will come forward.

GUBETTA (aside).

I would he might, by Jupiter! Donna Lucrezia would be prettily embarrassed.

(For some moments two men dressed in black have been walking upon the square, and watching.)

MAFFIO.

Gentlemen, yonder are some fellows of forbidding mien, who seem to observe us somewhat curiously. I think we should do well to separate. Brother Gennaro, no new madcap freaks.

GENNARO.

Fear not for me, my Maffio. Thy hand. Much pleasure to you, gentlemen, to-night!

(He enters his lodgings. The others disperse.)

SCENE IV

THE TWO MEN IN BLACK.

FIRST MAN.

What the devil dost thou here, Rustighello?

SECOND MAN.

I 'm waiting until thou dost take thy leave, Astolfo.

FIRST MAN.

Really?

SECOND MAN.

And what the devil dost thou here, Astolfo?

FIRST MAN.

I 'm waiting until thou dost take thy leave, Rustighello.

SECOND MAN.

With whom, pray, does thy business lie, Astolfo?

FIRST MAN.

With the youth who but now entered yonder house. And thine?

SECOND MAN.

With the same youth.

FIRST MAN.

The devil!

SECOND MAN.

What dost thou propose to do with him?

FIRST MAN.

To take him to the duchess. And thou?

SECOND MAN.

To take him to the duke.

FIRST MAN.

The devil!

SECOND MAN.

What has he to expect at the duchess's?

FIRST MAN.

Love, doubtless. And at the duke's?

SECOND MAN.

Probably the gallows.

FIRST MAN.

What 's to be done? He can't go to the duke and duchess both, or be at the same time a happy lover and hanged.

SECOND MAN.

Here 's a ducat. Let us toss up to see which of us shall have the man.

FIRST MAN.

Agreed.

SECOND MAN.

'Faith, if I lose, I 'll simply tell the duke I found the bird had flown. When all is said, I care but little for the duke's affairs.

(He tosses a ducat in the air.)

FIRST MAN.

Tail.

SECOND MAN (looking at the ground).

'T is head.

FIRST MAN.

Then let him be hanged. Take him. Farewell.

SECOND MAN.

Give you good-night.

(As soon as the other has disappeared, he opens the low door under the balcony, goes in, returns a moment later, accompanied by four sbirri, and knocks at the door of the house which Gennaro entered.)

Curtain.

ACT SECOND

THE COUPLE

FIRST PART

An apartment in the ducal palace at Ferrara. Hangings of Hungarian leather, stamped with gold arabesques. Superb furniture in the style of the latter part of the fifteenth century in Italy. The ducal chair of state, covered with red velvet embroidered with the crest of the house of Este. At one side a table covered with red velvet. At the rear of the stage a large door. At the right a small door. At the left another small door hidden by the hangings. Behind the last named door, in a small room which lies wholly upon the stage, can be seen the beginning of a spiral staircase leading down beneath the floor and lighted by a long and narrow barred window.

SCENE I

DON ALPHONSO D'ESTE, in a gorgeous costume of his own colors. RUSTIGHELLO, in a costume of the same colors, but of less costly material.

RUSTIGHELLO.

My lord duke, your first orders have been carried out. What is your pleasure now?

DON ALPHONSO.

Take this key and go to Numa's gallery. Count every panel in the wainscoting, from the large painted figure near the door, wherein is represented Hercules, Jupiter's son, one of my ancestors. When thou hast counted up to twenty-three, thou 'lt see a tiny opening hid betwixt the jaws of a gilded serpent of Milan. Therein insert the key; the panel then will

41

turn upon its hinges like a door. 'T was
Ludovic the Moor who made the panel thus.
Within the secret closet it conceals thou 'lt
see upon a crystal salver two flagons, one of
silver, one of gold, with two enamel cups.
Naught but pure water 's in the silver flagon ;
but in the other wine that has been *prepared*.
Disarrange naught, but bring the salver,
Rustighello, into yon cabinet, and if thou
hast ever heard men speak, while their teeth
chattered in affright, of that famed poison of
the Borgias, which, in a powder, is as white
and scintillant as fine Carrara marble ground
to dust, but which, when mixed with wine,
changes good Romorantin into Syracuse,
thou 'lt take good heed to keep thy fingers off
the golden flagon.

RUSTIGHELLO.

And is that all, my lord ?

DON ALPHONSO.

No ; thou wilt take thy keenest sword, and
stand behind the door within the cabinet, so
placed that thou canst hear whatever passes,
and canst come at my first call upon this
silver bell, the sound of which thou knowest.

(He points to a bell upon the table.)

If I call simply : "Rustighello !" thou 'lt
enter with the salver. If the bell rings,
thou 'lt enter with thy sword.

RUSTIGHELLO.

'T is well, my lord.

DON ALPHONSO.

Have thy sword naked in thy hand, so
thou 'lt not have the trouble to unsheath it.

RUSTIGHELLO.

'T is well.

DON ALPHONSO.

Take two swords, Rustighello ; one may
break. Now go.

(Exit Rustighello through the small door.)

AN USHER (enters by the door at the back of the
stage).

Our lady the duchess craves speech of our
lord the duke.

DON ALPHONSO.

Show my lady in.

SCENE II

DON ALPHONSO, DONNA LUCREZIA.

DONNA LUCREZIA (rushing upon the stage in great excitement).

My lord, my lord, this is most shameful, flagrant and most infamous. Some one of your retainers—dost know it, Don Alphonso? —has dared to mutilate your consort's name, engraved above the armorial bearings of my family on the façade of your own palace! 'T was done in broad daylight, and publicly— by whom? I know not, but 't is most shameful and insulting. My name has been transformed into a word of obloquy, and your Ferrara populace,—the most perfidious in all Italy, my lord—are sneering there at my emblazonment, as if they stood about a pillory. You surely cannot dream that I 'll sit meekly by and suffer it, my lord: and that I would not rather choose to die for good and all with one blow of a dagger, than die ten thousand deaths from the envenomed sting of sarcasm and banter? God's death! Signor, I undergo strange treatment here in your lordship of Ferrara! Ere now I have begun to weary of it, and you, methinks, are far too tranquil and too amiable the while your wife's good name is dragged through the gutters of your city's streets, and torn to shreds by calumny and insult. Flagrant reparation I must have for this. I warn you, my lord duke. Prepare to do me justice. Mark what I say, this is no laughing matter. Dost think, perchance, that there is no one in the world for whose esteem I care, and that my husband need be at no pains to be my knight? No, no, my lord, who marries must protect. Who gives his hand, gives with it his strong arm. I count upon you. Day after day insults are heaped upon me, and never do I see that you are moved. Does not the mire with which I am bespattered, Don Alphonso, bespatter you as well? Come, come, in God's name, knit your brows a bit, that I may see you once in all your life show some resentment on your wife's account! You love me dearly, so you sometimes say? love my fair fame no less! you 're jealous? be jealous of my glory! If by my dowry I increased twofold your inherited domains: if I did bring to you in marriage, not the gold rose alone, and benediction of the Holy Father, but certain things which occupy far more of the earth's surface,— Sienna, Rimini, Cesena, Spoleto, Piombino, and more towns than you yourself had castles, more duchies than you had of baronies: if I did make you the most puissant nobleman in Italy; not for that reason, signor, should you let your people rail at me, insult me, trumpet my name abroad, and your Ferrara display me to all Europe more scorned and more humiliated than your groom's valet's maid. I say that that 's no reason that your vile subjects should not let me pass among them without saying: "Ha! that woman!" And now, mark what I say, signor: it is my pleasure that this day's delict shall be looked into, and condignly punished: else will I make complaint to Valentinois who is at Forli with ten thousand troops. Now let us see if it is worth your while to leave your easy chair.

DON ALPHONSO.

Madame, the crime that you complain of is well known to me.

DONNA LUCREZIA.

What do I hear, my lord? The crime is known to you, and still the culprit 's not discovered?

DON ALPHONSO.

The culprit is discovered.

DONNA LUCREZIA.

Great God! if he 's discovered, how happens it he 's not arrested?

DON ALPHONSO.

He is arrested, madame.

DONNA LUCREZIA.

Upon my soul, if he 's indeed arrested, how happens it that he is not yet punished?

DON ALPHONSO.

He soon will be. I wished first to advise with you as to the punishment.

DONNA LUCREZIA.

And you did well, my lord. Where is he?

DON ALPHONSO.

Here.

DONNA LUCREZIA.

Ah, here! A palpable example must be made, you understand, my lord. The crime 's _lèse-majesté_. Such crimes always entail the falling of the hand that executes as well as of the head that plans them. Ah! he is here! I fain would see him.

DON ALPHONSO.

That 's easily arranged.

(Calling.)

Baptista!

(The usher enters.)

DONNA LUCREZIA.

Another word, my lord, before the culprit comes. Whoever he may be, be he of your city, or of your very household, Don Alphonso, give me your word of honor as crowned duke, that he shall not go out from here alive.

DON ALPHONSO.

You have my word. You have my word, madame, dost understand?

DONNA LUCREZIA.

'T is well. Why, yes, I understand. Now bring him in, and let me question him myself. My God! what is it that I 've done to these Ferrarans, that they persecute me thus?

DON ALPHONSO (to the usher).

Bring in the prisoner.

(The door at the rear of the stage is thrown open. Gennaro appears, disarmed, between two halberdiers. At the same moment Rustighello comes up the staircase in the little cabinet at the left behind the concealed door. He has in his hand a salver upon which are a gold flagon, a silver flagon, and two cups. He places the salver on the window-sill, draws his sword and stations himself behind the door.)

SCENE III

Tur Same: GENNARO.

DONNA LUCREZIA (aside).

Gennaro!

DON ALPHONSO (draws near to her and speaks in an undertone and with a smile).

Can it be, madame, that you know this man?

DONNA LUCREZIA (aside).

'T is Gennaro! O God! what a fatality! (She looks agonizingly at him. He turns his eyes away.)

GENNARO.

My lord duke, I am a simple captain, and address you with the respect to which you are entitled. Your Highness caused me to be seized this morning where I lodge. What is your pleasure with me?

DON ALPHONSO.

Signor Captain, the crime of *lèse-majesté* was committed this morning, opposite the house in which you live. The name of our beloved spouse and cousin, Donna Lucrezia Borgia, was insolently defaced upon the façade of our ducal palace. We seek the culprit.

DONNA LUCREZIA.

'T is not he! there's some mistake, my lord. 'T is not this youth.

DON ALPHONSO.

How can you know?

DONNA LUCREZIA.

I'm sure of what I say. This youth 's of Venice, not Ferrara. And so . .

DON ALPHONSO.

What does that prove?

DONNA LUCREZIA.

The deed was done this morning, and it 's within my knowledge that he passed the morning with one Fiammetta.

GENNARO.

Not so, madame.

DON ALPHONSO.

'T would seem your Highness is not well informed. Pray, let me question him. Captain Gennaro, are you he who did this thing?

DONNA LUCREZIA (in desperation).

I'm stifling here! Air! air! I must have air!

(She runs to a window, and as she passes Gennaro whispers hurriedly.)

Say that thou didst not do it!

DON ALPHONSO (aside).

She whispers to him.

GENNARO.

Don Alphonso, the fishers of Calabria, who reared me, and dipped me in the sea in childhood to make me strong and bold, taught me this maxim, which may lead one often to risk life, but never honor, "Do what thou sayest, and say what thou doest." Don Alphonso, I am the man you seek.

DON ALPHONSO (turning to Donna Lucrezia).

You have my word of honor as crowned duke, madame.

DONNA LUCREZIA.

I must say a word to you, my lord, in private.

(The duke motions to the usher and the guards to withdraw to the next room with the prisoner.)

SCENE IV

DONNA LUCREZIA, DON ALPHONSO.

DON ALPHONSO.

What would you with me, madame?

DONNA LUCREZIA.

This, Don Alphonso, that I would not that this youth should die.

DON ALPHONSO.

'T is but an instant since you entered here, angry and weeping, like a very tempest, and lodged complaint of a foul outrage put upon you; with shrieks and insult you cried out for the offender's head; demanded that I give my ducal word that he should not go forth from here alive, the which I loyally did give you, madame, and now you do not wish that he should die! By Jesus! madame, this passes comprehension!

DONNA LUCREZIA.

I do not choose that this young man shall die, my noble duke.

DON ALPHONSO.

Madame, those gentlemen who 've proved their gentle blood as I have done are little wont to leave their pledge in pawn. You have my word and I must needs redeem it. I swore the guilty man should die, and die he shall. But by my soul, you may, if you so please, select the kind of death.

DONNA LUCREZIA (smiling sweetly upon him).

Don Alphonso, Don Alphonso, what utter nonsense you and I are talking! It 's very true that I 'm a most unreasonable creature. My father spoiled me, that you know full well. From my childhood up my slightest whims have been obeyed. That which I longed for half an hour since, I 've ceased to long for now; it has been always so with me, as you know, Don Alphonso. Come sit you there, beside me, and let 's talk a while, frankly and lovingly, like man and wife, like two good friends.

DON ALPHONSO (assuming a gallant bearing).

You are my wife, Donna Lucrezia, and I am but too happy that it gives you pleasure to have me for an instant at your feet.

(He takes a seat beside her.)

DONNA LUCREZIA.

How good it is to understand each other! Do you know, Alphonso, that I do love you still as dearly as on the first day of our wedded life, the day when you made such a dazzling entry into Rome, between Signor di Valentinois, my brother, and Cardinal Hippolyte d'Este, yours? I was upon the balcony above St. Peter's steps. How well do I recall your beautiful white horse with trappings of chased gold, and the illustrious kingly mien with which you rode him!

DON ALPHONSO.

You were most beautiful yourself, madame, and fairly dazzling beneath your canopy of gold brocade.

DONNA LUCREZIA.

Oh! do not speak of me, my lord, when I would speak of you. Certain it is that all the princesses in Europe envied my fortune in espousing the noblest knight in Christendom. And I love you to-day, as if I were no more than sweet eighteen. You know I love you, do you not, Alphonso? Surely you never doubt it. I am cold at times, and absent; in that my nature is at fault, and not my heart. Listen, Alphonso; if your Highness would but scold me gently for it, I soon would mend my ways. How sweet it is to love as we do! Give me your hand,—and kiss me, Don Alphonso!—In very truth, if one does but reflect upon it, it is preposterous, that you and I, a prince and princess, seated side by side upon the most illustrious of ducal thrones, loving each other well, have been upon the point of quarreling, all for a paltry, pitiful Venetian captain! We must send the man away, and think no more of him. We'll let the rascal go where'er he pleases, will we not, Alphonso? The lion and the lioness won't lose their heads all for a wretched fly. Dost know, my lord, that if the ducal crown were offered in competition to the most gallant cavalier in all Ferrara, you would not cease to wear it. Wait, while I tell Baptista 't is your will that this Gennaro be forthwith driven from Ferrara.

DON ALPHONSO.

Nothing calls for haste.

DONNA LUCREZIA (playfully).

But I would like to think no more of him. Good my lord, let me conclude this matter as I choose.

DON ALPHONSO.

Nay, rather it must be concluded as I choose.

DONNA LUCREZIA.

And yet, Alphonso mine, you have no motive to desire this man's death.

DON ALPHONSO.

What of my word I gave to you? A king's word is a sacred thing.

DONNA LUCREZIA.

That 's very fine to fill the ears of the people. But as between ourselves, Alphonso, we know it means but little. The Holy Father promised Charles VIII. of France that Zizim should not die, and yet his Holiness did none the less contrive poor Zizim's death. The Duke of Valentinois became, upon his honor, hostage for that same youth to the same Charles, and then made his escape from the French camp when first occasion offered. You did yourself engage to restore Sienna to the Petrucci. You did it not, nor should have done it. Good lack! the history of all countries is filled with broken oaths. No king, no nation could endure a day if oaths must be so rigidly adhered to. Between ourselves, Alphonso, a sworn promise is never a necessity, save when there 's nothing else to take its place.

DON ALPHONSO.

And yet, Donna Lucrezia, an oath!

DONNA LUCREZIA.

A truce to all such paltry reasons. I am no silly girl. Rather be frank with me, my dear Alphonso, and tell me if aught inclines you to wish ill to this Gennaro. No? Why, then, grant me his life. You have already granted me his death. What matters it to you, if it 's my whim to pardon him? 'T was I whom he insulted.

DON ALPHONSO.

'T is just because he so insulted you, my love, that I 'll not pardon him.

DONNA LUCREZIA.

Alphonso, if you love me, you will not
deny me longer. What if it pleases me to try
my 'prentice hand at clemency? It is a way to
make myself beloved by your people; and
that 's my earnest wish. Mercy, Alphonso,
makes kings resemble Christ. Let us begin
to rule by mercy. Poor Italy has enough of
tyrants without us, from the baron, vicar of the
pope, e'en to the pope himself, God's vicar.
Let us have done with this, Alphonso. Set
this Gennaro free. It 's caprice if you choose,
but there is something sacred and worthy of
respect about a woman's caprice, when a
man's head is saved thereby.

DON ALPHONSO.

I cannot, dear Lucrezia.

DONNA LUCREZIA.

You cannot? Why, I pray to know, can
you not grant so slight a boon to me as this
young captain's life?

DON ALPHONSO.

You ask me why, my love?

DONNA LUCREZIA.

Yes, why?

DON ALPHONSO.

Because this captain is your lover, madame.

DONNA LUCREZIA.

Great Heaven!

DON ALPHONSO.

Because you went to seek him out at Venice!
Because you 'd gladly go to hell to seek him!
Because I followed you the while you followed
him! Because I saw you, masked and pant-
ing 'neath your mask, pursue him as a she-
wolf her prey! Because but now, this very
moment, you encompassed him with a glance
brimming o'er with tears and with the flame
of love! Because I doubt not, madame, that

ere this you have been false to me with
him! Because there 's been enough dishonor, shame and crime! Because it is full
time that I avenge my honor, and dig about
my bed a moat of blood! Mark what I say,
madame!

DONNA LUCREZIA.

Don Alphonso . . .

DON ALPHONSO.

Hold your peace. Henceforth, Lucrezia,
look well to your lovers! Station whatever
lackey you may choose as usher at the door
which opens into your apartment; but at the
door which gives egress therefrom, there 'll
be a porter of my choice—the hangman!

DONNA LUCREZIA.

My lord, I swear . . .

DON ALPHONSO.

Swear me no oaths. They 're very well to
fill the ears of the people. Give me no more
such wretched reasons.

DONNA LUCREZIA.

If you but knew . . .

DON ALPHONSO.

Hark ye, madame: I utterly detest your
whole abominable Borgia family, and you,
whom once I madly loved, I hate most
bitterly of all! Thus much I would say to
you thereon: that 't is a shameful thing, and
past belief, to see allied in our two persons,
the house of Este, which is far greater than the
house of Valois or of Tudor—to see, I say, the
house of Este united with the Borgia family,
who have no rightful claim to the name
Borgia, but properly are called Lenzuoli,
Lenzolio, or God knows what! I have the
utmost horror of your brother Cæsar, who has
the livid birthmarks on his face; Cæsar, who
slew your brother Giovanni! And for your

mother, Rose Vanozza, the old Spanish strumpet, whose life at Rome was no less scandalous than were her earlier years in Valencia. And as for your pretended nephews, the Dukes of Sermoneto and of Nepi! Fine dukes, forsooth! dukes made with stolen duchies! dukes of yesterday. Let me conclude. I have a horror of your father, who is pope, and has a harem like the Turkish Sultan Bajazet,—your father, who 's a very anti-Christ, who fills the galleys with illustrious persons and the Sacred College with banditti, so that on seeing them all clothed in red, cardinals and galley-slaves alike, one well might ask whether the cardinals were the galley-slaves, and the galley-slaves the cardinals! Now go!

DONNA LUCREZIA.

My lord! my lord! here on my bended knee, and with clasped hands, I beg of you, in the name of Jesus and of Mary, in your father's and your mother's names, my lord, to spare this captain's life.

DON ALPHONSO.

Here is true love indeed! You may act your pleasure with his dead body, madame, and that within an hour, my word for 't.

DONNA LUCREZIA.

Mercy for Gennaro!

DON ALPHONSO.

If you could read the firm determination of my heart, you 'd speak no more of him than if he were a corpse.

DONNA LUCREZIA (rising).

Then, look well to yourself, Alphonso of Ferrara, my fourth spouse!

DON ALPHONSO.

Oh! do not play the terrible with me, madame! Go to! I fear you not. I know your tricks. I 'll not be poisoned like your first husband, the poor Spanish gentleman, whose name I do not now remember, nor do you. I 'll not be driven off like Giovanni Sforza, Lord of Pesaro, your second husband, the poor imbecile! I 'll not be felled with halberd blows on any stairway under heaven, like your third husband, Alphonso of Aragon, puny child, whose blood did scarcely stain the steps more than pure water! A glorious trio! I, madame, am a man. The name of Hercules is often borne by members of my family. By Heaven! my city 's full, my whole domain is full of soldiers, and I myself am one, nor have I yet, like the poor King of Naples, sold all my trusty cannon to the pope, your holy father!

DONNA LUCREZIA.

You will repent these words, my lord. You forget who I am.

DON ALPHONSO.

Ah! no! be sure that I remember who you are, but I remember also where you are. You are the daughter of the pope, but you are not at Rome; you are the governor of Spoleto, but you are not at Spoleto; you are the wife, the vassal and the servant of Alphonso, Duke of Ferrara, and you are at Ferrara!

(Donna Lucrezia, livid with fear and wrath, gazes fixedly at the duke, and falls back before him until she reaches a chair, into which she falls, as if vanquished.)

Ah! that surprises you, you fear me, madame! hitherto 't was I who stood in fear of you. I purpose that it shall be thus henceforth, and to begin with, this, the first of your lovers upon whom I lay my hand, shall die!

DONNA LUCREZIA (in a faint voice).

Let us reason a little, Don Alphonso. If this be truly he who committed *lèse-majesté* against me, he cannot at the same time be my lover.

DON ALPHONSO.

Why not? in a fit of spite, of anger or of jealousy, for he perhaps is jealous too. But, after all, what matters it to me? I say this man shall die. It is my whim. This palace overflows with soldiers, who are devoted to me, and know none but me. Escape he cannot. You can do nothing, madame; I leave to you to choose the kind of death, so choose.

DONNA LUCREZIA (wringing her hands).

O God! O God! O God!

DON ALPHONSO.

You do not answer? I'll have him put to the sword in yonder cabinet.

(He starts to go out; she seizes his arm.)

DONNA LUCREZIA.

Stay!

DON ALPHONSO.

Would you prefer to pour for him yourself a glass of Syracuse?

DONNA LUCREZIA.

Gennaro!

DON ALPHONSO.

He must die.

DONNA LUCREZIA.

Not by the sword!

DON ALPHONSO.

The manner matters little. What do you choose?

DONNA LUCREZIA.

The other.

DON ALPHONSO.

You must take heed lest your hand go astray; you'll fill his glass yourself from the gold flagon that you know of. I shall be at hand. Imagine not that I shall leave you.

DONNA LUCREZIA.

I will do what you wish.

DON ALPHONSO.

Baptista!

(The usher enters.)

Bring in the prisoner.

DONNA LUCREZIA.

You are a fiendish man, my lord.

SCENE V

THE SAME: GENNARO, THE GUARDS.

DON ALPHONSO.

What 's this I hear, Signor Gennaro! That what you did this morning you did from mere bravado, and without malign intent, that madame, the duchess, pardons you, and that, moreover, you 're a gallant fellow. By my mother's soul, if so it be, you may return to Venice, safe and sound. May God forbid that I should be the means of fleecing the magnificent republic of a loyal servant, and Christendom of a trusty arm that wields a trusty sword, so long as there be Saracens and idol-worshipers about the shores of Candia and Cyprus!

GENNARO.

Upon my soul, my lord! I scarce expected this conclusion. But I thank your Highness. Clemency 's a royal virtue, and God on high will be most merciful to him who shows mercy here below.

DON ALPHONSO.

Find you the republic a good master, captain? Take one year with another, what 's your employment worth to you?

GENNARO.

I have a company, my lord, of fifty lances, which I myself maintain and uniform. The Most Serene Republic gives me an annual stipend of two thousand golden sequins, exclusive of all booty.

DON ALPHONSO.

If I should offer you four thousand, would you take service under me?

GENNARO.

I could not. I am pledged to the republic for five years to come.

DON ALPHONSO.

How pledged?

GENNARO.

By my plighted oath.

DON ALPHONSO (aside to Donna Lucrezia).

'T would seem that other people keep their oaths, madame.

(Aloud.)

We 'll say no more about it, Signor Gennaro.

GENNARO.

I have been guilty of no dastard's deed to save my life: but since your Highness deigns to spare it, I may now tell you this. The assault at Faenza some two years since doubtless still fills a place in my lord's memory? Duke Hercules of Este, your noble father, was in great peril from two of Valentinois' ruffians, whose swords were at his throat,—a mercenary saved his life.

DON ALPHONSO.

Yes, and the soldier never could be found.

GENNARO.

I am the man.

DON ALPHONSO.

Per Bacco! captain, that was a deed which well deserves to be rewarded. May I not beg you to accept this purse of golden sequins?

GENNARO.

We take an oath, on entering the republic's service, to take no gold from other sovereigns. However, with your Highness's good leave, I will distribute what the purse contains in my own name to these brave fellows here.

(Points to the guards.)

DON ALPHONSO.

Do so.

(Gennaro takes the purse.)

But surely you will drink with me, following the fashion of our ancestors, like the warm friends we are, a glass of my good wine of Syracuse.

GENNARO.

Gladly, my lord.

DON ALPHONSO.

And to do further honor to my father's savior, I beg that you, my lady, will with your own hands pour the wine for him.

(Gennaro bows and walks to the rear of the stage to distribute the money among the soldiers. The duke calls.)

Rustighello!

(Rustighello enters with the salver.)

Lay the salver there, upon the table. Good.

(Takes Donna Lucrezia's hand.)

Listen, madame, to what I have to say to this good fellow. Rustighello, go you back and take your place behind yon door, your drawn sword in your hand, and if you hear the tinkle of the bell, come in. Now go.

(Rustighello enters the cabinet, and is seen to take his stand behind the door.)

Madame, you will yourself fill the youth's glass, and you will be most careful to fill it from this golden flagon.

DONNA LUCREZIA (pale, and in a trembling voice).

Yes. If you but knew what you are doing at this moment, and what a monstrous thing it is, even you yourself, unnatural as you are, my lord, would shudder and turn pale!

DON ALPHONSO.

Take heed that you do not mistake the flagon.—Well, captain!

(Gennaro, having completed the distribution of the money, returns to the front of the stage. The duke fills one of the enamel cups from the silver flagon, and puts the cup to his lips.)

GENNARO.

I am o'erwhelmed with such abundant courtesy, my lord.

DON ALPHONSO.

Madame, fill Signor Gennaro's glass.— Captain, how old are you?

GENNARO. (He takes the other cup, and hands it to the duchess.)

Twenty years, my lord.

DON ALPHONSO (aside to the duchess, who makes a motion to pour from the silver flagon).

The golden flagon, madame!

(She takes the golden flagon in her hand, which trembles violently.)

At that age, captain, you should be in love?

GENNARO.

Who is not more or less in love, my lord?

DON ALPHONSO.

Dost know, madame, that 't would have been the sheerest cruelty to snatch away the captain from this life, from love, from the bright sun of Italy, from all the promise of his twenty years, his glorious trade of war and of adventure, wherein all royal houses take their rise, from fêtes and masquerades, from the gay carnivals of Venice, where he betrays so many husbands, and from the lovely women whom he perchance may love, and who can scarce help loving him—is it not so, madame? I prithee therefore fill the captain's cup.

(Aside.)

If you falter, I call Rustighello.

(She fills Gennaro's cup without a word.)

GENNARO.

Accept my thanks, my lord, for that you let me live for my poor mother.

DONNA LUCREZIA (aside).

Oh! horror!

DON ALPHONSO (drinking).

To your health, Captain Gennaro; may you live many happy years!

GENNARO.

May God give you the same, my lord!

(He drinks.)

DONNA LUCREZIA (aside).

Heaven!

DON ALPHONSO (aside).

'T is done.

(Aloud.)

Your pardon, if I leave you now, my captain. You may depart for Venice when you choose.

(In an undertone to Donna Lucrezia.)

Thank me, madame; you see I leave you tête-à-tête with him. You doubtless wish to say farewell. Stay with him during his last half hour, if it seems good to you.

(He goes out followed by the guards.)

SCENE VI

DONNA LUCREZIA, GENNARO.

(Rustighello can still be seen standing motionless behind the masked door.)

DONNA LUCREZIA.

Gennaro! you are poisoned!

GENNARO.

Poisoned, madame!

DONNA LUCREZIA.

Poisoned.

GENNARO.

I ought in truth to have suspected it, the wine being poured by you.

DONNA LUCREZIA.

Gennaro! do not load me with reproaches. Do not take from me the little strength I have, and which I greatly need for a brief moment. Listen. The duke is jealous of you, thinking you my lover. The duke gave me no choice but to see Rustighello poniard you before my eyes, or with my own hands to pour the poison for you. A fearful poison, too, Gennaro: a poison, the mere thought of which makes all Italians, who know the story of these twenty years past, tremble with horror.

GENNARO.

Ah, yes! the Borgia poison!

DONNA LUCREZIA.

You have drank of it. In this whole world none know the antidote save three—the pope, Valentinois, and I. See, take this phial, which I always carry hidden in my belt. In it, Gennaro, are life, health and safety. One drop, but one, upon your lips, and you are saved.

(She attempts to put the phial to Gennaro's lips, but he recoils.)

GENNARO (gazing earnestly at her).

Who can assure me, madame, that this is not the poison?

DONNA LUCREZIA (sinking despairingly upon a chair).

Oh! my God! my God!

GENNARO.

Is not your name Lucrezia Borgia? Think you that I forget the fate of Bajazet's young brother? Oh! but I know a little history. They made him think, poor lad, that he was poisoned by Charles VIII., and they gave him an antidote, of which he died. And the same hand that offered him the antidote, now holds that phial. And the same voice which bade him drink, now bids me do the same!

DONNA LUCREZIA.

Vile, wretched woman that I am!

GENNARO.

Listen, madame: I'm not deceived by your pretense of love. You have some sinister design upon me. That is apparent. You may know who I am. By Heaven! I read upon your face this moment that you do, and it 's most plain to see that you have some insuperable reason never to tell it me. Your family and mine have been allied, perhaps: it may be that your aim, in poisoning me thus, is not to be revenged on me, but on my mother: who can say 't is not?

DONNA LUCREZIA.

Your mother, Gennaro! Perchance your fancy shows her to you other than as she really is. What would you say if she should prove to be a sinful woman like myself?

GENNARO.

Do not slander her. Oh no! my mother is no woman such as you, Donna Lucrezia! Oh! in my heart and in my dreams I see and know her as she is; I have her image here, born with my life; I should not love her as I do, were she not more than worthy of my love; a son's heart cannot go astray anent his mother. I should detest her if 't were possible that she resembled you. But, no, no, no! Somewhat there is within me cries aloud that my dear mother 's no vile demon of debauchery, incest and poison, like you fine ladies of the present day. Oh God! I know full well that if there lives beneath the vault of heaven one woman, innocent and virtuous and saintlike, that woman is my mother! Oh! thus she must be, and not otherwise! You know her, doubtless, Donna Lucrezia, and you 'll not dare gainsay me!

DONNA LUCREZIA.

Not so, Gennaro, the woman, the mother you describe I do not know.

GENNARO.

In God's name, why do I speak thus before this woman? As if a mother's joy or grief were aught to you, Lucrezia Borgia! Never have you borne children, so 't is said, and well for you you have not! For, do you know, your children would deny you? What wretch could be so Heaven-abandoned as to own such a mother? To be Lucrezia Borgia's son! to call Lucrezia Borgia by the dear name of mother! Oh! . . .

DONNA LUCREZIA.

Gennaro! you are poisoned, and the duke, who thinks you dead ere this, may come at any moment. I should think only of your welfare and of your escape, but this that you are saying is so terrible, that I can do no otherwise than stand here, turned to stone, and listen.

GENNARO.

Madame . . .

DONNA LUCREZIA.

Come! we must make an end of this. Oh! curse me, crush me with your scorn; but you are poisoned—drink this instantly.

GENNARO.

What can I think, madame? The duke is loyal, and I saved his father's life. You I have bitterly insulted. You wish to be revenged on me.

DONNA LUCREZIA.

I, be revenged on thee, Gennaro! Were it essential for me to give my whole life to add one hour to thine, were it essential to shed all my blood to spare thee but one tear, were it essential for me to be pilloried to seat thee on a throne, were it essential for me to endure the pangs of hell to gain for thee one happy moment I would not hesitate, I would not murmur, I would be happy and would kiss thy feet, Gennaro! Oh! naught wilt thou ever know of my poor, miserable heart, save that thou fillest it! Time flies, Gennaro, the poison does its work; soon thou wilt feel it, and then, thou seest, a little longer, and 't will be too late. Life at this moment opens before thee two dark paths into the future, but in the one are fewer moments than years in the other. Thou must determine upon one of them. The alternative is terrible. Let me be thy guide. Have pity on thyself and me, Gennaro. Drink quickly, in God's name!

GENNARO.

So be it. If there's a crime in this, may it recoil upon your head. After all's said, whether you speak the truth or not, my life's not worth the trouble of discussing. Give me the phial.

(He takes it and drinks.)

DONNA LUCREZIA.

Saved! Now thou must depart for Venice as fast as horse can carry thee. Thou hast money?

GENNARO.

Yes.

DONNA LUCREZIA.

The duke believes thee dead. 'T will be an easy task to hide thy flight from him. Stay! Keep this phial, and carry it upon thee always. In times like these we live in, poison's at every board. Thou, more than all others, art in danger from it. Now go, and quickly.

(She leads him to the masked door, and partly opens it.)

Descend this staircase. It leads to a courtyard of the Negroni palace. Thou'lt find it easy to escape that way. Stay not until tomorrow morning, stay not until the sun has set, stay not an hour, no, nor half an hour! Take thy departure from Ferrara on the instant, as if 't were Sodom burning, and do not look behind thee! Farewell! Stay yet an instant. I've one last word to say to thee, Gennaro.

GENNARO.

Say on, madame.

DONNA LUCREZIA.

I say farewell to thee, Gennaro, now, forever—never to see thee more. I must no

longer dream of falling in with thee sometimes upon my path. It was the only happiness I had on earth. But it would be henceforth to risk thy head. And so we are forever parted in this life; alas! I know too well we shall be parted also in the other. Gennaro! wilt thou not say one kindly word to me before you leave me thus for all eternity?

GENNARO.

Madame . . .

DONNA LUCREZIA.

Consider, I have saved thy life.

GENNARO.

You tell me so. All this is most mysterious to me. I know not what to think. Madame, I can forgive you all, except one thing.

DONNA LUCREZIA.

And that?

GENNARO.

By all that you hold dear, by my own head, since I am dear to you, by the eternal welfare of my soul, swear that your crimes have not contributed to my poor mother's misery.

DONNA LUCREZIA.

All words are taken seriously by you, Gennaro. I cannot take that oath.

GENNARO.

O mother! mother! this is the wicked, fiendish woman, to whom thy misery is due!

DONNA LUCREZIA.

Gennaro!

GENNARO.

You have confessed it, madame! Farewell! My curse on thee!

DONNA LUCREZIA.

May Heaven's blessing rest on thee, Gennaro!

(He rushes off. She falls fainting upon a chair.)

SECOND PART

Scene as in Part Second of Act First. The square at Ferrara, with the ducal palace on one side, and the house occupied by Gennaro on the other. It is after nightfall.

SCENE I

DON ALPHONSO, RUSTIGHELLO, closely wrapped in cloaks.

RUSTIGHELLO.

So it was done, my lord. She gave him back to life by means of some, I know not what decoction, and helped him to escape through the courtyard of the Negroni palace.

DON ALPHONSO.

And thou didst suffer it?

RUSTIGHELLO.

How not? The door was bolted fast. I was a prisoner.

DON ALPHONSO.

Thou shouldst have broken down the door.

RUSTIGHELLO.

An oaken door, an iron bolt. A simple task, forsooth!

DON ALPHONSO.

It matters not! thou shouldst, I tell thee, have destroyed the bolt: thou shouldst have forced thy way into the room and slain him.

RUSTIGHELLO.

Suppose it had been possible for me to batter down the door, Donna Lucrezia with her own body would have sheltered him. I must have slain Donna Lucrezia, too.

59

DON ALPHONSO.

Indeed! and then?

RUSTIGHELLO.

My orders did not go to that extent.

DON ALPHONSO.

The most useful servants, Rustighello, are they who comprehend their royal master's meaning without compelling him to say the whole.

RUSTIGHELLO.

Then, too, I should have feared to set your Highness at odds with the pope.

DON ALPHONSO.

Imbecile!

RUSTIGHELLO.

'T was most embarrassing, my lord. To kill the daughter of the Holy Father!

DON ALPHONSO.

But without killing her couldst thou not have raised thy voice, have called to me and warned me, and thus have frustrated her lover's flight?

RUSTIGHELLO.

Oh, yes! and then to-morrow your Highness would be friends again with Donna Lucrezia, and two days hence Donna Lucrezia would have me hanged.

DON ALPHONSO.

Enough. Thou saidst that nothing is yet lost.

RUSTIGHELLO.

'T is true. You see a light in yonder window. Gennaro 's not yet gone. His servant, whom formerly the duchess owned, is now in my pay, and has told me all he knows. This moment he awaits his master behind the citadel with horses all equipped. Gennaro will come forth and join him in an instant.

DON ALPHONSO.

If that be so, let us conceal ourselves behind the corner of his house. 'T is very dark. We will attack him as he passes.

RUSTIGHELLO.

As you please.

DON ALPHONSO.

Is thy sword sharp?

RUSTIGHELLO.

It is.

DON ALPHONSO.

Thou hast a dagger?

RUSTIGHELLO.

There are two things not easy to be found under the sun, an Italian man without a dagger, and an Italian woman without a lover.

DON ALPHONSO.

'T is well. Have at him with both hands.

RUSTIGHELLO.

Why do you not, my lord duke, simply order his arrest, and have him hanged by sentence of the fiscal?

DON ALPHONSO.

He 's a Venetian subject, and that would be to declare war on the Republic. No. A dagger-thrust comes from one knows not where, and compromises no one. The poison would have been better still, but the poison missed its mark.

RUSTIGHELLO.

What say you then, my lord, to this? Shall I not take four *shirri* and dispatch him, and thus spare you the need of taking part in the affray?

DON ALPHONSO.

My friend, Signor Machiavelli, has often said to me, that at such times as this a prince had best trust no one but himself to do his work.

RUSTIGHELLO.

My lord, methinks I hear footsteps approaching.

DON ALPHONSO.

Let us stand close against the wall.

(They draw back into the shadow under the balcony. Maffio enters in holiday garb, humming a lively air, and knocks at Gennaro's door.)

SCENE II

DON ALPHONSO and RUSTIGHELLO, in hiding: MAFFIO, GENNARO.

MAFFIO.

Gennaro!

(*The door opens, and Gennaro appears.*)

GENNARO.

Is 't thou, Maffio? Wilt come in?

MAFFIO.

No. I have but two words to say to thee. Hast thou unalterably determined not to come with us this evening to supper with the Princess Negroni?

GENNARO.

I am not bidden.

MAFFIO.

I will present thee.

GENNARO.

There is another reason, Maffio. I cannot choose but tell thee. I am about to leave Ferrara.

MAFFIO.

What 's that? Thou leave Ferrara?

GENNARO.

Within the hour.

MAFFIO.

And wherefore?

GENNARO.

I 'll tell thee that at Venice.

MAFFIO.

A love affair?

GENNARO.

Even so, a love affair.

MAFFIO.

Thou 'rt dealing ill with me, Gennaro. We have sworn a mutual oath never to part, to be inseparable, to be true brothers, and now thou 'rt setting out without me.

GENNARO.

Come with me!

MAFFIO.

Rather come thou with me! 'T is better far to pass the night at table with pretty women, and jovial boon companions, than on the high road 'twixt the banditti and the dark ravines.

GENNARO.

Thou wert not over sure this morning of thy Princess Negroni.

MAFFIO.

I have made inquiry concerning her. Jeppo was right. She 's a charming creature, amiable and witty, and fond of poetry and music—nothing more. Come, come with me.

GENNARO.

I cannot.

MAFFIO.

What! Start at dead of night! 't is simply to invite assassination.

GENNARO.

Never fear. Farewell. Much pleasure to thee.

MAFFIO.

Brother Gennaro, I mislike the idea of thy journey.

GENNARO.

Brother Maffio, I mislike the idea of thy supper party.

MAFFIO.

Suppose some mishap should befall thee, and I not there!

GENNARO.

Who knows if I shall not reproach myself to-morrow for leaving thee to-night?

MAFFIO.

Hark ye, Gennaro, most certainly we should not part. Let us each yield a little to the other. Come thou with me this evening to the princess, and at break of day we will depart together. Dost thou agree?

GENNARO.

I needs must tell thee, Maffio, the motives of my abrupt departure. Thou then canst judge whether I 'm right or no.

(He takes Maffio aside and whispers in his ear.)

RUSTIGHELLO (under the balcony, aside to Don Alphonso).

Shall we fall upon them, my lord?

DON ALPHONSO.

Let 's see the end of this.

MAFFIO (laughing heartily at what he has heard from Gennaro).

Wouldst have me tell thee what I think of this, Gennaro? Thou hast been duped. There 's neither poison, nor its antidote, in the whole business. Pure comedy. The fair Lucrezia 's over head and ears in love with thee, and chose to have thee think that she had saved thy life, hoping thereby to lead thee gently on from gratitude to love. The duke 's a gallant fellow, incapable of poisoning or murdering any man on earth. Moreover,

thou didst save his father's life, and that he knows. The duchess would have thee take thy leave, that is most evident. Indeed, her amourette can much more handily be carried on at Venice than Ferrara. The husband always bothers her a bit. As for the supper at the princess's, 't will be delightful. Surely thou 'lt come. Zounds! man, we must be reasonable, and not make mountains out of molehills. Thou knowest me to be a discreet man and prudent counselor. Because there have been two or three notorious supper-parties, whereat the Borgias have done to death some of their dearest friends with poisoned wine, that surely is no reason for never supping more. That is no reason why we should scent poison in every bottle of good Syracuse, and spy Lucrezia Borgia lurking behind all the attractive princesses in Italy. Ghosts and moonshine! If it were so, none but children at the breast could feel assured of that which they were drinking, and thus could sup without anxiety. By Hercules, Gennaro! be thou a child, or be a man. Go to thy nurse again, or come to the supper.

GENNARO.

Indeed, it does seem strange to fly at night. It is as if I were afraid. Besides, if there is danger in remaining, I ought not to leave Maffio here alone. Let come what come may: one chance is worth another. 'T is said. Thou wilt present me to the Princess Negroni. I 'll go with thee.

MAFFIO (taking his hand).

Just God! This is a friend indeed!

(They go off; while they are still in sight moving toward the rear of the stage, Don Alphonso and Rustighello come out of their hiding-place.)

RUSTIGHELLO (with his drawn sword in his hand).

Well, my lord, why do you delay? They are but two. Do you give an account of your man, and I will look to the other.

DON ALPHONSO.

No, Rustighello. They are to go to supper with the Princess Negroni. If I am well informed . . .

(He seems to reflect for an instant: then bursts into laughter.)

By Heaven! that would serve my purpose even better, and would be an amusing episode. We 'll wait until to-morrow.

(They re-enter the palace.)

ACT THIRD

THE DEBAUCH

A superb apartment in the Palace Negroni. At the right a small door. At the rear very large folding doors. In the centre of the stage a table magnificently decorated in the style of the sixteenth century. Little black pages, dressed in a livery of gold brocade, are running hither and thither.

As the curtain rises there are fourteen guests at table—Jeppo, Maffio, Ascanio, Oloferno, Apostolo, Gennaro, and Gubetta, and seven lovely young women very handsomely dressed. All are eating or drinking, and laughing and talking gaily with their neighbors, except Gennaro, who is very silent and thoughtful.

SCENE I

JEPPO, MAFFIO, ASCANIO, OLOFERNO, APOSTOLO, GUBETTA, GENNARO, the Ladies and the Pages.

OLOFERNO (raising his glass).

All hail to the wine of Xeres! Xeres della Frontera is a corner of Paradise.

MAFFIO (glass in hand).

I very much prefer this wine to your prosy tales, Jeppo.

ASCANIO.

Jeppo invariably has an attack of story-telling when he 's in his cups.

DON APOSTOLO.

The other day it was at Venice at the palace of his Serene Highness the Doge Barbarigo: to-day 't is at Ferrara, at the palace of the divine Princess Negroni.

JEPPO.

Ah! but t' other day 't was a sad tale I told; to-day it is a cheerful one.

65

MAFFIO.

A cheerful story, Jeppo! How it happened that Don Siliceo, a gallant cavalier of thirty, who had wasted his substance at gaming, married the wealthy Marchioness Calpurnia, a damsel of forty-eight summers. By the body of Bacchus! You call that a cheerful story!

GUBETTA.

'T is a sad but common occurrence. A ruined man marries a woman gone to seed. We see it every day.

(He falls to eating again. From time to time some of the guests rise from the table and walk to the front of the stage and converse, while the debauch continues.)

PRINCESS NEGRONI (to Maffio, pointing to Gennaro).

Signor il Conte d'Orsini, your friend yonder seems much depressed.

MAFFIO.

He 's ever thus, madame. I pray you pardon me for having brought him hither, although you had not done him the honor to invite him. He is my brother in arms. He saved my life at the assault on Rimini. In the battle at the Bridge of Vicenza I received a sword-thrust which was aimed at him. We never part. We live together. A gipsy once foretold that we should die the self-same day.

THE NEGRONI (laughingly).

Did he say whether 't would be at night or in the morning?

MAFFIO.

He told us that 't would be in the morning.

THE NEGRONI (laughing more heartily than ever).

Your gipsy did not know what he was saying. And so you set much store by this youth?

MAFFIO.

I love him as dearly as man can love man.

THE NEGRONI.

Oh! then you 're all sufficient, each to the other. You are fortunate!

MAFFIO.

Friendship does not fill the whole heart, madame.

THE NEGRONI.

What is there, pray, that does fill the whole heart?

MAFFIO.

Love.

THE NEGRONI.

You always have love at your tongue's end.

MAFFIO.

You have it in your eyes.

THE NEGRONI.

What a strange man you are!

MAFFIO.

And you 're a lovely woman.

(He puts his arm about her.)

THE NEGRONI.

Signor il Conte d'Orsini, release me!

MAFFIO.

One kiss upon your hand?

THE NEGRONI.

Not one.

(She runs away from him.)

GUBETTA (approaching Maffio).

You seem to make good progress with the princess.

MAFFIO.

She always says me no.

GUBETTA.

In a woman's mouth "No" 's but the elder brother of "Yes."

JEPPO (joining them).

How dost thou find the princess, Maffio?

MAFFIO.

Simply adorable. Between ourselves she begins to raise the devil with my heart.

JEPPO.

And her supper?

MAFFIO.

A glorious success.

JEPPO.

The princess is a widow.

MAFFIO.

The first who comes can see that by her gayety.

JEPPO.

I hope that thou hast overcome thy distrust of her good cheer?

MAFFIO.

Distrust indeed! I was stark mad.

JEPPO (to Gubetta).

Signor di Belverana, you would not believe that Maffio was positively afraid to come to supper with the princess.

GUBETTA.

Afraid?—and wherefore?

JEPPO.

Because the Palace Negroni adjoins the Palace Borgia.

GUBETTA.

To the devil with the Borgias!—and let us drink!

JEPPO (aside to Maffio).

What most attracts me in this Belverana is that he does not love the Borgias.

MAFFIO (aside to Jeppo).

Indeed he never loses an occasion to send them to the devil with the utmost zest. And yet, dear Jeppo . . .

JEPPO.

Well?

MAFFIO.

I 've had an eye upon this pseudo-Spaniard since the festivities began. He has drunk naught but water.

JEPPO.

Aha! suspicion 's laying hold on thee again, my good friend Maffio. Thou art wearisomely monotonous when drunk.

MAFFIO.

Thou 'rt right perhaps. I 'm mad.

GUBETTA (returning to them, and scrutinizing Maffio from head to feet).

Do you know, Signor Maffio, that you are built to live full ninety years, and that you much resemble my own grandfather, who lived to that great age? he, like myself, was named Gil-Basilio-Fernan-Ireneo-Felipe- Frasco-Frasquito, Count of Belverana.

JEPPO (aside to Maffio).

I trust that thou 'lt no longer doubt his Spanish birth. He has no less than twenty Christian names. What a famous catalogue, Signor di Belverana!

GUBETTA.

Alas! our parents are wont to give us more names at our baptism than crowns at our marriage. But, pray, what do they find to laugh at over yonder?

(Aside.)

I must invent some pretext for the women to withdraw. What shall it be?

(He returns to the table and sits down.)

OLOFERNO (drinking).

By Hercules! my lords, I never knew a more delightful evening. Ladies, pray taste this wine. 'T is mellower than Lachrymae-Christi, and headier than wine of Cyprus. 'T is honest Syracuse, my lords!

GUBETTA (eating).

It 's plain that Oloferno 's drunk.

OLOFERNO.

Ladies, I must recite some verses that I 've lately made. I would I were a far cleverer poet that I might do full justice to this charming festival.

GUBETTA.

And I would I were far wealthier than I have the honor to be, that I might so entertain my friends.

OLOFERNO.

Nothing so delights the soul as to sing the praises of a lovely woman, and a dainty feast.

GUBETTA.

Unless it be to kiss the one and eat the other.

OLOFERNO.

Yes, I would like to be a poet. I would like to soar aloft to heaven. I would like to have a pair of wings . . .

GUBETTA.

Of a pheasant on my plate.

OLOFERNO.

I am inclined, however, to recite my sonnet.

GUBETTA.

By all the devils, Signor Marquis Oloferno Vitellozzo! I excuse you from reciting your sonnet. Let us drink in peace!

OLOFERNO.

You excuse me from reciting my sonnet?

GUBETTA.

As I excuse the dogs from biting me, the pope from blessing me, and the passers-by from throwing stones at me.

OLOFERNO.

God's death! you would insult me, it seems, Signor little Spaniard.

GUBETTA.

I would not insult you, huge Italian colossus that you are. I refuse to listen to your sonnet, nothing more. My palate thirsts much more for this good Cyprus, than do my ears for your poesy.

OLOFERNO.

I will nail your ears to your heels, Signor shabby Castilian.

GUBETTA.

You 're a ridiculous rascal! Fie! fie! was there ever such a boor? to get tipsy on Syracusan, and have every appearance of being fuddled with beer!

OLOFERNO.

Do you know that I 'll quarter you, by the living God!

GUBETTA (carving a pheasant).

I 'll not do the same by you. I never carve such large fowls.—Ladies, may I offer you a wing of this pheasant?

OLOFERNO (seizing a knife).

By God! I 'll disembowel the villain, though he be a greater man than the emperor.

THE WOMEN (rising from the table).

Heaven! they mean to fight!

THE MEN.

Fair and softly, Oloferno!

(They take the knife away from him as he is about to rush at Gubetta. Meanwhile the women make their exit through the door at the side.)

OLOFERNO (struggling to free himself).

Body of God!

GUBETTA.

So many of your lines end with "God," my worthy poet, that you have put the ladies to flight. You are an awkward lout.

JEPPO.

Indeed, they have gone: what the devil has become of them?

MAFFIO.

They were afraid. When knives gleam bright, the women take flight.

ASCANIO.

Pshaw! they will return.

OLOFERNO (threatening Gubetta).

I will seek thee out to-morrow, my little Belverana of the devil!

GUBETTA.

To-morrow, so be it, to your heart's content.

(Oloferno resumes his seat, trembling with anger. Gubetta laughs uproariously.)

The idiot! To frighten off the prettiest women in Ferrara with a knife hilted in a sonnet! To lose his head over his wretched verses! I verily believe that he has wings. He's not a man but a green goose. This creature, this Oloferno, roosts, and should sleep upon his feet!

JEPPO.

Softly, my friends, prithee make your peace. You shall cut each other's throats to-morrow morning in due form. By Jupiter! you shall at least fight like honest gentlemen, with swords and not with knives.

ASCANIO.

By the by, what did we with our swords?

DON APOSTOLO.

You forget that we were made to leave them in the reception-room.

GUBETTA.

A wise precaution, too—else should we have fallen to before the ladies: and even the tobacco-sodden Flemings of Flanders would have blushed for that!

GENNARO.

A wise precaution, in very truth.

MAFFIO.

Heaven save the mark! brother Gennaro, that's the first word thou 'st spoken since the feast began, and thou dost not drink! Can it be that thou art dreaming of Lucrezia Borgia? Gennaro, it must be that thou hast a love-intrigue with her! Deny it not!

GENNARO.

Pour me some wine, my Maffio! I 'll no more desert my friends at table than when under fire.

A BLACK PAGE (holding a flagon in either hand).

Cyprus or Syracuse, my lords?

MAFFIO.

For me the Syracuse. It's much the better.

(The page fills all the glasses.)

JEPPO.

A murrain on thee, Oloferno! Will not our friends return?

(He goes to each of the doors in succession.)

The doors are both secured on the outside, my lords!

MAFFIO.

Dost thou not feel somewhat disturbed thyself, Jeppo? They did not choose that we should follow them. That's very plain.

GENNARO.

Let us drink, my lords.

(They strike their glasses together.)

MAFFIO.

Thy health, Gennaro! and mayest thou find thy mother speedily!

GENNARO.

God hear thee, Maffio!

(All drink except Gubetta, who throws his wine over his shoulder.)

MAFFIO (aside to Jeppo).

Beyond a peradventure, Jeppo, I saw it then.

JEPPO.

Saw what?

MAFFIO.

The Spaniard did not drink.

JEPPO.

And if he did not?

MAFFIO.

He tossed his wine over his shoulder.

JEPPO.

He 's drunk, and so art thou.

MAFFIO.

It 's very possible.

GUBETTA.

A drinking song, my lords! I 'll sing you a drinking song that 's far beyond the Marquis Oloferno's sonnet. I swear by my good father's good old skull, that 't was not I who wrote the song, for I 'm no poet, and my wit 's not keen enough to set two rhymes a-pecking at each other at the tail of an idea. But here goes for the song. 'T is addressed to good St. Peter, the keeper of the gate of Paradise, and it is based upon the pleasant conceit that heaven belongs to drinking men.

JEPPO (aside to Maffio).

He 's more than tipsy, he 's downright drunk.

ALL (except Gennaro).

The song! the song!

GUBETTA (singing).

St. Peter, thy gates fling wide:
The toper waits outside.
His mighty voice will wake thy pride,
As he warbles: *Domino!*

ALL (in chorus, except Gennaro).

Gloria Domino!

GUBETTA.

The toper 's a jovial wight,
His paunch is so round and tight,
That no one can say when he heaves in sight,
If he 's man or barrel, O!

ALL (in chorus).

Gloria Domino!

(They clink their glasses with shouts of laughter. Suddenly voices are heard in the distance singing a funeral strain.)

VOICES (without).

Sanctum et terribile nomen ejus. Initium sapientiæ timor Domini.

JEPPO (roaring with laughter).

Listen, gentlemen! Diavolo! While we are singing drinking songs, the echo is singing vespers.

ALL.

Listen.

VOICES (without, a little nearer than before).

Nisi Dominus custodierit civitatem, frustra vigilat qui custodit eam.

(All laugh again.)

JEPPO.

The plain-chant pure and simple.

MAFFIO.

'T is some procession passing.

GENNARO.

At midnight! 't is a little late.

JEPPO.

Bah! go on, Signor de Belverana.

VOICES (without, but coming constantly nearer.)

Oculos habent et non videbunt. Nares habent, et non odorabunt. Aures habent, et non audient.

(They laugh more uproariously than ever.)

JEPPO.

What noisy fellows these monks are !

MAFFIO.

Pray look, Gennaro. The lamps are burning very low. In a moment we shall be in utter darkness.

(The lamps grow dim as if the oil were exhausted.)

VOICES (without, still nearer).

Manus habent, et non palpabunt, pedes habent et non ambulabunt, non clamabunt in gutture suo.

GENNARO.

Methinks the voices are drawing nearer.

JEPPO.

Indeed, it seems as if the procession must be directly beneath our windows.

MAFFIO.

They are chanting the prayers for the dead.

ASCANIO.

A funeral, doubtless.

JEPPO.

Let us drink the health of the man they 're burying.

GUBETTA.

Do you know that there are not several ?

JEPPO.

E'en so ; here 's a health to all of them !

APOSTOLO (to Gubetta).

Bravo !—Let us go on with our invocation to St. Peter.

GUBETTA.

Pray speak more courteously. We say: "To Signor St. Peter, most honorable usher and licensed turnkey of Paradise."

(He sings.)

As sure as the saints have ears,
Thy heavenly kingdom here 's
The drunkard's, who has no hopes or fears,
But sings his drinking song !

ALL.

But sings his drinking song !

GUBETTA.

If the sea of famed Cocagne,
Which laves thy broad domain,
Is made of good old wine of Spain,
Pray change us to fish ere long !

ALL (clinking their glasses with shouts of laughter).

Pray change us to fish ere long.

(The folding doors at the rear of the stage are silently thrown open to their full extent. Beyond them is seen a spacious hall with black hangings, lighted by a few torches, and with a tall silver cross at the farther end. A long line of black and white monks, whose eyes only can be seen through the holes in their hoods, file in through the door, torch in hand, intoning aloud, with ominous significance :

De profundis clamavi ad te, Domine !

They then take their places in silence along the sides of the dining hall, and stand motionless as statues, while the young men gaze at them in stupefaction.)

MAFFIO.

What can this mean ?

JEPPO (struggling to force a laugh).

It is mere pleasantry. I lay my horse against a swine, and my name of Liveretto against the name of Borgia, that our charming countesses have assumed this disguise to put us to the test, and that if we raise one of these hoods at hazard, we shall find beneath, the mischievous and blooming features of a lovely woman.—Here goes to make the trial.

(He laughingly raises one of the hoods, and stands as if turned to stone when his eyes fall upon the pallid countenance of a monk, who remains motionless, with his torch in his hand, and his eyes fixed on the ground.)

This is much more than strange !

MAFFIO.

I know not why my blood does fairly curdle in my veins.

THE MONKS (singing in shrill, piercing tones).

Conquassabit capita in terra multorum !

JEPPO.

What frightful trap is this ! Our swords ! our swords ! God's blood, my lords, we 're 'neath the devil's roof.

SCENE II

THE SAME: DONNA LUCREZIA.

DONNA LUCREZIA (appearing suddenly, dressed all in black, in the doorway).

You 're 'neath my roof!

ALL (except Gennaro, who is looking on from a corner of the stage where Donna Lucrezia does not see him).

Lucrezia Borgia!

DONNA LUCREZIA.

'T was but the other day that all of you, the very same who stand before me now, uttered that name in triumph. To-day you utter it in deadly terror. Yes, you well may gaze at me with eyes transfixed with fear. It is my very self, my lords. I come to tell you this—that you are poisoned, every one, and that there 's not a man among you all who has an hour to live. Stir not. The room adjoining this is filled with pikes. My turn has come. 'T is now for me to speak in thunder-tones and crush your heads beneath my heel! Jeppo Liveretto, go thou and seek Vitelli thy good uncle, whom I did order to be poniarded in the dungeons of the Vatican! Ascanio Petrucci, go seek thy cousin Pandolfo, murdered by me that I might steal his city! Oloferno Vitellozzo, thou knowest that Iago d'Appiani doth await thee, thy uncle whom I poisoned at a fête! Maffio Orsini, go thou unto the other world, and talk of me there with Gravina, thy brother, strangled by my command while he lay sleeping! Apostolo Gazella, thou sayest that 't was I who caused thy father, Francesco Gazella's head to fall, and set assassins on thy cousin, Alphonso of Aragon; go thou and dwell with them! Upon my soul! you honored me at Venice with a ball which I return by entertaining you at supper at Ferrara. A fête for a fête, my lords!

JEPPO.

A rude awakening this, my Maffio!

MAFFIO.

Let us think on God!

DONNA LUCREZIA.

Ah! my gallant friends of the last carnival, you scarce expected this conclusion. By Heaven! it seems to me that this is very like revenge! What do you say, my lords? Which of you claims to be an expert in revenge? Methinks that this is bravely near the mark. What say you? What think you of the plot, for a frail woman?

(To the monks.)

Fathers, conduct these gentlemen into the room adjoining, which has been made ready, confess them, and turn to good use the few brief instants they still have on earth, by saving what may yet be saved of each of them. My lords, I counsel those among you who have souls, to look to them. Be tranquil. They are in good hands. These worthy fathers are genuine friars from St. Sixtus, empowered by the Pope, our Holy Father, to bear me aid in functions of this nature. Even as I 've provided for your souls' welfare, so have I taken measures for the welfare of your bodies. Look.

(To the monks who are ranged in line in front of the door at the rear.)

Stand somewhat back, my fathers, so that these gentlemen may see.

(The monks stand aside and disclose to view five coffins, each covered with a black cloth, standing side by side beyond the door.)

The number is complete: five and no more. Ah! my young friends, you tear the heart out of a wretched woman, and fancy that she will not be revenged! There 's thine, Jeppo, Maffio, thine; Apostolo, Ascanio and Oloferno, yours, too, are there!

GENNARO (whom she has not yet seen, steps forward).

You 'll need a sixth, madame!

DONNA LUCREZIA.

Just Heaven! Gennaro!

GENNARO.

Himself.

DONNA LUCREZIA.

Let everyone withdraw. Leave us alone. Gubetta, whatsoever may occur, whatever you or anyone may hear without of that which passeth here, let no one enter!

GUBETTA.

So be it.

(The monks withdraw in procession, taking with them, between their lines, the five noblemen, trembling and despairing.)

SCENE III

GENNARO, DONNA LUCREZIA.

(There is no light in the room but that cast by a few flickering lamps. The doors are closed. Donna Lucrezia and Gennaro are left alone, and stand gazing at each other in silence for some moments, as if not knowing how to begin.)

DONNA LUCREZIA (speaking to herself).

It is in very truth Gennaro!

CHANT OF THE MONKS (without).

Nisi Dominus ædificaverit domum, in vanum laborant qui ædificant eam.

DONNA LUCREZIA.

Again, Gennaro! Always do I find you beneath the blows I strike! God in heaven! how happens it that you 're involved in this?

GENNARO.

I was suspicious of the whole affair.

DONNA LUCREZIA.

Again you 're poisoned. You will die!

GENNARO.

That 's as I choose. I have the antidote.

DONNA LUCREZIA.

Ah yes! May God be praised!

GENNARO.

One word, madame. You are well versed in matters of this sort. Is there enough elixir in this phial to save the gentlemen whom your monks did but now lead hence into their graves?

DONNA LUCREZIA (examining the phial).

There is but just enough for you, Gennaro.

GENNARO.

Could you not instantly procure it in abundance?

DONNA LUCREZIA.

I gave you all I had.

GENNARO.

'T is well.

DONNA LUCREZIA.

What do you there, Gennaro? In God's name, hasten! Pray, trifle not with things so terrible. One cannot take an antidote too soon. Drink, in the name of Heaven! My God! what fearful recklessness! Make haste to ensure the safety of your life. I will dismiss you from the palace by a secret door known to me alone. Still there is time to set all straight again. Horses can soon be saddled. Ere dawn to-morrow you will be far away from Ferrara. It is a place where frightful deeds are done. Drink and begone. You must live! You must be saved!

GENNARO (taking a knife from the table).

That is to say that you must die, madame.

DONNA LUCREZIA.

What 's that you say?

GENNARO.

I say that you have treacherously poisoned five gentlemen, my friends, my dearest friends, by Heaven! among them Maffio Orsini, my brother in arms, who saved my life in battle at Vicenza, and with whom I share and take revenge for every insult. I say that 't is an infamous thing you 've done, that 't is my bounden duty to avenge Maffio and the others, and that your hour has come!

DONNA LUCREZIA.

Great Heaven!

GENNARO.

Say your prayers, and make them short, madame. I 'm poisoned. I have no time to lose.

DONNA LUCREZIA.

God's providence! it cannot be. Gennaro murder me! Can it be possible?

GENNARO.

'T is stern reality, madame, and I swear to God that were I in your place I would betake myself to silent prayer, on bended knee and with hands clasped imploringly. Look, yonder 's an arm-chair that is most fit for that.

DONNA LUCREZIA.

No, no! I tell you that it is impossible. No, no! among the ghastliest thoughts that ever crossed my mind, this never found a place. Aha! you raise your knife! Gennaro, stay! there 's somewhat I must say to you.

GENNARO.

Say on, and quickly.

DONNA LUCREZIA.

Throw down thy knife, unhappy youth! I bid thee throw it down! If thou didst know. —Gennaro! Knowest thou who thou art? Knowest thou who I am? Thou knowest not how near I am to thee. Needs must I tell thee all? The same blood 's in thy veins and mine, Gennaro! Thy father was a Borgia, Giovanni, Duke of Gandia!

GENNARO.

Your brother! What! you are my aunt? Ah! madame!

DONNA LUCREZIA (aside).

His aunt!

GENNARO.

Ah! I am your nephew! and my poor mother 's the ill-fated Duchess of Gandia, whom all the Borgias have combined to render miserable! Donna Lucrezia, my mother in her letters speaks of you. You are of those unnatural kindred, of whom she writes to me with horror, who slew my father, and drowned her destiny in tears and blood. Ah! added to all the rest I have my father to avenge upon you, my mother to rescue from your schemes! And so you are my aunt! I am a Borgia! Oh! that drives me mad! Hearken to me, Donna Lucrezia Borgia; you have lived long, and your life 's filled so full of crime, that you must ere this have come to be execrable and hateful to yourself. Doubtless you are weary of your life? The time has come to make an end of it. In families like ours, where crime 's hereditary, and passes like the name from father to son, it always happens that the fatality is ended with a murder—most commonly a murder in the family, where kinsman murders kinsman, and thus the last in the long catalogue of crimes atones for all the others. No gentleman has ever been held blameworthy for lopping off a noxious branch from his ancestral tree. The Spaniard Mudarra slew his own uncle Rodriguez de Lara for less than you have done. That Spaniard has had universal praise for having slain his uncle, do you hear, my aunt? But I have said enough hereon! Commend your soul to God, if you believe in God, and in your soul.

DONNA LUCREZIA.

Gennaro! in pity for thyself! Thou art still innocent! Do not commit this crime!

GENNARO.

A crime! Oh! my brain whirls, and my mind wanders! Is it a crime? And even if I should commit a crime! By Heaven! I am a Borgia! To your knees, I say, my aunt! to your knees!

DONNA LUCREZIA.

Dost thou in truth say what is in thy mind, Gennaro? Is it thus thou dost repay my love for thee?

GENNARO.

Love!

DONNA LUCREZIA.

It is not possible. I choose to save thee from thyself. I 'll call for help.

GENNARO.

You will not open yonder door. You will not stir one step. As for your calling, that will never save you. Did you not a moment since with your own mouth command that no one should come in, whatever might be heard without of what transpired here?

DONNA LUCREZIA.

This is a very dastard's deed, Gennaro! To kill a woman, a defenseless woman! Oh! surely you have nobler sentiments than that in your man's heart! Listen to me: hereafter you may kill me if you choose, I set but little store by my life—but first my swelling bosom must o'erflow; 't is brim-full of anguish for the manner of thy treatment of me hitherto. Thou art still young, a child, in sooth, and youth is always too severe. Oh! if I needs must die, I would not it should be by thy dear hand. It is not possible that I should die by thy dear hand. Thou knowest not thyself how monstrous that would be. Besides, Gennaro, my hour has not come. 'T is true I have committed many evil deeds, I am a guilty, guilty woman; and just because I am that guilty woman, I must have time to own my faults and to repent. I must, I say, Gennaro, dost thou hear?

GENNARO.

You are my aunt. You are my father's sister. Donna Lucrezia Borgia, what have you done to my mother?

DONNA LUCREZIA.

Stay! Stay! My God! I cannot tell thee all. And then, even if I should tell thee all, I should perhaps but multiply tenfold thy horror and thy scorn for me! Listen yet an instant. Oh! I would that thou wouldst look with favor on me, repentant at thy feet. Thou wilt spare my life. Say, wilt thou not? Wouldst have me take the veil? Wouldst have me leave the world and entomb myself in a cloister? Suppose thou shouldst be told: "That wretched woman sleeps among the ashes with shaven head, she digs her grave with her own hands, and night and day prays God, not for herself, bitter as is her need, but for thee, who need it not; all this she does that thou some day mayest cast a pitying glance upon her, that thou mayest drop a tear on all the open wounds which rend her heart and soul, that thou mayest no more say to her, as thou hast said in tones more harsh than those of the last judgment: 'You are Lucrezia Borgia!'" Suppose this to be told to thee, Gennaro; then wouldst thou have the heart to spurn her? Oh, mercy! do not kill me, my Gennaro! Let us both live, thou to forgive my crimes, I to repent of them. Have some compassion on me! Surely it can in nothing profit thee to treat so pitilessly a poor, wretched woman, who craves a little pity, nothing more.

A little pity! Spare my life! And then,
thou seest, Gennaro (and this I say for thine
own sake) this that thou hast in mind would
be a base, unmanly deed, a fearful crime, a
murder! A man to slay a woman! a man
who 's made so much the stronger! Surely
thou wouldst not! no, thou wouldst not!

GENNARO (shaken in his purpose).

Madame . . .

DONNA LUCREZIA.

Ah! I know my prayer is granted! I read
it in thine eyes. Oh! let me weep here at thy
feet!

A VOICE (without).

Gennaro!

GENNARO.

Who calls?

THE VOICE.

Gennaro, my brother!

GENNARO.

'T is Maffio!

THE VOICE.

Gennaro! I am dying! Avenge me!

GENNARO (raising the knife).

'T is said. I listen to no more. You hear
him, madame; you must die!

DONNA LUCREZIA (struggling to hold his arm).

Mercy! mercy! one word more!

GENNARO.

Not one!

DONNA LUCREZIA.

Mercy! Listen to me!

GENNARO.

No!

DONNA LUCREZIA.

In Heaven's name!

GENNARO.

No!

(He strikes her.)

DONNA LUCREZIA.

Ah! thou hast killed me! Gennaro! I am
thy mother.

EDITION DEFINITIVE

NOTE I

In the original manuscript, the first page has this title :

LUCRÈCE BORGIA.

and below :

9th–20th July, 1832.

Played February 2d, 1833.

The second page has this title :

THE SUPPER AT FERRARA.

The first act was begun July 9th, and finished the 12th. The second act was begun on the 13th, and finished the 16th. The third act was begun on the 18th.

NOTE II

VARIANT READINGS

ACT FIRST. PART SECOND

SCENE IV

RUSTIGHELLO, ASTOLFO.

RUSTIGHELLO.

It 's past endurance ! There 's always sure to be a pack of worthless creatures, who interfere with what one does, and know no better than to thrust their noses into those matters one would keep secret. And after that, if one but goes to kill them for their insolence, they make a great show of astonishment, and seem not to have expected it. And yet it is the natural consequence. My secrets must be kept ; I do away with them who pry into them. That is the surest way ; there is no other.

ASTOLFO.

I do beseech thee, Rustighello . . .

79

RUSTIGHELLO.

What would become of governments, I pray to know, if every busybody might pry at will into affairs of state and then go babble with impunity of what he 'd seen. Thou 'rt making trouble for thyself, Astolfo!

ASTOLFO.

I leave the man to thee, Rustighello. Do with him as you please. But pray let me go hence. You surely do not mean to take my life! I am thy sister's husband. We are brothers.

RUSTIGHELLO.

What 's that to me? It 's plain that you are little versed in politics.

ASTOLFO.

Rustighello!

RUSTIGHELLO.

Bah! out upon thee, sniveler! Thou hast no knowledge of affairs, I tell thee! Thou wouldst have me fail in my duty. Begone, and come this way no more. Above all, not a word of all this to Donna Lucrezia.

ASTOLFO.

Never fear! Farewell, my good Rustighello! May Heaven and all its angels be with thee!

RUSTIGHELLO.

Go to the devil!

(Exit Astolfo.)

ACT SECOND. PART FIRST

SCENE VI

DONNA LUCREZIA, GENNARO.

.

GENNARO.

Oh my poor mother! my beloved mother! it seems to me that, as I stand in presence of a woman like to thee, thy image doth appear more gentle and more comforting. Alas, poor woman! they tore me from her arms when I was but a child! a new-born babe! O wretched woman, who did love no one on earth but me! She did not have me in my infancy, laughing and playing on her bed in the bright, morning sunshine. Other mothers hear the first lisping prattle of their little ones, they hold them as they take their first tottering steps, they are the first thing that they learn to love, they wipe the moisture from their little foreheads as they lie sleeping in their arms, and warm their wee feet in their bosoms, when they are cold; the joy of motherhood makes their pulses throb at every step in their darling's growth; yes, other mothers are happy indeed! But thou, alas, dear mother, hast had naught of all that. Thou hast no recollection of my childhood to brighten every hour of thy life. Ah! she has suffered bitterly, poor creature!

.   .

DONNA LUCREZIA.

Thy mother, were she here, Gennaro, would bid thee have pity upon me! She would tell thee that a woman 's a weak creature, to whom one never must refuse compassion, however guilty she may be. She would kneel before thee as I do, and crave thy mercy for Lucrezia Borgia. She would conjure thee to say one kindly word to me before we part forever. And when I say "one kindly word," I ask thee not to speak to me as one might do who loves me,—no, I am not so exigent as that—but tell me that thou dost not hate me, that thou dost not curse me, that when thou seest me thou dost not feel that thou must crush my head beneath thy heel as if I were a serpent—tell me that, only that—it is but little, is it not?—and I will be content, Gennaro.

ACT THIRD

In the first act, in the scene between Lucrezia and Gennaro, and after these words spoken by Gennaro :

" I have all my mother's letters here upon my heart . . . A mother's letters form an impenetrable cuirass !" the following rejoinder by Lucrezia is suggested in the margin :

" 'T would seem that that 's a thought which comes instinctively to one who loves. I also have some letters which are very dear to me, Gennaro, and I wear them upon my heart, as thou dost."

.　　.　　.　　.　　.　　.　　.　　.

SCENE LAST

GENNARO, DONNA LUCREZIA.

(She flies. He follows her. Both speak at once, without listening to each other.)

DONNA LUCREZIA.

Mercy! mercy! pardon!

GENNARO.

No pardon!

DONNA LUCREZIA.

My Gennaro!

GENNARO.

I am not thy Gennaro!

- (He seizes her by the hair)

DONNA LUCREZIA.

In Heaven's name!

GENNARO.

No!

(He strikes her.)

DONNA LUCREZIA.

Ah! . . .

(She falls upon a chair, with closed eyes, as if dead.)

GENNARO.
(Dropping the knife.)

God in heaven! what a fearful shriek! It is as if that shriek had waked me from a dream. What have I done? I 've killed a woman! 'T is a frightful thing for a man to kill a woman! 't is dastardly! A murder! there 's murder on me now! My hands are stained with blood! I have been guilty of a ghastly crime! Help! help! I must seek succor for the unhappy woman! No one comes! Am I alone in this great palace? My friends are there in yonder room, but at this moment it may be there are none but dead men there. But she is dying! Is it too late? Air! give her air! Merciful God! what have I done?

(He picks up the knife and cuts away Donna Lucrezia's dress. As he lays bare her breast, a packet of letters soaked with blood falls to the floor.)

What are these papers? Letters!

(He examines them.)

My handwriting! My God! it is indeed my handwriting!

(He looks through the letters and reads.)

" My mother !"—" my mother !"—" my dear mother !"—everywhere " my mother !" These are my letters to my mother! Saints in-heaven! how come they here, upon this woman's heart whom I have murdered? Oh! 't is a horrifying thought that comes into my mind! Can it be that I 've been led into a terrible mistake? This woman's love for me, the immeasurable tenderness of her words, her gaze forever fastened on my movements, her untiring forgiveness for all my brutal treatment of her—O my God! what does it mean?

(Throwing himself upon the body.)

Madame! madame! O Heaven! is she already dead? Madame! Ah! God be praised! she moves! her eyes are opening! God! how her wound doth bleed! Madame! answer me, madame!

DONNA LUCREZIA.

(Partly opening her eyes.)

My Gennaro! what wouldst thou with me ?

GENNARO.

Can it be that thou art my mother ?

DONNA LUCREZIA.

(Starting to her feet, as if by a galvanic shock.)

What dost thou say ?

GENNARO.

Are you my mother ?

DONNA LUCREZIA.

No! have no fear, Gennaro! I am not thy mother!

GENNARO.

Ah yes! you are !

DONNA LUCREZIA.

Heaven help me! who told thee so ?

GENNARO.

These letters !

DONNA LUCREZIA.

Thy letters !

GENNARO.

And now I see it in your eyes.

DONNA LUCREZIA.

Alas! alas! I wished to keep it from thee; I wished, for thy welfare, to bear my secret with me to the grave. But now thou knowest all! Yes, thou art my son, my son! my darling son! Ah! let me call thee by that name! for twenty years I have thirsted to call thee my son.

GENNARO

(Falling at her feet, sobbing bitterly.)

My mother !

DONNA LUCREZIA.

Thy cherished letters! give them to me that I may gaze on them once more, and kiss them! I did as thou didst, I put them on my heart; see how the dagger pierced them! They made a more penetrable cuirass than thou didst think, Gennaro!

GENNARO,

Oh! this will drive me mad! that you, who bore me in your womb, you, the thought of whom has been my sole delight since first I knew myself, you who have suffered torments for my sake, you, whose love for me is like the love of angels, that you, my mother, are thus restored to me! And yet 't is said there is a God in heaven. I find you covered with your own blood, a dagger buried in your breast, I find you foully murdered, mother! murdered! and by whom? by me! Oh! I am a miserable wretch! Oh! to think that 't was my hand that did this deed, and that I still do live and move and speak! to think that it is not a dream, that this knife is a knife, that this blood is blood, that this poor dying woman is my mother!

DONNA LUCREZIA.

(Gloomily.)

Gennaro, do not mourn so bitterly for Lucrezia Borgia.

GENNARO.

Lucrezia Borgia? Your name 's Lucrezia Borgia? Do I know if your name 's Lucrezia Borgia? My mother is my mother! that 's the end on 't. Why did you not tell me long ago you were my mother?

DONNA LUCREZIA.

Valentinois would not have let thee live an hour. And then I dreaded to expose thy filial affection to the shock my name would cause.

GENNARO.

Why not at least have told me just a moment since.

DONNA LUCREZIA.

I tried before the blow, but thou didst not understand me. After the blow, I could not bear to tell thee.

GENNARO.

Oh! mother! mother! Curse me.

DONNA LUCREZIA.

I forgive thee, my son! I forgive thee! Poor child, do not believe thyself more guilty than thou really art. Who so qualified to judge as I? Pray, who would dare to blame thee, if I do not complain? O my Gennaro, I do more than forgive thee, I thank thee! how could I die a happier death than this? There! lay thy head upon my knee, and calm thy sobs, my child! We must all die at last, and I die here by thee. Thou hast wounded me to the heart, but thou dost love me. My blood is flowing fast, but mingled with thy tears. Oh! I will say to God, if 't is my lot to stand before him, that thou art a good son.

GENNARO.

You forgive me? how kind and good you are! You must live! Let me call for help! You will be cured, my dearest mother! you will live and be happy!

DONNA LUCREZIA.

Live, no. Happy, I am already. Thou knowest that I am thy mother, and the knowledge does not make thee recoil from me in horror; thou lovest me, and weepest with me. I should be very hard to please, I promise thee, were I not happy!

GENNARO.

But you must live, dear mother.

DONNA LUCREZIA.

I must die. My chest is filling up, I feel it. My son, my adored son! oh! canst thou understand the joy it causes me to say to thee aloud: "my son?" My son, embrace me.

(He embraces her. She utters an exclamation of pain.)

Oh! my wound! What misery! the thing I most desired in all the world, to be clasped in my son's embrace, his breast against my own, causes me deadly suffering. But no matter! Embrace me, my son! the happiness is greater than the pain.

GENNARO.

Perhaps there still is hope. 'T would be unjust of Heaven to reunite us, only to bring upon us a more cruel separation, and tear you from my arms at once. Mother, a little help might save you. Let me fly . . .

DONNA LUCREZIA.

Do not leave me. Do not spoil the few moments that remain. Before others I could not call thee my son. How canst thou think that any human help could save me? Dost thou not notice that my voice is failing me? And see, my hand is cold already. Take it in thine. Gennaro, my son, I wish to die in thine arms. I am happy so. Do not weep; I suffer almost none at all: almost none at all, I assure thee. Dost thou not see me smile? Oh! I have been so miserably unhappy! this present hour, which seems to thee so ghastly and so horrible, my child, is the happiest hour I have ever known!

GENNARO.

(Despairingly.)

Mother! O! my God! my God! preserve my mother!

DONNA LUCREZIA.

(Suddenly bursting into sobs, and straining him to her heart.)

Alas! alas! 't is but too true! thou wilt soon lose thy mother, my poor child! Oh! how I pity thee, my son, for having to lose thy mother! What will become of thee when thou hast me no longer to watch over thee? O Heaven! I would that all the women in the world were here that I might commend thee to their care. The terrible Duke of Valentinois! Who is there to keep watch over my child when I am dead? Can it be true that I must die and part from thee forever, my Gennaro? A moment since I seemed resigned, but I was not. I did not wish to crush thee all at once. But now my grief 's more powerful than I. My heart bursts when I think that thou wilt be left alone. 'T is pitiful to die when one must leave a child behind one. Gennaro! my Gennaro! I know thee, and I know that thou needest to be loved. When my heart shall have ceased to beat, who is there who will love thee with an unselfish love, love thee for thyself, and for thyself alone, with no other thought than to love thee? Alas! 't is vain to tell you men, that no other woman in the world doth ever love you half so dearly as your mother. Dost thou really believe in other kinds of love, Gennaro? Thou weepest, thou canst not speak, my poor, dear child! Farewell! I feel the blood rising, and soon the end will come. Oh! for a little air! a breath of air! Thy hand! thy hand! Oh! I am choking! Come to me—close to my side.

GENNARO.

I am here, mother.

DONNA LUCREZIA.

Raise me. It seems to me that everything is expiated now, and that I may dare to raise my eyes to Heaven.

(She holds her hand above his head.)

O God! if such an one as I has still the right to bless thy creature, I bless the guileless offspring of my womb, my own Gennaro! Farewell, my son, farewell! Long be thy life, and happy! Ah! What didst thou throw upon the floor and stamp upon?

GENNARO.

The antidote.

ANOTHER VARIANT OF THE FINAL SCENE

GENNARO.

I 'll listen to no more. Enough of this.

(He seizes her by the hair and strikes her.)

DONNA LUCREZIA.

Gennaro! I am thy mother!

GENNARO.
(Trembling and letting the knife fall.)

My mother! Ah! you mock me!

DONNA LUCREZIA.

Thy mother! and thou hast slain me!

GENNARO.

Oh, no! it is not so! it cannot be! You my mother! In pity's name, tell me that you are not my mother!

DONNA LUCREZIA.
(Taking from her breast a bundle of letters, soaked with blood.)

There were letters upon my heart. These are they. Take them, Gennaro. Perchance my blood has not made them illegible. Dost recognize the writing?

GENNARO.
(Glancing at the letters.)

My letters!

DONNA LUCREZIA.

The dagger pierced them. They made a more penetrable cuirass than thou didst think, Gennaro.

GENNARO.

Ah yes! O Heaven! you are indeed my mother! I did not call to mind the incest. God in heaven! Why did you not tell me long ago?

DONNA LUCREZIA.

I was ashamed. Thy dagger's point alone, my child, could make me tell thee all. My secret gushed out from my heart with my blood. Shall I confess it? it was sweet to me to be beloved by thee in one aspect, while thou didst loathe me in another. Thy mother thou didst love, Gennaro; wouldst thou have loved Lucrezia Borgia?

GENNARO.

You, my mother!

DONNA LUCREZIA.

And then there was Valentinois—Valentinois, who slew thy father! My secret once divulged, even to thine ear alone, thou wouldst not have lived a day. Alas! even in the obscure station where I placed thee, at times I fancied that the tiger was prowling round thee, and I trembled, unhappy mother that I am, lest he should get scent of thee.

GENNARO.

I have killed my mother! You are my mother! What fearful crimes lay hidden in that word!

DONNA LUCREZIA.

An incestuous mother.

GENNARO.

Thy son a parricide!

DONNA LUCREZIA.

Gennaro!

GENNARO.

Yes, I am a parricide! 'T was I who did it, I who stand here and speak to thee! My God! how strange it seems to be a parricide!

DONNA LUCREZIA.

My son, come to thy senses!

GENNARO.

A parricide! Oh! can these walls permit me to stand here and fall not in upon me? I have been taught that parricides were beings so monstrous that marble ceilings fell upon their heads of their own motion. But I do walk and breathe and live! Curse me, my mother; stretch out your arm above my head! a mother's arm raised to call down curses on her son ought surely to make the heavens fall.

DONNA LUCREZIA.

My son, this murder is no crime of thine; 't is the sad consequence of my own sin.

GENNARO.

Has not a change come over my features? Tell me, is it not always so, when one 's a parricide? Look closely at me, mother! do I still resemble other men? It must be that I have a brand upon my brow! what is it like? Henceforth, people will draw aside to let me pass, will turn away their eyes, will lay no hand upon me, but let me pass like any cursed thing, the living prey of fate: the roofs where I have slept will crumble, my steps will leave no trace upon the sand or snow, whatever I may touch will vanish, and mothers will beat their children when I pass, that they may all their lives remember having seen me. Tell me, is it not terrible? So will it be with me. So it was of old with Cain. I shall be such a man as I have read of. Look, this blood upon my hands will not be wiped away. Look closely at me.

(Pointing to his forehead.)

I tell you it 's impossible that I have nothing there!

DONNA LUCREZIA.

Nothing, Gennaro! thy mind is wandering.

GENNARO.

There is a word written there, I say; I feel it!

DONNA LUCREZIA.

No. What word?

GENNARO.

What word? Parricide!

TRANSLATOR'S NOTE TO LUCREZIA BORGIA

This play was first performed at the Théâtre Porte-Saint-Martin on Saturday, February 2, 1833, and met with a most enthusiastic reception, which was especially significant as it was the first of Hugo's plays to be produced after the arbitrary act of the government prohibiting *Le Roi s'Amuse*.

"The success," says a writer, who is at no pains to conceal his unfriendliness for Victor Hugo, "was unanimous, and assumed the proportions of a triumph. Everything concurred to make the occasion a remarkable one; the power and pathos of the situations, the vigor and relief of the style, the richness of the setting, the powerful acting of Frédérick Lemaître, who took the part of Gennaro, and the tragic and truly royal beauty of Mademoiselle Georges." (M. Edmond Biré, *Victor Hugo après 1830*.

It is an interesting fact that M. Piccini, leader of the orchestra at the Porte-Saint-Martin, who composed music for the couplets sung at the Princess Negroni's supper-party, found a publisher who paid him 500 francs for it. It is said to have been the first time that the music of a melodrama obtained the honor of publication.

During the present century several authors have undertaken to lighten the burden of crime which rested upon the memory of Lucrezia Borgia for centuries: what success has attended the undertaking this is not the place to determine. A German author, Ferdinand Gregorovius, has made the most recent exhaustive inquiry into the subject, and the tendency of his two volumes entitled: "*Lucrezia Borgia, nach Urkunden und Correspondenzen ihrer eigenen Zeit*" (Stuttgart, 1875), is to discharge her from responsibility for many of the horrors commonly attributed to her. In the words of M. Paul de Saint-Victor, "she was neither a demon nor an angel; much farther removed from the demon than from the angel."

MARY TUDOR

SECOND DAY   SCENE FIRST

THE QUEEN

FABIANI.

I can be ... v ... th none but thee, Mary. I love none but thee.

THE QUEEN.

Art sure? Look in my eye. Art sure? Oh! sometimes I am jealous!
I fancy—where is the woman who has not such thoughts? I fancy sometimes
thou 'rt deceiving me. I fain would be invisible, that I might follow thee, and
always know what thou art doing, what thou art saying, where thou art. I 've
read in fairy tales of an enchanted ring, which renders him who weareth it
invisible: I 'd give my crown to have that ring. I dream incessantly that thou
art paying court to all the lovely maidens in the town. Oh! it must not be
that thou dost deceive me!

PREFACE

There are two ways of arousing the interest of the play-going public: by the great and by the true. The great appeals to the masses, the true to the individual. The aim therefore of the dramatic poet, whatever may be the general tenor of his opinions concerning his art, ought always to be, before everything, to represent the great, as Corneille does, or the true, like Molière: or better still, and this is the greatest triumph that genius can attain, to achieve the great and the true at once, the great in the true, the true in the great, like Shakespeare.

For, we may remark in passing, it was given to Shakespeare, and therein lies the sovereignty of his genius, to reconcile, to unite and to weld together time and again in his works, these two qualities, grandeur and truth, almost always set over against each other, or at least so clearly distinguished that the lack of either of them constitutes the opposite of the other. The stumbling-block of the true is the trivial: the stumbling-block of the great is the false. In all of Shakespeare's works there is grandeur which is true, and truth which is great. At the centre of all his creations we find the point of intersection between grandeur and truth: and where things that are great and things that are true come together, art has done its perfect work. Shakespeare, like Michael Angelo, seems to have been created to solve the interesting problem, the simple enunciation of which has an absurd sound:—how to remain always true to Nature, while overstepping her bounds at times. Shakespeare exaggerates proportions, but exhibits things in their proper relations. Marvelous omnipotence of the poet! he conceived characters greater than we, who live as we do. Hamlet, for example, is

as true to life as anyone of us, and far greater. Hamlet is colossal, and still true to life.
The fact is that Hamlet is not you, nor I, but all of us together. Hamlet is not *a* man,
but man.

Constantly to exalt the great through the agency of the true, and the true through the
agency of the great, such, in the opinion of the author of this drama, who reaffirms nevertheless such other opinions as he has taken occasion to exploit in such matters, such should be
the aim of the poet who writes for the stage. And these two words, *great* and *true*, embrace
everything. Truth includes morality, the great includes the beautiful.

The reader will not credit him with the presumption of thinking that he has himself ever
attained this result, or even that he ever could attain it, but he may be permitted to attest
publicly his own sincerity by declaring that he has never sought any other end in any of his
writing for the stage to this day. The new drama which is about to be produced is another
attempt to reach that glorious result. What is the thought which he has sought to develop in
Marie Tudor ? It is this. A queen who is also a woman. Great as queen. True as woman.

He has heretofore said in another place that the drama as he feels that it should be,
the drama as he would like to see it made by a man of genius, the drama according to
nineteenth century ideas, is not the lofty, impassioned and sublime Spanish tragic comedy of
Corneille ; it is not the abstract, amorous, idealistic and judiciously sad tragedy of Racine : it
is not the profound, acute, sagacious, but too pitilessly satirical comedy of Molière : it is not
the tragedy with philosophical leanings of Voltaire : it is not the comedy of revolutionary
days of Beaumarchais : it is not more than all of these, but it is all of these at once : or, I
should rather say, it is something different from any of them. It does not consist, as in the
works of these great men, in systematically and incessantly emphasizing a single aspect of
things, but in looking at everything in all aspects at once. If there were a man living to-day
who could realize our understanding of what the drama should be, his work would be an
epitome of the human heart, the human head, human passions and the human will ; it would
be the past brought to life again for the benefit of the present ; it would be the history our
fathers made brought face to face with the history we are making ; it would be a commingling
upon the stage of all those things which are mingled in real life ; there would be an *émeute*
here, a love scene there, and in the love scene a lesson for the people, and in the *émeute* an
appeal to the heart ; there would be laughter, there would be tears : good and evil, the high
and the low, fatality, providence, genius and chance, society, the world, nature, life ; and
over it all one would instinctively feel the presence of something great !

Such a drama, which would be an inexhaustible source of instruction to the spectators,
would be allowed entire liberty, because it would be of its very essence to abuse no privilege.
It would be so notoriously elevated, honest, straightforward and helpful, that it would never
be accused of seeking mere effect and noise, where its only purpose was to point a moral or
enforce a lesson. It might introduce François I. to Maguelonne's abode without arousing
suspicion ; it might make Didier's heart bleed with pity for Marion without alarming the most
strait-laced ; it might without being taxed with exaggeration and with being too emphatic
as the author of "Marie Tudor" has been, introduce frequently upon the stage that formidable triumvirate which appears so often in history : a queen, a favorite, and a headsman.

The man who produces such a drama must have two qualities, conscientiousness and genius. The present writer is well aware that he has only the first. He will go on nevertheless with what he has begun, hoping that others may do better than he. At the present day an immense public, growing always in intelligence, sympathizes with all the serious ventures of art. At the present day all high-minded criticism assists and encourages the poet. What captious critics have to say matters little. So let the poet come forward!

So far as the author of this drama is concerned, feeling sure of the future in store for one who goes steadily forward, and that his perseverance will some day be counted in his favor, in default of talent, he gazes out with serene and confident tranquility upon the throng which evening after evening honors his unworthy work with such deep interest and anxious attention. In the presence of that throng he feels the responsibility which rests upon him and accepts it with a clear conscience. Never, in his toil, does he for a single instant lose sight of the people whom the stage civilizes, of history which the stage explains, of the human heart to which the stage gives counsel. To-morrow he will lay aside the work that is done for the work that is to do: he will quit the noisy throng for the solitude of his study: a profound solitude, whither no evil influence from the outside world ever penetrates, where jocund youth, his friend, comes now and then to press his hand, where he is alone with his thoughts, his freedom and his will. His solitude will be more than ever dear to him, because it is only in solitude that one can work for the multitude. He will keep his mind, his thought and his work farther than ever removed from cliques and coteries: for he knows of something greater than cliques, namely parties: of something greater than parties, namely the people: of something greater than the people, namely mankind.

November 17, 1833.

DRAMATIS PERSONÆ

QUEEN MARY
JANE
GILBERT
FABIANO FABIANI
SIMON RENARD
JOSHUA FARNABY
A JEW
LORD CLINTON
LORD CHANDOS
LORD MONTACUTE
MASTER ÆNEAS DULVERTON
LORD GARDINER
A JAILER

LORDS, PAGES, GUARDS, THE EXECUTIONER

Scene—London.   *Time—1553.*

FIRST DAY

THE MAN OF THE PEOPLE

A lonely spot on the banks of the Thames. The ruins of an ancient parapet hide the brink of the stream. At the right a house of poor appearance. At the corner of the house a small figure of the Virgin, at whose feet a bunch of tow is burning in an iron cage. In the background, across the Thames, London. Two lofty buildings can be distinguished, the Tower of London, and Westminster. Night is just coming on.

SCENE 1

Several men standing in groups upon the shore, among them SIMON RENARD; JOHN BRIDGES, BARON CHANDOS; ROBERT CLINTON, BARON CLINTON; ANTHONY BROWN, VISCOUNT MONTACUTE.

LORD CHANDOS.

You are quite right, my lord. It must be that this damned Italian has bewitched the queen. She cannot do without him; she sees through his eyes only, has no joy save in him, and listens to no one but him. If she 's a whole day without seeing him, her eyes take on the same languishing expression they were used to wear when she loved Cardinal Pole.

SIMON RENARD.

She 's very much in love, in truth, and therefore very jealous.

LORD CHANDOS.

The Italian has bewitched her.

LORD MONTACUTE.

'T is said, indeed, that these Italians have philters for that purpose.

97

LORD CLINTON.

The Spaniards are famous for poisons that cause death, the Italians for poisons that breed love.

LORD CHANDOS.

This Fabiani then is Spaniard and Italian all in one. The queen's in love with him, and ill. He must have given her both kinds to drink.

LORD MONTACUTE.

But is he really Spaniard or Italian?

LORD CHANDOS.

It seems quite certain he was born in Italy in the Capitanate, and was reared in Spain. He claims close kinship with a great Spanish family. Lord Clinton has it all at his tongue's end.

LORD CLINTON.

A low adventurer. No Spaniard, nor Italian, still less an Englishman, thank God! These men who are of no country, have no mercy for a country when they rise to power.

LORD MONTACUTE.

Said you not, Chandos, that the queen is ill? That interferes not with the merry life she's leading with her favorite.

LORD CLINTON.

The merry life! the merry life! While the queen laughs, the people weep, and the favorite is gorged. The fellow feeds on silver and drinks gold! The queen has given him Lord Talbot's vast estates, the great Lord Talbot! The queen has made him Earl of Clanbrassil, and Baron Dinasmonddy, this Fabiano Fabiani, who says that he is of the Spanish family Peñalver, and when he says it, lies! He is a peer of England like yourselves, Chandos and Montacute, like Stanley, too, and Norfolk, like myself and like the king! He has the Garter as the King of Denmark has, and the Infant of Portugal, and Thomas Percy, Duke of Northumberland. And such a tyrant as this tyrant is who rules us from his bed! Never did England bear so harsh a burden. I have seen the like, but I am an old man. At Tyburn there are seventy new gallows; the funeral pyres are always glowing embers, never ashes; the headsman's axe is sharpened every morning, and dull again at night. Every day some once great nobleman is stricken down. Two days ago was Blantyre, Northcurry yesterday, to-day South Reppo, and to-morrow Tyrconnel. Next week, Chandos, your turn will come, and next month mine. My lords, my lords, it is a burning shame, an impious thing, that all these noble English heads should fall to suit the pleasure of an adventurer, sprung from God knows where, and who's not even of this country! 'T is an abominable thing, and unendurable, to think a Neapolitan favorite can draw as many chopping-blocks as suits his whim from under our queen's bed! They lead a merry life together, do you say? By Heaven! it's infamous! Ah yes! they lead a merry life, the turtle-doves, while the head-cutter at their door makes widows and orphans. Ah! their Italian guitar too often is accompanied by clanking chains. My lady queen! you send for singers from Avignon Cathedral; you have plays in your palace every day, and all the galleries filled with musicians. In God's name, madame, let there be less merry-making in your palace, an it please you, and less mourning in our homes; fewer mountebanks here and fewer headsmen there; fewer puppet-shows at Westminster, and fewer scaffolds at Tyburn!

LORD MONTACUTE.

Softly, my lord. We are all loyal subjects here. Lay naught upon the queen, all upon Fabiani.

SIMON RENARD (laying his hand upon Lord Clinton's shoulder).

Patience!

LORD CLINTON.

Patience! The word comes easily to your lips, Master Simon Renard. You have been governor of Amont in Franche-Comté, the emperor's subject, and his ambassador at London. You stand here for the Prince of Spain, the future husband of our queen. Your person is secure from Fabiani's schemes. But, do you see, with us it is a very different matter. To you Fabiani is the shepherd, to us the butcher.

(It has become quite dark.)

SIMON RENARD.

The man 's no less obnoxious to me than to you. Your fear is only for your life. Mine 's for my credit. That 's much the greater fear. I do not talk, I act. My wrath is not so violent as yours, my lord, but my hate 's keener. I will effect the ruin of the favorite.

LORD MONTACUTE.

Oh! how can it be done? I think of nothing else.

SIMON RENARD.

The favorites of queens are not made and unmade by daylight, but at night.

LORD CHANDOS.

This is a very dark and dismal one.

SIMON RENARD.

'T is most fit for what I have in mind to do.

LORD CHANDOS.

What is it, pray?

SIMON RENARD.

That you will see. Lord Chandos, when a woman reigns caprice is queen. At such times politics is not a game of skill, but one of chance. One can no longer count on anything. To-day has ceased to be the logical forerunner of to-morrow. Affairs no longer play at chess, but cards.

LORD CLINTON.

All this is very fine, but come we to the point. When may we hope to be delivered from the favorite, Monsieur le bailli? There 's need of haste. Tyrconnel is to lose his head to-morrow.

SIMON RENARD.

If I can find to-night the man I seek, Tyrconnel will sup with you to-morrow.

LORD CLINTON.

What do you mean? In that case what will have become of Fabiani?

SIMON RENARD.

Have you good eyes, my lord?

LORD CLINTON.

Yes, old as I am, and though it 's very dark.

SIMON RENARD.

Do you see London there, across the river?

LORD CLINTON.

Yes. But why?

SIMON RENARD.

Look carefully. From here we see the zenith and the nadir of every favorite's career, Westminster and the Tower of London.

LORD CLINTON.

Even so?

SIMON RENARD.

If God 's on my side, there is a man who while we 're talking is still there,

(He points to Westminster.)

and who to-morrow at this hour will be there.

(He points to the tower.)

LORD CLINTON.

May God be on your side!

LORD MONTACUTE.

The people hate him no less bitterly than we. How London will rejoice the day of his downfall!

LORD CHANDOS.

We place ourselves at your disposal, master bailli. Command us. What must we do?

SIMON RENARD (pointing to the house by the water).

You all observe this house. 'T is where one Gilbert dwells, a carver. Do not lose sight of it. Disperse with your retainers, but go not far away. Above all things, do nothing without me.

LORD CHANDOS.

'T is well.

(They all move off in different directions.)

SIMON RENARD (alone).

The man I need is very hard to find.

(He goes off. Jane and Gilbert enter, arm in arm, and walk toward the house. Joshua Farnaby, wrapped in a cloak, accompanies them.)

SCENE II

JANE, GILBERT, JOSHUA FARNABY.

JOSHUA.

I leave you here, my friends. 'T is late, and I must needs resume my duties as turnkey at the Tower of London. Ah! I am not free like you. A jailer, after all, is simply one variety of prisoner. Farewell, Jane. Farewell, Gilbert. 'Faith, my dear friends, how happy it makes me to see you happy! Come, Gilbert, when is to be the wedding?

GILBERT.

A week hence; eh, Jane?

JOSHUA.

Heyday! and Christmas but two days away. Christmas, the day of gifts and kindly wishes. But there is nothing I can wish for you. 'T would be impossible to wish more beauty to the bride, or more love to the bridegroom. You are happy indeed!

GILBERT.

Good Joshua! and art thou not happy?

JOSHUA.

As happy as unhappy. I have renounced it all. Look, Gilbert:

(He opens his cloak and shows a bunch of keys hanging at his belt.)

prison keys forever jingling at one's waist, speak, do you know, and talk of philosophical ideas of every sort. When I was young, I was like other youths, in love a day, ambitious a whole month, and mad the year through.

'T was under Henry Eighth that I was young. A strange man was that same Henry Eighth! a king who changed his wives as easily as a woman changes her dress. He threw aside the first, cut off the second's head, the third he disemboweled: as for the fourth, he pardoned her, and simply turned her out of doors, but to make matters even cut off the head of number five. I 'm not now telling you the history of Blue Beard, my pretty Jane, but of King Henry Eighth. In those days I took a hand in the religious wars, and fought on one side and the other. That was the wisest course a man could take. The question was a very knotty one. Were you for or against the pope? The king's people hanged those who were for him, but burned those who were against him. The indifferent, those who were neither for him or against him, they burned or hanged indifferently. Let him get out of it who could. Yes, the rope. No, the stake. Neither yes or no, the rope or the stake. I, who speak to you, have often smelled the smell of burning flesh, and I 'm by no means sure I did not have my neck stretched twice or thrice. Those were great days, equal almost to these. Yes, I fought through it all. The devil take me if I know now for whom or what I fought. When anybody speaks to me of Martin Luther or of Pope Paul the Third, I simply shrug my shoulders. You see, Gilbert, when one's hair is gray, 't is best not to recall the opinions for which one fought, or seek to see again the women to whom one made love at twenty. Both women and opinions seem very old and lean and toothless and wrinkled and foolish and ugly. There 's my story. Now I have withdrawn from the world. I am no longer the king's soldier or the pope's, but jailer at the Tower of London. I fight for no one now, but turn the key on everyone. I am a jailer and an old man. I 've one foot in the prison and the other in the grave. It is my place to gather up the fragments of all the ministers and all the favorites who come to grief in the queen's palace. It 's most diverting. And then I have a little child I dearly love, and you two whom I also love, and if you are happy, I am happy too!

GILBERT.

Why, then be happy, Joshua! What sayest thou, Jane?

JOSHUA.

I can do nothing to promote thy happiness, Jane everything. Thou lovest her! I shall be of no service to thee while I live. Happily thou art not of high rank enough ever to need the attention of the turnkeys of the Tower. Jane will acquit my debt with her own; for Jane and I owe everything to thee. Jane was a poor, abandoned orphan child; thou didst take her in and cherish her. One fine day I was drowning in the Thames; thou didst jump in and take me from the water.

GILBERT.

Oh, Joshua, why need you always speak of that?

JOSHUA.

To show that 't is our duty, Jane's and mine, to love thee well, I like a brother, and she—not like a sister!

JANE.

No, like a wife, I understand you, Joshua.

(She falls back into her reverie.)

GILBERT (aside to Joshua).

Look at her, Joshua! Is she not beautiful and bewitching, and would she not be worthy of a king? If thou didst but know! Thou canst not dream how dear she is to me!

JOSHUA.

Have a care. It 's most imprudent. A woman does not love like that. A child— that 's a different matter!

GILBERT.

What dost thou mean?

JOSHUA.

Nothing. I will be at your wedding a week hence. I hope that by that time the affairs of state will leave me more at liberty, and that 't will all be over.

GILBERT.

What? what 's that that will be over?

JOSHUA.

Ah! Gilbert, thou dost not concern thyself with matters of that sort. Thou art in love. Thou art of the people. And what hast thou, happy in thy humble station, to do with all the scheming that goes on above thee? But since thou askest me I 'll tell thee that there is hope that a week hence, perhaps before to-morrow at this hour, Fabiano Fabiani will be supplanted by another in the queen's good graces.

GILBERT.

Who is Fabiano Fabiani?

JOSHUA.

He 's the queen's lover; a very fascinating and notorious favorite, a favorite who 'll have you a man's head cut off who is obnoxious to him, before a procuress can say an *ave*, the most profitable favorite the Tower executioner has had for ten years past. For the executioner has ten silver crowns, you know, for every great lord's head, and sometimes double that when the head's owner is a man of eminence. Many there are who much desire to see Fabiani fall. It's very true that in my round of duty at the Tower the men I hear revile him are people out of humor, malcontents, whose heads are to come off within a month.

GILBERT.

Let the wolves prey on one another! What care we for the queen or the queen's favorite? What sayest thou, Jane?

JOSHUA.

Ah! there's a fine plot brewing against Fabiani. If he wins through it, he will be fortunate. I should not be surprised if there were something done to-night. I just saw Master Simon Renard walking yonder in deep thought.

GILBERT.

Who's Master Simon Renard?

JOSHUA.

How is it thou dost not know him? He is the emperor's right arm in London. The queen's to wed the Prince of Spain, and Renard's his ambassador to her. The queen detests this Simon Renard, but she fears him, and is powerless against him. He has already ruined several favorites. His instinct teaches him to ruin favorites. He sweeps the palace clean from time to time. A very shrewd and cunning fellow, who keeps informed of all that's going on, and always digs two or three tiers of underground intrigues beneath each new occurrence. As to Lord Paget—didst thou not ask me also who Lord Paget is?—he is a wily nobleman who was in politics under

Henry Eighth. He is a member of the Privy Council, and has acquired such ascendancy that the other ministers dare not breathe before him, except the chancellor, Lord Gardiner, who detests him. This Gardiner's a man of violent temper, and of illustrious birth, while Paget is a nobody, a cobbler's son. He is to be created Baron Paget of Beaudesert in Staffordshire.

GILBERT.

How trippingly this gossip runs off Joshua's tongue!

JOSHUA.

'Faith! simply because I hear the state prisoners talking.

(Simon Renard appears at the back of the stage.)

Mark this, Gilbert, that the best informed man as to the history of these times is the keeper of the Tower of London.

SIMON RENARD (who overhears the last words).

You are wrong, my master. The executioner's the man.

JOSHUA (aside to Jane and Gilbert).

Let us move away a little.

(Simon Renard walks slowly off the stage, and disappears.)

That's Master Simon Renard himself.

GILBERT.

All these people lurking about my house annoy me.

JOSHUA.

What the devil is he doing here? I must return at once. I fancy he's preparing work for me. Farewell, Gilbert. Farewell, my lovely Jane. I knew you when you were no taller than that.

GILBERT.

Farewell, Joshua. But what is it, pray, thou 'rt hiding there under thy cloak?

JOSHUA.

Aha! I have my little plot, as well.

GILBERT.

What plot?

JOSHUA.

Oh! trust a lover to forget! I just reminded you that two days hence is the day for gifts. The nobles are plotting a surprise for Fabiani; I am plotting, too. The queen, it may be, is about to give herself a brand-new favorite. I propose to give my child a doll.

(He takes a doll from underneath his cloak.)

Brand-new, too. We'll see which of the two will break her plaything first. God keep you, my dear friends!

GILBERT.

Farewell, Joshua.

(Joshua walks away, Gilbert seizes Jane's hand and kisses it passionately.)

JOSHUA (at the rear of the stage).

Oh! how great is providence! it gives to everyone his plaything, the doll to the child, the child to the man, the man to the woman, and the woman to the devil!

(Exit.)

SCENE III

GILBERT, JANE.

GILBERT.

I too must leave you. Good-night, dear Jane. Sweet sleep and pleasant dreams.

JANE.

Won't you come in with me this evening, Gilbert?

GILBERT.

I cannot. You know I told you, Jane, that I 've some work to finish at my shop to-night. A dagger-hilt to carve for one who calls himself Lord Clanbrassil; I never saw him, but he sent to me to ask that he might have it for to-morrow morning.

JANE.

Good-night, then, Gilbert. Until to-morrow.

GILBERT.

No, Jane, one moment more. Ah, me! how hard it is for me to part from you, even for these few hours! How true it is that you are all my life and all my joy! And yet I must return and work. We are so poor! I must not go in with you, for then I should remain; and still I cannot leave you, weak creature that I am! Come, sit we down a moment at the door upon this bench. It seems to me 't will be less difficult to go, than if I were to go into the house, and to your room. Give me your hand.

(He sits down and takes both her hands in his—she remains standing.)

Jane, dost thou love me?

JANE.

Ah! Gilbert, I owe everything to you! I know it now, although you long concealed it from me. When I was but a little child, scarce out of swaddling-clothes, I was abandoned by my parents, and you took me in. For sixteen years your arms have worked for me like any father's, your eyes watched over me with all a mother's care. What I should be without you, God alone can say! All that I have, you have given me; all that I am, you have made me.

GILBERT.

Jane, dost thou love me?

JANE.

Such absolute devotion, Gilbert! night and day alike you work for me; you 're wearing out your eyes, and shortening your life. To-night again, you mean to work all night. And never a reproach, never a harsh or angry word. You are so poor! yet you take pity on my most trivial girlish whims, and always gratify them. Gilbert, I cannot think of you that my eyes do not fill with tears. Sometimes you 've had no bread to eat, but I have had my ribbons.

GILBERT.

Jane, dost thou love me?

JANE.

I would like to kiss your feet, my Gilbert.

GILBERT.

But dost thou love me? dost thou love me? There 's nothing in all this to tell me thou dost love me. Those are the words I long to hear, dear Jane! Gratitude, always gratitude! I stamp upon it! love I will have or nothing! Death! For sixteen years, Jane, thou hast been my daughter, now thou 'rt to be my wife. I did adopt thee, now I wish to marry thee. To-morrow week, thou knowest, thou didst promise me. Thou didst consent. Thou art my own betrothed. Ah! thou didst love me when thou gavest me that promise. O Jane! there was a time—dost thou remember? when thou didst say to me: "I love thee!" raising thy lovely eyes to heaven. As thou wert then so I would have thee always. For months past it has seemed to me that there was something changed in thy demeanor, especially these last three weeks, when I have been obliged sometimes to be abroad at night. O Jane! I crave thy love. I am so wonted to the thought of it. And thou, who in the old days wert so blithe and joyous, art always sad now and preoccupied—not cold, poor child, thou dost thy utmost to avoid that; but I can plainly see the words of love no longer come instinctively and naturally as once they did. Why is it so? Is it that thou hast ceased to care for me? Doubtless I am an honest man, doubtless I am a clever craftsman—I know, I know—but I would rather be a thief and an assassin, and be loved by thee! Jane, if thou didst but know how I do love thee!

JANE.

I do know, Gilbert, and I weep to know.

GILBERT.

For joy, is 't not? Tell me it is for joy. Oh! I have need to think it so. There 's nothing in the world but to be loved. My heart is only a poor, humble workman's heart, and yet I must have my Jane's love. Why dost thou talk forever of what I 've done for thee? A single word of love from thee, my Jane, leaves all the gratitude for me to feel. I will commit a crime and sell my soul, whenever thou dost wish. But thou wilt be my wife, and thou dost love me? See, Jane—for a glance from thee I 'd give my trade and all my toil, for a smile my life, and for a kiss my soul!

JANE.

What a noble heart is yours, Gilbert!

GILBERT.

Listen, Jane! laugh if thou wilt; I 'm mad, for I am jealous! That 's the truth. Be not offended. For some time past I have seen, or seemed to see, many young gallants prowling hereabout. Jane, dost thou know that I am four and thirty years old? What misery for a poor loutish, ill-clad workingman like me, who is no longer young or handsome, to love a lovely, fascinating child of seventeen, who draws about her all the gilded and belaced fine gentlemen as light attracts the moths. Oh! I do suffer, doubt it not! Never in my thoughts do I dishonor thee, so pure and virtuous, thee, whose brow no lips but mine have ever touched. Only it seems to me at times that thou dost take too much delight in watching the queen's processions and the cavalcades, and all the gorgeous coats, beneath which are so few true hearts, so few pure souls. Forgive me! In God's name why do so many fine young gallants seek this spot? Why am I not young, handsome, noble, rich? Gilbert, the carver, nothing more. But they are Lord Chandos, Lord Gerald Fitz-Gerald, the Earl of Arundel, the Duke of Norfolk! Oh! how I hate them! I pass my life in carving for them the hilts of swords, the blades of which I 'd like right well to plunge into their breasts.

JANE.

Gilbert!

GILBERT.

Forgive me, Jane. Love makes one very wicked, does it not?

JANE.

No, very good. You are a good man, Gilbert.

GILBERT.

Oh! how I love thee! Every day more dearly. I would so gladly die for thee. Love me or love me not, 't is thine to choose. I am mad. Pray pardon me for all that I have said. 'T is late. and I must leave thee. Now, good-night! Great God! how hard it is to tear myself away! Now go in. Hast thou not the key?

JANE.

No, I 've not been able for some days to find it.

GILBERT.

Take mine. Farewell until to-morrow morning. Jane, do not forget. To-day I 'm still thy father; but a week hence, thy husband.

(He kisses her on the forehead, and exit.)

JANE (alone).

My husband! Oh! no, I will not commit that crime. Poor Gilbert! he loves me—and the other? Ah! had I not preferred vanity to love! Wretched girl that I am! On whom am I dependent now? Oh! I am very guilty and ungrateful! But I hear footsteps. I must go in at once.

(She enters the house.)

SCENE IV

GILBERT: A MAN (wrapped in a cloak, and wearing a yellow cap).

(The man holds Gilbert's hand.)

GILBERT.

Yes, I remember thee: thou art the Jew beggar whom I have seen prowling about this house for several days. What dost thou want with me? Why didst thou take my hand and lead me here?

THE MAN.

Because I have that to say to you, which I can say in no other place.

GILBERT.

Well, what is it? Say on. Waste no time.

THE MAN.

Listen, young man. Some sixteen years since, on the same night when my Lord Talbot, Earl of Waterford, was put to death by torchlight for the crimes of popery and rebellion, his partisans were cut to pieces here in London by the soldiers of King Henry Eighth. All night the firing continued in the streets. That night a young mechanic, much more intent upon his task than on the fighting, was working in his stall, the first as one steps on London Bridge. A low door at the right. Some marks of old red paint upon the wall. 'T was in the neighborhood of two o'clock. There was fighting thereabout, and bullets flew whistling across the Thames. Suddenly there was a knocking at the shop-door, through which a feeble light was cast by the workman's lamp. He opened. A strange man entered. In his arms he held a child in long clothes, shrieking with fear. He laid the child upon the table, saying: "This poor creature is fatherless and motherless." Then he went slowly out and closed the door behind him. Gilbert, the artisan, was fatherless and motherless as well. He took the child; the orphan boy adopted the orphan girl. He took her, he watched over her, he clothed her, fed her, brought her up and loved her. He gave himself without reserve to the poor little creature, brought to his shop by chance of civil war. He forgot everything for her, his youth, his youthful loves, his pleasure; he made the child the only object of his toil, of his affection, of his life, and thus he has gone on for sixteen years. Gilbert, the young mechanic was yourself; the child . . .

GILBERT.

Was Jane. All that thou sayest is true; but with what purpose dost thou say it?

THE MAN.

I forgot to say that to the infant's clothes was pinned a paper on which these words were writ: *Have pity on little Jane.*

GILBERT.

They were writ with blood. I have preserved the paper. I always carry it about me. But thou art fairly torturing me. Tell me thy purpose.

THE MAN.

'T is this. You see that I 'm familiar with your history. Gilbert, keep watch upon your house to-night.

GILBERT.

What dost thou mean by that?

THE MAN.

One word more. Go not to your work. Remain in this vicinity. Watch. I am neither friend nor foe to you; but I give you this warning. Now, the better not to prejudice yourself, leave me alone. Go you in that direction, and come if you should hear me call for help.

GILBERT.

What can this mean?

(Exit, slowly.)

SCENE V

THE MAN (alone).

The thing has fallen out most opportunely. I was in need of some one young and strong to bear me aid if it were necessary. This Gilbert is the very man. It seems to me I hear the sound of oars upon the water, and a guitar. Yes.

(He goes to the parapet.)

(A voice is heard in the distance, singing to the accompaniment of a guitar.)

When thou dost sing, at even,
Thy head upon my breast,
My thoughts, low murmuring, answer
The words thou warblest.
Thy soft refrain recalleth,
Life's fairest, happiest day;
    Sing, my beloved,
    Forever and for aye!

THE MAN.

That is my man.

THE VOICE.

(It draws nearer with each verse.)

When thou dost smile, love danceth,
And beameth in thine eye,
And from my fond heart fadeth
Distrust and jealousy.
Thy loyal smile evinceth
A heart as pure as day;
    Smile, my beloved,
    Forever and for aye!

When thou art calmly sleeping
Beneath my loving eye,
Thy perfumed breath's soft murmur
Is sweetest melody.
Thy loveliness unveiled
Eclipseth the sun's ray;
    Sleep, my beloved,
    Forever and for aye!

When thou dost say: I love thee!
Dear heart! it seemeth me,
That heaven's gates are opened,
And Paradise I see.
With love's flame ever kindled,
Thy glance doth shine alway;
    Love, my beloved,
    Forever and for aye!

Thus all of life, beloved,
Do these four words contain,
All joy that 's worth the having,
All pleasure without pain!
All that doth charm the senses
Or doth the passions move!
    To sing and smile, beloved,
    To slumber and to love!

THE MAN.

He steps ashore. Good. He dismisses the boatman. Excellent!

(Returning to the front of the stage.)

Here he comes.

(Enters Fabiano Fabiani in his cloak. He walks toward the door of the house.)

SCENE VI

THE MAN, FABIANI.

THE MAN (stopping Fabiani).

A word with you by your leave.

FABIANI.

Some one speaks to me, I think. Who is this fellow? Who art thou?

THE MAN.

Whoever you choose to have me.

FABIANI.

This lantern casts a wretched light. But thou wearest a yellow cap, I think, a Jew's cap. Art thou a Jew?

THE MAN.

Yes, a Jew. I 've something I must say to you.

FABIANI.

Thy name?

THE MAN.

I know your name and you do not know mine. That gives me the advantage over you, and by your leave I 'll keep it.

FABIANI.

Thou knowest my name? That is not true.

THE MAN.

I know your name, I say. At Naples you were called Signor Fabiani; at Madrid Don Fabiano; at London you are Fabiano Fabiani, Earl of Clanbrassil.

FABIANI.

May the devil fly away with you!

THE MAN.

May God have you in his keeping!

FABIANI.

I 'll have you beaten. I do not choose that my name should be known when I am out *incognito* at night.

THE MAN.

Especially when you are going where you 're going now.

FABIANI.

What dost thou mean?

THE MAN.

If the queen knew!

FABIANI.

I 'm going nowhere.

THE MAN.

Oh! yes, my lord! you 're on your way to visit the fair Jane, Gilbert the carver's fiancée.

FABIANI (aside).

The devil! this is a man to fear.

THE MAN.

Do you wish me to tell you more? you have seduced the girl, and she has received you twice at night within a month. To-night is the third time. The damsel awaits your coming.

FABIANI.

Hush! hush! dost thou want money for thy silence? what is thy price?

THE MAN.

We 'll come to that anon. First, my lord, do you wish that I should tell you why you seduced this girl?

FABIANI.

Zounds, man! because I fell in love with her.

THE MAN.

Not so. You did not fall in love with her.

FABIANI.

I did not fall in love with Jane?

THE MAN.

No more than with the queen. Love, no; self-interest, yes.

FABIANI.

Ah! rascal, thou art not a man, thou art my conscience, masquerading as a Jew.

THE MAN.

I mean to speak to you as your conscience should speak, my lord. Your affairs stand thus: You are the queen's favorite. The queen has given you the Garter, and raised you to the peerage with an earl's patent. Empty honors these! the Garter 's a mere bauble, the earldom but a word, the peerage but the right to have your head cut off. You must have something better than all that; you must have goodly estates and goodly villages, goodly castles, and goodly revenues in goodly golden guineas. Now Henry Eighth had confiscated the domains of Lord Talbot, beheaded sixteen years since. Queen Mary was prevailed upon to give Lord Talbot's vast estates to you. But that the gift should be a valid one, Lord Talbot must have died without heirs of his body. If there exists an heir or heiress of Lord Talbot, as he died for Queen Mary and her mother, Catharine of Aragon, as he was a papist, and the queen 's a papist, there can be little doubt that she would take

the property away from you, my lord, favorite though you be, and would restore it at the call of gratitude and duty and religion to such heir or heiress. You were but little troubled on that score. Lord Talbot had but one little girl, who vanished from her cradle at the time her father was beheaded, and who was dead, or so all England thought. But your spies have of late made this discovery—that on the night when my Lord Talbot and his party were exterminated by King Henry Eighth, a child was left mysteriously at a carver's stall on London Bridge, and that 't was more than probable that this child, who was called Jane, was Jane Talbot, Lord Talbot's missing daughter. 'T is true that written demonstration of her birth was not forthcoming; but it might come to light from day to day. It was, in truth, a most vexatious accident. To see one's self forced some day to restore, and to a little girl, Shrewsbury, Wexford, which is a goodly city, and the magnificent earldom of Waterford! 't would be a grievous thing. But what to do? You sought some means of ruining and crushing the poor girl. An honest man would have had her stabbed or poisoned. But you found a better way, my lord, you stole her honor.

FABIANI.

Insolent villain!

THE MAN.

It is your conscience speaks to you, my lord. Another would have taken the girl's life, you took her honor, and therewith her future. Queen Mary is a prude, though she has lovers.

FABIANI.

The fellow goes to the heart of everything!

THE MAN.

The queen's health is but poor, the queen may die, and in that case, you, her favorite, will go to ruin on her tomb. Indisputable proofs of the young girl's rank may come to light, and then, if the queen 's dead, Jane, dishonored though she is by you, will be acknowledged as Lord Talbot's heir. That possibility you have foreseen ; you are a well-favored young gallant, you have won her love, she has given herself to you, and as a last resort, you 'll marry her. Do not deny your plan, my lord, for I think it sublime. If I were not myself I would be you.

FABIANI.

Thanks.

THE MAN.

You 've managed the affair most cleverly. You have concealed your name. Therefore you 're in no danger from the queen. The poor girl thinks she has been seduced by one Amyas Paulet, a knight of Somersetshire.

FABIANI.

Ah! he knows all! But come, let 's to the point. What dost thou want from me?

THE MAN.

My lord, if some one had in his possession papers which prove the birth, the existence and the title of Lord Talbot's heiress, you would be left as poor as my forefather Job, and with no other castles, Don Fabiano, than your castles in Spain, the which would vex you sorely.

FABIANI.

True. But no one has those papers.

THE MAN.

Yes.

FABIANI.

Who?

THE MAN.

Myself.

FABIANI.

Thou, wretch! Go to! that is not true. All Jews are liars.

THE MAN.

I have the papers.

FABIANI.

Thou liest. Where hast thou them ?

THE MAN.

In my pocket.

FABIANI.

I believe thee not. Are they complete? Is no link missing ?

THE MAN.

Not one.

FABIANI.

Then I must have them !

THE MAN.

Softly.

FABIANI.

Give me the papers, Jew !

THE MAN.

Very good. You Jew, you wretched beggar whom I pass in the street, give me the town of Shrewsbury, the city of Wexford and the earldom of Waterford ! A little charity, in God's name !

FABIANI.

Those papers are everything to me and nothing to thee !

THE MAN.

Simon Renard and Lord Chandos will pay me well for them !

FABIANI.

Simon Renard and Lord Chandos are a pair of curs, and I will have thee hanged between them.

THE MAN.

Have you nothing different to propose to me ? Farewell.

FABIANI.

Here, Jew ! What wouldst thou I should give thee for the papers?

THE MAN.

Something you have upon you.

FABIANI.

My purse?

THE MAN.

For shame! Do you wish mine?

FABIANI.

What then?

THE MAN.

There is a document from which you never part. It bears Queen Mary's signature in blank, and when she gave it you she swore upon her Catholic crown to grant to him who should present it to her what boon soever he might crave at her hands. Give me that document and you shall have Jane Talbot's proofs of title. Paper for paper.

FABIANI.

What dost thou propose to do with the blank signature?

THE MAN.

Come! let us show our hands, my lord. I 've told you all about your own affairs, and now I 'll tell you mine. I am one of the leading Jewish usurers of Rue Kantersten at Brussels. I loan my money. That is my calling. I loan ten and receive back fifteen. I loan to everybody; I would loan to the devil or the pope. Some two months since one of my debtors died still in my debt. He was a former servant of the Talbot family, living in exile. The poor man left nothing but a few rags, and them I seized. Among those rags I found a box, and in the box were papers. My lord, they were Jane Talbot's papers, with her whole story told in most minute detail and fortified with proofs in expectation of the dawn of brighter days. Just at that time the Queen of England gave Jane Talbot's property to you. Now, I was

in great need of the Queen of England, to let me have ten thousand golden marks. I saw the chance to drive a trade with you. I came to England thus disguised. I watched your goings out and comings in myself. I played the spy myself upon Jane Talbot. I did myself all that I had to do. In that way I learned everything, and here I am. You shall have Jane Talbot's muniments if you give me the queen's blank signature. Then I will write above it that the queen gives me ten thousand golden marks. There 's somewhat owing me at the excise office here, but I 'll not haggle about that. Ten thousand golden marks, no more. I do not ask you for that sum, because there is but one crowned head that can afford to pay it. I trust that I have made my meaning plain. You see, my lord, that two such clever men as you and I have naught to gain by seeking to deceive each other. If plain-speaking were banished from the earth it ought to find a refuge in the tête-à-tête of two infernal rascals.

FABIANI.

Impossible. I cannot give thee the blank signature. Ten thousand golden marks! What would the queen say? And then, to-morrow I may be disgraced; this signature in blank is my protection; 't is my very head.

THE MAN.

What care I for that?

FABIANI.

Ask me for something else.

THE MAN.

I must have that.

FABIANI.

Give me Jane Talbot's papers, Jew.

THE MAN.

Give me the queen's blank signature, my lord.

FABIANI.

Out upon thee, accursed Jew! I needs must yield to thee.

(He takes a paper from his pocket.)

THE MAN.

Show me the queen's signature.

FABIANI.

Show me the Talbot papers.

THE MAN.

In due time.

(They approach the lantern. Fabiani, standing behind the Jew, holds the paper before his eyes with his left hand. The Jew scrutinizes it, and reads:)

"We, Mary, queen . . ." 'T is well. You see that I 'm like you, my lord. I foresaw everything.

FABIANI (drawing his dagger with his right hand and plunging it into the other's throat).

Save this!

THE MAN.

Oh! traitor! Help!

(He falls. As he falls, he throws a sealed packet behind him into the darkness, unseen by Fabiani.)

FABIANI (stooping over the body).

'Faith, I believe he 's dead! The papers— quick!

(He feels in the Jew's pockets.)

What 's this? he has nothing! nothing upon him! not a paper, the old miscreant! He lied! he deceived me! he stole from me! Do you hear that, damned Jew? Oh! he has nothing, and he 's dead! I have murdered him for nothing! These Jews are all alike. Lying and theft, that 's your Jew to the life. But come, we must get rid of this dead body; I cannot leave it here before this door.

(Walking to the back of the stage.)

I 'll see if my boatman is still there, and have him help me throw it in the Thames.

(He disappears behind the parapet.)

GILBERT (entering on the opposite side).

I thought I heard a cry for help.

(He sees the body on the ground under the lantern.)

Some one assassinated! What! the Jew!

THE MAN (raising himself partly from the ground).

Ah! Gilbert, you come too late.

(He points to the spot where he threw the package.)

Take that. It contains papers which prove that Jane, your fiancée, is the daughter and sole heiress of the last Lord Talbot. My murderer is Lord Clanbrassil, the queen's favorite. Oh! I am choking. Gilbert, avenge me and avenge thyself!

(He dies.)

GILBERT.

Dead! Avenge myself? What did he mean? Jane, Lord Talbot's daughter! Lord Clanbrassil, the queen's favorite! I cannot see my way.

(Shaking the body.)

Speak to me once more! He is quite dead.

SCENE VII

GILBERT, FABIANI.

FABIANI (returning).

Who 's there?

GILBERT.

A man 's been murdered here.

FABIANI.

No, a Jew.

GILBERT.

Who killed the man?

FABIANI.

Why, 'faith, 't was you or I.

GILBERT.

Sirrah!

FABIANI.

No witnesses. A body on the ground. Two men beside it. Which is the assassin? There 's naught to prove that it was either rather than the other, that it was I rather than you.

GILBERT.

Villain! you are the murderer!

FABIANI.

Well, yes, it 's true! I am. What then?

GILBERT.

I 'll go and call the constables.

FABIANI.

You 'll help me throw this body in the water.

GILBERT.

I 'll have you seized and punished.

FABIANI.

You 'll help me throw this body in the water.

GILBERT.

You are a shameless rascal.

FABIANI.

Take my advice; let us destroy all trace of this affair. You are more interested than myself.

GILBERT.

That is too much!

FABIANI.

One of us struck the blow. I am a great nobleman. You a mere passer-by, a nobody, a man of the people. A gentleman who kills a Jew pays four farthings fine, a man of the people who kills another is hanged.

GILBERT.

And you would dare . . .

FABIANI.

If you denounce me, I denounce you, and I shall be believed rather than you. In any case the chances are unequal. Four farthings fine for me, for you the gallows.

GILBERT.

No witnesses! no proof! Oh! my mind 's wandering! The villain has me in his grasp, indeed he has!

FABIANI.

Shall I help you throw the body in the river?

GILBERT.

You are the very devil!

(Gilbert takes the body by the head, Fabiani by the feet, and together they carry it to the parapet.)

FABIANI.

Yes. In good sooth, my dear fellow, I 'm no longer certain which of us two did really kill the man.

(They go down behind the parapet. Fabiani reappears.)

There, that 's well done. Good-night, comrade. Now go about your business.

(He walks toward the house, but turns again, seeing that Gilbert is following him.)

Well, what do you want? Some money for your trouble? On my conscience I owe you nothing; but take this.

(He offers his purse to Gilbert, whose first impulse prompts him to refuse it, but he finally accepts it as if he had changed his mind on reflection.)

Now, off with you. Well, what more do you expect?

GILBERT.

Nothing.

FABIANI.

'Faith, you may stand there if you choose! For you the lovely stars, for me the lovely damsel. God be with you!

(He walks up to the door of the house, and seems to be about to open it.)

GILBERT.

Where are you going?

FABIANI.

Heaven save the mark! I 'm going home.

GILBERT.

What 's that you say? Home?

FABIANI.

Yes.

GILBERT.

Which of us two is dreaming? But now you said to me that I was the Jew's murderer, and now you say this house is yours?

FABIANI.

Or my mistress's, which comes to the same thing.

GILBERT.

Repeat what you just said.

FABIANI.

I say, my friend, if you must know, that this is the abode of a charming girl named Jane, who is my mistress.

GILBERT.

And I, my lord, I say that thou liest! I say that thou 'rt a liar and assassin! I say that thou 'rt an insolent villain! I say that those were fatal words thou didst pronounce, for which we both must die, thou for having uttered, and I for having heard them!

FABIANI.

La, la! Who is this devil of a man?

GILBERT.

I am Gilbert, the carver. Jane is my betrothed.

FABIANI.

And I am Sir Amyas Paulet. Jane is my mistress.

GILBERT.

I say, thou liest! Thou art Lord Clanbrassil, the queen's favorite. Poor fool, to think I knew not that!

FABIANI (aside).

It seems that all the world knows me to-night! Another dangerous man to be got rid of.

GILBERT.

Tell me, instanter, that thou liest like a coward, and that Jane 's not thy mistress.

FABIANI.

Dost know her writing?

(He takes a letter from his pocket.)

Read this.

(Aside, as Gilbert convulsively unfolds the paper.)

It is important that he should go in and pick a quarrel with her; 't will give my people time to arrive.

GILBERT (reading).

"I shall be alone to-night, and you may come." Damnation! My lord, thou hast dishonored my betrothed, thou art a hellish villain! Give me satisfaction!

FABIANI (drawing his sword).

Willingly. But where 's thy sword?

GILBERT.

Ten thousand furies! Oh! to be of the common people, and to wear neither sword nor dagger at one's side! I 'll lie in wait for thee at night at some street corner, I 'll bury my nails in thy throat, and murder thee, vile wretch!

FABIANI.

La, la! You 're over violent, my friend!

GILBERT.

Oh! my lord, I 'll be revenged on thee!

FABIANI.

Thou! be revenged on me! thou so low and I so high! thou 'rt mad! I do defy thee.

GILBERT.

Thou defiest me?

FABIANI.

I do.

GILBERT.

Thou 'lt see.

FABIANI (aside).

The sun must not rise to-morrow for this man.

(Aloud.)

My friend, take my advice and go within. I grieve that thou hast discovered this; but I leave thee the damsel. Indeed, 't was not my purpose to pursue the affair. Go in.

(He throws a key at Gilbert's feet.)

Here is a key if thou hast none. Or if thou dost prefer, thou hast but to rap four times upon this shutter. Jane will think 't is I, and will admit thee. Good-night.

(Exit.)

SCENE VIII

GILBERT (alone).

He has gone! he is no longer here. I did not crush the man, and trample him beneath my feet! I had no choice but to let him go; I had no weapon!

(He spies the dagger with which Lord Clanbrassil killed the Jew, lying on the ground, and picks it up in a transport of rage.)

Ah! thou dost come too late! 't is likely thou wilt serve to kill none but myself. But whether thou didst fall from heaven or wert cast up from hell, 't is all the same to me, I bless thee. Jane has been false to me! She 's given herself to that vile caitiff! Jane is Lord Talbot's heiress, but she 's lost to me! Oh! God! within this hour more crushing blows have fallen on me than my poor head can bear!

(Simon Renard appears in the darkness at the back of the stage.)

Oh! to be revenged on him! to be revenged on this Lord Clanbrassil! If I go to the queen's palace, her lackeys will drive me forth with kicks and blows like any dog. Oh! I am mad. My brain is bursting! Little I care for death, could I but be revenged! I 'd give the last drop of my blood to be revenged. Is there no one in the world who cares to strike this bargain with me? who will insure my vengeance on Lord Clanbrassil, and take my life in payment?

SCENE IX

GILBERT, SIMON RENARD.

SIMON RENARD (stepping forward).

I.

GILBERT.

Thou! Who art thou?

SIMON RENARD.

I am the man thou seekest.

GILBERT.

Knowest thou who I am?

SIMON RENARD.

Thou art the man I need.

GILBERT.

I have but one idea left in my brain, dost thou know that? to be revenged on Lord Clanbrassil, and then die.

SIMON RENARD.

Thou shalt be revenged on Lord Clanbrassil, and thou shalt die.

GILBERT.

Whoever thou mayest be, I thank thee.

SIMON RENARD.

Yes, thou shalt have the vengeance that thou cravest. But do not forget on what condition. I must have thy life.

GILBERT.

Take it.

SIMON RENARD.

Is it agreed?

GILBERT.

It is.

SIMON RENARD.

Follow me.

GILBERT.

Whither?

SIMON RENARD.

Thou shalt soon know.

GILBERT.

Remember thou hast promised me my vengeance!

SIMON RENARD.

Remember thou hast promised me thy death!

SECOND DAY

THE QUEEN

A room in the queen's suite. A Bible lying open upon a *prie-Dieu*. The royal crown upon a stool. Doors at the sides. A wide door at the rear. A part of the wall at the rear of the stage is concealed by handsome high-warp tapestry.

SCENE I

THE QUEEN, in magnificent attire, reclining upon a couch. FABIANO FABIANI, seated beside her on a folding-chair. He also is superbly dressed and wears the insignia of the Garter.

FABIANI (sings, accompanying himself upon a guitar).

When thou art calmly sleeping,
　Beneath my loving eye,
Thy perfumed breath's soft murmur
　Is sweetest melody.
Thy loveliness unveiled
Eclipseth the sun's ray;
　Sleep, my beloved,
　Forever and for aye!

When thou dost say : I love thee !
　Dear heart ! it seemeth me,
That heaven's gates are opened,
　And Paradise I see.

With love's flame ever kindled,
Thy glance doth shine alway;
　Love, my beloved,
　Forever and for aye !

Thus all of life, beloved,
　Do these four words contain,
All joy that 's worth the having,
　All pleasure without pain !
All that doth charm the senses,
Or doth the passions move!
　To sing and smile, beloved,
　To slumber and to love !

(He lays the guitar on the floor.)

121

Ah! madame, I love you more than I can
say! but I detest this Renard, this Simon
Renard, who wields more power here than
your own self!

THE QUEEN.

You know that I am powerless, my lord.
He 's here as legate of the Prince of Spain,
my future spouse.

FABIANI.

Your future spouse!

THE QUEEN.

Tush! we 'll talk no more of that, my lord.
I love you; what more would you have?
And see, 't is time for you to go.

FABIANI.

Mary—one moment more.

THE QUEEN.

But 't is the hour for my Privy Council to
assemble. Till now the woman only has
been with you; 't is time the queen should
enter.

FABIANI.

I wish the woman would keep the queen
waiting at the door.

THE QUEEN.

You wish! you wish! Look up at me, my
lord. Thou hast a youthful, fascinating face,
Fabiano!

FABIANI.

The beauty, madame, is all yours. You
would need nothing but your beauty to be
omnipotent. There 's that upon your head
which says that you 're the queen, but 't is
writ still more plainly on your brow than on
your crown.

THE QUEEN.

You flatter me.

FABIANI.

I love thee.

THE QUEEN.

Thou dost love me, dost thou not? Thou
lovest none but me? Tell it me again like
that, and with thine eyes. Alas! we poor
women never know just what is taking place
in a man's heart. We have no choice but to
believe your eyes, and, Fabiano, the most
lovely eyes are oftentimes the most deceitful.
But in thine eyes, my lord, there 's such a
world of loyalty and candor and good faith
that 't is not possible that they should lie—
am I not right? Yes, yes, thy glance is honest
and sincere, my comely page. To use such
heavenly eyes as thine to cozen with would be
most villainous. Either thy dear eyes are an
angel's eyes, or they 're a very devil's.

FABIANI.

Neither a devil nor an angel. Simply a man
who loves you.

THE QUEEN.

Who loves the queen.

FABIANI.

Who loves Mary.

THE QUEEN.

Hark ye, Fabiano, so do I love thee. Thou
art young. I know that there are many lovely
women who have soft looks for thee. And
one may grow weary of a queen, as well as of
another. Nay, interrupt me not. If ever
thou dost lose thy heart to any other woman,
it is my wish that thou shouldst tell me so.
Perhaps if thou shouldst tell me I would pardon thee. Pray do not interrupt me. Thou
dost not know to what degree I love thee. I
scarce do know myself. There be moments,
it is true, when I would rather see thee lying
dead than happy with another! but there be
other moments when I would rather know
that thou wert happy. By Heaven! I know

not why they seek to have it go abroad that I 'm a cruel woman.

FABIANI.

I can be happy with none but thee, Mary. I love none but thee.

THE QUEEN.

Art sure? Look in my eye. Art sure? Oh! sometimes I am jealous! I fancy—where is the woman who has not such thoughts? I fancy sometimes thou 'rt deceiving me. I fain would be invisible, that I might follow thee, and always know what thou art doing, what thou art saying, where thou art. I 've read in fairy tales of an enchanted ring, which renders him who weareth it invisible; I 'd give my crown to have that ring. I dream incessantly that thou art paying court to all the lovely maidens in the town. Oh! it must not be that thou dost deceive me!

FABIANI.

Pray banish all such fancies from your mind, madame. I deceive you, my queen, my generous mistress! Then must I be the most ungrateful and most base of men. But surely I have given you no cause to deem me the most ungrateful and most base of men. I love thee, Mary! I adore thee! I 'd not so much as look at any other woman! I say I love thee! canst thou not read it in my eyes? Surely there is an accent of sincerity that should convince thee in my voice. Pray, look at me, and say if I 've the bearing of a man who 's false to thee. When a man plays a woman false, the treachery crops out. Women are not so easily deceived. And then what moment dost thou choose to say such things to me, my Mary? the moment when I love thee more than ever in my life. In truth meseems thou never wert so dear to me as now. I speak not to the queen. No, no! I snap my fingers at the queen! What is there that the queen can do to me? cut off my head—and what care I for that? But, Mary, thou canst break my heart. 'T is not thy majesty I love, but thou. 'T is thy fair white hand I kiss and worship, madame, not thy sceptre.

THE QUEEN.

Thanks, my Fabiano. Fare thee well. Alack, my lord, how young thou art! what beautiful black locks, and what a shapely head! Return within the hour.

FABIANI.

That which you call an hour, I call a century.

(Exit.)

(As soon as he has left the room, the queen rises hastily, runs to a masked door, which she opens, and admits Simon Renard.)

SCENE II

THE QUEEN.

Come in, monsieur le bailli. Did you remain at hand? and did you hear him?

SIMON RENARD.

Yes, madame.

THE QUEEN.

What do you say to it? Oh! he 's the vilest rascal, and the most false of men! What do you say?

SIMON RENARD.

I say, madame, that 't is most plain the fellow bears a name that ends in *i*.

THE QUEEN.

But are you sure that he goes to this woman's house by night? Have you seen him?

SIMON RENARD.

Myself — and Chandos, Montacute and Clinton. Ten witnesses.

THE QUEEN.

'T is downright infamous!

SIMON RENARD.

The queen will have still more convincing proof at once. The girl is here, as I have told your Majesty. I caused her apprehension at her house last night.

THE QUEEN.

Pray is not this a crime so grave that he must pay the forfeit of his head.

SIMON RENARD.

What, calling on a pretty girl at night? Why, no, madame. Your Majesty caused Throgmorton to be brought to book for the same crime. Throgmorton was acquitted.

THE QUEEN.

But I punished them who tried Throgmorton.

SIMON RENARD.

Seek to avoid the need to punish them who try Fabiani.

THE QUEEN.

Oh! how to be revenged upon the traitor?

SIMON RENARD.

Your Majesty does not desire to be revenged save in a certain way?

THE QUEEN.

The only way that 's not unworthy of me.

SIMON RENARD.

Throgmorton was acquitted, madame. There is but the one way; I have already named it to your Majesty. The man who 's yonder.

THE QUEEN.

Will he do everything I wish?

SIMON RENARD.

Yes, if you do everything he wishes.

THE QUEEN.

Will he give his life?

SIMON RENARD.

He will exact conditions. But he will give his life.

THE QUEEN.

Know you what are his wishes?

SIMON RENARD.

Identical with yours. To be revenged.

THE QUEEN.

Let him come in, and do you tarry within earshot.—Monsieur le bailli!

SIMON RENARD (returning).

Madame?

THE QUEEN.

Say to Lord Chandos that I bid him wait in the room adjoining with six men at arms, ready to come at call.—And the woman, too—let her be at hand to enter.—Now go.

(*Exit Renard.*)

THE QUEEN (alone).

Oh! this will be a terrible ordeal!

(*One of the doors at the side opens, and Simon Renard enters with Gilbert.*)

SCENE III

THE QUEEN, GILBERT, SIMON RENARD.

GILBERT.

In whose presence am I ?

SIMON RENARD.

The queen's.

GILBERT.

The queen !

THE QUEEN.

Yes, the queen. I am the queen. We have no time to waste in wonderment. You, sir, are one Gilbert, a carver. You live somewhere along the river bank with one Jane, whose fiancé you are, and who is false to you, and has for lover one Fabiano, who 's false to me. You crave revenge, and so do I. To that end I must have your life to do with as I choose. I must be sure that you will say whatever I may order you to say. You must henceforth know naught of false or true, of good or bad, of just or unjust, naught, in brief, but my will and my vengeance. You must let me act, and let yourself be acted on. Do you agree ?

GILBERT.

Madame.

THE QUEEN.

Thou shalt have thy revenge as well. But I forewarn thee thou must die, that 's all. Make thy conditions. If thou hast an old mother, and wouldst have me cover her table cloth with golden ingots, speak and it shall be done. Sell me thy life as dearly as thou wilt.

GILBERT.

I am no longer resolute to die, madame.

THE QUEEN.

What 's that?

GILBERT.

Your Majesty, I passed the night in thought. Nothing is absolutely proved. I saw a man who boasted that he was Jane's lover. Why might he not have lied ? I saw a key. Who says he did not steal it ? I saw a letter. Who says she did not write it under duress ? Indeed, I am not sure 't was writ by her hand, for it was dark, I was much agitated, and could not see. I cannot give my life, for it is hers. I believe nothing, I am sure of nothing. I did not see Jane.

THE QUEEN.

Certes, thou art in love. Thou art like me, and dost reject all proof. But if thou dost see this Jane of thine, if thou hearest her confess her guilt, wilt thou then do my will ?

GILBERT.

Yes. Upon one condition.

THE QUEEN.

Thou 'lt tell it me anon.

(To Simon Renard.)

The woman—admit her instantly.

(Renard goes off. The queen stations Gilbert behind a curtain, which cuts off a part of the rear of the room.)

Stand there.

(Jane enters, pale and trembling.)

DAY SECOND   SCENE IX

THE QUEEN

THE QUEEN (to the executioner, pointing to Fabiani).

Dost see that head, that charming youthful head, that head, which but this morning was to me the fairest and most precious treasure in the whole world!   Ah, well! that head—say, dost thou see it?—that head, I give to thee!

SCENE IV

THE QUEEN, JANE; GILBERT, behind the curtain.

THE QUEEN.

Come hither, girl. Dost thou know who we are?

JANE.

Yes, madame.

THE QUEEN.

And knowest thou who the man is who did seduce thee?

JANE.

Yes, madame.

THE QUEEN.

But he deceived thee. He feigned to be a gentleman named Amyas Paulet, did he not?

JANE.

Yes, madame.

THE QUEEN.

Thou knowest now that he is Fabiano Fabiani, Earl of Clanbrassil?

JANE.

Yes, madame.

THE QUEEN.

Last night, when thou wert arrested at thy home, thou hadst an assignation with him; thou wert expecting him, is it not true?

JANE (with clasped hands).

In God's name, madame!

THE QUEEN.

Answer me.

JANE (almost inaudibly).

Yes.

THE QUEEN.

Thou knowest there is now no hope either for him or thee?

JANE.

Naught but death. That is a hope.

THE QUEEN.

Tell me of thy affair with him. Where didst thou first fall in with him?

JANE.

The first time that I saw him, was . . . But what is to be gained by this? A wretched girl, of humble origin, poor and vain, light-headed and coquettish, who falls a victim to the wiles of a great nobleman. That 's the whole story. I have been seduced, dishonored, ruined. I can add nothing to that. God's mercy, madame! can you not see that every word I utter is death to me?

THE QUEEN.

'T is well.

JANE.

Oh! your wrath is terrible. I know it well, madame. My head is bowed already in anticipation of the punishment you have in store for me.

THE QUEEN.

I! punishment in store for thee! Dost think that I concern myself with thee, thou fool? Who art thou, wretched creature, that a queen should pause to think of thee? No, my account 's to settle with Fabiano. As for thee, woman, thy punishment devolves upon another than myself.

JANE.

So be it, madame; whoever he may be, to whom the duty is committed, however harsh the punishment, I will endure it all without complaint; nay, madame, I will even thank you, if you will mercifully grant the prayer I am about to offer. There is a man who took me in, a little orphan in the cradle, adopted me, supported me and brought me up, and loved me, and who loves me still; a man of whom I 'm utterly unworthy; a man to whom I have done grievous wrong, but whose image is deeply graven on my heart, as sacred and as cherished as God's own; a man who, doubtless, at this moment, even as I speak, is gazing on his desolate and ruined home, understanding nothing of what has come to pass, and tearing his hair in desperation. The boon I do entreat your Majesty to grant is this: that he may never understand, that I may disappear, and he not know what has become of me, nor what you did with me. Alas! I know not if I make my meaning clear, but you must understand, that I have a friend, a noble-hearted, generous friend, — poor Gilbert! yes, that is most true—who has esteem for me, and thinks me pure, and that I pray that he may never come to hate me and despise me. You understand me, do you not, madame? This man's esteem is dearer to me than my life, God knows. And then it would cause him such intolerable pain! The blow would be so sudden! At first he would refuse to credit it. Oh! madame! pray have pity upon him and me. He has in no way injured you. In Heaven's name let him know naught of this! In Heaven's name let him not know that I am guilty; he would kill himself. Let him not know that I am dead, for he would die.

THE QUEEN.

The man of whom you speak is listening to you; he is to judge you and to punish you.

(Gilbert steps forward.)

JANE.

Just Heaven! Gilbert!

GILBERT (to the queen).

My life is at your service, madame.

THE QUEEN.

'T is well. Have you conditions to propose?

GILBERT.

Yes, madame.

THE QUEEN.

What are they? We give our royal word that we will acquiesce in them.

GILBERT.

They are these, madame.—'T is but a simple matter. I do but pay a debt of gratitude, I owe one of your courtiers, who has employed me often in my trade of carver.

THE QUEEN.

Say on.

GILBERT.

This nobleman is carrying on a secret *liaison* with a woman whom he cannot marry, because she 's one of a proscribed race. This woman, who has lived hitherto in strict retirement, is the only daughter and sole heiress of the last Lord Talbot, beheaded under Henry Eighth.

THE QUEEN.

What 's that? Art sure of what thou sayest? John Talbot, the stanch Catholic nobleman, the loyal champion of my mother of Aragon, left a daughter, dost thou say? By my crown, if this is true, the child shall be my child. And what John Talbot did for Mary of England's mother, Mary of England will do for John Talbot's daughter.

GILBERT.

Then it will doubtless be a pleasure to your Majesty to restore to Lord Talbot's daughter her father's heritage?

THE QUEEN.

Yes, most assuredly, and to take it back from Fabiano! But are there proofs of the existence of this heir?

GILBERT.

There are.

THE QUEEN.

But even if we have no proofs, we will make proofs. We are not queen for nothing.

GILBERT.

Your Majesty will give back to Lord Talbot's daughter, her father's titles and estates, his name, his rank, his crest and his device. Your Majesty will cancel the decree of banishment, and guarantee her safety. Your Majesty will give her hand in marriage to this nobleman, who is the only man whom she can marry. On these conditions, madame, you may dispose of me, my will, my liberty, my life, according to your pleasure.

THE QUEEN.

'T is well. I will do what you ask.

GILBERT.

Your Majesty will do what I ask? The Queen of England swears to me, Gilbert, the carver, upon this crown here at my hand, and on the open Gospel yonder?

THE QUEEN.

Upon the royal crown here at thy hand, and on the Holy Gospel, I swear it!

GILBERT.

'T is done, madame. Order a grave prepared for me, a nuptial chamber for the bride and bridegroom. The nobleman of whom I speak is Fabiani, Earl of Clanbrassil. Lord Talbot's heiress is before you.

JANE.

What does he say?

THE QUEEN.

Is the man mad? What does this mean? Sirrah, reflect, that you are over bold to make sport of the Queen of England, that the royal apartment is a place where one must keep close watch upon the words one uses, and that there are occasions when the mouth causes the head to fall.

GILBERT.

My head you have already, madame. I have your oath.

THE QUEEN.

Surely you do not speak in sober earnest. Fabiano! Jane! Go to!

GILBERT.

Jane is Lord Talbot's daughter and sole heiress.

THE QUEEN.

Bah! dreams! imagination! madness! The proofs, have you the proofs?

GILBERT.

Complete.

(He takes a package from his pocket.)

Be pleased to read these papers.

THE QUEEN.

Dost think that I have time to read your papers? Did I ask you for your papers? What care I for your papers? Upon my soul, if they prove anything I'll throw them in the fire, and then naught will remain.

GILBERT.

But your oath, madame.

THE QUEEN.

My oath! my oath!

GILBERT.

Upon the crown and on the gospel, madame. That is to say, upon your head and on your soul, upon your life in this world and the other.

THE QUEEN.

But pray what wouldst thou have? I swear to thee that thou art raving mad!

GILBERT.

What would I have? Jane has lost her rank,—restore it to her! Jane has lost her honor,—restore it to her! Declare her Lord Talbot's daughter and Lord Clanbrassil's wife, and then my life is yours.

THE QUEEN.

Thy life! but what wouldst thou have me do with thy life now? I wanted it only to help me wreak my vengeance on that man, Fabiano. Thou dost not understand? Nor do I understand thee. Thou didst talk of vengeance! Is this the way thou takest vengeance? These common people are stupid beyond belief. And dost thou fancy I believe in thy absurd tale of an heiress of Lord Talbot? Papers! thou showest papers! I do not choose to look at them. Oho! a woman betrays thee, and thou dost play the generous lover! As thou choosest. I am not generous! My heart is bursting with rage and hatred. I will be revenged, and thou shalt aid me. Why, the man 's mad! he 's mad! he 's mad! Great God! why have I need of him? 'T is most embarrassing to have perforce to deal with such as he in matters of great concern.

GILBERT.

I have your word as the Most Catholic Queen. Lord Clanbrassil has ruined Jane, and he shall marry her!

THE QUEEN.

But if he doth refuse to marry her?

GILBERT.

You 'll force him to it, madame.

JANE.

Oh no! have pity on me, Gilbert!

GILBERT.

If the abandoned villain doth refuse, your Majesty may deal with him and me as suits your pleasure.

THE QUEEN (joyously).

Ah! that is all I ask!

GILBERT.

If that should happen, provided that the coronet of Countess Waterford shall formally be placed upon Jane Talbot's sacred and inviolable head, I, for my part, will do all the queen bids me do.

THE QUEEN.

All?

GILBERT.

Yes, all. Even a crime, if crime you must have done; or even treason, that is worse than crime; or a dastard deed, that 's worse than treason.

THE QUEEN.

Thou 'lt say whatever thou art bid to say? Thou 'lt die whatever death thou 'rt bid to die?

GILBERT.

Whatever death you bid me die.

JANE.

O God!

THE QUEEN.

Dost swear?

GILBERT.

I swear.

THE QUEEN.

The matter may be thus arranged. Enough. I have thy word, and thou hast mine. 'T is done.

(She seems to reflect a moment.)

(To Jane.)

Your presence here is useless; go you hence. We will recall you.

JANE.

O Gilbert ! what have you done? O Gilbert ! I am a miserable wretch, and dare not raise my eyes to yours. O Gilbert ! you are more than angel, for you have all the virtues of an angel, and all the virtuous passions of a man.

SCENE V

THE QUEEN, GILBERT: afterwards SIMON RENARD, LORD CHANDOS and Guards.

THE QUEEN (to Gilbert).

Hast thou a weapon on thy person? a knife, a dagger, anything?

GILBERT (drawing Lord Clanbrassil's dagger from his breast).

A dagger? yes, madame.

THE QUEEN.

Good. Keep it in thy hand.

(She hastily seizes his arm.)

Monsieur le bailli d'Amont! Lord Chandos!

(Enter Simon Renard and Lord Chandos with the guards.)

Seize this man! He drew his dagger on me! I caught his arm as it was raised to strike. He 's an assassin!

GILBERT.

Madame.

THE QUEEN (aside, to Gilbert).

Hast thou so soon forgotten our agreement? is it thus thou doest what thou 'rt bid?

(Aloud.)

I call you all to witness that he still has the dagger in his hand. Monsieur le bailli, what is the name of the executioner at the Tower?

SIMON RENARD.

McDermott; he is an Irishman

THE QUEEN.

Let him be summoned hither. I have somewhat to say to him.

SIMON RENARD.

Yourself?

THE QUEEN.

Myself.

SIMON RENARD.

The queen speak with the executioner?

THE QUEEN.

Yes, the queen will speak with the executioner. The head will speak with the hand. Therefore send.

(One of the guards goes out.)

Lord Chandos, and you, gentlemen, will answer to me for this man. Keep him there, behind you, in your ranks. That is to happen here which he must witness. Monsieur le bailli d'Amont, is Lord Clanbrassil at the palace?

SIMON RENARD.

He 's in the Painted Chamber, waiting until it be the queen's pleasure that he wait upon her.

THE QUEEN.

He suspects nothing?

SIMON RENARD.

Nothing.

THE QUEEN (to Lord Chandos).

Let him come in.

SIMON RENARD.

The whole court is likewise in attendance. Shall none be introduced before Lord Clanbrassil?

THE QUEEN.

Which of our peers are they who hate Fabiani?

SIMON RENARD.

All.

THE QUEEN.

But they who most do hate him?

SIMON RENARD.

Montacute, Clinton, Somerset, the Earl of Derby, Gerald Fitz-Gerald, Lord Paget and the Lord Chancellor.

THE QUEEN (to Lord Chandos).

Admit all these, save the Lord Chancellor. Go.

(Chandos goes out.)

(To Simon Renard.)

The worthy chancellor-bishop has no more love for Fabiani than the others, but he 's a man of scruples.

(She spies the papers, which Gilbert has placed upon the table.)

Ah! I must cast a glance over these papers.

(While she is examining them, the door at the rear of the stage is thrown open. The noblemen named by Simon Renard enter with deep reverences.)

SCENE VI

THE SAME: LORD CLINTON and the other noblemen.

THE QUEEN.

Good-morrow, gentlemen. My lords, God have you in his keeping!

(To Lord Montacute.)

Anthony Brown, 't is ever in my recollection that you did worthily uphold my interests 'gainst Jean de Montmorency and Monsieur de Toulouse, in my negotiations with the emperor, my uncle. Lord Paget, you will receive to-day your letters patent as Baron Paget of Beaudesert, in Stafford. What 's this? Why, here is our old friend, Lord Clinton! We are always your good friend, my lord. 'T was you who did stamp out the uprising of Sir Thomas Wyatt, on Saint-James's plain. May we all remember it, my lords. That day the crown of England was saved by a bridge which gave my troops access to the rebels, and by a wall which barred the rebels' access to myself. The bridge was London Bridge. The wall was my Lord Clinton.

LORD CLINTON (aside, to Simon Renard).

'T is six months since the queen last spoke to me. How kind she is to-day!

SIMON RENARD (aside, to Lord Clinton).

Patience, my lord. You 'll find her in a moment kinder still.

THE QUEEN (to Lord Chandos).

Admit my Lord Clanbrassil.

(To Simon Renard.)

When he has been here some few minutes—

(She speaks to him in an undertone, pointing to the door by which Jane went out.)

SIMON RENARD.

'T is well, madame.

(Enters Fabiani.)

SCENE VII

THE SAME : FABIANI.

THE QUEEN.

Ah! here he is!

(She continues to speak low to Simon Renard.)

FABIANI (aside, and looking about, everybody having saluted him).

What can this mean? None but my ene-mies are here this morning. The queen is whispering with Simon Renard. She laughs! the devil! that bodes no good to me!

THE QUEEN (graciously, to Fabiani).

God have you in his keeping, my lord!

FABIANI (seizing her hand, and kissing it).

Madame . . .
(Aside.)

She smiles on me. The danger's not for me.

THE QUEEN (still with a gracious air).

I would speak with you.

(She walks to the front of the stage with him.)

FABIANI.

And I would speak with you, madame. I have words of reproach for you. To banish me, to keep me at a distance for so long a time! Ah! it would not be so, if in the hours of absence you thought of me as I think of you.

THE QUEEN.

You are unjust. Since we last parted my mind has been engrossed with you.

FABIANI.

Can it be true? Am I so blest? Say it once more.

THE QUEEN (smiling as before).

I swear it.

FABIANI.

You love me, then, as I love you?

THE QUEEN.

Yes, my lord. 'T is certain I have thought of none but you. And I resolved to give you an agreeable surprise on your return.

FABIANI.

What manner of surprise?

THE QUEEN.

A meeting that will give you pleasure.

FABIANI.

A meeting! and with whom?

THE QUEEN.

Guess. Can you not guess?

FABIANI.

No, madame.

THE QUEEN.

Look behind you.

(He turns and sees Jane standing on the threshold of the small door, which is open.)

FABIANI (aside).

Jane!

JANE (aside).

'T is he!

THE QUEEN (still smiling).

My lord, do you know this young woman?

FABIANI.

No, madame!

THE QUEEN.

Young woman, do you know my lord?

JANE.

Truth before life. Yes, madame.

THE QUEEN.

And so, my lord, you do not know this woman?

FABIANI.

Madame, this is a plot to ruin me. I am surrounded by my enemies. This woman doubtless is in league with them. I know her not, madame! I know not who she is, madame!

THE QUEEN (striking him across the face with her fan).

Ah! thou dastard! thou dost betray one, and deny the other! Thou knowest not, thou sayest, who she is! And dost thou wish that I should tell thee? She is Jane Talbot, John Talbot's daughter, the gallant Catholic lord who died upon the scaffold in my mother's cause. She is Jane Talbot, and my cousin; Countess of Shrewsbury, Wexford and Waterford, and peeress of England! Such is this woman! Lord Paget, Lord Keeper of the Seal, we bid you mark well our words. The Queen of England formally doth recognize this woman as Jane, the only daughter and sole heiress of the last Earl of Waterford.

(Holding up the papers.)

Here are the muniments of title and the proofs, to which you will cause the great seal to be affixed. Such is our pleasure.

(To Fabiani.)

Yes, Countess of Waterford! and that is fully proved! and thou 'lt restore her patrimony to her, villain. Ah! thou knowest not this woman! thou knowest not who this woman is! Be it so. I tell thee, she is Jane Talbot! And must I tell thee more?

(She looks him squarely in the face, and mutters low, between her teeth.)

Coward! she is thy mistress!

FABIANI.

Madame . . .

THE QUEEN.

That 's what she is. Now, let us see what thou art. Thou art a soulless, heartless, mindless man! thou art a scoundrel and a craven cur! thou art—Pardy, my lords, you have no need to move away. It matters not to me that you should overhear what I 'm about to say to yonder fellow. I do not drop my voice, that I can see. Fabiano, thou art a villain, a traitor to me, a dastard to her, a lying hound, the vilest, worst of men! 'T is true that I have made thee Earl of Clanbrassil, Baron of Dinasmonddy, and what else? Baron of Dartmouth in County Devon. Oh well! I was stark mad! I crave your pardon, my lords, for having forced you to submit to the indignity of being elbowed by this man! Thou, a gentleman! thou, a belted knight! thou, a peer of England! Why, do but compare thyself an instant with these who stand about thee, caitiff! look if thou wouldst see true gentlemen! There 's Bridges, Baron Chandos! there 's Seymour, Duke of Somerset! and there the Stanleys, who have been Earls of Derby since fourteen eighty-five! There are the Clintons too, who have been Barons Clinton since twelve hundred ninety-eight! Dost thou imagine, pray, that thou dost in aught resemble such as they? Thou sayest that thou art akin to the great Spanish family of Peñalver, but that 's a lie; thou 'rt nothing but a base Italian, a nobody, less than a nobody! son of a hosier of Larino!—

Yes, gentlemen, a hosier's son! I knew it, and I said it not aloud; I hid it, and pretended to believe him when he prated of his noble birth. For so are we women made. By Heaven, I would that there were women here, 't would be a useful lesson for them. Oh! the villain! the villain! he deceives one woman, and denies the other! Infamous! yes, surely thou art doubly infamous! What 's this! While I 've been speaking, he has dared to stand! To thy knees, Fabiani! My lords, force this man to his knees!

FABIANI.

Madame . . .

THE QUEEN.

Vile churl, whom I have loaded down with favors! Base Neapolitan lackey, whom I have made a gilded knight and peer of England! Ah! I might well have looked for what has come to pass! I was forewarned that this would be the end. But I am always thus, wedded to my own will, and then I find too late that I was wrong. It is my fault. Italian, that means scoundrel! Neapolitan, that means dastard! My father never did make use of an Italian, that he did not repent it. This Fabiani! Thou seest, Lady Jane, unhappy child, what manner of man he is to whom thou gav'st thyself! But I 'll avenge thee, never fear! Oh! I should have known that nothing can be found in an Italian's pocket but a stiletto, and nothing in his soul but treachery!

FABIANI.

Madame, I swear . . .

THE QUEEN.

And now he seeks to perjure himself! he will be base and vile until the end; he 'll make us blush before these gentlemen to the very last, us poor, weak women who have loved him! but he will not raise his head!

FABIANI.

Yes, madame, I will raise my head. I see full well that I am lost. My death is predetermined. You will use any means—the dagger, poison . . .

THE QUEEN (seizing his hands and drawing him hurriedly to the front of the stage).

The dagger! poison! What dost thou say, Italian? a treacherous, cowardly revenge, revenge behind one's back, revenge as it is practiced in thy country! No, Signor Fabiani, neither the dagger nor poison. In God's name, have I to conceal myself? to lurk about street corners in the dark, and make myself small when I avenge myself? No, by my soul! I choose the broad daylight, my lord, dost understand? the radiant sunlight at high noon, the public square, the axe and block, the people in the streets and at the windows, and on the house-tops—a hundred thousand witnesses. I choose to strike fear to the heart, dost understand, my lord? that my good subjects shall see a striking, splendid, awe-inspiring spectacle, and shall say among themselves: "'T was a woman who was insulted, but 't is a queen who 's wreaking vengeance for the insult!" I long to see this envied favorite, this handsome, impudent young gallant, whom I have clothed in velvet and in satin, aghast and trembling, bent double on his knees on a black cloth, feet bare, hands bound, hooted and jeered at by the crowd, abandoned to the headsman's tender mercies. I long to put a rope around that snow-white neck, on which I once did clasp a golden necklet. I 've seen how this Fabiani looks upon a throne, I long to see how he will look upon a scaffold.

FABIANI.

Madame . . .

THE QUEEN.

Not a word! No! not another word! Thou art indeed inevitably lost. Thou 'lt mount the scaffold like Northumberland and Suffolk. 'T will be a spectacle as welcome as another to set before my loyal town of London. Thou knowest how that good town of mine detests thee. I' faith, it is a goodly thing, when one has vengeance in one's heart, to be the lady Mary, Queen of England, daughter of Henry Eighth, and mistress of the four seas! And when thou 'rt on the scaffold, Fabiani, thou mayest, an it please thee, like Northumberland, make a long speech to the people, or a long prayer to God, like Suffolk, to give thy pardon time to arrive; Heaven is my witness that thou art a traitor, and that no pardon shall arrive for thee! The base-born churl, who talked to me of love, and called me "thou" this very morning! God 'a mercy, gentlemen, it seems to cause you wonder that I speak thus before you, but I repeat, what matters it to me?

(To Lord Somerset.)

Do you, my lord duke, as Constable of the Tower, demand the caitiff's sword.

FABIANI.

Here is my sword, but I protest. Even though it be fully proved that I 've deceived a woman or seduced her . . .

THE QUEEN.

What 's that? prithee, what care I that thou hast seduced a woman? These gentlemen will bear me witness that it 's all one to me!

FABIANI.

Seduction is no capital offense, madame. Your Majesty failed to secure Throgmorton's condemnation on a like charge.

THE QUEEN.

He defies us now, I verily believe! the worm becomes a viper. Who told thee, pray, thou wast accused of that?

FABIANI.

Of what else am I accused? I am not English born, I am no subject of your Majesty. I am a subject of the King of Naples, and vassal of the Holy Father. I 'll call upon his legate, the most eminent Cardinal Pole, to demand my liberty. I cannot be brought to trial, save for a crime committed, a real crime. What is my crime?

THE QUEEN.

Thou askest what thy crime is?

FABIANI.

Yes, madame.

THE QUEEN.

You all do hear the question that is put to me, my lords. You all shall hear my answer. Mark it well, and look well to yourselves, for you will see that I have but to stamp my foot upon the ground to make a scaffold spring thereout. Chandos! Chandos! throw open the great door! Summon the court! Let everyone come in!

(The folding doors at the rear are thrown open. The whole court enters.)

SCENE VIII

THE SAME: THE LORD CHANCELLOR, and the whole court.

THE QUEEN.

Come in, come in, my lords. It gives me much real pleasure to see you all to-day. Good, good! this way, you men of the law, nearer, nearer! Where are the sergeants-at-arms of the Lord's House, Harriot and Herbert? Ah! there you are, gentlemen. Welcome. Draw your swords. 'T is well. Now place yourselves at this man's right and left. He is your prisoner.

FABIANI.

Madame, what is my crime?

THE QUEEN.

Lord Gardiner, my learned friend, and Lord High Chancellor of England, we bid you with all diligence convene the twelve lords commissioners of the Star Chamber, whom we regret not to see here among us. Strange things are happening within these walls. Listen, my lords. Already has the Princess Elizabeth set astir more than one enemy against our throne. There was the plot of Pietro Caro, who led the uprising at Exeter, and who maintained a secret correspondence with Elizabeth by means of a cipher cut on a guitar. There was the treasonous scheme of Thomas Wyatt who set all Kent aflame. There was the rebellion of the Duke of Suffolk, who was found hiding in a hollow tree after his partisans were routed. To-day there was a new scheme in the wind.

Listen all. To-day, this morning, a man made his appearance at my audience. After a few words interchanged he drew a dagger on me. I caught his arm in time. Lord Chandos and the bailli of Amont seized the man. He swore he was incited to the crime by Lord Clanbrassil.

FABIANI.

By me? That cannot be. Oh! but this is most abominable! That man does not exist. That man cannot be found. Who is the man? where is he?

THE QUEEN.

He is here.

GILBERT (coming out from among the soldiers, behind whom he has remained, concealed from sight, up to this time).

I am the man.

THE QUEEN.

In consequence of this man's declarations, we, Mary, queen, do charge this other man, Fabiano Fabiani, Earl of Clanbrassil, with high treason, and attempted regicide upon our royal, consecrated person, and summon him to answer before the Star Chamber.

FABIANI.

I, regicide! 't is a monstrous thing! Oh! my mind wanders, and my sight grows dim! What snare is this? Whoever thou mayest be, thou miscreant, dost thou dare affirm the truth of what the queen has said?

GILBERT.

I do.

FABIANI

That I incited thee to regicide?

GILBERT.

Yes.

FABIANI.

Yes! always yes! ten thousand curses! Is it possible that you can fail to see how false this is, my lords? This man is fresh from hell. Villain! thou mayest destroy me, but thou dost not know that thou destroyest thyself at the same time. The crime with which thou chargest me is on thy head as well. Thou 'lt cause my death, but thou wilt die. With a single word, insensate fool, thou causest two heads to fall, my own and thine.

GILBERT.

I know it.

FABIANI.

My lords, this man is paid . . .

GILBERT.

By you. Here is the purse filled with gold, you gave me for the crime. Your coat of arms and cipher are worked upon it.

FABIANI.

Just Heaven! But the dagger 's not forthcoming with which this man essayed, 't is said, to strike the queen. Where is the dagger?

LORD CHANDOS.

Here it is.

GILBERT (to Fabiani).

'T is yours. You gave it me for that. The scabbard will be found in your apartments.

THE LORD CHANCELLOR.

Earl of Clanbrassil, what have you to reply? Do you recognize this man?

FABIANI.

No.

GILBERT.

In truth, he has not seen me save at night. Let me say two words in his ear, madame. That will assist his memory.

(He draws near Fabiani.)

To-day thou recognizest nobody, my lord, no more the man thou hast insulted than the woman thou hast seduced. Ah! the queen will be revenged, but the man of the people will be revenged as well. Thou didst defy me, if I mistake not. Now thou art fast between two vengeances, my lord. What dost thou say to that? I am Gilbert, the carver.

FABIANI.

Yes, I recognize you. I recognize this man, my lords. The moment that I find I have this man to deal with, I have no more to say.

THE QUEEN.

He confesses!

THE LORD CHANCELLOR (to Gilbert).

According to the Norman law, and the statute of the twenty-fifth year of King Henry Eighth, in cases of *lèse-majesté* in the first degree, confession does not absolve the accomplice. Forget not that it is a case wherein the queen has not the power to pardon, and that you must die upon the scaffold with him whom you accuse. Consider well. Do you reiterate all that you have said?

GILBERT.

I know that I shall die, and I reiterate it.

JANE (aside).

Merciful God! if all this is a dream, 't is a most frightful one.

THE LORD CHANCELLOR (to Gilbert).

Do you agree to ratify your declarations with your hand upon the Gospel?

(He offers the Gospel to Gilbert, who lays his hand upon it.)

GILBERT.

I swear, my hand upon the Holy Gospel, and with impending death before my eyes, that that man 's an assassin ; that this dagger, which is his, has helped commit a crime ; that this purse, which is his, was given me by him for the crime. That is the truth, so help me God!

THE LORD CHANCELLOR (to Fabiani).

My lord, what have you to say ?

FABIANI.

Nothing.—I am lost !

SIMON RENARD (in an undertone to the queen).

Your Majesty sent to require the presence of the executioner. He is without.

THE QUEEN.

Good. Let him come in.

(*The courtiers stand aside, and the executioner appears in the door-way, clad in red and black, and with a long sword in its sheath, over his shoulder.*)

SCENE IX

THE SAME: THE EXECUTIONER.

THE QUEEN.

My Lord Duke of Somerset, these two men to the Tower. My Lord Chancellor Gardiner, let their trial be begun to-morrow before the twelve commissioners of the Star Chamber, and may God help old England! It is our pleasure that they both be tried before we set out for Oxford, whither we go to open Parliament, and for Windsor, where we shall celebrate the Easter festival.

(To the executioner.)

Come nearer thou. I am much pleased to see thee. Thou art a faithful servitor. Thou art advanced in years, thou hast already seen three reigns. 'T is ancient usage that the sovereign of this kingdom should give thee on succeeding to the throne the most splendid gift within her power. My father, Henry Eighth, gave thee the diamond clasp wherewith his cloak was fastened. My brother, Edward Sixth, gave thee a goblet of chased gold. Now 't is my turn. I have as yet made thee no present. 'T is meet that I should do so now. Draw near.

(Pointing to Fabiani.)

Dost see that head, that charming youthful head, that head, which but this morning was to me the fairest and most precious treasure in the whole world! Ah, well! that head—say, dost thou see it?—that head, I give to thee!

THIRD DAY

WHICH OF THE TWO?

FIRST PART

An apartment in the Tower of London. Ogive arches supported by heavy pillars. At the right and left low doors leading to two dungeons. At the right, a window supposed to look upon the Thames ; at the left a window supposed to look into the street. On each side a masked door in the wall. At the rear a gallery with a wide balcony looking into the outer courtyard of the Tower.

SCENE 1

GILBERT, JOSHUA.

GILBERT.

Well ?

JOSHUA.

Alas !

GILBERT.

Is there no hope ?

JOSHUA.

No hope.

(Gilbert goes to the window.)

Oh ! thou 'lt see nothing from the window.

GILBERT.

Thou hast made inquiry, hast thou not ?

JOSHUA.

I am but too sure.

143

GILBERT.

It is for Fabiani?

JOSHUA.

It is for Fabiani.

GILBERT.

Oh! what a happy man! There is a curse upon me!

JOSHUA.

Poor Gilbert! thy turn will come. To-day, 't is he, to-morrow 't will be thou.

GILBERT.

What dost thou mean? We fail to understand each other. To what dost thou refer?

JOSHUA.

To the scaffold that is being erected at this moment.

GILBERT.

And I am asking thee concerning Jane.

JOSHUA.

Concerning Jane?

GILBERT.

Yes, Jane! and only Jane! What care I for the rest? Hast thou then forgotten everything? Dost thou not remember how, for a month past, with my face glued to the bars of my dungeon, whence I can see the street, I have watched her, pale and in mourning, walking to and fro from morn till night at the foot of this turret, which contains two men, myself and Fabiani? And dost thou not recall my doubts, my anguish, my perplexity? For which of the two men comes she hither? I ask myself that question night and day, poor wretch! I asked it of thyself, Joshua, and thou didst promise me last night to try to see her and to speak with her. Oh! tell me! hast thou learned aught? Is it for me she comes, or is it for Fabiani?

JOSHUA.

I have learned that Fabiani 's surely to lose his head to-day, and thou to-morrow, and I confess that since that moment, I have been like a madman, Gilbert. The scaffold has put Jane out of my thoughts. Thy death . . .

GILBERT.

My death! What meanest thou by that? 'T is death to me to know that Jane no longer loves me. I have been dead from the first day I ceased to be beloved. Ah! dead in very truth, my Joshua! All that survives of me since then is hardly worth the trouble they will take to-morrow. My friend, thou canst form no conception what it is to love. If one had said to me two months ago: " Your spotless Jane, your love, your pride, your treasure, your pure, white lily, will give herself to another: will you still care for her?" I would have answered: " No, I 'll none of her! better a thousand times death for her and me!" And I would have trampled under foot the man who dared say that thing to me. But now I say, yes. I do care for her. To-day, thou seest, Jane is no longer the pure, spotless Jane whom I adored, the Jane whose brow I scarce dared let my lips breathe upon. I know full well that Jane has given herself to another—a villain, too— and still it 's all the same to me—I love her! my heart is broken, but I love her! I would I might but kiss the hem of her dress, and ask her to forgive me if she wished me to; and if she were in the gutter with them whose home is there, how I would rush to lift her up, and press her to my heart! Joshua, I would give,—not a hundred years of my life, for I have but a single day,—but the eternity which will be mine to-morrow, to see her smile on me once more, but once before I die, and say to me those blessed words which she used once to say: " I love thee !" Ah ! Joshua, Joshua, such is a man's heart who loves. You think that you would kill the woman who deceives you? But, no, you would not kill her, but would lie at her feet, after as before, only you would be sad at heart. You think me weak? Pray what should I have gained by killing Jane? Oh ! my heart 's full of thoughts that are beyond endurance ! If she but loved me still, what should I care for all that she has done? But she loves Fabiani ! she loves Fabiani ! 't is for him she comes ! There is but one thing beyond doubt, and that is, that I long for death. Have pity on me, Joshua.

JOSHUA.

Fabiani will be put to death to-day.

GILBERT.

And I to-morrow?

JOSHUA.

God is the supreme judge.

GILBERT.

To-day I shall be revenged on him: to-morrow he will be revenged on me.

JOSHUA.

My brother, here comes the Deputy Constable of the Tower, Master Æneas Dulverton. Thou must go in. I 'll see thee again this evening, brother.

GILBERT.

Oh ! to die unloved ! to die unwept ! Jane ! Jane ! Jane !

(He goes into his cell.)

JOSHUA.

Poor Gilbert ! Great God ! who would have dreamed such things would ever happen?

(He goes out.   Enter Simon Renard and Master Æneas.)

SCENE II

SIMON RENARD, MASTER ÆNEAS DULVERTON.

SIMON RENARD.

'T is, as you say, most strange; but what would you? the queen is mad and knows not what she wants. One can count on nothing, -for she is a woman. Consider, pray, what brings her hither? The female heart is an enigma of which King François First wrote the solution on the window pane at Chambord:

> Souvent femme varie
> Bien fol est qui s'y fie.

Look you, Master Æneas, we are old friends. It is essential that this thing shall end to-day. All depends upon your action here. If you receive instructions . . .

(He whispers hastily in Æneas's ear.)

spin the thing out, and manage cleverly to make it fail. Give me but two hours before me this evening, and what I seek is done; to-morrow the favorite is no more; I am all-powerful, and the day after you are Lieutenant of the Tower and a baronet. Is it agreed?

MASTER ÆNEAS.

Agreed.

SIMON RENARD.

'T is well. I hear footsteps. We must not be seen together. Go you that way. I go to meet the queen.

(They separate.)

SCENE III

A JAILER enters, looking carefully around, then introduces LADY JANE.

THE JAILER.

Here you are where you wished to be, my lady. Here are the doors of the two dungeons. Now my reward, so please you.

(Jane takes off her diamond bracelet and gives it to him.)

JANE.

Take this.

THE JAILER.

Thanks. Do not betray me.

(He goes out.)

JANE (alone).

Just Heaven! what shall I do now? 'T was I who ruined him, and 't is for me to save him. I can never do it. A woman can do nothing. The scaffold! the scaffold! oh! 't is horrible. Come, no more tears, but deeds! Have pity on me, O my God! I think that some one comes. Who speaks? I know that voice. It is the queen's. Ah! all is lost!

(She conceals herself behind a pillar. Enter the queen and Simon Renard.)

SCENE IV

THE QUEEN, SIMON RENARD; JANE (concealed).

THE QUEEN.

And so my change of purpose doth surprise you! 'T is true I am no longer like myself. But even so, what matters it? It is not now my wish that he should die.

SIMON RENARD.

Your Majesty, however, gave order yesterday that the execution should take place to-day.

THE QUEEN.

Even as I gave order on the previous day that the execution should take place yesterday. Even as I gave order on the Sunday that the execution should take place on Monday. To-day it is my pleasure that the execution shall take place to-morrow.

SIMON RENARD.

Indeed, 't is true that since the second Sunday of this Advent season, when the Star Chamber's judgment was pronounced, and the condemned were brought back to the Tower, preceded by the executioner, his axe's point turned toward their faces, we 've had three weeks of this; each day your Majesty postpones the execution till the morrow.

THE QUEEN.

Well, do you not understand what that implies? must I put it all in words, and must I, a woman, lay my heart bare before you, because it is my lot to be a queen, and yours to represent the Prince of Spain, my future husband? By Heaven, monsieur, you do not know, you men, that a woman's heart has its modesty no less than her body. If you must know, and since you fail to understand, or so pretend, 't is true that I from day to day defer Fabiani's execution till the next day, because each morning my resolution fails me at the thought that the Tower bell is soon to give the signal for his death; because I feel my pulses slacken at the thought that the axe is being sharpened for him; because my heart stops beating at the thought that soon the coffin-lid will be nailed down upon him; because I am a woman, and am weak and foolish; because, God help me, I do love the man! Have you enough of reasons? Are you content? Do you now understand? Oh! I will some day find a way to be revenged on you for all that you have made me say.

SIMON RENARD.

It is full time, however, to have done with Fabiani. You are to espouse the Prince of Spain, my royal master, madame.

THE QUEEN.

If the Prince of Spain is not content, let him but say so, we will find another spouse, we have no lack of suitors. The King of the Romans' son, the Prince of Piedmont, the Infant of Portugal, Cardinal Pole, the King of Denmark, and Lord Courtenay are every whit as nobly born as he.

SIMON RENARD.

Lord Courtenay! Lord Courtenay!

THE QUEEN.

An English earl, monsieur, is quite the equal of a Spanish prince. Moreover, Lord Courtenay traces his descent from the Emperors of the East. But then, be angry, if you choose.

SIMON RENARD.

Fabiani has incurred the hatred of everyone who has a heart, in London.

THE QUEEN.

Except myself.

SIMON RENARD.

The citizens are in full accord with the nobility concerning him. If he 's not put to death this very day, even as your Majesty did promise . . .

THE QUEEN.

Well?

SIMON RENARD.

There will be rioting among the people.

THE QUEEN.

I have my guards.

SIMON RENARD.

There will be plots among the nobles.

THE QUEEN.

I have the headsman.

SIMON RENARD.

Your Majesty made oath upon your mother's Book of Hours that you would not pardon him.

THE QUEEN.

Here is my signature in blank which he has sent to me, wherein I swear by my imperial crown that I will pardon him. My father's crown is no less sacred than my mother's Book of Hours. One oath destroys the other. Besides, who said that I propose to pardon him?

SIMON RENARD.

He most audaciously deceived you, madame.

THE QUEEN.

What 's that to me? All men do the same. I do not choose that he shall die. Look you, my lord—monsieur le bailli. I would say— Great Heaven! my mind 's in such a ferment that I no longer know to whom I speak! I know all that you would say to me. That he is a base churl, a coward and a villain. I know it well, and blush to know it. But what would you have me do? I might, perhaps, love an honorable man less dearly. And then, too, who are all you others? Are you better men than he? You would remind me that he is a favorite, and that the English nation loves not favorites. Do I not know that you would overthrow him only to set up in his place the Earl of Kildare, that Irish simpleton? You say that twenty heads a day are cut off through his agency. What 's that to you? And prate not to me of the Prince of Spain. Your chagrin 's not for him. Nor talk about the discontent of M. de Noailles, the French ambassador. M. de Noailles is an idiot, and so I 'll tell him to his face. Besides, I am a woman. I would and I would not. I am not always of one mind. This man's life is necessary to my life. Do not assume that air of virginal simplicity and candor, I beseech you, for I know all your schemes. Between ourselves, you know, and so do I, that he did not commit the crime for which he was condemned. 'T was put upon him. It is my will that Fabiani shall not die. Am I the mistress here, or no? Come, monsieur le bailli, shall we not talk of something else?

SIMON RENARD.

I will withdraw, madame. All the nobility has spoken by my voice.

THE QUEEN.

What care I for the nobility?

SIMON RENARD (aside).

We must try the people.

(He makes a deep obeisance, and goes out.)

THE QUEEN (alone).

His face wore a strange expression as he took his leave. The fellow is quite capable of stirring up sedition. I must in all haste to the Guildhall. Without there!

(Enter Master Æneas and Joshua.)

SCENE V

THE QUEEN, MASTER ÆNEAS, JOSHUA.

THE QUEEN.

Is 't you, Master Æneas? You and this good fellow must find out a way to effect Lord Clanbrassil's escape upon the instant.

MASTER ÆNEAS.

Madame . . .

THE QUEEN.

But no, I trust you not. I recollect that you are of his enemies. God in Heaven! are there none near me save the enemies of him I love? I 'll lay my crown this turnkey, who 's a stranger to me, detests him like the rest.

JOSHUA.

'T is true, madame.

THE QUEEN.

My God! my God! this Simon Renard is more king than I am queen. What! no one here whom I can safely trust! no one to whom to give full power to insure Fabiani's flight!

JANE (coming out from behind the pillar).

Yes, madame, I.

JOSHUA (aside).

Jane!

THE QUEEN.

Thou! who art thou? Is it you, Jane Talbot? How came you here? But it matters not, since you are here! you come to save Fabiani. Thanks! I ought to hate you, Jane, I should be jealous of you, I have a thousand reasons for it. But no, I love you for loving him. Before the scaffold, there 's an end of jealousy, and naught but love remains. You are like me, you have forgiven him. These men can never understand how that can be. Let us speak plainly, Lady Jane. We are both miserably unhappy, is 't not so? Fabiani must be permitted to escape. I have none but you, and I must needs take you. I cannot doubt at least that your heart 's in the work. Take it upon yourself. You, sirs, will faithfully obey my Lady Jane in everything, and you will answer to me with your heads for the due execution of her orders. Embrace me, girl!

JANE.

The Thames flows at the foot of the Tower on this side. There is a secret egress there which I have noticed. A boat in readiness at that point, and he may escape by the river. 'T is the surest way.

MASTER ÆNEAS.

'T will be impossible to have a boat in waiting there within an hour.

JANE.

That seems very long.

MASTER ÆNEAS.

An hour is soon gone. Then, too, an hour hence it will be dark. That will be better, if her Majesty desires the escape to be kept secret.

THE QUEEN.

It may be that you 're right. So be
it then, an hour hence. I leave you, Lady
Jane. I must to the Guildhall. Save
Fabiani !

JANE.

Have no fear, madame.

(The queen goes out ; Jane looks after her.)

JOSHUA (at the front of the stage).

Gilbert was right, 't is all for Fabiani !

SCENE VI

THE SAME, without the queen.

JANE (to Master Æneas).

You heard the queen's commands. A boat here at the foot of the Tower, the keys of the secret corridors, a hat and cloak.

MASTER ÆNEAS.

Impossible to have all those before 't is dark. An hour hence, my lady.

JANE.

'T is well. Go, leave me with this man.

(Master Æneas goes out. Jane follows him with her eyes.)

JOSHUA (aside, at the front of the stage).

This man! But surely she who has forgotten Gilbert will not remember Joshua.

(He walks toward Fabiani's cell, and sets about opening the door.)

JANE.

What do you there?

JOSHUA.

I am anticipating your command, my lady, and opening this door.

JANE.

What door is that?

JOSHUA.

The door of my lord Fabiani's dungeon.

JANE.

And this?

JOSHUA.

The door of another man's dungeon.

JANE.

Who is this other?

JOSHUA.

Another condemned man, one whom you do not know; a working man named Gilbert!

JANE.

Open this door.

JOSHUA (after opening the door).

Gilbert!

SCENE VII

JANE, GILBERT, JOSHUA.

GILBERT (inside the cell).

What do you want with me?

(He appears in the doorway, espies Jane, and leans against the wall to save himself from falling.)

Jane! Lady Jane Talbot!

JANE (on her knees, without looking up at him).

Gilbert, I come to save you.

GILBERT.

To save me!

JANE.

Listen. Be merciful, and do not overwhelm me with reproaches. I know all that you would say to me. 'T is just, but do not say it. I must save you now. All is in readiness. Escape is sure. Consent to let me save your life, as if I were another than myself. I ask no more than that. You need not recognize me afterward. You need not know what has become of me. Do not forgive me, only let me save you. Will you, Gilbert?

GILBERT.

I thank you, but 't is useless. What is it to me that you would like to save my life, my Lady Jane, if you have ceased to love me?

JANE.

Oh! Gilbert, do I hear aright? oh! can it be that you still deign to occupy yourself with what takes place in this poor heart of mine? can it be that the affection I may entertain for any man is still of interest to you, and seems to make it worth your while to ask about it? I thought that you cared nothing for it, and that your scorn for me was so profound, that it made you indifferent to what I might do with my heart. Oh! Gilbert, if you but knew the joy your words have caused me! 'T is like a ray of sunshine in my darkness! I pray you, listen to me! If I still dared approach you, if I dared touch your clothing, if I dared take your hand in mine, if I dared raise my eyes to yours and to Heaven as I used to do, dost know what I would say, here on my knees, weeping upon thy feet, my voice choked with sobs, and in my heart such joy as angels know? I would say: "Gilbert, I love thee!"

GILBERT (throwing his arms passionately about her).

Thou lovest me?

JANE.

Yes, I love thee!

GILBERT.

Thou lovest me! She loves me, O my God! 't is true; 't is she herself who says it; 't was her mouth spake the words, O God in Heaven!

JANE.

My Gilbert!

GILBERT.

Sayest thou, thou hast made preparations for my escape. Quick! quick! life! I long for life! Jane loves me! These walls press heavily upon my head and crush me! I must have air! I 'm stifling here! Let us fly quickly! Let us go, Jane! I must live now, for I am loved!

JANE.

Not yet. We must have a boat. We must await the darkness. But fear not, thou art saved. Within the hour, we shall be outside these walls. The queen is at the Guildhall, and will not return so soon. I am mistress here. I will explain it all to thee.

GILBERT.

An hour to wait! that is a weary while. Oh! I am in such haste to seize on life and happiness once more. Jane, Jane, thou art here! I shall live! thou lovest me! I have come back from hell! Hold me, in God's name, or I shall commit some folly. I could laugh and sing. Say, dost thou love me?

JANE.

Yes, I do love thee! yes, I do love thee! And—believe me, Gilbert, I speak the truth, as if I were on my death-bed. I have loved none but thee. Even in my sin, even in my crime, I loved thee! I scarce had fallen into the arms of the demon who betrayed me, ere I wept for my good angel.

GILBERT.

Forgotten! forgiven! Say no more, Jane. Oh! what care we for the past? Who could resist thy voice? What man is there who could do otherwise than I? Oh! yes, I freely pardon everything, my darling child. The essence of true love is indulgence and forgiveness. Jane, despair and jealousy dried with their fire the tears that filled my eyes, but I forgive thee, and I thank thee; thou art to me the one bright shining star in the whole world, at every word thou utterest I feel one more grief die, and a new joy up-springing in my heart. Jane, raise your head, stand on your feet, and look at me. I say you are my darling child.

JANE.

Still the same generous heart! still, Gilbert, my beloved.

GILBERT.

Oh! would I were even now away, far, far away, and free with thee! Oh! will the night never come? The boat is not yet here! Jane, we will leave London instantly, this very night. We will leave England. We will go to Venice. Men of my trade grow rich and prosper there. Thou wilt be mine. But oh! great Heaven! I 'm mad; I had forgotten the name thou bearest. It is too great a name, my Jane.

JANE.

What dost thou mean?

GILBERT.

Lord Talbot's daughter!

JANE.

I know a prouder title.

GILBERT.

What?

JANE.

Gilbert the carver's wife.

GILBERT.

Jane! . . .

JANE.

Oh! no! oh! think not that I ask it of thee. I know too well my own unworthiness. I cannot raise my eyes so high. I 'll not impose on thy forgiving spirit to that point. Gilbert, the poor carver, will not contract a misalliance with the Countess of Waterford. No, I will follow thee and love thee, I will never leave thee. I will lie by day at thy feet, and by night outside thy door. I will watch thee at thy work, assist thee, and give thee what thou mayest need. I will be to thee something less than sister, something more than dog. And if thou dost marry, Gilbert—for it will please God that thou shalt find at last a stainless wife, and pure, and worthy of thee—if thou dost marry, and if thy wife is kind and will consent, I 'll be her maid. If she 'll have none of me, I 'll go my way, and die where'er I may. Except in that event I will not leave thee. If thou dost not marry, I will remain with thee; I will be very gentle and resigned, thou 'lt see, and if the world likes not to see me with thee, the world may say what it will. I have no further cause to blush, thou seest, for I am a poor, lost girl!

GILBERT (falling at her feet).

Thou art an angel! thou art my wife!

JANE.

Thy wife! Thou 'lt pardon then only as God pardons, by purifying. Ah! blessed be thou, Gilbert, for laying that crown upon my brow!

(Gilbert rises and folds her in his arms. While they are clasped in each other's arms, Joshua draws near and takes Jane's hand.)

JOSHUA.

'T is Joshua, Lady Jane.

GILBERT.

Good Joshua!

JOSHUA.

A moment since you did not recognize me.

JANE.

Because I could begin with none but him.

(Joshua kisses her hand.)

GILBERT (embracing her).

What bliss! oh! can it be that all this happiness is real?

(For a few moments a confused uproar, with loud shouting, has been audible, but at a distance. It has begun to grow dark.)

JOSHUA.

What is that noise?

(He goes to the window looking into the street.)

JANE.

God grant that nothing untoward may happen!

JOSHUA.

There 's a great crowd without. Mattocks and pikes and torches! The queen's pensioners on horseback, and in battle-order. All are coming this way. What an uproar! The devil! 't is very like a riot.

JANE.

God grant it be not directed against Gilbert!

DISTANT SHOUTS.

Fabiani! death to Fabiani!

JANE.

Do you hear?

JOSHUA.

Yes.

JANE.

What do they say?

JOSHUA.

I cannot distinguish.

JANE.

Oh! my God! my God!

(Master Æneas and a boatman rush hastily in through the masked door.)

SCENE VIII

THE SAME: MASTER ÆNEAS, A BOATMAN.

MASTER ÆNEAS.

My lord Fabiani! my lord! not an instant to lose! It has gone abroad that the queen wished to save your life. The people of London have risen against you. A quarter of an hour hence you will be torn in pieces. Save yourself, my lord! Here are a cloak and hat. Here are the keys! Here is a boatman! Do not forget you owe all this to me. Make haste, my lord!

(In an undertone, to the boatman.)

You need be in no hurry.

JANE. (She hurriedly puts the hat and cloak on Gilbert.)

(Aside, to Joshua.)

Great Heaven! if only this man does not recognize . . .

MASTER ÆNEAS (looking in Gilbert's face).

What 's this! This is not Lord Clanbrassil! You are not executing the queen's orders, my lady! You are assisting another to escape!

JANE.

All is lost! I should have foreseen this! Ah! God! kind sir, 't is true, have pity . . .

MASTER ÆNEAS (in a low voice, to Jane).

Silence! Go on! I have said nothing and seen nothing.

(He walks toward the rear of the stage with an air of indifference.)

JANE.

What does he say? Ah! Providence is on our side! It seems that everybody wishes to save Gilbert.

JOSHUA.

No, Lady Jane. Everybody wishes to destroy Fabiani.

(During this whole scene the cries without have constantly increased.)

JANE.

Let us make haste, Gilbert! Come quickly!

JOSHUA.

Let him go alone.

JANE.

Leave him?

JOSHUA.

For a moment. No women in the boat, if you wish him to reach a place of safety. It is still too light. You are dressed in white. The danger passed, you 'll meet again. Come you with me, through this door; he through that.

JANE.

Joshua is right. Where shall we meet, my Gilbert?

GILBERT.

Under the first arch of London Bridge.

JANE.

'T is well. Go quickly. The noise grows louder. I would have thee far away.

JOSHUA.

I Iere are the keys. There are twelve doors to open and close between here and the river. Enough for a good quarter hour.

JANE.

A quarter hour! twelve doors! 't is frightful!

GILBERT (embracing her).

Farewell, dear Jane. A few moments more of separation, and we shall be joined for life.

JANE.

For eternity!

(To the boatman.)

Friend, I commend him to you.

MASTER ÆNEAS (in an undertone, to the boatman).

For fear of accident, be not too fast.

(Gilbert goes out with the boatman.)

JOSHUA.

He is saved! Now for ourselves! I must close this door.

(He closes the door of Gilbert's cell.)

'T is done. Come this way, quickly!

(He goes out with Jane through the other masked door.)

MASTER ÆNEAS (alone).

So Fabiani remains in the trap! You 're a very clever little woman whom Master Simon Renard would have paid handsomely. But how will the queen take the way the affair has turned? I trust that she 'll not lay the blame on me.

(Simon Renard and the queen come hurriedly in by way of the gallery. The uproar without has steadily increased. It has become quite dark. Shouts of "death," the glare of torches, and the muttered roar of the crowd. Clashing of weapons, reports of fire-arms, and neighing of horses. The queen is attended by Clarencieux King-at-arms, bearing the royal banner, and Garter King-at-arms bearing the banner of the Order of the Garter.)

SCENE IX

THE QUEEN, SIMON RENARD, MASTER ÆNEAS, LORD CLINTON, THE TWO KINGS-AT-ARMS, Lords, Pages, etc.

THE QUEEN (in an undertone to Master Æneas).

Has Fabiani escaped?

MASTER ÆNEAS.

Not yet.

THE QUEEN.

Not yet!

(She gazes fixedly at him with a terrifying expression.)

MASTER ÆNEAS (aside).

The devil!

SHOUTS OF THE PEOPLE (without).

Death to Fabiani!

SIMON RENARD.

Your Majesty must instantly make choice what course to adopt, madame. The people wish for that man's death. London is all aflame. The tower is surrounded. The riot has assumed formidable proportions. The nobles of the ban have been cut in pieces at London Bridge. The pensioners still hold their ground; but none the less your Majesty was tracked from street to street, from Guildhall to the Tower. The partisans of Madame Elizabeth are mingled with the populace. One feels that they are there from the bad temper that prevails. All this looks very black. What are your Majesty's commands?

SHOUTS OF THE MOB.

Fabiani! Death to Fabiani!

(They grow louder and come constantly nearer.)

THE QUEEN.

"Death to Fabiani!" Do you hear the varlets howl, my lords? We needs must throw a man to them. The good people are hungry.

SIMON RENARD.

What are your Majesty's commands?

THE QUEEN.

God's death, my lords, meseems you all do tremble as you stand about me. Pray, must a woman teach you your trade of gentlemen? To horse, my lords, to horse! Can it be that this *canaille* holds you back? Since when were swords afraid of clubs?

SIMON RENARD.

Do not, I pray you, let the émeute go farther. Yield, madame, while there still is time. Now you may say "*canaille*," within the hour you will be compelled to say "the people."

(The shouts increase in violence, and the uproar comes nearer.)

THE QUEEN.

Within the hour!

SIMON RENARD (goes to the gallery and returns).

Within the quarter, madame. Already the first courtyard of the Tower is forced. One step more and the people will be here.

THE PEOPLE.

To the Tower! To the Tower! Fabiani! Death to Fabiani!

THE QUEEN.

How truly has it been said that the people are terrible! Fabiano!

SIMON RENARD.

Do you wish to see him torn in pieces before your very eyes an instant hence?

THE QUEEN.

Why, by my soul, my lords, 't is infamous that none of you will stir! In Heaven's name, defend me!

LORD CLINTON.

You, madame, yes; Fabiani, no.

THE QUEEN.

Just Heaven! Well, if I must, I must; I 'll say aloud, Fabiano 's innocent! Fabiano 's guiltless of the crime for which he was condemned. 'T was I, myself, and this man here, and Gilbert the carver who imagined and invented the whole plot. Pure comedy. Dare to gainsay me, monsieur le bailli! Now, my lords, will you defend him? He 's innocent, I tell you! By my head, by my crown, by my God, by my mother's soul, he 's guiltless of the crime! That is as true as it is true that you stand there, Lord Clinton. Defend him. Stamp out these vermin, as you stamped out Tom Wyatt and his crew, my brave Clinton, good Robert, my old friend. I swear to you that it is false that Fabiano sought to assassinate your queen.

LORD CLINTON.

Ah! but there 's another queen he sought to assassinate—England.

(The cries without continue.)

THE QUEEN.

The balcony! throw open the balcony! I will myself convince the populace that he 's not guilty!

SIMON RENARD.

Convince them that he 's not Italian.

THE QUEEN.

To think that 't is a Simon Renard, Cardinal Granvelle's creature, who dares beard me thus! Throw open the door of yonder dungeon! Fabiano 's there. I would see him and speak with him.

SIMON RENARD (in an undertone).

What are you doing? In his own interest, it 's ill-advised to let the whole world know where he is.

THE PEOPLE.

Down with Fabiani! Long live Elizabeth!

SIMON RENARD.

Ah! now they shout: "Long live Elizabeth!"

THE QUEEN.

My God! my God!

SIMON RENARD.

Make your choice, madame:

(He points with one hand to the door of the dungeon.)

either that head to the populace,

(With the other hand he points to the crown on the queen's head.)

or that crown to Madame Elizabeth.

THE PEOPLE.

Death! death! Fabiani! Elizabeth!

(A stone crashes through a window near where the queen stands.)

SIMON RENARD.

Your Majesty is ruining yourself, and without saving him. The second courtyard 's forced. What is the queen's will?

THE QUEEN.

You are all cowards! and Clinton first of all! Ah! Clinton, I 'll remember this, my friend!

SIMON RENARD.

What is the queen's will?

THE QUEEN.

Oh! to be abandoned thus by all! to have told everything and gained nothing by it! Pray what sort of gentlemen are these? This rabble is most infamous! I would that I could trample them beneath my feet. It seems that there are times when a queen 's but a woman! You shall all pay me dear for this, my lords!

SIMON RENARD.

What is the queen's will?

THE QUEEN (overwhelmed).

Whatever you choose. Do what you will. You are an assassin!

(Aside.)

Oh! Fabiano!

SIMON RENARD.

What, ho! Clarence! Garter! Master Æneas, throw open the windows of the balcony.

(The balcony at the rear is thrown open. Simon Renard goes out with Clarencieux at his right, and Garter at his left. The uproar without is tremendous.)

THE PEOPLE.

Fabiani! Fabiani!

SIMON RENARD (on the balcony, facing the people).

In the queen's name!

THE KINGS-AT-ARMS.

In the queen's name!

(Profound silence without.)

SIMON RENARD.

Friends, the queen gives you to know that on this night, an hour after curfew, Fabiano Fabiani, Earl of Clanbrassil, covered from head to foot with a black veil, gagged with an iron gag, a torch of yellow wax of three pounds weight in his hand, will be conducted from the Tower of London by torchlight to the Old City Market, there to be publicly beheaded by way of reparation for the crimes of high treason in the first degree and regicidal plot against her Majesty's imperial person.

(A great burst of applause without.)

THE PEOPLE.

Long live the queen! Death to Fabiani!

SIMON RENARD (continuing).

And to the end that no one in the whole city of London may be in ignorance of what is happening, the queen has given order thus: During the progress of the condemned man from the Tower to the Old Market, the great bell of the Tower shall be rung. Just at the moment of the execution, a cannon shall be three times discharged; the first time when he ascends the scaffold, the second when he takes his place on the black cloth, the third when his head falls.

(Renewed applause.)

THE PEOPLE.

Illuminate! illuminate!

SIMON RENARD.

To-night the Tower and the city will be illuminated with bonfires and torches in token of rejoicing. I have said.

(Applause.)

God preserve the ancient charter of England!

THE KINGS-AT-ARMS.

God preserve the ancient charter of England!

THE PEOPLE.

Death to Fabiani! Long live Mary! long live the queen!

(The doors leading to the balcony are closed again. Simon Renard returns to the queen.)

SIMON RENARD.

What I have done will never be forgiven by Princess Elizabeth.

THE QUEEN.

Nor by Queen Mary. Leave me, monsieur.

(She dismisses all those present with a gesture.)

SIMON RENARD (in an undertone, to Master Æneas).

Master Æneas, look you to the execution.

MASTER ÆNEAS.

Depend on me.

(Simon Renard goes out. As Master Æneas is about to follow him, the queen runs to him, seizes him by the arm, and leads him back excitedly to the front of the stage.)

SCENE X

THE QUEEN, MASTER ÆNEAS.

CRIES WITHOUT.

Death to Fabiani! Fabiani! Fabiani!

THE QUEEN.

Which of the two heads, thinkest thou, is in the greatest danger at this moment, Fabiani's or thine own?

MASTER ÆNEAS.

Madame . . .

THE QUEEN.

Thou art a traitor!

MASTER ÆNEAS.

Madame . . .

(Aside.)

The devil!

THE QUEEN.

I 'll hear no excuses. By my mother's soul I swear that if Fabiano dies, thou too shalt die!

MASTER ÆNEAS.

But, madame . . .

THE QUEEN.

Save Fabiani, and thou 'lt save thyself. Not otherwise.

CRIES.

Death to Fabiani! Fabiani!

MASTER ÆNEAS.

Save Lord Clanbrassil! But the mob is here. It is impossible. What means? . . .

THE QUEEN.

Cudgel thy brains.

MASTER ÆNEAS.

What shall I do, in God's name?

THE QUEEN.

Do as if 't were for thyself.

MASTER ÆNEAS.

But the people will remain under arms until the execution. To appease their rage some-one must be beheaded.

THE QUEEN.

Whosoever thou wilt.

MASTER ÆNEAS.

Whosoever I will! One moment, madame. The execution will take place at night, by torchlight, the culprit covered with a black veil and gagged, the rabble kept at a distance from the scaffold by the pikemen, as always. 'T is enough that they see some head fall. The thing is possible. If only the boatman is still there! I told him not to hurry.

(He goes to the window looking on the Thames.)

He is still there! but it was time.

(He leans out the window, torch in hand, waving his handkerchief, then turns to the queen.)

'T is well. I 'll answer to you for my lord Fabiani, madame.

THE QUEEN.

With thy head?

MASTER ÆNEAS.

With my head!

THIRD DAY

WHICH OF THE TWO?

SECOND PART

A large hall, in which two staircases end, one ascending, the other descending. The landing of each of the staircases occupies a portion of the rear of the stage. The one which ascends passes out of sight among the flies, the other passes out of sight under the stage. The spectator cannot see where they come from, nor whither they lead.

The hall is draped in mourning in a curious way; the walls at the right and left, and the ceiling in black cloth with a great white cross; the wall at the rear, facing the audience, in white cloth with a great black cross. The black hangings and the white are both continued as far as can be seen, under the two staircases. At the right and left, altars draped in black and white, as if for funeral services. Tall candles. No priests. A few flickering lamps, hanging from the ceiling here and there, cast a dim light upon the hall and staircases. The hall is really lighted by the white cloth at the rear, through which a reddish light shines, as if there were an immense fiery furnace behind it. The hall is paved with tombstones. As the curtain rises the motionless shadow of the queen is traced in silhouette upon the transparent cloth.

SCENE I

JANE, JOSHUA.

(They enter cautiously, raising part of the black hangings, through some concealed door.)

JANE.

Where are we, Joshua?

JOSHUA.

On the great landing of the staircase which those condemned to die descend when on their way to execution.

JANE.

Is there no way for us to leave the Tower?

JOSHUA.

The people are watching all the exits. They purpose to make certain of their victim this time. No one can go out before the execution.

JANE.

The proclamation that was made upon the balcony is ringing still in my ears. Did you hear it, when we were below? All this is horrible, Joshua!

JOSHUA.

Ah! I have seen many such.

JANE.

God grant that Gilbert made good his escape! Think you that he is safe, Joshua?

JOSHUA.

Safe! I am sure of it.

JANE.

Art quite sure, dear Joshua?

JOSHUA.

The Tower was not surrounded on the water-side. And then the riot, when he must have gone, was not what it has since become. It was no paltry riot, do you know!

JANE.

You 're sure that he is safe?

JOSHUA.

And that he 's waiting for you at this moment under the first arch of London Bridge, where you will join him before midnight.

JANE.

Ah me! he 'll have an anxious time of waiting.

(She spies the queen's shadow.)

Great Heaven! Joshua, what 's that?

JOSHUA (in an undertone, taking her hand).

Hush! 'T is the lioness on the watch.

(While Jane is gazing in terror at the silhouette, a voice is heard in the distance, apparently coming from above, pronouncing these words, slowly and distinctly:)

THE VOICE.

He who walks behind me, covered with this black veil, is the great and powerful nobleman, Fabiano Fabiani, Earl of Clanbrassil, Baron of Dinasmonddy, and Baron of Dartmouth in Devonshire, who is to be beheaded on the Market-place of London for the crimes of regicide and high treason. May God have mercy on his soul!

ANOTHER VOICE.

Pray for him!

JANE (trembling).

Joshua, do you hear?

JOSHUA.

Yes, I hear these same things every day.

(A ghostly procession appears upon the staircase, and spreads out over the stairs as it slowly descends. At the head, a man dressed in black, carrying a white banner with a black cross. Then Master Æneas Dulverton in an ample black cloak with his white constable's staff in his hand. Then a group of halberdiers, clothed in red. Then the executioner, axe on shoulder, with the edge turned toward the figure following him. Then a man entirely shrouded in a great black veil which drags about his feet. Of him nothing can be seen save one bare arm, passed through an aperture in the shroud, with a lighted torch of yellow wax in the hand. Beside him is a priest in the costume worn on All Souls' Day. Then a group of halberdiers in red. Then a man dressed in white, carrying a black banner with a white cross. At the right and left, files of halberdiers, with torches.)

JANE.

Joshua, do you see?

JOSHUA.

Yes, I see these same things every day.

(The procession halts as it comes out upon the stage.)

MASTER ÆNEAS.

He who walks behind me, covered with this black veil, is the great and powerful nobleman, Fabiano Fabiani, Earl of Clanbrassil, Baron of Dinasmonddy, and Baron of Dartmouth in Devonshire, who is to be beheaded on the Market-place of London for the crimes of regicide and high treason. May God have mercy on his soul!

THE TWO BANNER-BEARERS.

Pray for him!

(The procession passes slowly across the rear of the stage.)

JANE.

This is a horrifying sight, my Joshua. It makes my blood run cold.

JOSHUA.

The villain Fabiani!

JANE.

Peace, Joshua! a villain, if you choose, but most unfortunate!

(The procession reaches the other staircase. Simon Renard, who has appeared at the top of that staircase a few moments before, and watched the whole proceeding, stands aside to let it pass. The procession passes under the arch of the staircase, and gradually disappears. Jane looks after it, in terror.)

SIMON RENARD (after the procession has disappeared).

What does this mean? Was it in truth Fabiani? I thought him not so tall. Can it be that Master Æneas . . . ? Methinks the queen detained him for a moment. We must look to this!

(He darts down the stairs after the procession.)

VOICE (farther and farther away).

He who walks behind me, covered with this black veil, is the great and powerful nobleman, Fabiano Fabiani, Earl of Clanbrassil, Baron of Dinasmonddy, and Baron of Dartmouth in Devonshire, who is to be beheaded on the Market-place of London for the crimes of regicide and high treason. May God have mercy on his soul!

OTHER VOICES (almost inaudible).

Pray for him!

JOSHUA.

The great bell will in a moment announce that he has left the Tower. It will perhaps be practicable now for you to make your escape. I must try to find out a way. Wait for me here; I will return anon.

JANE.

You leave me, Joshua? Alone here, I shall be afraid.

JOSHUA.

You could not without danger go with me about the Tower. I must find some way to effect your exit. Reflect that Gilbert waits for you.

JANE.

Gilbert! anything for Gilbert! Go!

(Exit Joshua.)

Oh! what a terrifying spectacle! and when I think 't would have been thus with Gilbert!

(She kneels upon the steps of one of the altars.)

I thank thee, God! thou art indeed a Savior! Thou hast saved Gilbert!

(The hangings at the rear are drawn aside. The queen appears, and walks slowly toward the front of the stage, without seeing Jane, who turns her head.)

Great Heaven! the queen!

SCENE II

JANE, THE QUEEN.

(Jane crouches against the altar, and gazes at the queen in terror and stupefaction.)

THE QUEEN. (She stands for some moments in silence at the front of the stage, pale, and with her eyes fixed on vacancy, as if buried in gloomy reflections. At last she heaves a deep sigh.)

Oh! this populace!

(She looks around with some uneasiness, and her glance falls upon Jane.)

Some one here! What, 't is thou, girl! you, Lady Jane! I frighten you. Go to! fear nothing. Æneas the turnkey betrayed us, did you know? You need have no fear. I have already told thee, child, that thou hast naught to fear from me. The very circumstance that did undo thee a month since, to-day is thy salvation. Thou lovest Fabiano. There are none but thou and I in all the world whose hearts lead us to him, none but thou and I who love him. We are sisters.

JANE.

Madame . . .

THE QUEEN.

Yes, thou and I, two women, are all that he has on his side, poor fellow. All others are against him! a whole city, a whole people, a whole world! 'T is an unequal contest of love 'gainst hate. Our love for Fabiano is melancholy, terrified, despairing; it has thy pale brow, it has my tearful eyes; it hides beside a black-draped altar, it prays with thy lips, and blasphemes with mine. Their hate for Fabiani is arrogant, elated and triumphant, 't is armed and conquering; it has the court, it has the populace, it has these swarms of men who fill the streets, it vents itself in shouts of death, and shouts of joy in the same moment, is domineering, haughty and omnipotent, and sets a whole town ablaze with bonfires around a scaffold! The love is here, —two women clad in mourning in a tomb. The hate is there!

(With a sudden, violent movement she draws aside the white cloth at the rear, disclosing a balcony, and beyond the balcony, as far as the eye can see, the city of London brilliantly illuminated, the night being intensely dark. That portion of the Tower which can be seen is also splendidly illuminated. Jane gazes in amazement at this dazzling spectacle, the reflection of which lights up the stage.)

Oh! infamous city! rebellious city! accursed city! oh! execrable city, which soaks its festal robes in blood, and holds the torch to light the executioner! Thou fearest it, Jane, dost thou not? Does it not seem to thee as to myself that it is basely mocking us, and gazing with its hundred thousand flaming eyeballs at us, poor, weak, abandoned women that we are, undone, alone here in this sepulchre? Jane, dost thou hear the shameless city laugh and roar? Oh! England! England to him who will destroy this London! Oh! had I but the power to change these torches to live brands, these lights to flames, and this illuminated city to a burning city!

(A terrific uproar is heard without. Applause, confused shouts: "He comes! There he is! Death to Fabiani!" The great bell of the Tower begins to toll. At the sound the queen laughs a ghastly laugh.)

JANE.

Merciful God! the unhappy man is coming out! You laugh, madame?

THE QUEEN.

Yes, I laugh!

(She laughs.)

Yes, and in an instant thou wilt laugh! But first I must replace these hangings. It seems to me each moment that we 're not alone, and that yon frightful city sees and hears us.

(She lets down the white curtain, and returns to Jane.)

Now that he 's gone, now that there 's no more danger, I may tell thee. But laugh, I say; let us both laugh at this revolting rabble who drink blood. Oh! it is charming! Jane, thou tremblest for Fabiano? fear not, but laugh with me I tell thee! Jane, the man they have, the man who is to die, the man they take for Fabiano, is not Fabiano!

(She laughs.)

JANE.

Not Fabiano!

THE QUEEN.

No!

JANE.

Who, then, in God's name?

THE QUEEN.

The other.

JANE.

What other?

THE QUEEN.

You know, you know the man, that workman, who—at all events, what matters it?

JANE (trembling from head to foot).

Gilbert?

THE QUEEN.

Yes, Gilbert. That 's the name.

JANE.

Madame! oh! no, madame! oh! say that 't is not he! Gilbert! that would be too horrible! He has escaped!

THE QUEEN.

He was escaping, when they seized him, that is true. They put him under the black veil instead of Fabiano. 'T is a night execution. The people will see nothing. Have no fear.

JANE (with a heart-rending shriek).

Ah! madame! 't is Gilbert whom I love!

THE QUEEN.

What! what sayest thou? Hast lost thy reason? Didst thou, too, deceive me? So 't is this Gilbert whom thou lovest? Well, what 's that to me?

JANE (overwhelmed with anguish, and sobbing bitterly, drags herself on her knees to the queen's feet, with clasped hands. The great bell tolls throughout the scene).

Madame, in pity's name! in God's name, madame! by your crown, madame—by your mother, by the angels! Gilbert! Gilbert! I shall go mad! Madame, save Gilbert! He is my life; he is my husband; he . . . I 've told you he did everything for me, adopted me and brought me up, and at my cradle took my father's place, who died for your mother. Madame, you see that I am only a poor, weak girl, and that you must not be too harsh with me. What you just said to me dealt me so terrible a blow that I can scarcely say where I do find the strength to speak to you. I plead as best I may. But you must stop the execution. At once. Postpone the execution. Defer it till to-morrow. Time to reflect, no more. The populace can wait until to-morrow. Then we will see what we will do. Nay, do not shake your head. Be not alarmed for your Fabiano. You may put me in his place. Under the black veil. At night. Who will know me? But Gilbert must be saved! What matters it to you, whether 't is he or I? But 't is enough that I prefer to die!—Oh! my God! that bell! that awful bell! Each stroke upon that bell is one step toward the scaffold! Each stroke upon that bell is echoed in my heart. Do what I ask, madame. Have pity! There is no danger for your Fabiano. Let me kiss your hands. I love you, madame. I have not told you so, but I do love you dearly. You are a great queen. See how I kiss your lovely hands. Oh! an order to defer the execution! There is still time. I promise you that it is possible. They go but slowly. 'T is a long distance from the Tower to the Old Market. The man on the balcony said that they would go by Charing Cross. There is a shorter way. A mounted man might still arrive in time. In Heaven's name, madame, have pity! Pray, put yourself in my place; suppose that I were queen, and you the poor girl; then you would weep as I do, and I would grant your prayer. Mercy, madame! Oh! this is what I feared, that tears would choke my voice. Do not delay. Defer the execution. There is no danger in it, madame. No danger for Fabiano. I swear to you. Can it be, madame, that you do not see that you must do what I say?

THE QUEEN (deeply moved, raising her from the floor).

I would I could, poor child. Ah! thou dost weep, yes, even as I wept; that which thou feelest I have felt, my agony makes me sympathize with thine. Look, thou seest I am weeping, too. 'T is most unfortunate, poor child! Doubtless, it seems as if another might have filled his place. Tyrconnel, for example; but he is too well known, 't was

necessary to have some obscure man. He was the only one at hand. I make this explanation so that thou mayest understand. Ah! such fatalities there are. One finds one's self involved in them, and can do nothing.

JANE.

Yes, madame, I listen to you. I still have many things to say to you. But I would like the order to suspend the execution to be signed, and the man gone. That would be something done, you see. Then we can talk more at our ease. Oh! that bell! that tireless bell!

THE QUEEN.

What you desire is impossible, Lady Jane.

JANE.

No, it is possible. A man on horseback. There is a shorter way. By the river bank. I will go, myself. 'T is possible. 'T is easy. You see that I speak calmly.

THE QUEEN.

But the people would not. They would return and massacre every person in the Tower. And Fabiano is still here. Pray understand. Thou art trembling like a leaf, poor child, and I am like thee, I am trembling too. Do thou put thyself in my place. But no, I could not take the trouble to explain it all to thee. Thou seest that I do all I can. Think no more of this Gilbert, Jane! It is all over. Resign thyself!

JANE.

Over! no, it is not all over! So long as yonder fearful bell keeps ringing, it will not be all over. Resign myself to Gilbert's death! Do you imagine that I will let my Gilbert die in this way? No, madame. Ah! but my trouble 's thrown away! You do not listen to me. Ah! well, if the Queen of England hears me not, the populace will hear me.

They are kind at heart, you know. There are still people in the courtyard. You may do with me after as you choose. I 'm going now to tell them that they 've been deceived, and that 't is Gilbert, a craftsman like themselves, and not Fabiani !

THE QUEEN.

Stay, wretched child !

(She seizes her arm, and gazes threateningly at her.)

Ah! thus thou takest it ! I am kind and gentle, and I weep with thee, and lo ! thou dost transform thyself into a raving madwoman ! Why, my love is as great as thine, and my hand is stronger. Thou shalt not stir. Thy lover ! What care I for thy lover ? In God's name, are all the women in all England to come to me to settle with them for their lovers ? I' faith I save my own as best I can, at the expense of anyone who is at hand. Look you to yours.

JANE.

Let me go ! My curse upon you, wicked woman !

THE QUEEN.

Hold thy peace !

JANE.

No, I 'll not hold my peace ! Would you that I should tell you the thought that 's in my mind ? I do not think the man who 's on his way to execution is Gilbert.

THE QUEEN.

What sayest thou ?

JANE.

I know not, but it seems to me that when I saw him pass, shrouded in the black veil, if it had been Gilbert, some instinct would have told me so, something would have risen in rebellion in my heart, and cried to me ! " Gilbert ! 't is Gilbert ! " But I felt no such movement ; it is not Gilbert !

THE QUEEN.

What dost thou say ? Ah, God ! thou art insane, and what thou sayest is rank-idiocy, and still it terrifies me ! Thou hast set astir one of the secret misgivings of my heart. Why did this riot hinder me from overlooking everything myself ? Why did I trust to others than myself to look to Fabiano's safety ? Æneas Dulverton 's a traitor. It may be that Simon Renard's hand was in it. If only I have not been betrayed a second time by Fabiano's enemies ! God grant it was not really Fabiano ! Ho there ! a messenger ! a messenger !

(Two jailers appear.)

(To the first.)

Hasten, you. Here is my signet-ring. Say that the execution is to be deferred. To the Old Market ! to the Old Market ! There is a shorter road, Jane, didst thou say ?

JANE.

By the river bank.

THE QUEEN (to the jailer).

Go by the river bank. A horse. Ride at full speed !

(The jailer goes out.)

(To the second jailer.)

Go you at once to Edward the Confessor's tower. There there are two cells for those condemned to death. In one of them there is a man. Bring him to me upon the instant.

(The jailer goes out.)

Ah! how I tremble ! my feet will scarce support me, and I had not the strength to go myself. Ah ! thou dost make me mad as thou art ! See, wretched girl ! thou hast made me as miserable as thou art thyself. I curse thee as thou didst curse me. Just God ! will the messenger be in time ? What terrible suspense ! I cannot see. My mind is all confusion. For whom does the bell toll ? Is it for Gilbert ? is it for Fabiano ?

JANE.

The bell has stopped.

THE QUEEN.

That means that the procession has reached the place of execution. The man will not have arrived in time.

(A distant cannon shot is heard.)

JANE.

Great Heaven !

THE QUEEN.

He is ascending the scaffold.

(A second report.)

He is kneeling.

JANE.

How horrible !

(A third report.)

BOTH.

Ah !

THE QUEEN.

But one of them is living now. A moment more and we shall know which one it is. O God, grant that he who soon will join us here may be Fabiano !

JANE.

O God, grant that it may be Gilbert !

(The curtain at the rear is thrown back, and Simon Renard appears, leading Gilbert by the hand.)

Gilbert !

(They rush into each other's arms.)

THE QUEEN.

And Fabiano ?

SIMON RENARD.

Dead.

THE QUEEN.

Dead ? Dead ! Who dared ?

SIMON RENARD.

I, madame. I have saved the queen and England.

EDITION DEFINITIVE

NOTE I

From memoranda upon the original manuscript, it would appear that the "First Day" of "Mary Tudor" was begun August 12th, 1833, and finished on the 16th. The "Second Day," begun August 17th, was finished August 23d, at 12.45 A. M. The "Third Day," begun August 25th, was finished September 1st, at 8 P. M.

NOTE II

VARIANT READINGS

FIRST DAY

SCENE IV

GILBERT, A MAN.

.   .   .

GILBERT.

What is thy purpose?

THE MAN.

This: Gilbert, the girl thou didst adopt in infancy, whom thou didst rear to womanhood, whom thou hast toiled for night and day these sixteen years, this girl whom thou dost love, and whom thou dost propose to take to wife . . .

GILBERT.

Well, what of her?

THE MAN.

To-day, to-night, this very hour, she awaits a lover.

GILBERT.

Jew! thou art a Jew! thou art a miserable dog of a Jew! thou liest!

THE MAN.

This very night.

GILBERT.

Jew! this that thou sayest thou must prove to me, or by my soul I 'll take thy head between my hands, and cut thy tongue out with thy teeth!

THE MAN.

Listen . . .

GILBERT.

Not a word! The proof! the proof!

THE MAN.

Thou shalt have it.

GILBERT.

When?

THE MAN.

At once.

GILBERT.

Oh! if this be false, my curse upon thee! if it be true, still be my curse upon thee! But 't is not true. Thou liest! Jane! Jane, my beloved! What liars be these execrable Jews!

THE MAN.

Dost thou not hear the beat of oars upon the river?

GILBERT.

Yes.

THE MAN.

(He walks to the parapet.)

'T is he, 't is the man whom she awaits. He steps ashore, he dismisses the boatman, he comes this way.

GILBERT.

I swear to thee that what thou sayest means death to one of us: to thee, if 't is false, to me, if 't is true.

THE MAN.

Stand in the shadow, so placed that thou canst hear our conversation, and lend me thy help at need.

SCENE V

FABIANO, THE MAN.

.   .

FABIANO.

In God's name, is no secret unknown to thee?

THE MAN.

To know everybody's secrets is my profession, my whole life.

FABIANO.

What is thy method, pray?

THE MAN.

That is my secret, and I take good care that nobody shall know it.

THIRD DAY. PART FIRST

SCENE I

GILBERT, JOSHUA.

. . .

GILBERT.

. . . I long for death. Have pity on me, Joshua.

JOSHUA.

Gilbert, thou 'rt mad! think no more of that woman who has destroyed two men. Alas! thou hast but little time before thee to think of her. This is no time for thee to think of women, Gilbert, but of God.

GILBERT.

(Speaking to himself.)

Fabiani's cell is there, and mine is here. For whom does she come hither? Of course, for Fabiani. The day we were condemned to death, when we had passed through that long, crowded corridor, returning to the Tower, as we marched solemnly along, preceded by the executioner holding his axe's edge toward our faces, as is always done with men condemned to death, a shriek rang out just as we left the corridor, a heart-rending, woman's shriek. I recognized the voice : 't was Jane's! For which of us was that shriek uttered? Ah! Joshua, thou dost shake thy head. For Fabiani!

SCENE VII

GILBERT, JANE, JOSHUA.

GILBERT.

Jane! Lady Jane Talbot!

JANE.

(Trembling.)

Gilbert, I am no longer aught to you; you turn away your eyes, and justly, for in your eyes I am nothing more than a woman whom you may have known once on a time, a person whom you may have passed in the street, but for whom you no longer have a glance to spare. Oh! do not shake your head. I feel that I am hateful in your sight, but listen, I pray you, for a moment; let me assure your safety. I swear to you that I will never seek to see you afterward. To-morrow, or to-night, your eyes shall look upon me for the last time. Gilbert, I swear that it shall be so. God pity me!

. . .

JANE.

I scarce had fallen into the arms of the demon who betrayed me, ere I wept for my good angel! To-day I cannot understand how I, whom Gilbert deigned to love, could have become the victim of that villain's wiles. Ah! I must have been a miserable, wicked creature!

GILBERT.

Why dost thou still speak of that, when I have told thee thrice that I forgive thee? didst thou not hear? Thou lovest me. 'T is all forgotten.

JANE.

Still the same generous heart! Ah! you are the only one whose heart is generous! Do I love thee! Oh, God! I pray thee give me words to tell him how I love him! You do not know how deep and single-hearted, how desperate, is the love which knows remorse for wrongs inflicted on the beloved one! The day on which you sacrificed yourself for me, the day on which I saw you taken to the Tower, the day on which I heard the judgment read that sentenced you to death, and me as well—but why run through them one by one? Day after day and every day, not one excepted, my heart 's been filled with thee, filled with remorse and love and grief immeasurable! At night I could not sleep. I 'd rise and lay my head against the wall and think of thee. All day I stood about the Tower walls with no thought in my mind save flight, escape and life for Gilbert! Moments there were when those who saw me there might well have thought I was a statue. Sometimes, because it rained, the passers-by sought to lead me away. Oh! Gilbert, I do love thee! doubt it not. In my eyes thou art beautiful, thou art so noble-hearted. To me all men are nothing beside thee; thou canst not doubt it. Great Heaven! how I love thee! Perchance thou dost not yet believe me. I have deceived thee once. I did so grievously insult thee. But what I say is most sincerely said. Oh! answer me, in pity's name! hast thou not still one shred of trust in me? Oh! words, words are worse than nothing; Gilbert, I wish that one could open a door into one's heart, and say to the man one loves: "Look in!" There are so many, many things which I, in my position, would say to thee, things which I feel, but cannot put in words. There is no way to prove to thee how truly thou art all in all to me, and how humiliated and embarrassed and repentant I stand before thee! I would my voice might strike caressingly upon thine ear, and make thee happy. Oh! thou shalt not die! we will fly together! thou art mine! we love each other! Who would have told me that this morning? What a blessed change! I 'm foolish, am I not? Gilbert, I do despise and loathe myself so bitterly that it seems impossible that thou shouldst love me and esteem me. Thou canst not dream how miserable I have been! Give me thy hand. I love thee! I love thee! Look in my eyes; they tell thee that I love thee. Look at my tears; they tell thee I am happy. Oh! give me courage to speak thus to thee! My heart, the poor betrayed girl's heart, is overflowing. Once I had wings as thou hast. Now I have lost them. How can it be that thou still carest for me? How can it be that thou dost still set store by my love? Say it is true that thou dost still set store by it, and that thou dost not say it in pity simply. Art sure thou lovest me? God is my witness that my heart is overfilled with joy. Thou comest from heaven, Gilbert!

GILBERT.

Oh! Jane! there 's naught I can reply to such words, spoken as thou speakest them! My heart is bursting. I feel as if I must die with rapture. What care we for the past? Who could resist thy voice? who could do otherwise than I do? Ah, yes! I pardon thee with all my heart, my darling child.

.   .   .   .

GILBERT.

(He goes to the window and looks out.)

The boat 's not there.

JANE.

The man who promised to procure it, required an hour.

GILBERT.

The hour is made of years, not of minutes! I long to be outside the walls! I say I long to be outside! Now I no longer wish to die. Those men who are at work upon a scaffold for me make me shudder. Thou hast made me a coward by telling me thou lovest me.

JANE.

Gilbert, if thou wert dead, I too, should die.

TRANSLATOR'S NOTE TO MARY TUDOR

This play was first produced at the Porte-Saint-Martin on November 6th, 1833. The friends and enemies of the author were out in force, and the performance was attended by the disorderly scenes which commonly marked the first appearance of a drama written by Victor Hugo. The general verdict seems to have been unfavorable to the play, and it can hardly be said to have achieved success. It was reproduced at the same theatre forty years later, on September 27th, 1873.

In a note to the edition of 1836, the author says: "In order that the reader may satisfy himself once for all of the degree to which the author is faithful to the facts of history in his works, and of the quantity and quality of the investigations made by him for each of his dramas, he deems it his duty to print here, as a specimen, a list of the books and documents he consulted before writing *Marie Tudor*."

Then follows a very long list of works, familiar and unfamiliar, beginning with the *Historia et Annales Henrici VII.*, by FRANC. BARONUM, "who can be no other than our old friend, Francis Bacon," says an English biographer of Hugo.

It must be said that, notwithstanding his preparatory labors in this field, historical accuracy is not the most prominent characteristic of the play of Mary Tudor. While some of the characters introduced, other than the queen herself, are historical personages, notably Simon Renard and Gardiner, the bigoted and cruel Chancellor; and while some of the allusions are to incidents that actually happened during Mary's reign—for instance the Wyatt rebellion, and the acquittal of Sir Nicholas Throgmorton (but on a charge of conspiracy, not of seduction), there is no historical authority for the main incidents of the play, nor for representing Mary's character as it is here represented. Even her harshest critics among Protestant historians have always borne witness to her irreproachable morals, and the late Mr. James Anthony Froude, who certainly cannot be accused of partiality in her regard, says: "She had reigned little more than five years, and she descended into the grave amidst curses deeper than the acclamations which had welcomed her accession. In that brief time she had swathed her name in the horrid epithet which will cling to it forever; and yet from the passions which in general tempt sovereigns into crime, she was entirely free; to the time of her accession she had lived a blameless, and, in many respects, a noble life; and few men or women have lived, less capable of doing knowingly a wrong thing."

ANGELO, TYRANT OF PADUA

SECOND DAY

SECOND DAY

THE CRUCIFIX

CATARINA (alone).

I wish I could recall the words. Oh! I would sell my soul to hear him sing them just once more; even though I could not see him, though he were as far away as anyone could wish. But his voice! to hear his voice!

RODOLFO (upon the balcony).

(Sings.)

My heart to thine is freely given,
I cannot live apart from thee;
The bond divine was forged in heaven,
That joins us for eternity.

PREFACE

In view of the present status of all those momentous questions, which go to the very roots of society, it long ago occurred to the author of this drama that it might be profitable as well as elevating to develop upon the stage something like the following plan :—

Given a plot dealing wholly with the affections, to present two serious, sorrowful figures, the woman in society and the woman not in society, that is to say, in two living examples, all women and woman. To represent these two women, who embody in themselves all woman-kind, as often moved by noble impulses, but always unhappy. To defend the one against despotism, the other against contempt. To point out the temptations which the virtuous instinct of the one resists, and the suffering with which the other washes away her stains. To place the blame where it belongs, that is to say, upon man, who is the stronger, and upon the constitution of society, which is absurd. In these two typical hearts to cause the resentment of the woman to yield to the pious veneration of the daughter, the love of a lover to the love of a mother, hatred to devotion, passion to a sense of duty. In opposition to these two women, thus imagined, to place two men, the husband and the lover, the despot and the exile, and to exhibit in them, by divers collateral developments of the plot, all the relations, regular and irregular, that man can sustain with woman on the one hand and society on the other. And then, over against this group, which craves and possesses and suffers, at times radiant, and at times overspread with gloom, to place the envious man, the fatal witness, who is always on hand, whom Providence stations on the outskirts of all societies, all governments, all prosperous careers, all human passions; the tireless enemy of everyone above him;

changing his form according to the time and place, but always the same at heart; a spy at Venice, a eunuch at Constantinople, a pamphleteer at Paris. To station him, as Providence stations him, in the shadow, gnashing his teeth at every smile, this clever and abandoned wretch, who has no power save to injure, for all the doors that are closed to his love are open to his vengeance. Lastly, above the three men, between the two women, to place the dead Christ upon the cross, as a sacred bond, a symbol, an intercessor and counselor. To nail all this human suffering to the back of the crucifix.

Then, of all these elements, thus arranged, to make a drama; not concerned altogether with royalties, lest the possible application be lost sight of in the grandeur of the proportions; not altogether on the middle-class level, lest the insignificance of the characters interfere with the development of the idea; but dealing with persons of princely rank and with domestic incidents: with the former, because the drama should be great; with the latter because it should be true to life. And in this work, for the gratification of the craving of the mind to feel the past in the present and the present in the past, to mingle the divine element with the human, and the historical element with the social. To picture, by the way, àpropos of this idea, not man and woman alone, not these three men and these two women alone, but a whole century, a whole country, a whole civilization, a whole people. To build upon this thought, following the lines of history, a plot so simple and so true, so instinct with life and vivid, that it can serve to hide the thought itself from the eyes of the audience, as the flesh hides the bones.

That is what the author of this drama has sought to do. His sole regret is that the thought did not come to one better fitted than he to develop it.

To-day, in the face of success clearly due to this underlying thought, a success which has exceeded all his hopes, he feels the need of setting forth his thought in its entirety to the sympathetic and enlightened multitude who gather evening after evening to witness his work, with an interest which places a heavy responsibility upon him.

It cannot be said too often for anyone who has reflected upon the needs of society, to which the endeavors of true art ought always to correspond, that to-day more than ever before the theatre is a place of instruction. The drama, as the author of this work would like to make it, and as a man of genius might make it, ought to impart philosophy to the audience, direction to the thoughts, muscles, blood and life to poetry, an unbiased opinion to thinking men, a cooling drink to thirsty souls, a balm to hidden wounds, to everyone good counsel, and to all a law.

It goes without saying that the essential conditions of art should be, first of all and in every respect, complied with. Curiosity, interest, amusement, laughter, tears, unflagging observation of whatever is true to nature, and the marvelous envelope of style, all these the drama must have, else it would be no drama; but to be complete, it must have also the desire to instruct, coincident with the desire to please. Shrink not from fascinating the audience with your drama, but let the lesson be within it, so that it may always be found when one chooses to dissect the lovely, entrancing, poetic, impassioned creation of your brain, gorgeously clad in gold and silk and velvet. In the most captivating drama there should always be a serious undercurrent of thought, just as there always is a skeleton in the loveliest woman.

The author, as will be seen, does not gloss over any of the stern duties of the dramatic poet. He will perhaps some day attempt, in a special work, to explain in detail what he has sought to accomplish in each of the dramas he has produced during the past seven years. In presence of so vast a problem as that of the stage of the nineteenth century, he is deeply conscious of his own insufficiency; but he will persevere none the less in the work he has begun. With all his insignificance, how could he draw back, encouraged as he has been by the approval of the choicest minds, by the applause of the multitude, and by the loyal sympathy of all the eminent men who are numbered among the critics of to day? He will go on then with firm tread; and whenever he deems it necessary to expound to all the world, in its smallest details, a useful idea, relating to society or to mankind at large, he will place the stage over it like a microscope.

In the age in which we live the horizon of art is greatly widened. In the old days the poet spoke of "the public;" to-day he speaks of "the people."

May 7, 1833.

DRAMATIS PERSONÆ

ANGELO MALIPIERI, Podesta

CATARINA BRAGADINI

THISBE

RODOLFO

HOMODEI

ANAFESTO GALEOFA

ORDELAFO

ORFEO

GABOARDO

REGINELLA

DAPHNE

A BLACK PAGE

A NIGHT WATCHMAN

AN USHER

THE DEAN OF ST. ANTHONY'S

THE ARCHPRIEST

Scene—Padua, 1549.   Francisco Donato, Doge.

FIRST DAY

THE KEY

A garden, illuminated for an evening party. At the right, a palace brilliantly lighted, with a door opening upon the garden, and a balcony with arched openings, on which the guests can be seen walking to and fro. Music within the palace. Beside the door a stone bench. At the left another bench, upon which the form of a man sleeping can be distinguished in the darkness. In the background, above the trees, the silhouette of Padua, as it was in the sixteenth century, against a clear sky. Toward the close of the act day breaks.

SCENE I

THISBE, in a rich party dress: ANGELO MALIPIERI, with the ducal vest and the gold stole : HOMODEI, asleep ; he wears a long brown woolen frock, buttoned in front, and red small-clothes ; a guitar lies beside him.

THISBE.

Yes, you are master here, monsignore, the mighty podesta ; the lives and deaths of all are in your hands, you are omnipotent and your will is law. Venice did send you hither, and where'er your face is seen, it is as if one saw the majestic features of the Serene Republic. When you pass through a street, the windows close, the passers-by slink off, and all who are within the houses tremble. Alas ! these timid Paduans have scarcely more self-confidence and pride when you are by, than if they were the rabble of Constantinople, and you the Turk. Yes, so it is. But I have been at Brescia. Ah ! 't is another matter there. Venice would never dare to maltreat Brescia as she does Padua. Brescia would defend herself. When the Venetian arm is raised to strike, Brescia bites, but Padua licks the hand. It is a burning shame. But though you be everybody's master here, and claim that title over me as well, listen to me, monsignore, while I speak frankly to you. Not on affairs of state, do not fear that, but on your own affairs. I say, monsignore, you are a strange man, you pass my comprehension, for you 're in love with me, and still are jealous of your wife !

ANGELO.

Jealous of you as well, signora.

THISBE.

Indeed you have no need to tell me so. And yet you have no right, for I do not belong to you. I pass here for your mistress, your omnipotent mistress, but none the less I am not, as you know.

ANGELO.

Your fête is most magnificent, signora.

THISBE.

Oh ! I am only a poor actress, permitted to give fêtes to senators ; I strive to entertain our master, but my efforts meet with ill success to-day. Your face is gloomier than my mask is black. 'T is vain for me to multiply torches and girandoles, the shadow still remains upon your brow. You do not pay in gayety, monsignore, for the music that I furnish for your pleasure. Come, laugh a bit, in God's name !

ANGELO.

Yes, I will laugh. Said you not that the young man who came with you to Padua was your brother ?

THISBE.

Yes, and then ?

ANGELO.

You spoke with him but now. Who was the other man, with whom he was ?

THISBE.

His friend, one Anafesto Galeofa, of Vicenza.

ANGELO.

And your brother's name ?

THISBE.

Rodolfo, monsignore, Rodolfo. Twenty times already I have told you that. Pray have you nothing more agreeable to say to me ?

ANGELO.

Forgive me, Thisbe, I will ask you no more questions. Do you know with what marvelous charm you played Rosmonda yesterday, and that this city 's very fortunate to have you, and that all Italy is lost in admiration of you, Thisbe, and envious of these Paduans whom you compassionate so deeply ? Oh ! this applauding crowd is a sore trial to me. I die of jealousy to see you stared at by so many eyes. Ah ! Thisbe ! Pray, who was that masked man with whom I saw you talking in the corridor this evening ?

THISBE.

" Forgive me, Thisbe, I will ask you no more questions." Very good ! That man, monsignore, was Virgilio Tasca.

ANGELO.

My lieutenant ?

THISBE.

Your sbirro.

ANGELO.

What business did you have with him ?

THISBE.

You would be rightly served if I chose not to tell you.

ANGELO.

Thisbe !

THISBE.

No, no, I 'll be indulgent ; this is the story. You know that I am a mere nobody, a daughter of the people, an actress, a thing that you caress to-day, and trample on to-morrow, all in sport. Well, humble as I am, I had a mother. Do you know what it is to have a mother? had you a mother? Do you know what it is to be a child, a poor, weak, naked, miserable, hungry child, alone in all the world, and then to feel beside you and about you and above you, walking when you walk, stopping when you stop, and smiling when you weep, a woman—no, you are still too young to know that she 's a woman—an angel, who watches over you, who teaches you to talk and laugh and love! who warms your fingers in her hands, your body on her knees, your heart against her heart! who gives you of her milk when you are young, and of her bread when you are older, and of her life all the time! whom you call mother, and who calls you, "my son," so sweetly that the words rejoice God's heart? Well, I had such a mother. She was a poor woman, with no husband, who sang ballads in the public squares of Brescia. I used to go with her. We lived on money that was thrown to us. Thus I began. My mother's custom was to stand beside Gatta-Melatta's statue. One day, it seems that in the song she sang—but did not understand—there was some slur on the signoria of Venice, which much amused some of an ambassador's retainers, who were standing by. A senator passed by. He looked and listened, and said to the officer who followed him: "That woman to the gallows!" In the Venetian state that is soon done. My mother was seized upon the instant. She said nothing,—where was the use?—but kissed me, and a great tear fell upon my forehead; she took her crucifix and let them bind her. I can still see that crucifix of polished copper. My name, *Thisbe*, was roughly written at the foot with a dagger-point. I was sixteen then;

I watched them bind my mother, unable to cry out or speak or weep, as cold and rigid and lifeless as if I were dreaming. The crowd was silent, too. But there was with the senator a young girl, whose hand he held, his daughter doubtless, and suddenly she overflowed with sympathy. A lovely girl, monsignore. Poor child! she threw herself at his feet, and wept so bitterly, such supplicating tears, and from such lovely eyes, that she obtained my mother's pardon. Yes, monsignore. When my mother was unbound, she took her crucifix, and gave it to the lovely child: "Signorina, keep this crucifix," she said, "'t will bring you luck!" Since then my mother, blessed soul, has died. I have grown rich, and I would give the world to see that child once more, that angel who did save my mother's life. She is a woman now, and therefore wretched. Who knows? perhaps she may have need of me. In every city that I visit, I send for the sbirro or barigel or captain of police and tell him my story; and to him who finds the woman that I seek I will give ten thousand golden sequins. That 's why you saw me in the corridor just now talking with Virgilio Tasca, your barigel. Are you content?

ANGELO.

Ten thousand golden sequins! But what in Heaven's name will you give the woman herself when you have found her?

THISBE.

My life, if she will have it.

ANGELO.

How will you recognize her?

THISBE.

By my mother's crucifix.

ANGELO.

Bah! she will have lost it.

THISBE.

Oh, no! one does not lose what comes to one in that way.

ANGELO. (He spies Homodei.)

Signora! Signora! there 's a man yonder! do you know that there 's a man yonder? Who is the man?

THISBE (laughing heartily).

Why, yes, of course I know there 's a man yonder. And he 's sleeping too! and such a sleep! Pray be not so alarmed at sight of him. It 's my poor Homodei.

ANGELO.

Homodei! who the devil 's Homodei?

THISBE.

Homodei 's a man, monsignore, just as I, Thisbe, am a woman. Homodei, monsignore, is a guitarist, whom the primicerius of Saint-Mark's, one of my warmest friends, sent lately to me with a letter, which I will show you, jealous creature! And with the letter came a present.

ANGELO.

Eh! What 's that?

THISBE.

A genuine Venetian present. A casket which contains naught but two flagons, one white, the other black. In the white flagon is a most powerful narcotic which causes sleep like death for twelve long hours. In the black flagon there is poison, that fearful poison which Malaspina administered to the pope in an aloes pellet, as you have heard. The primicerius wrote to me that I might find it useful on occasion. A charming gift you see. The reverend primicerius also said that the poor fellow who did bring the letter and the present was an idiot. He has been here—surely you must have seen him—for a full fortnight,

eating in the pantry, sleeping in any corner, as his wont is, playing and singing, awaiting his departure for Vicenza. He comes from Venice. Ah me! my mother used to roam about in the same way. I will keep him here until he choose to go. He entertained my guests some little time this evening. But the festivities do not amuse him, and he 's gone to sleep. That 's all there is to that.

ANGELO.

You answer to me for this man?

THISBE.

Go to, you are pleased to joke! A mighty cause for such a show of terror! a guitar-player, an idiot, a sleeping man! Signor podesta, in Heaven's name what is the matter with you? You pass your life in asking questions about this and that one, and you take offense at everything. Is it jealousy, or fear?

ANGELO.

Both.

THISBE.

Jealousy I can understand, for you feel called upon to watch two women. But fear! you, the sole master, who do yourself rule the whole town by fear!

ANGELO.

The best of reasons wherefore I myself should tremble.

(He goes close to her, and speaks in a low voice.)

Listen, Thisbe. As you have said, my power has no limit here. I am the sovereign lord and despot of this town. I am the podesta, whom Venice fastens upon Padua, the tiger's claw upon the lamb. Yes, I am omnipotent. But, absolute as I am, above me, Thisbe, there 's a power, mighty and terrible, and shrouded in mystery: 't is Venice. Venice, you needs must know, means the state inquisition, the Council of Ten. Oh! that Council of Ten! let us speak of it in whispers, Thisbe, for it may be listening somewhere here. Men who are known to none of us, and who know us all; men who are visible in no state ceremony, but (whose agency is visible) at every scaffold; men in whose hands are all our heads, your head and mine, the doge's too, but men who wear no gown or stole, nothing to designate them to the eye, nothing to make it possible for one to say: "That man is of the Ten;" some mystic symbol worn beneath their frock, no more; agents everywhere, sbirri everywhere and headsmen everywhere; men who do not show to the Venetians other features than those forbidding mouths of bronze, that stand always open beneath the porches of Saint-Mark's; ominous mouths, deemed by the rabble dumb, but which speak none the less, and speak in loud and fearful tones, saying to every passer-by: "Denounce!" He who is once denounced is seized; once seized, and all is said. At Venice everything is done mysteriously and secretly and *surely.* Condemned, beheaded; naught to be seen, naught to be said; impossible to cry out, useless to look; the victim has a gag, the executioner a mask. What was I saying of the scaffold but a moment since? I was wrong. At Venice one dies not upon the scaffold; one disappears. Suddenly a man is missing in a family. What has become of him? The leads of Saint-Mark's, the wells, the Orfano canal can say. Sometimes the noise of something falling in the water is heard at night. Pass quickly then! Add to these horrors balls and festivals, music and torches, gondolas, theatres, and five months of carnival, and there 's your Venice. You, Thisbe, my lovely Thalia, know but this side; I, Angelo, the Senator, know the other. You see, in

every palace, in the doge's, in my own, unknown to him who dwells therein, there is a secret passage, a constant traitor to all the halls and rooms and alcoves, a dark corridor to which others than yourself have access, and which you feel winding about you, uncertain where it lies; a mysterious mine, where men are ever going to and fro intent on something. And private hatreds too, that one must reckon with, are crouching in that darkness. Often at night I sit upright in bed and listen, and hear footsteps in the wall. Under such fearful pressure am I living, Thisbe. I am over Padua, but this is over me. My mission is to humble Padua. My orders are to make myself dreaded and feared. I am a despot only on condition that I am a tyrant. In God's name never sue for mercy for any one, whoever he may be, to me who can deny you nothing, or you will be my ruin. Full freedom is accorded me to punish, none at all to pardon. Yes, so it is. Tyrant of Padua, I am the slave of Venice. I am well watched, you see! Oh! the Council of Ten! Place a single workman in a cellar and bid him make a lock; ere the lock 's finished the key is in the pocket of the Ten. Signora, the valet who serves me is a spy upon me, the friend who greets me is a spy upon me, the priest who hears me in confession is a spy upon me, the woman who says to me: "I love thee!"—yes, Thisbe—she, too, is a spy upon me.

THISBE.

Ah! signor!

ANGELO.

You never told me that you loved me, Thisbe; I do not speak of you. I say again that everyone who looks at me is an eye of the Council of Ten, everyone who listens to me is an ear of the Council of Ten, everyone who touches me is a hand of the

Council of Ten, a formidable hand, which feels about at first a long while, and then seizes suddenly. Oh! magnificent podesta as I am, I am not sure I may not see some wretched sbirro appear to-morrow without warning in my room, and bid me follow him; and he will be naught but a wretched sbirro, and I shall follow him! Whither? to some deep cavern, whence he will come forth without me. To be of Venice is to have one's life hanging by a thread. A dark and difficult position is this I occupy, signora, leaning over this fiery furnace which you call Padua, my face covered always with a mask, doing my tyrant's work, surrounded by precautions, and by risks and terrors, constantly in dread of an explosion, and trembling every moment lest I be stricken dead by my work, as the alchemist by his poison. Pity me, signora, and do not ask me why I tremble.

THISBE.

Ah! God! yours is indeed a terrible position!

ANGELO.

Yes, I am the tool wherewith one people inflicts torture on another. Such tools are soon worn out, and often break, my Thisbe. Ah! I am very wretched! There is but one bright spot in the world for me, and that is you. And yet I feel sure that you love me not. At least you love no other?

THISBE.

No, no. Be calm.

ANGELO.

I mislike the tone in which you say that "no."

THISBE.

I' faith, I say it as I can.

ANGELO.

Oh! be not mine,—I can be reconciled to that,—but in God's name be not another's, Thisbe! Pray God I never learn that any other . . .

THISBE.

Think you that you are handsome when you look like that?

ANGELO.

When will you love me, Thisbe?

THISBE.

When all Padua loves you.

ANGELO.

Alas!—Even so, remain at Padua; I do not wish you to leave Padua, do you hear? If you go hence, my life goes with you. Malediction! some one comes this way. We have been seen talking together for a long while. Even that may cause distrust at Venice. I leave you.

(He stops and points to Homodei.)

You answer to me for that man?

THISBE.

As for a child who might lie sleeping there.

ANGELO.

Your brother comes. I leave you with him.

(Exit Angelo.)

SCENE II

THISBE: RODOLFO, dressed in sober black, with a black feather in his cap: HOMODEI, still asleep.

THISBE.

Ah! 't is Rodolfo! yes, 't is Rodolfo! Come, for I love thee!

(She turns in the direction in which Angelo went off.)

No, shallow tyrant, he is not my brother, but my lover. Come to me, Rodolfo, my brave soldier, my generous, noble-hearted exile. Look in my eyes. Thou art so fair, and I do love thee!

RODOLFO.

Thisbe . . .

THISBE.

Why didst thou wish to come to Padua? Now, as thou seest, we are trapped. We cannot leave the city. In thy position, wherever thou dost go thou needs must say that thou art my brother. This podesta 's in love with thy poor Thisbe; he has us in his grasp, and will not let us go. I never cease to tremble lest he discover who thou really art. And oh! what torture 't is! But never fear! this tyrant shall have none of me. Thou hast no fear of that, Rodolfo? And yet I would that thou wouldst fear it. I would that thou wouldst once be jealous of me.

RODOLFO.

You are a noble-hearted, fascinating woman.

THISBE.

Ah! but I am jealous of thee! oh! so jealous! This Angelo Malipieri, this Venetian, who also prates of jealousy, doth actually fancy he is jealous, and mixes up all sorts of other things therewith. Ah! monsignore, when one is jealous, one does not think of Venice or the Ten, of sbirri, spies, or the canal Orfano; one has but one thing in his thoughts, and that his jealousy! I cannot bear to see thee speak to other women, my Rodolfo, even so much as to speak to them; it drives me mad. What right have they to words from thee? Oh! a rival! never give me a rival! I would kill her! For see, I love thee! Thou art the only man that I have ever loved. My life has long been sad, but now 't is radiant. Thou art my light. Thy love is like a sun new risen for me. Other men have found me cold as ice. Oh! why did I not know thee ten years since? It seems to me that all those portions of my body that have died of cold would still be living. What happiness that we can be alone and talk an instant! What madness to have come to Padua! We live in such constraint. Dear Rodolfo! Yes, yes! he is my lover! What do I say? my brother! I am fairly mad with joy when I can speak thus at my ease with thee; thou seest that I 'm mad! Dost thou love me?

RODOLFO.

Who would not love you, Thisbe?

THISBE.

If you say "you" to me once more, I shall be angry. Good lack! I must go show myself a moment to my guests. For some time it has seemed to me that thou art melancholy. Tell me it is not so.

RODOLFO.

No, Thisbe.

THISBE.

Thou art not jealous?

RODOLFO.

No.

THISBE.

Ah! but I wish thee to be jealous. Else it must be because thou lov'st me not. But come, no moping, Thisbe. Look, how I tremble still, and thou art not alarmed? does no one here know that thou art not my brother?

RODOLFO.

No one, save Anafesto.

THISBE.

Thy friend. Oh! he is trustworthy.

(*Enter Anafesto Galeofa.*)

Here is the man himself. I will entrust thee to him for a few moments.

(*Laughingly to Anafesto.*)

Signor Anafesto, look to it that he speak not to any woman.

ANAFESTO (*smiling*).

Have no fear, signora.

(*Exit Thisbe.*)

SCENE III

RODOLFO, ANAFESTO: HOMODEI, still asleep.

ANAFESTO (looking after Thisbe).

Oh! she is lovely! Rodolfo, thou 'rt a lucky fellow, for she loves thee.

RODOLFO.

I am unlucky, Anafesto, for I do not love her.

ANAFESTO.

What! what dost thou say?

RODOLFO (noticing Homodei).

Who 's the man sleeping yonder?

ANAFESTO.

Only that poor musician : thou knowest him?

RODOLFO.

Ah, yes! the idiot.

ANAFESTO.

Thou dost not love Thisbe? can it be? what didst thou say to me a moment since?

RODOLFO.

Did I say that? Forget it.

ANAFESTO.

Thisbe! Adorable creature!

RODOLFO.

Adorable indeed. I love her not.

ANAFESTO.

What?

RODOLFO.

Question me not.

ANAFESTO.

I, thy friend?

THISBE (returning, runs to Rodolfo, with a smile).

I return to say a single word to thee ; I love thee! Now I am off again.

(She runs off.)

ANAFESTO (looking after her).

Poor Thisbe!

RODOLFO.

There is at the very centre of my being a secret known to me alone.

ANAFESTO.

Some day thou wilt confide it to thy friend, Rodolfo, wilt thou not? Thou 'rt very sad to-day.

RODOLFO.

Yes. Leave me a moment.

(Exit Anafesto. Rodolfo takes his seat upon the stone bench by the door, and lets his head fall in his hands. When Anafesto is out of sight, Homodei opens his eyes, rises and walks slowly to where Rodolfo sits, lost in thought, and stands behind him.)

SCENE IV

RODOLFO, HOMODEI.

(Homodei lays his hand upon Rodolfo's shoulder. Rodolfo turns and gazes wonderingly at him.)

HOMODEI.

Your name is not Rodolfo. Your name is Ezzelino da Romana. You are of an ancient family that once reigned at Padua, and was banished thence two hundred years ago. You roam about from this city to that, sometimes risking thy head in the Venetian State. Some seven years since, in Venice city—you then were twenty years old—you saw one day a damsel of surpassing beauty in a church—the church of Saint George the Great. You did not follow her; to follow a woman in Venice is to invite a blow from a stiletto; but you went very often to the church. You were possessed with love for her, and she for you. In ignorance of her name (for you have never known it, nor do you know it yet—to you she has no name but Catarina) you found a way to write to her, and she to answer. You induced her to meet you at a woman's house, pious Cecilia's. You loved each other to distraction, but she retained her purity unsullied. The maiden was of noble birth. You know no more of her than that. A nobly born Venetian woman can marry none but a Venetian noble or a king. You are no Venetian, and you are no longer king. You are an exile, furthermore, and so could not aspire to her hand. One day she failed to meet you as agreed. Pious Cecilia told you they had forced a husband on her. You were no better able to ascertain the husband's name, than formerly the father's. You left Venice. From that day you have traversed Italy from end to end to escape the love that still does follow you. You have passed your time in pleasure and in folly and in vice. In vain. You have struggled to love other women, and have even thought that you did love them, this actress, Thisbe, for example. Still in vain. The old love inevitably reappears beneath the new. Three months ago you came to Padua with Thisbe, who gave out that you were her brother. Monsignore Angelo Malipieri, the podesta, is over head and ears in love with her, and you—this is what has befallen you. One evening, 't was the sixteenth of February, a woman closely veiled passed you upon the Ponte Molino, took you by the hand, and led you to the street called Sampiero. On that street are the ruins of the old Palazzo Magaruffi, demolished by your ancestor, Ezzelino III.; among the ruins there is a poor house, and in that house you found the fair Venetian whom you have loved, and who has loved you, too, for seven years. From that day on you met three times each week in that same house. She has been always faithful to her love and to her honor, to you and to her husband. Her name, however, she still keeps from you; she is Catarina,

nothing more. Last month your happiness
was rudely interrupted. One day she failed
to meet you. 'T is five weeks now that you 've
not seen her, and that means that her husband
is suspicious of her and keeps her under
lock and key. 'T will soon be dawn. You
seek her everywhere, but cannot find her:
you will never find her. Would you like to
see her this evening?

RODOLFO (looking earnestly at him).

Who are you?

HOMODEI.

Ah! questions? Expect no answer. And
so you have no wish to see this girl to-night?

RODOLFO.

Yes! yes! indeed I wish to see her! In
Heaven's name, let me but see her for an
instant, and then die!

HOMODEI.

You shall see her.

RODOLFO.

Where?

HOMODEI.

At her home.

RODOLFO.

But tell me, pray, who is she? what 's her
name?

HOMODEI.

I 'll tell you at her home.

RODOLFO.

Ah! you come from heaven.

HOMODEI.

I know naught of that. To-night, at moon-
rise—at midnight, that is simpler,—be at the
corner of Palazzo Alberto di Baon on Santo-
Urbano. I will be there and take you to her.
At midnight.

RODOLFO.

A thousand thanks! And will you not tell
me who you are?

HOMODEI.

Who am I? An idiot.

(Exit Homodei.)

RODOLFO (alone).

Who is this man? But then, what matters
it? Midnight! at midnight! How long it
seems from now to midnight! Oh! Catarina,
for the hour of bliss he promises me, I would
have given him my life!

(Enter Thisbe.)

SCENE V

RODOLFO, THISBE.

THISBE.

'T is I once more, Rodolfo. Good-morning! I could no longer stay away from thee. I cannot bear to be apart from thee, I follow thee where'er thou goest. I think and live by thee alone. I am the shadow of thy body, and thou the soul of mine.

RODOLFO.

Have a care, Thisbe! Mine is an accursed family. There is a prophecy concerning us, a fatal prophecy which almost never lacks fulfillment from generation to generation. We cause the death of those who love us.

THISBE.

Oh, well, thou shalt cause my death. Why not? If only thou dost love me?

RODOLFO.

Thisbe . . .

THISBE.

In that case you will weep for me. I ask no more than that.

RODOLFO.

Thisbe, you deserve an angel's love.

(He kisses her hand, and walks slowly away.)

THISBE (alone).

Well, well! how quickly he doth leave me! Rodolfo! He has gone. What can be the matter?

(She looks toward the bench.)

Ah! Homodei is awake.

(Homodei appears at the back of the stage.)

SCENE VI

THISBE, HOMODEI.

HOMODEI.

Rodolfo's name is Ezzelino, the adventurer is a prince, the idiot 's a shrewd fellow, the sleeping man a cat that watches, eyes closed, ears open.

THISBE.

What does he say?

HOMODEI (pointing to his guitar).

This guitar has strings which do give forth such notes as one may choose. A man's heart, a woman's heart have strings as well, whereon who will may play.

THISBE.

What does that mean?

HOMODEI.

It means that if perchance, you lose to-day a handsome youth with a black feather in his cap, signora, I know the place where you may find him once again to-night.

THISBE.

With a woman?

HOMODEI.

Fair.

THISBE.

What meanest thou? who art thou?

HOMODEI.

I have no idea.

THISBE.

Thou art not what I thought. Wretched creature that I am. The podesta suspected that thou wert a man to be feared. Who art thou? oh! who art thou? Rodolfo with a woman! and to-night! That is what thou wouldst say, is 't not? is that what thou wouldst say?

HOMODEI.

I have no idea.

THISBE.

Thou liest! 'T is impossible, for my Rodolfo loves me.

HOMODEI.

I have no idea.

THISBE.

Ah! villain! Ah! thou liest! How he doth lie! Thou art suborned. My God! in that case even I have enemies! Rodolfo loves me well. Go to, thou canst not frighten me. I do believe thee not. It must e'en make thee wild to see that what thou sayest has no effect on me.

HOMODEI.

You have remarked, no doubt, that Monsignore Angelo Malipieri, the podesta, wears a small golden charm of most artistic workmanship, attached to the chain about his neck. That charm 's a key. Pretend a longing for it as a bauble. Ask him to give it you without a word of what we mean to do with it.

TIISBE.

A key thou sayest? I will not ask it of him. I will ask nothing of him. Infamous wretch, who sought to make me doubt Rodolfo! I do not want the key. Begone, I will not listen to thee.

HOMODEI.

Here comes the podesta himself. When you once have the key, I will explain to you how to make use of it to-night. I will return a quarter of an hour hence.

TIISBE.

Didst thou not hear me, villain? I tell thee that I do not want the key. My confidence in my Rodolfo's absolute. I care nothing for the key, and I'll not say a word about it to the podesta. Do not return, 't is useless. I believe thee not.

HOMODEI.

In a quarter of an hour.

(Exit Homodei. Enters Angelo.)

SCENE VII

THISBE, ANGELO.

THISBE.

Ah! there you are, monsignore. Are you seeking someone?

ANGELO.

Yes, Virgilio Tasca, to whom I had a word to say.

THISBE.

Are you still jealous?

ANGELO.

Still, signora.

THISBE.

You are foolish. Why be jealous? I do not understand this jealousy. If I should love a man, most surely I would not be jealous of him.

ANGELO.

Do you love someone?

THISBE.

I should say as much!

ANGELO.

Whom?

THISBE.

You.

ANGELO.

You love me! Is it possible? Oh! do not mock me, for the love of God! Oh! say to me again what you just said.

THISBE.

I love you.

(He draws close to her ecstatically. She takes in her hand the chain he wears around his neck.)

Ah! what is this little chain? I had not noticed it before. How pretty! And so artistically done! Why, 't was chased by Benvenuto! Lovely! Pray, what is it? Is it a fit adornment for a woman?

ANGELO.

Ah! Thisbe, you have filled my heart with joy with that one word!

THISBE.

'T is well, 't is well. But tell me, pray, what this is.

ANGELO.

That is a key.

THISBE.

Oho! a key. I never should have guessed it. Oh! yes, I see, it 's used to open something. Yes, yes! a key.

ANGELO.

Yes, Thisbe dear.

THISBE.

Oh, well, if it 's a key, I do not care for it; keep it yourself.

ANGELO.

What! did you care for it, my Thisbe?

THISBE.

A little; as a beautiful chased bauble.

ANGELO.

Take it, pray!

(He detaches the key from the chain.)

THISBE.

No. Had I known it was a key, I 'd not have mentioned it. I do not care for it, I tell you. Perhaps you use it.

ANGELO.

Very rarely. Besides, I have another. You may safely take it, I promise you.

THISBE.

No. I no longer have the desire for it. Pray can one open doors with such a key? it 's very small.

ANGELO.

That makes no difference; these keys are made for secret locks. This one will open several doors, that of a certain bedroom among others.

THISBE.

Indeed! Well, since you really urge me, I will take it.

(She takes the key.)

ANGELO.

Oh! thanks! What happiness! you have accepted something from me! a thousand thanks!

THISBE.

I' faith, I remember that the French ambassador, M. de Montluc, had one almost its counterpart. Did you know M. le Maréchal de Montluc? A man of great gifts was he not? Ah! I forgot; you nobles cannot speak to the ambassadors. No matter, he had no patience with the Huguenots, this M. de Montluc. If ever they fell in his way! He was an ardent Catholic. Look, monsignore, I think that is Virgilio Tasca looking for you in the gallery.

ANGELO.

You think so?

THISBE.

Had you not something that you wished to say to him?

ANGELO.

A curse on him for tearing me away from you!

THISBE (pointing to the gallery).

That way.

ANGELO (kissing her hand).

Ah! Thisbe, you do love me?

THISBE.

That way, that way. Tasca is waiting for you.

(Exit Angelo. Homodei appears at the back of the stage. Thisbe runs to him.)

SCENE VIII

THISBE, HOMODEI.

THISBE.

I have the key!

HOMODEI.

Let me see.

(*He scrutinizes the key.*)

Yes, this is it. In the podesta's palace there is a gallery that looks upon the Ponte Molino. Hide yourself there this evening, behind the furniture, or tapestry, or where you will. At two o'clock I 'll seek you there.

THISBE (*giving him her purse*).

Thou shalt have better recompense ere long; but meanwhile take this purse.

HOMODEI.

That 's as you please. But hear me through. At two o'clock I 'll seek you there. I will point out to you the first door you will have to open with this key. Then I shall leave you. You can do the rest without me, for there is naught to do but to walk straight ahead.

THISBE.

What shall I find after the first door?

HOMODEI.

A second, which this same key will open.

THISBE.

And after the second?

HOMODEI.

A third. This key will open all.

THISBE.

And after the third?

HOMODEI.

That you will see.

SECOND DAY

THE CRUCIFIX

A room richly hung in scarlet with raised gold figures. In a corner at the left a superb bed upon a raised platform, under a canopy upheld by twisted columns. At the four corners of the canopy hang crimson curtains which can be drawn so close as to conceal the bed entirely. In a corner at the right an open window. On the same side a door hidden by the hangings; near it a *pri-Dieu*, above which a crucifix in polished copper is fastened to the wall. At the back large folding-doors. Between them and the bed another small door handsomely carved. A table, chairs, torches, and a large sideboard. Without, gardens, steeples, and bright moonlight. A lute lies upon the table.

SCENE I

DAPHNE, REGINELLA, afterwards HOMODEI.

REGINELLA.

Yes, Daphne, 't is beyond all doubt. Troilo, the night-usher, told me. It happened very recently, on my lady's last journey to Venice. A paltry sbirro, an infamous sbirro, dared to fall in love with her, to write to her, and seek to see her, Daphne. Is it not past belief? My lady ordered him turned out of doors, and she did well.

DAPHNE (opening the door near the prie-Dieu).

She did, indeed, my Reginella. But she is waiting for her Book of Hours, you know.

REGINELLA (looking over some books upon the table).

As for the other thing, that is more terrible, and I am also sure of that. Because he warned his master that he found a spy lurking in the house, poor Palimuro died suddenly the same

evening. Poison, you understand. I recom-
mend you to be very prudent. First of all one
must be very careful what one says here in this
palace. There 's always someone listening in
the wall.

DAPHNE.

Come, pray make haste, and we will talk
another time. My lady 's waiting.

REGINELLA (still turning over the books, with her
eyes fixed on the table).

If you are in such haste, go you before.
I 'll follow you.

(Daphne goes off and closes the door, unseen by
Reginella.)

Yes, Daphne, I most earnestly do counsel
silence in this cursed palace. There is no
room but this where one is safe. But here, at
least, we need have no fear. Here we can
say whatever we may choose. It is the only
spot where, when one speaks, one can be sure
of not being overheard.

(As she utters the last words, the sideboard against
the wall at the right turns upon a pivot, giving
entrance to Homodei, unseen by her, and closes
again.)

HOMODEI.

It is the only spot where, when one speaks,
one can be sure of not being overheard.

REGINELLA (turning toward him).

Heaven !

HOMODEI.

Silence !

(He opens his frock and discovers a black velvet
doublet, whereon are embroidered the letters
C. D. X. Reginella gazes at the letters and the man
in terror.)

When a man sees one of us, and afterwards
by the least sign does make it possible for
anyone on earth to guess what he has seen,
that man 's a dead man before sunset. We
are talked about among the people, and thou
must know that what I say is true.

REGINELLA.

Jesus ! By what door did he enter ?

HOMODEI.

By no door.

REGINELLA.

Jesus !

HOMODEI.

Reply to all my questions, and seek not to
deceive me upon any point. Thy life depends
upon it. Where does this door lead ?

(Pointing to the folding-doors.)

REGINELLA.

Into monsignore's sleeping-room.

HOMODEI.

And this ?

(Pointing to the small door near the large one.)

REGINELLA.

To a secret staircase which gives access to
the galleries of the palace. Monsignore has
the only key to it.

HOMODEI (pointing to the door near the prie-Dieu).

And this ?

REGINELLA.

To the signora's oratory.

HOMODEI.

Is there another exit from the oratory ?

REGINELLA.

No. The oratory 's in a turret. There 's
naught but one barred window there.

HOMODEI (going to the window).

And that is on a level with this one. 'T is
well. Full eighty feet of perpendicular wall,
and the Brenta at the foot. The grating is of
little use. But there 's a little stairway in the
oratory. Whither does it lead ?

REGINELLA.

To my room, which is Daphne's also, monsignore.

HOMODEI.

Is there another exit from that room?

REGINELLA.

No, monsignore. A barred window, and no other door than that which leads down to the oratory.

HOMODEI.

As soon as thy mistress has retired, thou wilt go to thy room and remain there, hearing and seeing nothing.

REGINELLA.

I will obey, monsignore.

HOMODEI.

Where is thy mistress?

REGINELLA.

In the oratory. She is praying there.

HOMODEI.

Will she return here when her prayer is done?

REGINELLA.

Yes, monsignore.

HOMODEI.

Not within the half-hour?

REGINELLA.

No, monsignore.

HOMODEI.

'T is well. Now go. Silence, before everything! Nothing of that which may take place here doth concern thee. Whatever happens, do thou not say a word. If the cat plays with the mouse, what is 't to thee? Thou hast not seen me, thou dost not know that I exist. Dost understand? If thou dost risk a word, I shall hear it; a wink, I shall see it; a gesture, signal, or pressure of the hand, I shall feel it. Now go.

REGINELLA.

Oh Heaven! In God's name, who is to die?

HOMODEI.

Thou art, if thou dost lisp a word of this.

(At a sign from Homodei she goes off through the small door near the prie-Dieu. When she has gone, Homodei walks to the sideboard, which turns upon itself once more, and affords a glimpse of a dark corridor.)

Monsignore Rodolfo, you may come now. Nine steps to ascend.

(Steps are heard upon the staircase which the sideboard conceals. Rodolfo appears.)

SCENE II

HOMODEI, RODOLFO (wrapped in a cloak).

HOMODEI.

Come in.

RODOLFO.

Where am I?

HOMODEI.

Where are you? Perhaps upon the flooring of your scaffold.

RODOLFO.

What do you mean by that?

HOMODEI.

Has it not reached your ears that there is in Padua a certain room, a room to be avoided, which, though filled with flowers and sweet perfumes, and perhaps with love, no man can enter, whosoe'er he be, noble or subject, young or old, because to enter there, or but to set the door ajar, is a crime punishable with death?

RODOLFO.

Yes, 't is the podesta's wife's chamber.

HOMODEI.

Even so.

RODOLFO.

Well, and you say that chamber . . .

HOMODEI.

You are in it now.

RODOLFO.

In the podesta's wife's chamber?

HOMODEI.

Yes.

RODOLFO.

And the woman I love? . . .

HOMODEI.

Is Catarina Bragadini, wife of Angelo Malipieri, Podesta of Padua.

RODOLFO.

Can it be possible? Catarina Bragadini, wife of the podesta!

HOMODEI.

If your heart fails you, there is still time; the open door 's before you, you may go.

RODOLFO.

For myself I have no fear, but for her. Who will vouch for your good faith?

HOMODEI.

If you will have it so, I 'll tell you *what* will vouch for me. A week ago, ('t was very late at night) you crossed the square of San Prodocimo. You were alone. You heard the clash of swords and shouts behind the church. You ran in that direction.

RODOLFO.

Yes, and I rescued a masked man from three assassins who were just about to make an end of him.

HOMODEI.

And he went his way without so much as telling you his name or thanking you. That masked man was myself. Since that night,

Monsignore Ezzolino, I have wished you well. You know me not, but I know you. I have sought to bring you and her you love together. 'T is gratitude. Nothing but gratitude. Now, do you trust me?

RODOLFO.

Yes! and I do thank thee from my heart. I feared some treachery on her account. There was a heavy weight upon my heart, but now thou hast removed it. Ah! thou art my friend, my friend for life! Thou hast done more for me than I did do for thee. I could not live much longer without seeing Catarina. I should have killed myself and damned myself for all eternity. I did but save thy life, but thou hast saved my heart and soul!

HOMODEI.

And so you will remain?

RODOLFO.

Will I remain? will I remain? I trust to thee, I tell thee! Oh! to see her once more! though for but an hour or a minute, to see her once more! Pray dost thou understand what it is to me, to see her once more? Where is she?

HOMODEI.

Yonder, in her oratory.

RODOLFO.

Where shall I see her?

HOMODEI.

Here.

RODOLFO.

And when?

HOMODEI.

A quarter of an hour hence.

RODOLFO.

Thank God!

HOMODEI (pointing to the different doors one after another).

Mark what I say. There at the end, is the podesta's sleeping room. At this moment he is sleeping, and there are none in the whole palace now awake, save Donna Catarina and ourselves. I think that you do run but little risk to-night. As to the means of entrance that we used, I cannot now divulge the secret which is known to me alone. but in the morning you will find it easy to escape.

(He walks to the rear of the stage.)

This then is the husband's door. As for yourself, Signor Rodolfo, the lover,

(He points to the window.)

't is my advice to you not to have recourse to that means of exit under any circumstances. Eighty feet sheer, and the river at the bottom. Now, I will leave you.

RODOLFO.

Thou saidst in quarter of an hour?

HOMODEI.

Yes.

RODOLFO.

Will she come alone?

HOMODEI.

Perhaps she will not. Stand out of sight for a few moments.

RODOLFO.

Where?

HOMODEI.

Behind the bed. No! see, upon the balcony. You will reveal your presence when you think fit. I think I hear chairs moving in the oratory. Signora Catarina will soon be here. 'T is time for us to part. Farewell.

RODOLFO.

Whoever thou art, after such a service, thou mayest dispose of all I have, my property, my life!

(He steps out upon the balcony and disappears.)

HOMODEI (returning to the front of the stage).

That is no longer yours, monsignore.

(He looks to see if Rodolfo can see him, then takes a letter from his breast and places it upon the table. He goes off through the secret entrance, which closes after him. Enter through the oratory door Catarina and Daphne. Catarina in the costume of a noble Venetian.)

SCENE III

CATARINA, DAPHNE: RODOLFO (out of sight upon the balcony).

CATARINA.

Above a month! Know'st thou, Daphne, that 't is above a month? Ah! 't is all over. If I could but sleep, I might, perchance, behold him in my dreams. But sleep I cannot. Where is Reginella?

DAPHNE.

She went up to her room a moment since, and is at prayer. Shall I bid her come and serve madame?

CATARINA.

Let her serve God. Let her pray on. Alas! prayer is of no avail to me.

DAPHNE.

Shall I close the window?

CATARINA.

It is because my suffering is too keen, poor Daphne. 'T is five long weeks, five never-ending weeks, that I 've not seen him! No, do not close the window. The air refreshes me. My head is burning. Lay thy hand upon it. And I shall never see him more! I am confined and watched,—to all intent imprisoned. 'T is ended. To enter this room is a capital offense. Oh! I would far rather never see him. To see him here! I tremble at the thought. Alas! my God, my God, was my love then so blameworthy? Why did he come to Padua? Why did I yield again to the allurement of that happiness which was so soon to end? I passed an

hour with him now and again. That hour, short as it was and so soon flown, was the one opening through which a little air and sunshine came into my life. Now all is sealed. I shall not ever see again the face whence my light came to me. Oh! my Rodolfo! Tell me, Daphne, dost thou not truly think that I shall never see him more?

DAPHNE.

My lady . . .

CATARINA.

And I am not as other women are. Parties and gallantry and merry-making are naught to me. These seven years, Daphne, I have had in my heart but the one thought, love; but the one feeling, love; but the one name, Rodolfo. When I do look within myself, I find Rodolfo there, always Rodolfo, nothing but Rodolfo! My soul is made after his image. As thou canst see, it could not well be otherwise. These seven years I have loved him dearly. I was very young. How pitilessly they force one into marriage! As for my husband, I simply dare not speak to him. Thinkst thou that that gives promise of a happy life? What a plight is mine! If my dear mother were but with me still!

DAPHNE.

In God's name, banish all these gloomy thoughts, my lady.

CATARINA.

Oh! Daphne, he and I have passed many blissful hours together on evenings such as this is. Can it be that all this that I say to thee of him I should not say? It cannot be, am I not right? But my grief saddens thee, and I would not cause thee pain. Go thou and sleep. Go and join Reginella.

DAPHNE.

But will madame . . .

CATARINA.

Yes, I will be my own maid to-night. Sweet sleep to thee, good Daphne. Go.

DAPHNE.

May Heaven have you in his keeping, madame!

(She goes off through the door leading to the oratory.)

SCENE IV

CATARINA (alone).

There was a song he used to sing. He used to sing it, sitting at my feet, and in a voice so wondrous sweet! Oh! there are moments when it seems that I must see him. I would give all my blood to see him. There was one verse above all, which was meant for me.

(She takes up the guitar.)

This was the air, I think.

(She plays a few measures of a plaintive air.)

I wish I could recall the words. Oh! I would sell my soul to hear him sing them just once more ; even though I could not see him, though he were as far away as anyone could wish. But his voice! to hear his voice!

RODOLFO (upon the balcony).

(Sings.)

My heart to thine is freely given,
   I cannot live apart from thee ;
The bond divine was forged in heaven,
   That joins us for eternity.
Thou harmony, and I the viol,
   Thou the zephyr, I the tree,
I the lip, and thou the smile,
   Thou beauty, and I, love for thee.

CATARINA (letting the guitar fall).

Just Heaven!

RODOLFO (still out of sight).

While the hours
   Flow on apace,
My tearful song
   Doth pass along
Thy laughing face.

CATARINA.

Rodolfo!

RODOLFO (appearing at the window, and throwing his cloak behind him upon the balcony).

Catarina!

(He throws himself at her feet.)

CATARINA.

You here? You here? Ah! God! I die with joy and terror. Rodolfo! do you know where you are? Do you perchance imagine that this is a room like other rooms, unhappy man! Your head 's in danger here!

RODOLFO.

What matters it to me? I should have died for lack of seeing you ; I much prefer to die for having seen you.

CATARINA.

Thou hast done well. Yes, thou wert right to come. My head 's in danger, too. But thou art with me, and what boots the rest? One hour with thee, then let the ceiling crumble, if it will!

RODOLFO.

Heaven will protect us, too. All in the palace are asleep, and there 's no reason why I should not go hence as I came.

CATARINA.

How didst thou come?

RODOLFO.

With the assistance of a man whose life I lately saved. I will explain it all to you. I am sure of the means that I employed.

CATARINA.

Sure? If thou art sure, that is enough. God's love! pray, look at me, and let me see thy face!

RODOLFO.

Catarina!

CATARINA.

Let us think no more of aught save our two selves, thou of me, and I of thee. Thou dost find me much altered, dost thou not? I 'll tell thee why: it is because I have done naught but weep for five long weeks. And thou, what hast thou done throughout those weeks? Hast thou not been sad and unhappy, too? What change has our separation wrought in thee? Tell me, I pray thee. Speak to me. I long to have thee speak to me.

RODOLFO.

O Catarina! to be parted from thee is to have clouds before one's eyes, and in one's heart an aching void; to feel that one is dying day by day; to be without a light in a dark dungeon, without a star at night; to cease to live, or think, or know! What have I done, sayest thou? I know not. What I have felt thou knowest now.

CATARINA.

And I the same! and I the same! and I the same! Ah! now I know our hearts have not been parted. I fain would tell thee many things. But where begin? I am in prison. I cannot go out. I have suffered bitterly. Thou must not be surprised that I did not throw myself at once upon thy neck; thy presence here was such a shock. Great Heaven! when I heard thy voice, I cannot tell thee my emotion; I knew not where I was.

Come, sit thee down, as in the old days. But let us talk in whispers. Thou wilt remain till morning. Daphne will show thee how to leave the palace. Oh! what blissful hours! Now, I have no fear at all, for thou hast fully reassured me. How glad I am to see thee! Between Paradise and thee, I would choose thee. Ask Daphne to tell thee of my weeping. She has been most devoted to me, the poor girl! Thou shalt thank her for it. And Reginella, too. But tell me, hast thou found out my name at last? Ah! thou 'rt dismayed at nothing. I know of nothing that thou wouldst not do when thou hast one desire in thy heart. Say, wilt thou have a way to come again?

RODOLFO.

Yes. How could I live without it? Catarina, my heart is bursting as I listen to thee. Fear nothing. See how calm the night. All is love within us, all is repose about us. Two hearts like ours, which overflow into each other, Catarina, have that about them that 's so beautiful and holy, that God would not bring distress upon them. I love thee and thou lovest me, and God sees us. We three alone are waking at this hour. Fear nothing.

CATARINA.

No. And there are moments when one remembers nothing. When one is happy, dazed with happiness. Listen, Rodolfo: when we are parted I am only a poor captive, and thou a poor exile; together we give the angels cause to envy us! Oh, no! they are not so near heaven as we. Rodolfo, one does not die of joy, or I should have died ere this. My head is in a whirl. Just now I plied thee with a thousand questions, and not a single word of what I asked can I remember. Dost thou remember? Tell me, is it not a dream? Art thou there, in very truth?

RODOLFO.

Dear heart!

CATARINA.

No; do not speak to me, let me collect my thoughts, and look at thee, my soul! and tell myself that thou art there. Soon I will answer thee. One has such moments when one longs to gaze at the man one loves, and say to him: "Hush, I am looking at thee! hush, I do love thee! hush, for I am happy!"

(He kisses her hand. She turns and spies the letter on the table.)

What's that? My God! Here is a paper that brings me to myself! A letter! Didst thou put it there?

RODOLFO.

No. It must have been the man who came with me.

CATARINA.

A man came with thee! Who was he? Let us see what the letter is.

(She hurriedly tears it open, and reads.)

"There are people who get tipsy on nothing but Cyprus. There are others who enjoy nothing but refined vengeance. A sbirro in love, my lady, is of small account, but a sbirro revenging himself is another matter."

RODOLFO.

Great God! what does that mean?

CATARINA.

I know the hand. 'T was written by an infamous villain who dared to love me and to tell me so, to come to my apartments one day at Venice, and whom I turned out of doors. His name is Homodei.

RODOLFO.

'T is he.

CATARINA.

He is a spy of the Council of Ten.

RODOLFO.

Heaven help us!

CATARINA.

We are lost. A snare was set for us, and we are caught in it.

(She goes to the balcony and looks out.)

Ah! God!

RODOLFO.

What is it?

CATARINA.

Put out that torch. Quickly.

RODOLFO (extinguishing the torch).

What dost thou see?

CATARINA.

The gallery that overlooks the Ponte Molino.

RODOLFO.

Well?

CATARINA.

I saw a light appear and disappear there.

RODOLFO.

Wretched madman that I am! Catarina, I am the sole cause of thy ruin.

CATARINA.

Rodolfo, I would have come to thee, as thou didst come to me.

(She listens at the small door at the rear.)

Hush! listen! I think I hear a noise in the corridor. Yes, a door opens, and I hear footsteps. How didst thou come in?

RODOLFO.

Through a masked door which the demon closed behind him.

CATARINA.

What shall we do?

RODOLFO.

That door?

CATARINA.

Leads to my husband's room.

RODOLFO.

The window?

CATARINA.

A bottomless abyss.

RODOLFO.

And this door?

CATARINA.

Leads to my oratory, from which there's no way out. No chance of flight. No matter, go in there.

(She opens the door, Rodolfo rushes in, and she closes it behind him.)

I'll lock it with a double turn.

(She removes the key and conceals it in her bosom.)

Who knows what might not happen? He might perhaps seek to come to my assistance. Then he would rush out to his destruction.

(She goes to the small door at the rear.)

I can hear nothing now. Yes, someone walking. Now they stop. To listen, doubtless. Ah! I will pretend to be asleep.

(She removes her dress and throws herself upon the bed.)

Merciful God! how I tremble! Someone is putting a key in the lock. Oh! I do not wish to see who comes!

(She draws the curtains close. The door opens.)

SCENE V

CATARINA, THISBE.

(Enters Thisbe, pale as death, carrying a light. She comes slowly forward, looking on all sides. Upon reaching the table she examines the recently extinguished torch.)

THISBE.

The torch still smokes.

(She turns, spies the bed, runs to it and draws aside the curtain.)

She is alone. She feigns to be asleep.

(She makes the tour of the room, examining the doors and the wall.)

This is the husband's door.

(The back of her hand comes in contact with the door of the oratory, which is hidden by the hangings.)

There's a door here.

(Catarina has sat up in bed, and is watching her in amazement.)

CATARINA.

What does this mean?

THISBE.

Mean? What does it mean? Hark ye, I'll tell you what it means. It means that the podesta's mistress has the podesta's wife safe in her hands.

CATARINA.

Just Heaven!

THISBE.

What does it mean, my lady? It means that a poor actress, a stage-girl, a *ballerina*, as we are dubbed by you, has in her clutches a great lady, a married woman, a respected woman, virtue personified! Yes; has her in her clutches, has her nails and teeth fastened in her flesh. It means that she can work her will upon this same great lady, upon her fair, unsullied reputation, and that she'll tear her and her good name to rags and tatters! Ah! my noble dames, I know not what may happen, but this I know: that I have one of you under my feet! and that I will not let her go! and that she may be well assured of that! and that't were better for her that God's lightning struck her down, than to see my face looking into hers! Upon my soul, my lady, 't is passing bold for you to dare to raise your eyes to mine, when you've a lover hiding in your room.

CATARINA.

Signora . . .

THISBE.

Yes, hiding!

CATARINA.

You are mistaken.

THISBE.

Go to, do not deny it. He was here. The chairs in which you sat still bear the imprint of your forms. You should at least have smoothed away the wrinkles. What did you say? a thousand tender things, no doubt? a thousand charming things, no doubt? "I love thee! I adore thee! I am thine!" Ah! touch me not, my lady!

CATARINA.

I cannot comprehend.

THISBE.

And you are no whit better than ourselves. What we say to a man aloud in broad daylight, you stammer to him with shamed face at night. The hours only are changed. We take your husbands, and you take our lovers. We are rivals. Good. Let us fight it out! Ah! tawdry tinsel, hypocrites, traitors, soiled virtues, false creatures that you are! Per Bacco, no! You are not fit to hold a candle to us! We deceive nobody! You deceive everybody; your families, your husbands, and, if you could, you would deceive the good God himself! Oh! these virtuous women who go veiled through the streets! They are on their way to church, so stand aside, and bow and lick the dust before them! No, do not stand aside, nor bow, nor lick the dust, but go right up to them, tear off the veil; behind the veil there is a mask; tear off the mask; behind the mask there is a lying mouth! But it 's all one to me. I am the mistress of the podesta, and you his wife, and I will ruin you!

CATARINA.

Great God! signora . . .

THISBE.

Where is he?

CATARINA.

Who?

THISBE.

He.

CATARINA.

I am alone. Alone, upon my soul. All alone. I do not understand a word of what you ask me. I know you not, but your words freeze my blood with terror. What I have done to injure you, I know not. I cannot think that you have any interest in this.

THISBE.

That I 've an interest in this! I lean to the opinion that I have! You doubt it! These virtuous dames are most incredulous!

Think you that I would speak to you as I have spoken, were not my heart consumed with rage? What is all this that I have said to you to me? What is 't to me that you are a great lady, and I an actress? It 's all the same to me, for I am fair as you! Hatred is rankling in my heart, I tell thee, and I insult thee as I may. Where is the man? Tell me his name. I wish to see the man! Oh! when I think that she was feigning sleep! Upon my soul, 't is downright infamous!

CATARINA.

O God! merciful God! what will become of me? In Heaven's name, signora! if you knew . . .

THISBE.

I know that yonder is a door! I 'm sure that he is there.

CATARINA.

It is my oratory. Nothing more. There is no one there, I swear. If you but knew! you have been misled in my regard. I live a most retired life, alone, hidden from all eyes.

THISBE.

The veil!

CATARINA.

It is my oratory, I assure you. There 's nothing there beside my prie-Dieu, and Book of Hours.

THISBE.

The mask!

CATARINA.

I swear that there is no one hidden there, signora!

THISBE.

The lying mouth!

CATARINA.

Signora . . .

THISBE.

Enough. Why, you are mad to talk in this way, when your whole bearing 's that of a guilty, frightened creature. You do not put

enough assurance into your denials. Come,
come, my lady, leave your bed, rage and
bluster, if you dare, and then play injured
innocence !

(Suddenly she spies the cloak on the floor by the balcony ; she runs and picks it up.)

Ah ! now it 's no longer possible. Here 's
his cloak.

CATARINA.

Heaven help me !

THISBE.

No, it 's not a cloak, is it? It 's not a
man's cloak? Unluckily, one cannot tell its
owner, for all these cloaks are much alike.
Come, look to yourself, and tell me the man's
name !

CATARINA.

I know not what you mean.

THISBE.

That is your oratory, you say? Open the
door.

CATARINA.

Why so ?

THISBE.

I wish to pray. Open !

CATARINA.

I have lost the key.

THISBE.

Open, I say !

CATARINA.

I do not know who has the key.

THISBE.

Ah ! it must be that your husband has it !
Monsignore Angelo ! Angelo ! Angelo !

(She attempts to run to the door at the rear. Catarina
throws herself in front of her, and holds her back.)

CATARINA.

No ! you shall not go to that door ! No,
you shall not ! I have in no way injured you.

I cannot see what you can have against me. You
will not ruin me, signora. You will have pity
on me. Stay but a moment. You shall see.
I will explain. An instant only. Since you
came in I have been dazed and terrified ; and
then your words, all that you have said ;
really I am bewildered, and some things I did
not understand ; you told me that you were
an actress and I a great lady, and that 's all I
know. I swear that there is no one there.
You did not mention that vile sbirro, and yet
I know that he is at the bottom of it all. He
is a fearful man, and has deceived you. A
spy. A spy is not to be believed ! Oh !
listen to me for an instant. Surely one woman
cannot refuse to listen to another for an instant.
If 't were a man he might not be so kind.
But do you be merciful. You are too lovely to
be cruel. I was saying that this spy, this sbirro,
is a vile creature. We need but to understand
each other, then you would bitterly regret that
you had caused my death. Do not arouse my
husband. He would have me put to death.
If you knew my position, you would pity me.
I am not guilty, really, not very guilty. I
may perhaps have been imprudent, but I have
no mother now. Upon my word, I have no
mother. Oh ! have mercy on me, and do not
go to yonder door, I beg you, I beg you, I
beg you !

THISBE.

Enough ! No ! I 'll hear no more ! Monsignore ! Monsignore !

CATARINA.

Stay ! stay ! for the love of God ! You do
not know that he will kill me ! At least, give
me an instant, one short instant, to pray
God ! No, I 'll not leave this room. See, I
will kneel here

(She points to the copper crucifix above the prie-Dieu.)

before this crucifix.

(Thisbe's eyes are fixed upon the crucifix.)

Oh! come, in pity's name, and pray beside me. Say, will you? And then, if you still wish my death, if the good God leaves that thought in your heart, you may do what you will.

THISBE.

(She pounces upon the crucifix, and tears it from the wall.)

What is this crucifix? Whence came it to your hands? From whom had you it? Who gave it you?

CATARINA.

What? That crucifix? Oh! this is past belief! Surely it can avail you nothing to question me about that crucifix.

THISBE.

How came it in your hands? tell me at once!

(She draws near the torch which stands upon a buffet near the balcony, and examines the crucifix. Catarina follows her.)

CATARINA.

A woman gave it me. You are looking at the name carved at the bottom—a name, I do not know,—*Thisbe*, I think. 'T was a poor woman who was to be put to death. I asked mercy for her, and as it was my father who condemned her, he granted my petition. It was at Brescia. I was a mere child. Oh! do not bring destruction on my head, signora, but have mercy on me! The woman thereupon gave me the crucifix, saying that 't would bring me luck. That 's the whole story. I swear to you that that is all. But what is it to you? Why question me about these useless things? Oh! my strength is spent!

THISBE (aside).

God's mercy! O my mother!

(The door at the rear of the stage opens. Angelo appears, in his night-dress.)

CATARINA (returning to the front of the stage).

My husband! I am lost!

SCENE VI

ANGELO.

(He does not see Thisbe, who has remained near the balcony.)

What does this mean, my lady? Methought I heard a noise here in your room.

CATARINA.

Monsignore . . .

ANGELO.

How happens it that you are not in bed at this hour?

CATARINA.

Because . . .

ANGELO.

Great Heaven! how you tremble! There 's someone with you!

THISBE (coming forward).

Yes, I, monsignore.

ANGELO.

Thisbe! You!

THISBE.

Yes, I.

ANGELO.

You here! at midnight! How happens it that you are here, that you are here at this hour, and that my lady . . .

THISBE.

Is trembling from head to foot? I 'll tell you, monsignore. It is well worth the trouble.

CATARINA (aside).

Woe 's me! the end has come.

THISBE.

In two words, 't is this. You were to be assassinated to-morrow morning.

ANGELO.

Assassinated!

THISBE.

Yes, upon your way from your palace to mine. You know that 't is your habit in the morning to go out alone. I received warning of the plot to-night, and hastened hither to warn my lady so that she might prevent your going forth to-morrow. That 's why I 'm here, why I am here at midnight, and why my lady trembles so.

CATARINA (aside).

Great God! who can this woman be?

ANGELO.

Is it possible? But after all it 's not surprising to me. You see that I was right when I described to you the perils that surround me. Who told you of the plot?

THISBE.

A man unknown to me, who first of all obtained my promise that I would take no measures to detain him. I kept my promise.

ANGELO.

You did wrong. 'T was well enough to promise, but you should have caused the man's arrest. How did you succeed in gaining entrance to the palace?

THISBE.

The stranger let me in. He found a way to open a small wicket under the Ponte Molino.

ANGELO.

Upon my word! and by what means did you reach these apartments?

THISBE.

Ah! but the key you gave me yesterday.

ANGELO.

I think I did not tell you that it would give you access to this room.

THISBE.

You did, indeed. You have forgotten.

ANGELO.

(His eye falls upon the cloak.)

Whose is that cloak?

THISBE.

A cloak that the man loaned me to wear when I entered the palace. I had his hat also, but what I did with it I know not.

ANGELO.

To think that such men go and come at will in my abode! Ah! what a life is mine. Some portion of my gown is always caught in one trap or another. Tell me, Thisbe . . .

THISBE.

Oh! pray postpone all further questions till to-morrow, monsignore. To-night we have saved your life, and you should be content with that. You do not even thank my lady and myself.

ANGELO.

Forgive me, Thisbe.

THISBE.

My litter is awaiting me below. Will you give me your hand to take me to it? We will let my lady go to sleep.

ANGELO.

At your service, Signora Thisbe. We will go through my apartment, by your leave, that I may get my sword.

(He goes to the great door at the rear.)

Hola! Bring lights!

THISBE (leading Catarina to the front of the stage).

Let him escape at once. By the same way I entered. Here's the key.

(She turns toward the oratory.)

Oh! that door! Oh! how I suffer! Not even to be certain that 't is he!

ANGELO (returning).

Signora, I await your orders.

THISBE (aside).

Oh! if I could but see him pass! But no! I must away! Ah! me!

(To Angelo.)

Come, monsignore.

CATARINA (following them with her eyes).

Is this a dream?

THIRD DAY

WHITE FOR BLACK

CATARINA.

Rodolfo!

RODOLFO. (*He runs to her and takes her in his arms.*)

(*Catarina.*) Great God! Thou here and living? How can this be?

Just Heaven!

(*Turning to Thisbe.*)

What have I done?

THIRD DAY

WHITE FOR BLACK

CATARINA.

Rudolfo !

RODOLFO. (He runs to her and takes her in his arms.)

Catarina !   Great God !   Thou here and living ?   How can this be ?
Just Heaven !

(Turning to Thisbe.)

What have I done ?

THIRD DAY

WHITE FOR BLACK

FIRST PART

The interior of a wretched hovel. A few pieces of rough furniture. A rush basket, half woven, in a corner. At the rear, a door. In the corner at the left a window, half closed with a rotten shutter. On the same side a long window entirely closed. On the opposite side, a door, and a high chimney-piece, which fills the right-hand corner. Beside the long window ropes and hurdles lying against the wall, and a pile of large stones.

SCENE I

HOMODEI, ORDELAFO.

ORDELAFO.

Look, Homodei, it 's from that window.

(Pointing to the long, closed window.)

The river flows beneath it. Whenever the serene signoria or the podesta wish to be rid of someone, they bring that someone here, dead or alive, lay him on a hurdle, tie four good stones to the four corners, and toss the whole thing through that window. The river does the rest. You have the Orfano canal at Venice, and here at Padua we have the Brenta. Can it be that you don't know this house?

HOMODEI.

I am a new-comer here. I don't as yet know all the customs of the place. However, this house is very well situated for what I want to do. In a lonely spot, and on the road that Reginella needs must take to return to the palace.

ORDELAFO.

Who is this Reginella?

HOMODEI.

There! there! confine yourself to answering my questions. Who lives in this house?

ORDELAFO.

Two bull-dogs with human faces, named Orfeo and Gaboardo. You'll see them in a moment.

HOMODEI.

What do they here?

ORDELAFO.

Night executions, disappearances of dead bodies, and the whole current of secret affairs which follows the course of the Brenta. But to resume. You were saying that the affair had fallen through.

HOMODEI.

Yes.

ORDELAFO.

What an idiot you were to think that all you needed was to set a woman on her!

HOMODEI.

You know not what you say. When one has an idea which involves a person's death, the very best weapon for which to use it as a handle is a woman's jealousy. Women, you see, are generally eager for revenge. I cannot understand what passed through this one's head. Let no one ever speak to me again of actresses as knowing how to drive a dagger home. Their tragedy is all worked out upon the stage.

ORDELAFO.

In your place I would have gone straight to the podesta, and said: "Your wife . . ."

HOMODEI.

In my place you would not have gone straight to the podesta, and you would not have said:—"Your wife;" for you know as well as I that the most illustrious Council of Ten forbids us all, myself no less than you, to have any dealings whatsoever with the podesta, until such time as we are bidden to arrest him. You know full well that I can neither speak to the podesta, nor write to him, on peril of my life, and that I am closely watched. Who knows? Perhaps it is yourself that watches me!

ORDELAFO.

Homodei, we are friends!

HOMODEI.

So much the worse. I am not supposed to suspect you.

ORDELAFO.

Oh! my dear friend Homodei!

HOMODEI.

But then, you see, I do suspect you.

ORDELAFO.

I know not what I have done to you.

HOMODEI.

Nothing but ask foolish questions. And then I'm in no pleasant mood. Good! we are friends. Give me your hand.

ORDELAFO.

So you renounce all thought of vengeance?

HOMODEI.

Renounce my life, rather! Ordelafo, you have never loved a woman, you know not what it is to love a woman, and have her turn you out of doors and humble you and buffet you with your own name, by calling you a spy when you are a spy. Oh! in such case, what one feels for that woman, for that Catarina, is not love you see, nor hate, but a love that hates! A fearful, burning, thirsty passion, which drinks from but one cup, revenge! I'll be revenged on her. I'll seize her, and drag her by the feet into the tomb! I'll do it, Ordelafo!

ORDELAFO.

Your plan has failed. How will you do it?

HOMODEI.

I have another plan already.

(He goes to the window at the rear.)

Look, Ordelafo! you can help me. Come hither. Dost see a woman yonder in a red mantle, coming this way?

ORDELAFO.

What then?

HOMODEI.

Go out as if you did not notice her. When you meet her, you will let her pass, then turn and softly follow her. When she's before the house—be sure and leave the door ajar—give her a sudden push against the door. 'T will yield, and I will help you bring her in the house. The rest is my affair.

ORDELAFO.

Agreed.

HOMODEI.

Is anyone in sight?

(He looks out.)

No, not a soul. If she shrieks, let her shriek. Go.

(Exit Ordelafo.)

HOMODEI *(alone).*

This house is excellently placed. The pope might be assassinated here, and no Christian hear his cries.

(Footsteps near the door. It flies open, and Reginella appears, gagged with a handkerchief. Ordelafo is pushing her into the house.)

SCENE II

HOMODEI, ORDELAFO, REGINELLA.

ORDELAFO.

I gagged her to make doubly sure.

HOMODEI.

You did well.

(*He removes the gag.*)

REGINELLA (in deadly terror).

Heaven's mercy, monsignore!

HOMODEI.

Nonsense, be not afraid. You weary me. Be calm, and answer. Since you know me, you cannot fear me. I spoke with you last night, you know. I am the man. Certes, I did you no harm then. Your name is Reginella. 'T was you who used to guide Signor Rodolfo to his assignations with Signora Catarina in the old Magaruffi Palace. This morning, about an hour since, Rodolfo met you near the Ponte Altina, not far from here. He handed you a letter for your mistress.

REGINELLA.

Monsignore . . .

HOMODEI.

Give me the letter.

REGINELLA.

Here it is.

HOMODEI.

Good.

(*He tears the letter open.*)

REGINELLA.

You break the seal, monsignore?

HOMODEI.

I know not why you call me monsignore. I am a spy. It is mere craven fear, and does not flatter me.

(*He reads the letter.*)

That will do. He did not sign it, more 's the pity. I must find a way to let the podesta know his name.

(*A key is thrust into the lock. A man dressed in gray enters. Gray hair, great, coarse hands, and a dirty face. There is a general appearance of griminess about him.*)

HOMODEI.

Who is this man?

ORDELAFO.

One of the bull-dogs, of whom I spoke to you. This one answers to the name of Orfeo. The other will soon be here. As he is awake all night, he sleeps by day.

(*The man approaches Homodei, and scrutinizes him with a savage expression.*)

Let him know who you are.

(*Homodei half opens his frock. At sight of the three letters the man puts his hand to his cap.*)

ORDELAFO (to Orfeo).

Go and lie down.

(*He retires into a corner without a word.*)

HOMODEI.

Is there another exit from the house?

ORDELAFO.

Yes. Through that door. It opens on the Strada Scalona.

HOMODEI.

Go you out that way with the girl, and walk her about all day.

(Exit Ordelafo and Reginella.)

(Orfeo is still at the rear of the stage in the shadow, sitting beside a basket he is weaving.)

HOMODEI (aside).

I have already made great progress. But this letter! how can I send it to Malipieri? and how acquaint him with Rodolfo's name? Meanwhile I must not keep the letter on my person. Where can I put it safely out of sight?

(He spies a table with a drawer.)

Can I lock this drawer? Yes. 'T is well.

(He puts the letter in the drawer and takes the key.)

Orfeo!

(The man rises and approaches him.)

Is not Orfeo your name? I am going hence. Keep good watch to-night, you and your comrade. It may be that someone will be brought to you to be put out of sight. A woman.

ORFEO.

The Brenta 's there.

(He returns to his corner.)

HOMODEI (resuming his seat).

Oh! how vexatious to be unable to write to the podesta or speak to him! How that would simplify the thing!

(He rests his elbows upon the table and his head upon his hands, as if in deep thought.)

(At this moment Rodolfo's face appears at the window at the rear.)

RODOLFO.

Methinks that that man much resembles . . .

(He opens the shutter a little farther.)

I am not mistaken. 'T is he. 'T is that villain, Homodei! Yes, there he sits.

(He closes the shutter and disappears.)

HOMODEI (rising).

Well, I must find some way to inform the podesta. Ah! the key of the drawer. Have I it? Yes. 'T is well.

(Exit by the door at the rear of the stage, which closes after him.)

(Loud voices without.)

FIRST VOICE.

Defend yourself, villain!

SECOND VOICE.

Who is it? you, signor!

FIRST VOICE.

Defend yourself, I say!

SECOND VOICE.

Signor Rodolfo!

FIRST VOICE.

Defend yourself, vile caitiff! or I will kill you like a dog!

(The clash of swords is heard.)

ORFEO (alone in the hovel, raising his head).

It seems to me that someone 's being killed out there.

(He resumes his weaving.)

SECOND VOICE.

Ah!

FIRST VOICE.

You owe me your life, Homodei, pay it now.

SECOND VOICE.

Ah!

(The noise ceases. Someone walks rapidly away.)

ORFEO (still at his weaving).

There is one dead.

(Several violent blows at the door.)

Who 's there?

A VOICE (outside).

I. Open.

ORFEO.

Ah! is it you, Gaboardo?

(He opens the door. Enters Gaboardo, carrying Homodei, whose legs drag on the ground. Gaboardo is the counterpart of Orfeo.)

SCENE III

ORFEO, GABOARDO, HOMODEI.

ORFEO (examining Homodei).

The devil! 't is the man who was here just now.

GABOARDO.

'T was a young gentleman who killed him, and made off at a great pace when I came up. A fine young man, i' faith !

ORFEO.

Is he quite dead ?

GABOARDO.

He looks it.

ORFEO.

Shake him a bit. Hardly any blood has come from the wound.

GABOARDO.

He 's none the better for that.

HOMODEI (opening his eyes).

Oh ! Where am I ? I am choking ! Is it you, Orfeo ? Is that you, comrade ? Oh ! Take my purse, here, in my pocket. 'T is for you.

(Orfeo fumbles in his pockets.)

GABOARDO (to Orfeo).

No ; don't take the trouble. I have already taken it.

HOMODEI.

I understand that you have taken it. 'T is well. You seem quick witted. I will explain to you what you must do. There 's a key also in my pocket. Oh ! you torture me ! No matter, take it. Good. 'T is the key of yonder drawer. Go you and open it. What is your name ?

GABOARDO.

Gaboardo.

HOMODEI.

Gaboardo. Good. Open the drawer. There is a paper there. Bring it to me. Good. You must take this paper to the podesta. Dost hear ? dost understand ? To the podesta. This paper. Oh ! I am dead. Something to write with—quick !

ORFEO.

Write ! What is that ?

GABOARDO.

We have nothing.

HOMODEI (in a frenzy).

Nothing to write with ! Ah !

(He falls back, then sits up again.)

Well, listen to me. Listen, Gaboardo. You will seek out the podesta, Monsignore Malipieri, with this paper, which is a letter. Dost hear ? He will give you a hundred golden sequins ! Dost hear ? You will say to the podesta that this letter was written by his wife by his wife's lover—oh ! I am choking !—whose name 's Rodolfo. Whose name 's Rodolfo. Remember that. Oh ! I am dying, but my vengeance will live after me. If 't is you who bury me, pray leave my right arm above ground, uplifted, to typify my vengeance. Rodolfo, you understand? Come, what have I said to you? Repeat it.

GABOARDO.

You said someone would give us a hundred gold sequins.

HOMODEI.

No! not that. Hold my head higher so that I can speak. Now listen. The podesta will not give you the hundred sequins unless you tell him.—Ah! Listen. Carry him the letter: the podesta. His wife has a lover. Tell him that. Who wrote the letter. Tell him that. Whose name 's Rodolfo. Tell him that. Ah! I feel that I am suffocating. This means death. Raise my head once more.

O misery! to die and have no one to whom to intrust my vengeance but these imbeciles! Dost understand? Rod—Rod—olfo.

(His head falls back.)

GABOARDO.

Dead. Now for the podesta. A hundred golden sequins. The devil! Have I the letter? Yes. Do you remember all he said, Orfeo? Tell the podesta that his wife has a lover, who wrote this letter, and whose name is——. What did he say?

ORFEO.

He said Roderigo.

GABOARDO.

No; he said Pandolfo.

THIRD DAY

WHITE FOR BLACK

SECOND PART

Catarina's apartment. The curtains are drawn close around the platform.

SCENE I

ANGELO, TWO PRIESTS.

ANGELO (to the first priest).

Signor Decano, of Saint Anthony's of Padua, you will forthwith cause the nave and choir and high altar of your church to be hung with black. Two hours hence—two hours hence—you will perform a solemn service for the soul's repose of an illustrious personage who will depart this world at that precise moment. You will be present at the service with your whole chapter. You will cause the saint's shrine to be uncovered. You will light three hundred white wax candles, as for a queen's demise. You will select six hundred poor persons, each one to receive a silver ducat and a gold sequin. On the black hangings there will be no other blazonry than the arms of Malipieri and of Bragadini. The escutcheon of Malipieri is of gold with the eagle's talon; that of Bragadini silver and azure with the red cross.

231

THE DEAN.

Mighty podesta.

ANGELO.

Tush ! You will go down at once with all your clergy, cross and banner at their head, to the vaults of this ducal palace, where are the tombs of the Romanas. A stone has been raised there, and a grave newly dug. You will bless the grave. Lose no time. You will also pray for me.

THE DEAN.

Is it one of your kindred, monsignore ?

ANGELO.

Go !

(The dean bows low and goes off through the door at the rear. The other priest prepares to follow him, but Angelo detains him.)

Do you remain, Signor Archpriest. There is in yonder oratory a person whom you must confess at once.

THE ARCHPRIEST.

A condemned man, monsignore ?

ANGELO.

A woman.

THE ARCHPRIEST.

Am I to prepare this woman for her death ?

ANGELO.

Yes. I will lead you thither.

(An usher enters.)

THE USHER.

Your Excellency caused Signora Thisbe to be sent for. She is here.

ANGELO.

Let her come in and await me here an instant.

(Exit the usher. The podesta opens the door of the oratory, and motions to the archpriest to go in. On the threshold he stops him.)

Signor Archpriest, upon your life, when you go hence, be mindful not to say to any one on earth the woman's name whom you are now to see.

(He enters the oratory with the priest. The door at the rear opens, and Thisbe is ushered in.)

THISBE (to the usher).

Do you know why he sends for me ?

THE USHER.

Signora, no.

(Exit the usher.)

SCENE II

THISBE (alone).

Ah! this room! once again I am in this room! What can the podesta want with me? The palace wears an ominous appearance this morning. What matters it to me? I would give my life to know the truth. Ah! that door! It gives me a strange feeling to see that door again by daylight! It was behind that door that the man was. But who? Who was behind that door? Can I be sure that it was he? I have not even seen the spy again. Oh! this uncertainty! this frightful phantom which besets me and gazes askance at me, with neither smiles or tears! If I were sure it was Rodolfo—as sure I well might be with such convincing proofs—Oh! I would crush him. I would denounce him to the podesta. No. But I would be revenged upon that woman. No. Then I would kill myself. Ah! yes, for were I sure Rodolfo loves me not, sure that he has deceived me, sure that he loves another, in God's name what should I have to do with life? 't would have no charm for me, and I would die. But unrevenged? Why not? Ah, yes! I say that at this moment, but I know 't is very possible that I may yet take my revenge. Can I be answerable for what might take place in my heart if it were proved to me that last night's lover was Rodolfo? O God! preserve me from an outbreak of jealous fury! O Rodolfo! Catarina! Oh! if 't were true, what should I do? what should I do? Whom should I kill? them or myself? I cannot say.

(Enters Angelo.)

SCENE III

THISBE, ANGELO.

THISBE.

You sent for me, monsignore.

ANGELO.

Yes, Thisbe. I must speak with you. I absolutely must speak with you. And of matters of great gravity. I told you that in my life some snare is laid each day, some treachery devised, a dagger-thrust to be received, or a blow of the headsman's axe to be administered. In a word, my wife has a lover.

THISBE.

Whose name is . . . ?

ANGELO.

Who was with her last night when we were here.

THISBE.

Whose name is . . . ?

ANGELO.

Thus 't was discovered. A certain man, a spy of the Ten—these spies of the Ten, you know, do hold a strange position with reference to us podestas of the mainland. The Council forbids them, on their lives, to write to us, or speak to us, or have relations of any sort with us until the day that they are bidden to arrest us. One of these spies, then, was found poniarded this morning, on the river bank, close by the Ponte Altina. The two night-watchmen found him. Was it a duel? or an ambuscade? They do not know. The spy could say but a few words. He was dying, and as ill-luck would have it, he is dead! When he was stricken down, he had, so it would seem, presence of mind sufficient to retain possession of a letter which he had intercepted, doubtless, and which he delivered to the night-watchmen to be conveyed to me. The letter has been handed me by them. It is a letter written to my wife by a lover.

THISBE.

Whose name is . . . ?

ANGELO.

The letter is not signed. You ask me the lover's name? 'T is that which most embarrasses me. The murdered man told the name to the night-watchmen. But they, the idiots, have forgotten it! They cannot agree at all regarding it. One says Roderigo, the other Pandolfo.

THISBE.

Have you the letter?

ANGELO (putting his hand in his breast).

Yes, I have it with me. I sent for you expressly to show it you. If by any chance you know the writing, you will tell me whose it is.

(He takes out the letter.)

Here it is.

THISBE.

Give it me.

ANGELO (crumpling the letter in his hands).

But I am in frightful trouble, Thisbe! There is a man who has dared—has dared to lift his eyes to a Malipieri's wife! There is a man who has dared to make a blot on the Venetian Book of Gold at its fairest page, the page that bears my name! my name! Malipieri! There is a man who was in this room last night, and who perhaps trod on the very spot where I now stand! There is a vile wretch who wrote this letter, and I may not lay my hand upon him! I may not nail my vengeance over the insult put upon me! I may not cause his blood to flow in streams upon this floor! Oh! I would give my father's sword and ten years of my life, and my right hand, to know who wrote this letter!

THISBE.

Pray let me see the letter.

ANGELO (passes it to her).

Take it.

THISBE (unfolds the letter and glances at it).

(Aside.)

'T is Rodolfo!

ANGELO.

Do you know the hand?

THISBE.

Let me read it.

"Catarina, my poor love, thou seest that God protects us. We were saved last night as by a miracle from thy husband and that woman."

(Aside.)

That woman!

"I love thee, my own Catarina. Thou art the only woman I have ever loved. Fear not for me, my safety is assured."

ANGELO.

Well, do you know the hand?

THISBE (returning the letter).

No, monsignore.

ANGELO.

You do not? And what say you to the letter? It cannot be a man who has come recently to Padua, for 't is the language of a long-standing flame. Oh! I will have the whole city searched, for I must find the fellow! What is your counsel, Thisbe?

THISBE.

Search.

ANGELO.

I have given orders that no one be admitted to the palace to-day save you and your brother, whom you may need to see. All others will be seized and brought before me. I will question them myself. Meanwhile I have one-half of my revenge here at my hand, and I propose to take it. .

THISBE.

What do you mean?

ANGELO.

To put my wife to death.

THISBE.

Your wife!

ANGELO.

Yes, all is ready. Within the hour Catarina Bragadini will be beheaded, as 't is meet she should be.

THISBE.

Beheaded!

ANGELO.

In this room.

THISBE.

In this room!

ANGELO.

Listen. My dishonored bed becomes her tomb. The woman must die, for I have so resolved. My resolution was too dispassionately formed to be relaxed. There is no anger in my heart to be appeased by prayers. Were my best friend, if friend I had, to intercede for her, I should distrust my friend.

That 's the whole story. Let us talk of it, if you choose. And then, you see, I hate the woman, Thisbe ! A woman to whom I let myself be married for family reasons—because my affairs were sadly disordered in my embassies,—and to please my uncle, the Bishop of Castello ; a woman whose face is always sad and her whole bearing woe-begone before me ! and who has never borne me children ! Moreover hatred 's in the blood and the traditions of our family. A Malipieri must always hate someone. On that day when the Lion of Saint Mark's flies from his pedestal, hatred will spread her wings of bronze, and fly from the Malipieri heart. My grandsire hated Marquis Azzo, and had him drowned by night in the wells of Venice. My father hated the procurator Badoër, and had him poisoned at a banquet given by Queen Cornaro. I hate that woman. I would not have harmed her ; but she is guilty. So much the worse for her. She shall be punished. 'T is possible that I am in no wise better than she, but she must die. Her death is necessary. My mind is fixed. I tell you that the woman shall die. Mercy for her ! though my own mother's bones should plead for it, they 'd not obtain it !

THISBE.

But does the most serene Signoria of Venice give you permission ?

ANGELO.

None at all to pardon, but unrestricted power to punish.

THISBE.

And your wife's family, the Bragadinis ?

ANGELO.

Will thank me.

THISBE.

Your mind 's made up, you say, and she must die. 'T is well. I approve your purpose.

But since the whole affair is still unknown, and since no name has been pronounced, could you not spare your wife a moment's suffering, this palace a blood-stain, and yourself publicity and gossip? The headsman is a witness, and one witness is too many.

ANGELO.

True. Poison would be far better. But a swift poison 's necessary, and, if you 'll believe me, I have none such at hand.

THISBE.

But I have.

ANGELO.

Where ?

THISBE.

At my apartments.

ANGELO.

What is the poison ?

THISBE.

The Malaspina poison. You remember ? the box the primicerius of Saint Mark's did send me.

ANGELO.

Yes, you have told me of it heretofore. It is a sure poison, swift in its effects. Yes, you are right. 'T is better that the whole affair be kept between ourselves. Hark ye, Thisbe, I have full confidence in you. You understand that this that I am forced to do is lawful. I but avenge mine honor, and every man would do in my place as I do. This is a dark and difficult affair in which I am embarked. I have no friend therein save you. I can confide in none but you. Speedy execution and secrecy are for this woman's interest as well as for my own. Help me. I need your help. I ask it of you. Do you agree ?

THISBE.

Yes.

ANGELO.

Let the woman disappear in such wise that no one will know how she disappears, or why. A grave is dug, a service chanted, but no one knows for whom. I 'll have the body carried off by these same men, the two night-watchmen, whom I have under lock and key. Yes, you are right, and we will throw a veil over the whole affair. Send for the poison.

THISBE.

I alone know where it is. I must go myself.

ANGELO.

Go; I await you.

(Exit Thisbe.)

Yes, 't is better so. The crime was done under cover of the darkness, let darkness veil the punishment.

(The door of the oratory opens. The archpriest comes out with downcast eyes and with his arms crossed upon his breast. He walks slowly across the room. As he is about to pass through the door at the rear, Angelo turns toward him.)

Is she prepared?

THE ARCHPRIEST.

Yes, monsignore.

(Exit the archpriest. Catarina appears at the oratory door.)

SCENE IV

ANGELO, CATARINA.

CATARINA.

Prepared for what ?

ANGELO.

To die.

CATARINA.

To die !   Can it be true ? can it be possible ?
Oh ! I cannot accustom myself to the thought !
Die !   No, I am not prepared.   I am not prepared.   My lord, I am in no respect prepared
to die !

ANGELO.

How much time must you have to be prepared ?

CATARINA.

Oh ! I do not know—a long, long time !

ANGELO.

Pray, is your courage like to fail you, my
lady ?

CATARINA.

To die so suddenly !   Why, I have done
nothing to deserve death, surely I have done
nothing !   My lord, my lord, another day !
No, not a day, for I am sure that I shall be no
braver on the morrow.   Life, life !   Spare my
life !   A cloister, if you choose !   Ah ! tell
me if 't is indeed impossible that you should
spare my life ?

ANGELO.

No.   I may spare your life, I have already
told you, upon one condition.

CATARINA.

What is the condition ?   I have forgotten.

ANGELO.

Who wrote this letter ?   Name the man to
me !   Place him in my power !

CATARINA (wringing her hands).

My God !

ANGELO.

Well, you do not reply.

CATARINA.

Yes.   I do reply ; my God !

ANGELO.

Pray, come to some decision, madame !

CATARINA.

I was cold in yonder oratory.   I am very
cold.   •

ANGELO.

Hark ye, my lady.   It is my wish to be
most kind to you.   You have an hour still
before you ; an hour, that is yours to do with
as you please, and during which you will be
left alone.   No one will enter here.   Devote
the hour to reflection.   I place the letter on
the table.   Write the man's name beneath,
and you are saved.   Catarina Bragadini, the
mouth that speaks to you is made of marble ; you must unmask the man or die.   You
have an hour in which to make your choice.

CATARINA.

Oh ! a day !

ANGELO.

One hour.

(Exit Angelo.)

SCENE V

CATARINA (alone).

This door.

(She runs to the door.)

Ah ! I hear him bolt it on the other side !

(She goes to the window.)

This window . . .

(She looks out.)

Oh ! how high it is !

(She falls upon a chair.)

To die ! God's mercy ! 't is a fearful thought when it comes thus suddenly upon you at the moment when you least expect it ! To have but one short hour to live, and then to tell one's self : " I have but one hour more !" Ah ! to know how horrible it is one must needs have it happen to one's self ! I ache in every limb. Even this arm-chair hurts me.

(She rises.)

My bed would rest me more, I think, if I could have one instant of oblivion !

(She goes to the bed.)

One instant of repose !

(She draws the curtain aside and recoils in horror. Where the bed stood there stands a block covered with a black cloth, and an axe.)

Great Heaven ! what do I see ? Oh ! this is too horrible !

(She draws the curtain together again convulsively.)

Oh ! I cannot endure the sight ! My God ! and 't is for me ! My God ! I am alone here with that horror !

(She drags herself to the chair.)

Behind me ! 't is behind me ! Oh ! I dare not turn my head. Mercy ! mercy ! Ah ! 't is no dream, you see that what is happening here is stern reality, for there are fearful things behind the curtain !

(The little door at the rear opens. Rodolfo appears.)

SCENE VI

CATARINA, RODOLFO.

CATARINA (aside).

Just Heaven ! Rodolfo !

RODOLFO (running to her).

Yes, Catarina, it is I. For a brief moment. Thou art alone. What bliss ! But thou art deathly pale, and hast an anxious look !

CATARINA.

Well may I have, and thou so rash and heedless, to come here in broad daylight at this time !

RODOLFO.

Ah ! I was too ill at ease. I could not stay away.

CATARINA.

Why ill at ease ?

RODOLFO.

I 'll tell you, Catarina, my beloved. Ah ! in good sooth it makes me very happy to find you in such tranquil mood.

CATARINA.

How did you gain admission ?

RODOLFO.

The key thou gavest me thyself.

CATARINA.

I know ; but to the palace ?

RODOLFO.

That is one thing that makes me anxious. I came in without difficulty, but fear that I shall not go out so easily.

CATARINA.

Why not ?

RODOLFO.

The *grande-capitano* informed me at the palace gate that no one could go out before nightfall.

CATARINA.

No one before nightfall !

(Aside.)

No possible escape ! God help us !

RODOLFO.

Sbirri are posted on every corridor. The palace is as closely guarded as a prison. I managed to slip into the great gallery, and came to you. Have I thy word that nothing is toward ?

CATARINA.

No. Nothing, nothing ; fear not, my Rodolfo. Here everything is quite as usual. Look about. Thou seest that nothing in the room is disarranged. But go at once. I tremble lest the podesta return.

RODOLFO.

No, Catarina. Fear nothing in that quarter. The podesta is at this moment down yonder on the Ponte Molino. He 's questioning some people who have been arrested. Ah ! I was very anxious, Catarina ! Everything to-day wears a strange aspect, the city no less so than the palace. Bands of archers and of Venetian cernides are marching through the

streets. St. Anthony's church is hung with
black, and the offices for the dead are being
chanted there. For whom? No one can say.
Do you know?

CATARINA.

No.

RODOLFO.

I could not make my way into the church.
The city seems in a sort of stupor. Everybody speaks beneath his breath. 'T is sure
that something terrible is happening somewhere. Where? I have no idea. It is not
here, and that is all I need to know. Dear
love, here in thy solitude, thou hadst no
thought of this.

CATARINA.

No.

RODOLFO.

Indeed, what matters it to us? Tell me,
hast thou recovered from last night's excitement? What an adventure! I still am all
at sea concerning it. Catarina, I have rid
you of the sbirro Homodei. He 'll do thee
no more harm.

CATARINA.

Thinkest thou so?

RODOLFO.

He 's dead. Catarina! there certainly is
something wrong with thee, thou seemest so
sad. Catarina! thou art hiding nothing from
me? At least, no harm has come to thee?
Ah! they should have my life before thine!

CATARINA.

No, there is nothing. I swear to thee that
there is nothing. 'T is only that I wish that
thou wert far away. I am alarmed for thee.

RODOLFO.

What wert thou doing when I came?

CATARINA.

In God's name, set your mind at rest,
my own Rodolfo; I was not sad, far from it.
I was trying to recall the air you sing so
beautifully. See, I have my guitar still here.

RODOLFO.

I wrote to thee this morning. I met
Reginella, and handed her the letter. It was
not intercepted? It reached thy hand?

CATARINA.

It reached my hand so surely, that 't is
here.

(She shows him the letter.)

RODOLFO.

Ah! thou hast it! 'T is well. One is
always anxious when one writes.

CATARINA.

All the issues from the palace guarded!
No one to go forth before nightfall!

RODOLFO.

No one, as I told thee. Such are the
orders.

CATARINA.

Come, now you have seen me and have
spoken to me; your mind is set at rest; you
see that if the city is excited all is tranquil
here. Go, my Rodolfo, in Heaven's name!
Suppose the podesta should come! Go,
quickly! Since thou must needs abide till
evening in the palace, I will myself arrange
thy cloak about thee. So. Thy hat upon
thy head. And then, in presence of the
sbirri, assume an easy, unconcerned demeanor.
Seek not to avoid them, and take no precautions—precautions cause suspicion. And
if, perchance, some spy or anyone should lay
a snare for thee, and seek to make thee write
something, find some excuse, and do not
write.

RODOLFO.

Why that last caution, Catarina?

CATARINA.

Why? Because I do not wish that they should see your writing. 'T is a whim of mine. You know that women have these whims, my dear. I thank thee for having come, for having come to me and stayed with me; it has given me the greatest joy to see thee. Thou seest that I am calm and joyous and content, and that I have thy letter and my guitar Now go quickly. I wish that you would go. One other word.

RODOLFO.

What, my beloved?

CATARINA.

Thou knowest, Rodolfo, that I have never yielded in aught to thee. Surely thou knowest it.

RODOLFO.

Even so.

CATARINA.

To-day 't is I who ask thee for a kiss, Rodolfo.

RODOLFO (throwing his arms about her).

Oh! this is heaven!

CATARINA.

I see it opening before me.

RODOLFO.

O rapture!

CATARINA.

Art thou happy?

RODOLFO.

Yes.

CATARINA.

Now go, Rodolfo, mine.

RODOLFO.

A thousand thanks!

CATARINA.

Farewell!—Rodolfo!

(Rodolfo, who is at the door, stops.)

I love thee!

(Exit Rodolfo.)

SCENE VII

CATARINA (alone).

To fly with him! I thought upon it for a moment. Oh God! to fly with him! impossible! I should have brought destruction on him to no purpose. Oh! if only nothing happens to him! if only the sbirri do not arrest him! if only they let him go this evening! No, there is no reason why suspicion should fall upon him. Save him, my God!

(She listens at the door leading into the corridor.)

I can still hear his steps. My own beloved! They grow fainter. Now I hear nothing. 'T is over. Go in safety, my Rodolfo!

(The great door opens.)

Heaven help me!

(Enter Angelo and Thisbe.)

SCENE VIII

CATARINA, ANGELO, THISBE.

CATARINA (aside).

Who is this woman ? The woman of last night !

ANGELO.

Have you reflected well, my lady ?

CATARINA.

Yes, my lord.

ANGELO.

You must die or deliver to me the man who wrote the letter. Have you decided to give up the man, my lady ?

CATARINA.

Not for a single instant have I thought of it, my lord.

THISBE (aside).

Thou art a brave and noble-hearted woman, Catarina !

(Angelo signals to Thisbe, who hands him a silver phial. He places it upon the table.)

ANGELO.

Then you will drink the contents of this phial ?

CATARINA.

Is it poison ?

ANGELO.

It is, madame.

CATARINA.

O God in heaven ! some day thou wilt judge this man. I pray thy pardon for him.

ANGELO.

Madame, the Proveditore Urseolo, a Bragadini, one of your ancestors, did put to death Marcella Galbaï, his wife, in the same way, for the same crime.

CATARINA.

Let us speak plainly. There is no question here of Bragadinis. You are a villain ! How coolly you come hither with poison in your hand ! Guilty ? No, I am not. At least, not as you think. But I 'll not stoop to justify myself. And you, who always lie, would not believe me. Upon my soul, I utterly despise you ! You took me to wife for my money, because I was rich, because my family has water-rights in the *cilernas* of Venice. You said: "I 'll take this girl, she 'll bring me in a hundred thousand ducats yearly." And what manner of life have I lived with you these five years past ? You love me not. Yet you are jealous. You keep me in a prison. You have mistresses, that is your privilege. Men can do anything. Always harsh and stern with me. Never a kind word. Talking incessantly about your ancestors, about the doges that have been of your family, and ridiculing mine. Think you that that 's the way to make a woman happy ? Oh ! one must needs have suffered all that I have suffered, to understand the lot of womankind. Yes, my lord, ere I knew you, I loved a man whom I still love. You murder me for that. If you 've that right you must agree that these are fearful times of ours. Ah! you are very happy, are you not? to have a letter, a scrap of paper, a pretext! Very good! You try me, sentence me and execute me. In the dark. In secret. By poison. The strength is on your side. It is a dastard's deed!

(Turning to Thisbe.)

What think you of this man, signora?

ANGELO.

Beware!

CATARINA (to Thisbe).

And who are you? What have you to do with me? This is a noble deed that you are doing. You are my husband's avowed mistress, and 't is your interest to ruin me; you set your spies upon me, took me unawares, and now you put your foot upon my neck. You aid my husband in his abominable scheme. Who knows! Perhaps 't is you who furnish him the poison!

(To Angelo.)

What think you of this woman, my lord?

ANGELO.

Madame . . .

CATARINA.

In sooth, this is a most execrable country, of which we three are subjects! An odious republic is that wherein a man can trample with impunity upon a woman, as you are doing now, my lord; and wherein other men will say to him: "Thou doest well." Foscari had his daughter put to death; Loredano his wife; Bragadini . . . Pray, is it not rank infamy? All Venice is at this moment in this room; all Venice in your two persons! Nothing is lacking.

(She points to Angelo.)

Venice, the despot, there.

(She points to Thisbe.)

Venice, the harlot, here.

(To Thisbe.)

If I do go too far in what I say, signora, so much the worse for you! Why are you here?

ANGELO (grasping her arm).

Come, let 's have done with this, my lady!

CATARINA (approaching the table on which stands the phial).

I will do what you wish,

(She puts out her hand toward the phial.)

if there is no escape . . .

(She recoils.)

No, no, it is too horrible! I will not do it! I could never do it! Pray think on what you do, before it is too late. You, whose power is limitless, reflect. A woman, a solitary and deserted woman, who has no strength, who has no power to defend herself, who has no relatives at hand. No family, or friends! And you would murder her! would poison her by stealth here in a corner of your house! O mother! mother! mother!

THISBE.

Poor woman!

CATARINA.

You said, "poor woman," madame! you said it! I heard you say it! Oh! do not tell me that you did not say it! Then you have pity for me, madame! Oh! pray do not resist your feeling of compassion! You see that I am to be murdered! Are you, too, in the plot? It is not possible! Oh, no! you are not, are you? Stay, I will explain the affair to you, and tell you the whole story. Then you will speak to the podesta. You 'll say to him that this he 's doing is a fearful thing. That I should say so is to be expected, but from your lips 't will have much more effect. Sometimes a single word from a third person

is quite enough to bring a man to reason. If
I insulted you a moment since, I pray you,
pardon me. Signora, I have never done
aught that was wrong, really wrong. I have
been always chaste. You understand me, that
I see. Alas! I cannot say it to my husband.
Men, you know, are never willing to believe
us. And yet we sometimes tell them things
that are most true. I pray you, madame, do
not tell me to have courage. Pray, am I con-
strained to be courageous? I am not ashamed
that I am naught but a weak woman, to whom
you should show mercy. I weep because I
am afraid to die. 'T is not my fault.

ANGELO.

Madame, I can no longer wait your pleasure.

CATARINA.

Aha! you interrupt me.

(To Thisbe.)

See how he interrupts me. It is not fair.
He sees that what I say to you is like to move
your pity, and so he cuts me short.

(To Angelo.)

You are a monster!

ANGELO.

This is too much! Catarina Bragadini, the
crime demands due punishment, the open
grave demands a coffin, the outraged husband
demands a dead wife. All the words that
thou dost utter are absolutely thrown away—I
swear it by God in heaven!

(He points to the poison.)

Will you drink it, madame?

CATARINA.

No!

ANGELO.

No? Then I recur to my first plan. The
swords! the swords! Troïlo! let some one go
—No. I will go myself.

(He rushes violently through the door at the rear of
the stage, and is heard to secure it on the other
side.)

SCENE IX

CATARINA, THISBE.

THISBE.

Listen ! Quickly ! we have but an instant. Since he loves you, your welfare only must be looked to. Do what he wishes, or you 're lost. I cannot explain myself more clearly. You are not prudent. Just now I inadvertently exclaimed : "Poor woman !" And you at once, like a mad woman, repeated it aloud before the podesta, and thereby risked arousing his suspicions. If I should tell you all, you are so wrought up that you 'd do some foolish thing, and all would then be lost. Yield to his will, and drink. Swords do not pardon. Resist no longer. What would you have me say to you? 'T is you who are beloved, and 't is my wish that some one should be under obligation to me. You do not realize how to say this that I am saying to you tears my very heart !

CATARINA.

Signora.

THISBE.

Do as he bids you do. No more resistance. Not a word. Above all, do nothing to disturb the confidence your husband has in me. Do you understand? I dare not tell you more, because of your mania for repeating everything. There 's a poor woman in this room, who 's soon to die, but 't is not you. Do you agree ?

CATARINA.

I will do as you wish, signora.

THISBE.

'T is well. I hear him returning.

(She throws herself against the door at the rear, just as it is opened.)

Alone ! alone ! come in alone !

(Enters Angelo. Sbirri can be seen through the door, standing with bare swords in the adjoining room. The door is closed.)

SCENE X

CATARINA, THISBE, ANGELO.

THISBE.

She will take the poison.

ANGELO (to Catarina).

Then do so on the instant, madame.

CATARINA (taking the phial).

(To Thisbe.)

I know that you 're my husband's mistress. If your secret thoughts be treacherous, and based upon your wish to see me dead, and fill my place, which you are mad to envy me, 't would be a most abominable thing, madame, and hard though it be to die at twenty-two, I would far rather do what I do now, than take your guilt upon my soul.

(She drinks.)

THISBE (aside).

Great God! how many useless words!

ANGELO (goes to the door at the rear of the stage and half opens it).

You may go.

CATARINA.

Oh! that draught doth freeze my blood!

(Gazing earnestly at Thisbe.)

Ah! signora!

(To Angelo.)

Are you content, my lord? I feel that death is near. I fear you now no more. I tell you now, demon, as I shall tell my God a moment hence: I have loved a man, but I am pure.

ANGELO.

I believe you not, madame.

THISBE (aside).

But I believe her.

CATARINA.

I feel my senses leaving me. No, not that chair. Lay not your hand upon me. I have already told you, you 're a villain!

(She walks unsteadily toward her oratory.)

I wish to die upon my knees, before yonder altar. To die alone, at peace, without your eyes upon me.

(She reaches the door and leans against the framework.)

I wish to die, praying to God.

(To Angelo.)

For you, my lord.

(She enters the oratory.)

ANGELO.

Troïlo!

(Enters the usher.)

Take from my purse the key of my secret room. There you will find two men. Bring them to me without a word to them.

(Exit the usher.)

(To Thisbe.)

Now I must go and question those who have been arrested. When I have spoken with the night-watchmen, Thisbe, I 'll trust to you to look to what remains to do. But above all things, secrecy!

(Enter Orfeo and Gaboardo, shown in by the usher, who withdraws at once.)

SCENE XI

ANGELO, THISBE, ORFEO, GABOARDO.

ANGELO (to the night-watchmen).

You have been many times employed to do night executions in this palace. You know the crypt where the tombs are?

GABOARDO.

Yes, monsignore.

ANGELO.

Are the passages leading thither so well concealed, that to-day for instance, when the palace overflows with soldiers, you can go down into the crypt, and thence go from the palace without being seen by anyone?

GABOARDO.

We can go in and out without being seen by anyone, monsignore.

ANGELO.

'T is well.

(He partly opens the door of the oratory.)

There lies a woman dead in there. You are to take her secretly into the crypt. There

you will find one tile displaced, and a grave freshly dug beneath it. You will bestow the woman in the grave, and then replace the tile. You understand?

GABOARDO.

Yes, monsignore.

ANGELO.

You must needs pass through my apartment. I 'll go and see that no one 's there.

(To Thisbe.)

Pray see that everything is done in secret.

(Exit Angelo.)

THISBE (taking a purse from her girdle).

Two hundred golden sequins in this purse. For you. To-morrow morning twice that sum if you do faithfully all that I bid you do.

GABOARDO (taking the purse).

It 's a bargain, my lady. Where must we go?

THISBE.

First to the crypt.

THIRD DAY

WHITE FOR BLACK

THIRD PART

A bed-room — At the rear a curtained alcove with a bed. A door on each side of the alcove ; that at the right is hidden by the hangings. Tables, chairs, on which are thrown masks, fans, open jewel-boxes, and theatrical costumes.

SCENE I
THISBE, GABOARDO, ORFEO, A BLACK PAGE.

(CATARINA upon the bed, enveloped in a winding-sheet ; the copper crucifix can be seen upon her breast.)

(Thisbe takes a mirror and uncovers Catarina's colorless face.)

THISBE (to the page).

Come nearer with thy torch.

(She holds the mirror in front of Catarina's lips.)

My mind 's at rest.

(She draws the curtains of the alcove.)

(To the night watchmen.)

You are quite sure that no one saw you on your way hither from the palace ?

GABOARDO.

The night is very dark. The city is deserted at this hour. You know that we met not a soul, my lady. You saw us put the coffin in the grave and cover it with the tile. Have no fear. We know not if the woman 's

251

dead, but one thing is certain, and that is that everyone believes she's fast in the tomb. You can do what you choose with her.

THISBE.

Very good.

(To the page.)

Where are the man's clothes I bade you have in readiness?

THE PAGE (pointing to a package in the shadow).

They are here, my lady.

THISBE.

And the two horses that I ordered—are they in the courtyard?

THE PAGE.

Saddled and bridled.

THISBE.

Are they good horses?

THE PAGE.

I 'll answer for them, my lady.

THISBE.

'T is well.

(To the night-watchmen.)

Tell me, you fellows, how long a time one needs, well-mounted, to pass the frontier of the Venetian State?

GABOARDO.

That depends. The shortest way is to go straight to Montebacco; that belongs to the pope. Three hours will do it. It 's a fine road.

THISBE.

Enough. Now go. Silence concerning this affair. Return to-morrow for the reward I promised you.

(Exeunt Orfeo and Gaboardo.)

(To the page.)

Go you, and make the door secure. Let no one enter upon any pretext.

THE PAGE.

Signor Rodolfo has his private entrance, madame. Shall I secure that also?

THISBE.

No, leave it unsecured. If he comes, let him enter. But he alone, no other. Be sure that not a soul in the whole world makes his way hither, above all if Rodolfo comes. Do not you yourself come in unless I summon you. Now leave me.

(Exit the page.)

SCENE II

THISBE : CATARINA in the alcove.

THISBE.

I think that 't will not be much longer now. She did not wish to die. I understand. When one is well assured that one is loved! But on the other hand, rather than live unloved,

(Turning toward the bed.)

thou wouldst have met death joyfully, wouldst thou not? Oh! my head 's burning up! These three nights now I have not slept. Night before last, my party, last night, their meeting at which I surprised them, to-night . . . Ah! when to-morrow night comes, I shall sleep!

(She glances at the theatrical paraphernalia scattered about.)

Oh! yes, we actresses are very fortunate! How they applaud us on the stage! "How beautifully you played Rosmonda, signora!" The fools! Yes, they admire us, and think us beautiful, and smother us with flowers, but the heart bleeds beneath. Oh! Rodolfo!

Rodolfo! Belief in his love for me was necessary to my life. When I believed in it, I often used to think that, if I died, I should be glad to die beside him, to die in such a way that he could never thenceforth tear from his heart my memory, and that my shade would ever after stand beside him, between all other women and himself! Oh! death is nothing; to be forgot is everything. I do not wish him to forget me. Alas! see to what I have come! see to what depths I 've fallen! And this is what the world has done for me! This is what love has done for me!

(She goes to the alcove, draws the curtains aside, gazes fixedly for some moments at the motionless Catarina, and takes the crucifix.)

Ah! if this crucifix has brought good luck to anyone on earth, it has not to thy daughter, mother!

(She places the crucifix on the table. The masked door opens. Enters Rodolfo.)

SCENE III

THISBE.

You, Rodolfo! Ah! so much the better! I 've something I must say to you. Listen.

RODOLFO.

And I have something I must say to you as well, and you will listen first to me, madame!

THISBE.

Rodolfo!

RODOLFO.

Are you alone, madame?

THISBE.

Alone.

RODOLFO.

Give orders to admit no one.

THISBE.

They are already given.

RODOLFO.

Allow me to secure these doors.

(He fastens the two doors with bolts.)

THISBE.

I await what you have to say to me.

RODOLFO.

Whence come you? Why are you so pale? What have you done to-day? tell me! What have those hands of yours done? tell me! Where have you passed the execrable hours of this day? tell me. No, do not tell me, but let me tell you. Do not reply, do not deny, do not invent or falsify. I know all! I tell you, I know all! You 'll see that I know all, madame! Daphne was there, within two steps of you, separated only by a door; Daphne was there, in the oratory, and saw everything, and heard everything; she was there, almost beside you, and heard and saw! And these are the words you used. Said the podesta: "I have no poison," whereupon you said: "But I have!" "I have!" "I have!" Said you that, yes or no? Come, lie a bit! Ah! you have poison, have you! Even so; I have a knife!

(He draws a dagger from his breast.)

THISBE.

Rodolfo!

RODOLFO.

You have a quarter of an hour to prepare for death, madame!

THISBE.

Ah! you will kill me! 'T is the first thought that comes to you! Your purpose is to kill me, with your own hand, at once, without delay, without being sure of what I 've done? You find it in your heart to come so easily to such a resolution? You care for me no more than that? You kill me, because you love another! Oh! Rodolfo, is it true (oh! tell me with your own lips) that you did ever love me?

RODOLFO.

Never.

THISBE.

Ah! 't is that word that kills me, cruel man! thy dagger will but complete the work.

RODOLFO.

Love for you! No, I have none, nor ever had! Thank God that I can boast of that! The utmost that I ever felt for you was pity.

THISBE.

Ingrate! And, one word more, tell me, didst thou love her?

RODOLFO.

Her! did I love her! Oh! listen to this, since it is torture to you, wretch! Did I love her! a pure and chaste and saintly creature, a woman who is herself an altar, light of my eyes, my life, my blood, my treasure and my solace, my constant thought, my soul— that 's how I loved her!

THISBE.

Then I have done well.

RODOLFO.

You have done well?

THISBE.

Yes, I have done well. But art thou sure of what I 've done?

RODOLFO.

I am not sure, you say! This is the second time you 've said it. But Daphne was there, I tell you once again, Daphne was there, and what she told me is ringing in my ears yet: "Signor, signor, there were but those three in the room, the podesta, she, and another woman, a fearful woman whom the podesta called Thisbe. Signor, for two long hours, two hours of agony and terror, signor, they kept her there, poor soul, weeping and praying and imploring, pleading for mercy, pleading for life"—thou didst plead for life, Catarina, my beloved !—"on her knees, with hands clasped beseechingly, and prostrate at their feet—and they said no! And 't was the woman Thisbe who went to fetch the poison! 't was she who forced madame to drink it; and she it was who carried off the poor dead body, signor; that woman, that monster, Thisbe!" Where have you put it, madame? "That 's what this Thisbe did!" And yet you say I am not sure!

(He takes a handkerchief from his breast.)

This handkerchief I found in Catarina's room; whose is it? yours!

(Pointing to the crucifix.)

This crucifix I find here in your room; whose is it? hers! And am I sure! Come, pray and weep and beg for mercy, and do whatever else you have to do, and let 's have done with it!

THISBE.

Rodolfo!

RODOLFO.

What have you to say to justify yourself? Speak quickly! Waste no time!

THISBE.

Nothing, Rodolfo. All this that thou hast been told is true. Believe it all. Rodolfo, thy visit is most opportune; I longed to die, and cast about to find some means of dying in thy presence, at thy feet. To die by thy hand! Ah! it is more, far more, than I had dared to hope. To die by thy hand! and I shall fall, perchance, into thy arms. I thank thee. I am sure, at least, that thou wilt hear my last words. My last sigh thou wilt have, although thou carest naught for it. Life has no charm for me. Thou dost not love me, therefore kill me. It is the only thing that thou canst now do for me, my Rodolfo. And so thou wilt relieve me of my burden. Agreed. I thank thee from my heart.

RODOLFO.

Madame . . .

THISBE.

'T is thus. Have patience with me but an instant. I have been always greatly to be pitied. These are not idle words, but the overflowing of a swelling heart. The world has little sympathy for us women of the stage; the world is wrong. It knows naught of the virtue and the courage we often have. Think'st thou that I should set great store by life? Consider that I was sent into the streets to beg when a mere child. And then, at sixteen years, I was left penniless. I was taken from the street by men of rank, and sank from depths of misery to depths of shame. Starvation or pollution. I know what you would say; "better die of hunger!" but I did suffer bitterly. Oh! yes, the sympathy is all for the great ladies. If they weep, you console them. If they do evil, you make excuses for them. And then, how they complain! But for us anything is too good. We are overwhelmed with obloquy. "Come, poor woman! move on. Of what dost thou complain? The whole world is against thee? Well, wert thou not made to suffer, strumpet?" — Rodolfo, surely thou canst feel that I in my position did sorely need to find a heart that understood my own. If I have no one in the world who loves me, pray tell me what to thy thinking would become of me? I say this, thinking not to move thee; I know that that is hopeless now. But I do love thee! O Rodolfo! how passionately this poor girl doth love thee thou wilt not know till I am dead; when I am here no more. Six months have passed since I first knew thee; six months that thy glance has been my whole life, thy smile my joy, thy breath my very soul! Judge of my misery! in these six months not for one single instant

have I dreamed, even though the dream was necessary to my life, that thou didst love me. Thou knowest how I forever wearied thee with jealous doubts; there were a thousand signs that tore my heart. Now it is all explained. I blame thee not, for 't is no fault of thine. I know that thy thoughts have been wholly hers for seven years. I was a distraction, a mere pastime to you, nothing more. 'T is clear as day. I blame thee not. But what wouldst thou have me do? Live on without thy love I cannot. For one must breathe, and 't is by thee I breathe. Ah! thou art not so much as listening to me! Does it weary thee to have me speak to thee? Oh! I am so wretched and unhappy that I think, upon my soul, that any-one who saw me now might pity me!

RODOLFO.

Am I sure! The podesta went off to seek four sbirri, and meanwhile you whispered in her ear some dreadful words which made her take the poison! Woman, do you not see that my mind 's wandering? Woman, where is Catarina? Answer me. Say, is it true that thou hast murdered her, hast poisoned her? Where is she? answer! where is she? Know, madame, that she 's the only woman I have ever loved! the only one, the only one, do you hear? the only one!

THISBE.

The only one! the only one! Ah! 't is cruel to strike so many blows! In pity's name!

(She points to the dagger in his hand.)

deal me the last with this and quickly!

RODOLFO.

Where is Catarina? the only woman I have ever loved! yes, the only one!

THISBE.

Ah! thou art pitiless! thou dost break my heart! Well, then I hate her, dost thou hear? I hate that woman! What thou wert told is true; I did revenge myself, I poisoned her, I killed her.

RODOLFO.

Ah! you confess it! remember that, you 've confessed it with your own lips! By Heaven! I do believe you boast of it, unhappy woman!

THISBE.

I do, and what I 've done, I 'd do again! Strike!

RODOLFO (in terrible wrath).

Madame . . .

THISBE.

I say, I killed her! Strike!

RODOLFO.

Vile creature!

(He stabs her.)

THISBE (as she falls).

Ah! to the heart! Thou hast stabbed me to the heart! 'T is well. My Rodolfo, thy hand!

(She takes his hand and kisses it.)

Oh! thanks! Thou hast delivered me! Let me keep thy hand. Thou seest that I 've no wish to do thee ill. Rodolfo, my beloved, thou couldst not see thyself when thou didst enter, but I could not endure the thought of living after the way in which thou saidst: "you have a quarter of an hour," raising thy knife. Now that I am about to die, be kind to me, and say a pitying word. I think that so thou wouldst do well.

RODOLFO.

Madame . . .

THISBE.

One word of pity! Wilt thou not?

(A voice is heard behind the curtains of the alcove.)

CATARINA.

Where am I, Rodolfo?

RODOLFO.

What do I hear? Whose voice is that?

(He turns and sees the pale face of Catarina, who has drawn the curtains partly aside.)

CATARINA.

Rodolfo!

RODOLFO. (He runs to her and takes her in his arms.)

Catarina! Great God! Thou here and living? How can this be? Just Heaven!

(Turning to Thisbe.)

What have I done?

THISBE (dragging herself toward them with a smile).

Nothing. Thou hast done nothing. I did it all. I wished to die. I drove thy hand to do it.

RODOLFO.

Catarina! thou alive! God's providence! By whom wert thou saved?

THISBE.

By me for thee.

RODOLFO.

Thisbe! Help! help! Wretch that I am!

THISBE.

No. Help would be useless, I am sure of it. Thanks! Oh! yield to thy joy as if I were not here. I wish not to embarrass you. I know full well that thou shouldst be content. I deceived the podesta. 'T was a narcotic I administered, and not a poison. Everyone thinks her dead; but she was simply sleeping. Below are horses all prepared for your departure, and male clothes for her. Be off at once. In three hours you will be without Venetian territory. Be happy. She is set free. Dead to the podesta. Living for thee. Think'st thou I planned it well?

RODOLFO.

Catarina! Thisbe!

(He falls on his knees with his eyes fixed on the dying Thisbe.)

THISBE (in a voice which grows rapidly weaker).

I am dying. Thou wilt think sometimes of me, wilt thou not? and then wilt say: "Oh well, all said and done poor Thisbe was a good-hearted girl." Oh! that will make me leap for joy, even in my tomb! Adieu! Permit me, my lady, once more to call him my Rodolfo! Farewell, my Rodolfo! Now go quickly. I die. Live thou. My blessing on thy head!

(She dies.)

EDITION DEFINITIVE

NOTE I

The "First Day" of "Angelo" was begun February 2d, 1835, and finished February 6th, at noon. The "Second Day" was begun February 6th, and finished February 11th. The "Third Day" was begun February 12th, and finished February 19th, at 10 A. M.

NOTE II

VARIANT READINGS

FIRST DAY

SCENE II

RODOLFO, THISBE.

THISBE.

Oh! what misery! I am confined in the same cage with this podesta! Dost thou recall the dog we saw at Florence caged with the tiger? I am that poor dog, Rodolfo.

SECOND DAY

SCENE V

CATARINA, THISBE.

(Thisbe enters, torch in hand.)

THISBE.

The light is out. There 's no one here.

(She goes to the bed.)

She is alone. If what my guide informed me is to be believed, it 's certain that no one can leave the room.

(Aloud.)

Come, madame, do not pretend to be asleep. What 's the use? Do you imagine that I am your dupe? Open your eyes. I have to speak with you.

CATARINA.

(Sitting up in bed.)

A woman! Who is this woman? Who are you, signora?

THISBE.

Your enemy.

CATARINA.

What do you mean by that? By whose advice have you come hither? Do you not know that anyone who enters here, woman or man, does thereby risk his head? Your life is in my hands.

THISBE.

And yours in mine.

CATARINA.

Know you to whom you speak? I am the podesta's wife.

THISBE.

And I his mistress.

THIRD DAY. PART SECOND

SCENE VI

RODOLFO, CATARINA.

·

RODOLFO.

Thou seest that God's on our side. I have a key that gives me access to thee! And when I think that I perchance may see thee every day! What bliss! 'T is sure that God is on our side.

CATARINA.   ·

Thinkst thou so?

RODOLFO.

How calm and lovely everything about thee! There's something sanctifying in the very atmosphere, Catarina, by which one feels that thou dost dwell here night and day. The room is filled with all the perfumes of thy soul. What lovely trees without! and oh! the lovely springtime! and the lovely sunshine! Here everything is peaceable and pure. It is the only blessed nook in this accursed city. Ah! yes, accursed, indeed! To-day, for instance—thou hast no suspicion of it—Venice, or Padua herself, is consummating some great crime within these walls. Something's toward. The city's in a stupor. The streets are all patrolled by archers. No one speaks above a whisper. At this very moment something terrible is surely taking place somewhere.

SCENE VIII

CATARINA, ANGELO, THISBE.

·   ·   ·   ·

ANGELO.

You will drink this.

CATARINA.

'T is poison?

ANGELO.

Yes, madame.

CATARINA.

How many soldiers have you in the ante-chamber? how many in the palace? how many in the street? how many throughout the city? how many of your men are there,

(Looking at Thisbe.)

and women, in league against me? Ah! this is poison! and I am to drink it! A woman, helpless in a chamber with two executioners! The poison 's there! the husband says: " Drink!" Oh! no one would believe that that could happen which is happening here, but so it is!

. . . .

You had at first another plan, but you prefer the poison. 'T is more secret. And so I am to disappear, to pass away into the darkness, and no one know what has become of me. I am a stone that you toss in the water. The waters meet again above me, and leave no sign.

. . .

CATARINA.

(To Thisbe.)

To die at my age! does it not rouse your pity? I have no courage, I confess it; and wouldst thou have courage, wert thou in my place? In God's name, speak to the podesta! I pray, speak to him. I have not given you the name of him who wrote the letter. Will you do it? Listen a moment, madame. When I have laid the thing before you as it is, you will see that it 's a sad story. I never have been happy. For seven years I have been in love. Long before I was married. I should not have been forced to marry, had my mother lived!

THIRD DAY. PART THIRD

SCENE I

THISBE: CATARINA (asleep).

THISBE.

(Turning toward the bed.)

Rather than live unloved, thou wouldst have met death joyfully, wouldst thou not? If thou hadst felt that thy life had no roots in any other heart, what wouldst thou then have done? Oh! thou wouldst not have had the courage to finish out thy day; thou wouldst have owned thyself wearied by the anticipation of so long a journey to be traveled all alone, and thou wouldst have said unto the tomb: "I long to sleep!"

(She opens a small casket which stands upon the table.)

Yes, of the two decoctions that were in this casket, a powerful narcotic and a deadly poison, but one remains. To-morrow, neither will remain.

TRANSLATOR'S NOTE TO ANGELO

Justly or unjustly, Victor Hugo laid the responsibility for the ill-success of *Marie Tudor* at the door of M. Harel, Director of the Théâtre Porte-Saint-Martin; they quarreled upon that subject, and by mutual consent the contract between them which called for the production of three of Hugo's dramas at that theatre was rescinded—two only, *Lucrèce Borgia* and *Marie Tudor*, having been produced.

Tudor was produced in November, 1833, and early in the following month the author was at work on *Angelo*, which did not receive its first performance, however, until April, 1835, when it was produced on the stage of the Théâtre-Français.

From *Victor Hugo Raconté par un Témoin de Sa Vie*, a work supposed to have been inspired by the great poet and dramatist, if not actually written by him, we extract the following paragraph concerning *Angelo*.

" The drama, as originally written, had five acts. The death of Homodei took place on the stage. Rodolfo followed the spy to a resort of bandits, where there was a scene of drunkenness and bloodshed. After the play was read to the committee, MM. Taylor and Jouslin de Lasalle waited upon the author; the act in the bandits' den worried them; *Le Roi S'Amuse* owed its downfall in part to Saltabadil's hovel, and Homodei's hovel would be the ruin of *Angelo;* it was not indispensable to the drama; *Homodei's* death could be narrated in a few words; they induced the author to suppress the act."

The work here cited contains many interesting details concerning the first production of *Angelo*. Mademoiselle Mars, who had created the rôle of Donna Sol in *Hernani*, was still a member of the company at the Français, although somewhat past her prime, but it was necessary to look elsewhere for an actress to take the second leading female part, and Madame Dorval was engaged.

Mademoiselle Mars was allowed to take her choice between the two rôles, Catarina and Thisbe.

" Catarina, married and chaste, was marvelously adapted to the straightforward, decorous talent of Mademoiselle Mars; but Thisbe, the child of the streets, of violent passions and irregular life, seemed made for the freer Bohemian talent of Madame Dorval. *Therefore* Mademoiselle Mars preferred the rôle of Thisbe."

(Victor Hugo Raconté, etc.)

" Therefore," because Mademoiselle Mars was inclined to be a little jealous, and when Madame Dorval, who was the personification of good nature and unselfishness, purposely held herself back at rehearsal, " Mademoiselle Mars congratulated herself upon her cleverness in selecting a rôle which was little suited to her talent, for how much less suited was Catarina to the capacity of Madame Dorval ! The idea of that immodest, shameless woman in a chaste and dignified part ! She was in great danger of being hissed. But at one rehearsal Madame Dorval forgot herself, and played with such power, that Mademoiselle Mars's hopes faded away on the spot. She could not restrain herself, and in the third act, interrupted Catarina's angry outburst against Angelo and Thisbe.

" ' Tell me, Monsieur Hugo, what attitude you wish me to assume, while madame is insulting me in this charming fashion ? Do you not think that this tirade of hers is over long ?'

" ' No longer, madame, than the one you address to her in the preceding act.'

" ' Oh ! for my part,' said Madame Dorval, ' I don't consider madame's insults too long. When the lines are so fine it 's as much pleasure to me to listen to them as to say them myself.' "

The first performance resulted in the unqualified success of both of the great artists, and neither had any reason to be jealous of the other. Upon the records of the Théâtre-Français may be read to-day, in connection with this performance, the words : " Great success ; Mmes. Mars and Dorval recalled."

The prohibition of *Marion de Lorme* in 1829, before its production was the basis of the first of Victor Hugo's *dramatic* lawsuits; the prohibition of *Le Roi S'Amuse* after its first performance in 1832, was the basis of the second; and a breach of contract by the government of the Théâtre-Français, in failing to produce *Angelo* and *Hernani* the stipulated number of times, was the basis of the third and last lawsuit, in 1837.

When *Angelo* was revived at the Français in 1850, the rôle of Thisbe was assumed by Madame Rachel.